CLASH

Spinward Fringe Broadcast 17

RANDOLPH LALONDE

Books by Randolph Lalonde

FANTASY

Highshield

Brightwill

NEM: Awakening

NEM: Crimson Shores

SCIENCE FICTION

THE SPINWARD FRINGE SERIES

Spinward Fringe Broadcast 0: Origins

Spinward Fringe Broadcast 1 and 2: Resurrection and Awakening

Spinward Fringe Broadcast 3: Triton

Spinward Fringe Broadcast 4: Frontline

Spinward Fringe Broadcast 5: Fracture

Spinward Fringe Broadcast 6: Fragments

The Expendable Few: A Spinward Fringe Novel

Spinward Fringe Broadcast 7: Framework

Spinward Fringe Broadcast 8: Renegades

Spinward Fringe Broadcast 9: Warpath

Spinward Fringe Broadcast 10: Freeground

Spinward Fringe Broadcast 10.5: Carnie's Tale

Spinward Fringe Broadcast 11: Revenge

Spinward Fringe Broadcast 12: Invasion

www.RandolphLalonde.com

Spinward Fringe Broadcast 17: Clash

EBook ISBN: 978-1-988175-55-3
Print Edition ISBN: 978-1-988175-56-0

Cover graphics provided by: Selfpubbookcovers.com

Thank you for purchasing this book.

If you would like to purchase, preview other books by Randolph Lalonde or contact the author for any reason please visit my website.
www.RandolphLalonde.com

Before We Begin

It has been a while since Hunters: Spinward Fringe Broadcast 16, was released. I spent some time away from the series to practice my skills in other genres and to explore different ideas.

This happens from time to time, and when I come back to write another novel in the main Spinward Fringe series I always find that working in other genres or with other characters has improved my skills and refreshed my mind.

I wrote another fantasy novel called NEM: Crimson Shores which completed a story that I started with NEM: Awakening. I promised myself and many readers that the second book in that new series would have a much more satisfying ending, and that it would come soon, so I wrote it while it was fresh in my mind.

While I was getting ready to write Clash, the last pieces of a puzzle came together for another book: Psycho Electric. I had been thinking about writing that novel for about ten years, and couldn't resist finally penning it. As intended, it's a one shot, full length cyberpunk novel that takes place in the Spinward Fringe Universe. If you're wondering about where it sits on the timeline, it takes place right before this book, but isn't directly connected to it. It features a new location close to earth and stars almost all new characters. I wouldn't say that it's required reading before you dive into Clash. I do recommend you check out the ebook or audiobook version sometime, though. I'm proud of both of them. David Berlekamp's performance is especially good.

Before I got to work on the book you're about to read I wrote one more thing as a warm up. It's sort of a prelude in a way. An idea came up while I was talking to David. We were talking about how a missile or bullet fired in space would drift until it was interfered with. A single bullet could ruin someone's day after drifting for five hundred years or more. He was also using lines from a popular video game to demonstrate his drill sergeant voice, a mode of speech he'd use in the Psycho Electric audiobook later.

I had a thought then. What if there was a special unit that took responsibility for the perpetually floating munitions of war? The idea of the Bullet Chasers was born, and after a couple weeks, I had finished writing the short novelette known as The Last of the Bullet Chasers. I recommend you read that before you begin Clash, but you certainly don't have to. It does introduce a few new characters to the series, but you won't be lost if you skip that short for now. I think the story is great fun though, and I like how it brought me back to the main Spinward Fringe series.

So, my creative wandering is finished for now. I've finished Clash, which moves the series forward in a direction I like a great deal, and I'm getting ready to write Samurai Squadron, the next book in the main Spinward Fringe series. I'm looking forward to it.

I would like to thank my Patreon members, who supported me while I wrote this and other novels over the last two years. They also helped find a few dozen typos in the early manuscript.

I'd also like to thank everyone who buys my books and talks them up to whoever will listen.

With no further delay, I hope you enjoy this book!

- RL

Chapter 1

The Recuperation of the Cefa System

ALICE VALENT'S SHIP, the Clever Dream, was destroyed three months and two weeks ago. Since then Haven Fleet assigned her to another task, one that she wouldn't have chosen.

The differences in her life and the hope that she could take control again were on her mind as she stood near the middle of a long bridge that was made in the oldest of styles. Fine brick and mortar were formed into a long arc over an expansive palace flower garden. The Davari Refuge's blossoms below lent an earthy, sweet fragrance to the warm night air. The city of Erivis had been her home for nearly three months, and there was no telling how long she would be stuck there after the coronation of the Lecini King, the ruler of the Cefa System.

It took over two months for Alice to find enjoyment in her

new assignment as the guardian of Prince Philip. The majority of the people who survived the Order of Eden Occupation were calling for him to become king. His family ruled over a golden period that lasted at least a century in the solar system. The populace wanted it back regardless of the fact that he was only seventeen standard years old.

Even though the majority of the solar system's population wanted him and his family to oversee the government and become the ultimate rulers again, some were still against it. Until it was her job to make sure that the Prince was safe she never realized that dissidents could become violent when they didn't feel their voices were heard. The Order of Eden didn't want him to take the throne either. Stability in the Cefa System seemed to be against their plan. The close tie they had to the Haven Government may have been the reason, but Alice suspected there was more to it.

Was the hybrid monarchy democracy something that Alice understood? Eventually, technically, yes, but she wouldn't want to live under a government where a monarch could dismiss regional governors, regardless of what the people wanted. The pure civilian democracy of the Haven Government was much better in her opinion. While she was serving in the Cefa System, she had the opportunity to remotely vote in a major election and five referendums, and it was encouraging to see the Haven democracy work.

None of that changed the fact that guarding the Prince felt like a punishment after everything she accomplished in the Rose System, specifically on Planet Rodus. Stealing three brand new Next Generation Order of Eden destroyers with a small band of allies was a landmark victory. She even provided Haven Fleet with one to study.

She was sure that her assignment in the Cefa system was

punitive along with her demotion to Commander. After stealing the Advanced Destroyers she'd released an android named Rogue into the wild. Her demotion didn't feel right. Alice was confident that she knew what Rogue would do, that she'd be out there, trying to destroy the Order of Eden however she could.

No matter what Alice told the convened authority reviewing the creation of Rogue, she couldn't convince them that it wouldn't come back to haunt them. They were stuck on the fact that Rogue was made using the most advanced technology in the fleet. If that wasn't bad enough, no one could figure out how the data that brought her full autonomy on survived in Alice's head. Everything everyone, including Alice, believed led them to think that the dormant data that came to life in the android was self-deleted long ago.

When it was all said and done, Alice was lucky to be demoted one step down from Captain to Commander in the Special Operations Combat Unit. S.O.C.U. was sent to the Cefa System to oversee the rebuilding of the government and the massive wormhole gate there. When Alice begrudgingly followed orders, rejoining them in the Cefa System, she thought she'd be assigned to explore the planets, asteroid belts or the centuries-old gate station there.

She was wrong. Commodore Vrex, her superior officer, put her in briefings about the Rogue android for three weeks. By the time she was finished, most of her crew was reassigned and she was demoted. Her father couldn't do anything without putting noses out of joint as Alice's new superior officer, Captain Poole, decided that she should help run the security for the remaining members of the Lacini Royal Family. The thinking there was that she might get along with the Prince, and Poole wouldn't let go of the idea that Alice was the closest thing to a princess that Haven Fleet had. Her mother and father were part owners of the entire Haven solar system, after all.

To Alice's relief, the Prince wasn't an insufferable brat. To her horror, he requested her as his personal guard on the first day. Regardless of rank, or that she was commanding three squads of soldiers, she was assigned to be at his side whenever he was awake. It was a direct order from Captain Poole. Rumours immediately started to fly around the online tabloids. Alice made sure that she was always in uniform - not in civilian dress - when she was out of her quarters. She kept things professional and civil whenever she was talking to anyone, not just the Prince and his people. None of that mattered. Tabloids went crazy, even creating fake imagery of her staring longingly at him when he wasn't looking, and worse. It didn't help that the Prince formed a quick crush, and the rest of her duty on Lacini became a balancing act between making sure that he stayed out of danger during political and public engagements while Alice tried to politely keep her distance.

As the memory of the worst night, only a few evenings ago, crept up on her again, Alice shuddered. It wasn't worth remembering, but it was difficult to forget. Alice tried to focus on the present, on the vacation weekend that was just starting. It was the first real time off since she started guarding the Prince.

To her relief, the sounds of boot steps coming up the far arc of the flower garden's bridge completely returned her attention to the present. She checked her well-fitted powder blue dress again, adjusting it at the waist. It split into two broad panels at the hips and was designed for the kind of dancing that took place in Lacini royal courts often, which was a combination of old-world Spanish styles. She tried to learn a few steps weeks ago with Faloo, and they had great fun, but neither of them showed much potential. The instructor seemed to take pleasure in telling Faloo that, as a burrowing Nafalli, she was too broad and furry. She also critizised Alice for being too short.

Still, Alice loved the fashion that the ancient dance styles inspired. It was elegant, not too showy, with a little flair. The colour was her personal touch because Noah loved it on her, and it suited her red, chin-length ringlets. A style choice she made because curly hair was very popular in Lacini, and it reminded her of her mother.

Noah Lucas's head and shoulders crested the curve of the bridge and she was grinning the instant Alice spotted his big smile. She stood there for a moment, making eye contact, watching him take her in. He'd left his trench coat behind, and wore a long-sleeved, navy tunic over thick black trousers. That was a style he picked up from Rodus, and she assumed he'd shaped his vacsuit that way instead of buying the clothes. How he got it, and what he spent didn't matter nearly as much as how it suited him. His dirty blonde hair brushed the stiff open collar, and the shirt clung to his shoulders and chest. He was carrying a rose that was gently glowing shifting shades of red.

Alice ran to him with a happy squeal. That was another thing she liked about dresses that were made for dancing; they were easier to move in, and with no complications from its cloth, she leapt at him. There was no doubt in her mind that he'd catch her as she made full-body contact and then wrapped her legs and arms around his waist.

It had been over three months since they'd seen each other in person. Even meeting in sims wasn't enough anymore. The empathic sense she'd honed while listening for threats around the Prince and providing lie detection services was completely useless in digital environments.

Without that sense, there was still an indescribably wonderful feeling of being with Noah. Feeling him wrap his arms around her, his body firmly against hers and being nose to nose with his grinning face for real was what she needed then. "I could get used to that," Noah laughed softly before giving her a brief kiss.

"I missed you a little," Alice teased, running her fingers up his neck into his dirty blonde hair.

"Uh-huh. Right," he teased. "Are you sure? I saw a headline the other day…"

"Oh, no, you've been reading the tabs? Even out at the Shattered End?" she asked, fighting her rising embarrassment.

His eyes darted around for a second, he was accessing menus that she couldn't see, and then a hologram of an article came up. The headline read; HAVENLY PRINCESS HUMILIATES PRINCE PHILIP.

The image was straight from the Prince's birthday party, where he proposed to her in front of every remaining member of his family and the leaders of political parties from across the Cefa Solar System. "Yeah, that happened, but in my defence, I had no idea he would propose. The whole idea was ridiculous." She kissed him then, and said; "I'm all yours."

"Well, if he's not good enough for you, but I am, then I'm feeling pretty…" he was interrupted again as Alice flicked the hologram away and squeezed his waist with her thighs. "That's a hell of a grip."

"It's been almost two weeks, I'm sure he's over it. As far as extra-curricular stuff, I've had nothing to do in my spare time but work out, study, pass new Fleet qualifier tests and sleep. Running security is about being alert, using your head and staying well rested. Well, I can't be seen in public doing anything interesting either, so…"

"And you've never been more bored in your life. I can tell, even when we were in sims. I like the daily calls lately though, sorry I couldn't take all of 'em."

"No worries. I know you're not on the same kind of schedule I am. Really glad you're here," she kissed him softly, enjoying the moment so much that she was sure she was blushing, practically glowing for all to see. Then she asked; "Did you bring me something?"

He stared into her eyes blankly for a moment then said; "Oh yeah." The rose he'd obviously bought at the entrance of the garden was uncrushed, and he presented it to her like the most precious thing in the galaxy. "They grow them here. It's the ever-bloom kind."

That was something Alice didn't expect. She hadn't noticed the pod attached to the stem. "So I can plant this wherever I go and it'll stay alive." She was tempted to scold him for spending so much platinum on it but appreciated the delicate glowing petals instead. "Thank you."

He watched her admire the flower. "I have another gift for you, but it's not legal here, so it'll have to wait," he said as he watched her admire the flower.

"What is it?" she asked with a playful gasp.

"No, you'll have to wait. I had to leave it on the Corsair though, so it's not far away." It was obvious that Noah was enjoying teasing her.

"Give me a hint?" Alice pressed.

"Brat. Nope," he laughed softly.

"Fine," she said, rolling her eyes but smiling all the same. "We'll visit the Corsair tomorrow. Thank you for the rose." Alice rewarded him with a long, prolonged kiss, enjoying the feeling of his lips on hers. When they finished she whispered. "I have a room overlooking the gardens. What do you think of having dinner on the balcony and then going in for the night?" she bit her lip and watched him, finding it difficult to hold her empathic ability in check.

"Well, I thought we'd check out a couple clubs, maybe see if there are any afterparties," he started to ramble. Then, probably seeing that her jaw was slowly dropping in either frustration or shock, he squeezed her, kissed her on the cheek and nodded. "I'm messing with you." Then, more tenderly, he said; "If you're sure tonight's…"

"I've never been more sure," Alice burst. "Have you seen this place? I don't think any of the dating cyberscapes we saw live up to it. It's so romantic here that I'm sure the conception rate on this island must be crazy. I'm on the verge of skipping dinner altogether and jumping you in the bushes."

Noah laughed so hard that she was sure everyone strolling in the enormous garden below could hear him. It was so good to see him relaxed, happy to be with her. "Well, why not? It doesn't look like there are a lot of people down there, we could find a spot."

Alice was fairly sure he was teasing. Two could play that game. "Okay."

His jaw dropped for a moment then it started to raise into a smile as he started walking slowly, holding her up. "Now we're talking."

Was he really taking her seriously? Alice glanced at an older woman who might have heard enough of the exchange to know what was going on. She was smiling, her feathered hat exaggerating a knowing little nod as she passed. "There are thorns in most of those bushes, so you know."

"Thank you," Alice told her, blushing furiously.

"Well, I guess we're going upstairs. Should I carry you to the hotel, or?" Noah asked.

Taking care not to push her dress too far out of place, Alice slipped down to her feet with his help. Hand in hand they started walking down the other side of the bridge. "It's a palace, actually. This garden is a part of the grounds in the southern section."

"A part? How big is this place?"

"The whole island is reserved land. The only people allowed here are royals and their guests, so, um, big. A little smaller than Haven Shore. The security has been pretty easy to maintain here, the problems start when we leave," Alice replied. "I'd still rather be running around the Rose System and hanging out with the Captains though. This place is great for a weekend, but I wouldn't live here. Speaking of weekends, tell me you can stay all three days?"

"Elyub, Theo and Knud are handling everything right now, so you've got me for a week if you want," Noah replied.

"The coronation is coming up at the end of the week, so everything's going to go nuts starting on Tuesday morning. I mean, you could stay, but you'd be stuck on the Corsair most of the time."

"So, we have the weekend," Noah said with a smile as he took her hand and grazed the back of it with a tickling kiss.

Her command and control unit - a transparent version that looked more like a thick bracelet that matched her dress - flashed red and buzzed. There was also a sensation from it that projected urgency up the nerves in her arm. That was something that was usually deactivated since empaths and telepaths sensed that sort of thing more intensely. "Seriously?" Alice grumbled, yanked out of the moment.

"Could it be about your dad?" Noah asked.

"Probably not. How much trouble could he be getting into in extended debriefing? I mean, maybe he escaped, he must be climbing the walls after two weeks." Alice activated it, accepting the call.

"Alice!" it was Faloo, her big brown eyes were wide with alarm. "I know you said you were off this weekend, but it's morning in Haven Shore, and your father's about to be sentenced for something. No one knows what, but Hart News is going crazy. He's going to make some kind of pre-sentencing statement, and they've said that no one else is allowed to."

"What? Which court?" Alice asked.

"It's a Tribunal of the Admiralty, called by Haven Fleet Convening Authority. I think that's the top Fleet court," Faloo said. "I'm sorry, Alice."

"Put it through, and…" Alice started, her mind racing to figure out what he was being sentenced for. There were a few things, really. The execution of Wheeler came to mind first.

Faloo interrupted her. "There's something else. Everyone from SOCU is being recalled to the Haven System. The new orders should come up on your Com-Con. I blocked them at first along with the rest of your messages, but I think it's pretty important, so…"

"You did the right thing, Faloo, thank you," Alice said in a rush as she saw the message from Captain Poole in red and black letters. She checked it, making sure that Noah could see, and shook her head. "I'm off-world in the morning. Dame is coming in the Clever Dream Two. The funny thing is; I still haven't been given or assigned a replacement for the Clever Dream, and she's been with Samurai Squadron."

"I know, Easy's been keeping in touch with her…" Noah's left command and control bracer flashed red and he checked it. "Where are you being told to report to?"

"Freeground Station," Alice said.

"Looks like I'll be meeting you there. I hope they don't do an inspection of the Corsair, or want it back. The hold is full of..." he hesitated, looking worried, then went on. "...well, between your present and my cargo, I could get into trouble."

"What's in there?" Alice said, looking up the Haven News feed.

"Well, I've got some platinum to hide, I thought maybe I could stash a few tons in a vault on Lacini. It's nice and civilised here with Haven Fleet guarding the place and real law enforcement," Noah said with a shrug.

"A few tons of platinum?"

"Registered and molecularly stamped. The really valuable kind," he nodded. "About fifteen tons."

"That's what you made in three months?" Alice asked, equally impressed and shocked.

"Well, it's about three-quarters of my cut," he replied sheepishly.

"If you're rejoining the fleet, you can put that in a vault on Tamber. I put all my stuff from my old apartment in secure storage, and no one gets in there. I thought it was overkill for some furniture and a few personal things, but it would be perfect for a huge pile of plat. Or use the new facility on Unity. I bet my mother can get you space there even if you're still playing outlaw."

"In a research vault? Well, it would be secure," he mused.

Alice got verification for her orders and was stunned for a moment before she showed him. "It's official. I can't believe it. My entire security staff and everyone else under Commodore Vrex, then Captain Poole are getting yanked without saying so much as a farewell to the Royal Staff."

"You seem disappointed," Noah said carefully.

"Well, I guess, a little. I mean, I don't want to be here, but I thought I'd be part of the coronation security team. You know, I thought I'd get to see things through to the next step. There was a whole other team training the royal guards, and I guessed that they'd take over when they were ready."

"Are they?" Noah asked.

"No," Alice scoffed. "The best of them are from the last King's detail. They're great, but there are only five of them. The rest were killed during the Order occupation. Philip will have to stay on this island if he wants to be safe. I wouldn't store your plat here either."

"I gathered that," Noah said with a nod.

"I'm glad you're here," she said, leaning against him as she scrolled through the news posts, searching. Alice found the feed of the court where her father was walking in from a side door, making his way to the podium. "What did you get yourself into now, Dad?" she asked as they both watched a hologram of the proceedings. Seeing Ayan and Minh-Chu in a gallery set aside for family made her scowl so hard that it made her brow hurt. "I should be there. Why didn't anyone tell me?"

Chapter 2

The Statement

ALICE FELT a chill as she started watching the proceedings. Noah put an arm around her and she leaned against him, setting her command and control bracelet to project a hologram of the courtroom around them. The scent of the flowers drifting up from below, the warm air, and palatial surroundings faded as she focused on her father as he stood at a podium in front of three presiding Admirals.

"He's using an older appearance. This is how his face looked before he lost the framework system," Alice explained to Noah, who nodded silently. The uniform seemed stripped down to the minimum with no marking indicating his current assignment, and no equipment or gun belt. Only the rank of Admiral, the emblem of Haven Fleet, and a sword passing through a circle that marked him as one of the new founders of the haven System were on his jacket. It, like the one-piece, fitted vacsuit beneath was perfectly black except for a red line running up the side.

The judges don't do him the honour of reading the charges themselves. Instead, an unnamed clerk with a piercing voice that made her wince did so. "Admiral Jacob Valent has pleaded no contest to the following charge: Murder by proxy in the first degree."

As the gallery's hush broke with the rumble of a thousand people talking at once, Alice considered that. She knew the military code well, and her heart sank as she realized what he'd plead guilty to. "Oh, no, it's the Mary Virus he released on Obyn," she whispered. Memories of being in the Cefa System when it struck, of watching the first Yawen and several other crew members getting killed, and of her retribution came flooding back. Her father was light years away when the Order of Eden ships in the Cefa System faltered, and she took full advantage. Using the arsenal on her ship, the Clever Dream, she launched volleys that most likely killed thousands of enemy marines. To some that would be seen as a victory, as an act that weakened the Order's grasp on the Cefa System. To others it was cruel, taking advantage of an enemy that had been rendered defenceless. Alice often leaned towards the latter, but her sympathy for the Order of Eden and the people who served it was severely limited, so she rarely lost sleep over it.

"My client will waive the reading of the charges," Liara, the Communications Officer who had served under Jacob Valent on two ships, said from the defendant's table as she stood.

"Decorum! Decorum in the court!" shouted Admiral Unlo Kulsh as the recording of a harsh bell clanging filled the room. His broad Mergillian mouth was twisted in an expression that made him seem insulted, like he took the rumbling of the gallery personally.

They were silenced, and Admiral Limeen Doolth, the calmest of the trio, sitting in the middle, stroked the fur under her chin. The Nafalli's coat had whitened since Alice had last seen her. "The full reading of the charges are waived, but I believe it's important that they are outlined accurately so the context of Jacob Valent's statement is clear. My fellow judge, Admiral Damari Mathias, will read the summary that we've prepared."

Alice didn't know much about that Admiral, only that she'd come from a world near the Irish Union, and had a long, well-known history of service with the military forces there. She'd also refused any rollback treatments, preferring to age naturally while she was in good health. Mathias' expression was passive as she read the summarized charge. "This information was recently declassified to demystify the charges against Jacob Valent. I would like to preface this summary of events and charges by saying that Admiral Jacob Valent has cooperated by providing evidence for the record, and that has already been taken into consideration."

"Is that what he's been doing for two weeks? Giving them everything they need to hang him?" Alice muttered quietly. It wasn't easy to watch without getting angry at the judges, her father, and even the friends he had with him. She should have been told that something was going on, that her father was in trouble. Barring that, someone, like the Defence Minister who was one of his oldest friends, should have put a stop to it. Instead of raving about it to Noah, she kept her thoughts to herself and continued to watch.

Admiral Mathias continued in a tone that was official and devoid of emotional weight. "In preparation for a raid on the planet Obyn against an Order of Eden base, Admiral Jacob Valent ordered the creation of the Mary Virus. He specifically instructed a subordinate to create an artificial intelligence that would, without limitations, attack any computer system that it identified as belonging to the Order of Eden Military Organization. Furthermore, it was created to spread quickly using every Hyper Transmitter communications relay system. The Mary Virus was later released during the following raid on Obyn. Haven Fleet, Mergillian and British Alliance Intelligence have determined that this led to an eventual megadeath - that is the killing of at least a million people - across tens of thousands of Order of Eden military ships, bases and other installations. This includes incidents where our allies were given opportunities to destroy defenceless ships in the Cefa, Iyagda, and other solar systems within hours of the transmission of the artificial intelligence-driven Mary Virus. These facts have been confirmed by Admiral Jacob Valent's own records. They have not been confirmed by any representative from the Order of Eden or any of their allies, who uniformly deny that the Mary Virus was present in any of their systems."

"They contacted them about this?" Alice was stunned and didn't know what to think.

"Sounds like the Order was too proud to admit that someone got the better of them though," Noah said. "That probably helped his case."

In the gallery behind her father, Alice saw reactions ranging between shock and anger. "Thank God he did it!" shouted one of the people at the back. "He should do it again!" he added as a chorus of voices rose up in agreement.

"Decorum!" shouted Admiral Kulsh as a pair of bailiffs moved closer to the man and the gallery calmed.

"To continue," Admiral Mathias said, clearing her throat.

"The work of the aforementioned intelligence services has proven that the deaths of hundreds of thousands of Order of Eden soldiers, contract workers and officers took place thanks to failed life support and other essential systems. This act, made by Admiral Jacob Valent, reinforces the importance of the Standard Galactic Law known as The Eden Law. In short, it is meant to prevent the release of unsuitably restricted artificial intelligence into a networked system with malicious intent. After weeks of examining evidence, and considering the defendant's history, we are ready for the sentencing phase of this process."

Admiral Doolth's long muzzle turned back towards Alice's father. "We understand that you're ready to make a statement, Admiral."

"I am," Jake said clearly, loudly.

"Then you may proceed," Admiral Doolth said. Alice thought she was a close friend of her mother's, and liked the Nafalli. It was surreal watching her direct the sentencing, almost nightmarish.

"I would like to make a brief statement and enter a document into the record before he begins," Liara said. A trained lawyer, Alice always appreciated how intelligent and polite she was.

"You may proceed, Commander," Admiral Doolth said.

Liara pressed a button on her terminal and a list appeared large against the wall beside her. Hundreds of names started scrolling slowly. "This is a list of officers who wanted to appear and make statements before sentencing for Admiral Valent today. They range from Ensigns who have only served with him a short time to Admirals who have not always agreed with Admiral Valent, but have great respect for him. There are also several people on this list who have been his long-time friends and have intimate knowledge of his character, including our own Defence Minister, Terry Ozark McPatrick. I request that this list be read aloud."

The Tribunal of Admirals spoke with each other quickly for a minute in an obscuring field that kept the sound from carrying and made them appear blurry so no one could read their lips. Then the field dropped and Admiral Kulsh said; "Your request is denied. A redacted version of this list will be made available for the public, and the Tribunal acknowledges its significance."

"Now you may make your statement, Admiral Valent," Admiral Doolth said after failing to hide her irritation at the Mergillian Admiral beside her.

"Before I start, I'd like to thank everyone who volunteered to speak on my behalf," Alice's father said. "It seems most of the people who have served beside and under me wanted to be here."

"Please keep your statements focused on yourself and on this matter, Admiral," Admiral Methias said flatly.

"I apologize, Admiral," Alice's father said before continuing. He took a moment to look at the Admirals sitting on the bench in front of him, to his right where Liara was sitting, then further back to Ayan and Minh-Chu. Finally, as the gallery waited in silence, he faced the judges again and said; "I only regret that my actions may have taken innocent lives. The details of my mission on the day that I released the Mary Virus are largely classified, so I can't explain the conditions I was under when I made the decision to break Standard Galactic and Haven Fleet Uniform Law. I can tell you why I did it instead, and I'll keep it short."

"Don't get yourself into more trouble, Dad," Alice said under her breath as she stared at the holographic broadcast.

"How could he get into more trouble?" Noah asked.

"Oh, if anyone could find a way to make things worse…" Alice trailed off as her father started to speak.

"There have been times in my life when I've felt completely surrounded by the enemy. When hope hung by a string so slender, that you can only see it in a certain light. It was a time like that when I decided to have the Mary Virus made. Only, there was a difference. I wasn't alone. My crew, my friends, and hundreds of thousands of people at home were all in jeopardy with me. The Order of Eden seemed like an indomitable force against which we may win a few battles, but would never win a war. I felt it was crucial to take every opportunity to do them such great harm that everyone in the galaxy would see that they were vulnerable. That one person could make a difference against an armada that was growing, spreading and taking more territory every day. A normal virus could be stopped in one system or computer network, so I needed something that would aggressively adapt, and I knew my staff could produce it. I ordered them to create a weaponized artificial intelligence that could evade detection, and defeat countermeasures. I deployed it myself at a time that I thought was most effective and, while I can't foresee a situation where I would do it again, I don't regret the harm that program did to our enemy, the Order of Eden. The last of the Order ships in the Iyagda System faltered and failed, giving the British Alliance the opportunity they needed to take control of that space. The ships in the Cefa System were crippled, breaking their hold there as well. Several other victories across the galaxy have been reported. Hundreds of millions of people saw the Order of Eden falter and fail right in front of them."

There was a murmur of supporting voices in the gallery

that was silenced as several members of the military police looked their way. "I don't know if he should try to justify this," Noah said. "I mean, I'm not against what he did, but…"

"I know, I hope he's not going that way," Alice agreed.

Admiral Jacob Valent went on; "A lot has happened since then. I have had time to consider my actions and can tell you that, even though I believe the Mary Virus won Haven Fleet and our allies several great victories, the ends do not justify the means. Standard Galactic Laws serve a purpose. They restrict us from committing the most far-reaching and cruel crimes. I understand that thousands of innocent lives were lost because they were adjacent to Order of Eden assets. More than one warship fell out of orbit in the Cefa Solar System, causing harm to their environment and killing bystanders. That's only one example, one I've come to know well while I was overseeing the security of the Cefa Solar System recently. There were other ways, less direct ways of accomplishing the same thing I did with the Mary Virus, and I regret that I didn't try harder to use those legal means. I am at the mercy of this court and would like to make a final statement as a Haven Fleet Admiral."

It was then, as the Tribunal Admirals were discussing something no one could hear or see, that Alice made a mistake. She looked up the standard punishment for breaking the Eden Law and found that over seventy percent of offenders were executed. She dismissed the little search window and tried not to think about it.

"You may proceed," Admiral Kulsh said. "But I advise caution against hubris."

Admiral Valent nodded then looked directly into a holographic recorder that was hovering nearby. It looked like he was staring right at Alice and every other viewer watching the broadcast. "I have the honour of being one of the new founders of the Haven System and Haven Fleet. As we enter into new alliances, grow, and evolve into an honourable fighting force that could not make me more proud, I fear that we are over-prioritizing defence. We cannot win the war against the Order of Eden, the Edxi or any other enemy who is actively trying to do us harm while nearly all our focus is on the Haven System. There are other places, nearby solar systems, that need our help. In their desperation and our absence, some of them are embracing the Order of Eden. That is because the Order of Eden in this region has an intelligent leader that knows how to not only conduct a shooting war, but a cultural one. The Order presents themselves as the saviours of humanity and under the right circumstances, they are convincing."

Admiral Valent took a moment to let the gallery murmur, then went on. "We must get to people in need first, approach them diplomatically and offer them meaningful aid. When we arrive late, after the Order of Eden, we have to be prepared to fight with all our intelligence, our vigour, and with only the best motivations and methods. Compassion must come first as we offer to help people on their terms whenever possible. We have to learn about the societies we're saving so we don't become like the Order of Eden. Our enemy erases culture and replaces it with rampant consumerism that pushes entire planets into debt so they are forced into servitude. That can never be our way."

"How can a bounty hunter talk about compassion?" a red-faced man near the front of the gallery shouted as Admiral Jacob Valent paused for a moment.

Alice found herself clenching her teeth at having a part of her father's past brought up. It was an inconvenient part taken out of context. If they knew that her father picked his targets carefully, always tried to hunt people who deserved it, and was fair when he couldn't, maybe it wouldn't be so frustrating. "Everyone has a past, asshole," she whispered.

Admiral Valent's expression hardened as he went on. "I said it once already: I am proud of Haven Fleet, but now I think the spectre of cowardice is beginning to loom over some of its leadership. We have taken back the Haven Solar System and now make every effort to shore up its defences. That's difficult, it takes time, but we have turned inward and if we're not careful, we will become isolated while our enemies close in around us. I have seen it happen before. We need to explore while we maintain our defences. We need to connect to other cultures and show our generous intentions while we learn about them. Lastly, we must fight the inequity and abuse that the Order of Eden will inflict on humanity. We must stop the message of superiority that they are spreading like a virus that will lead to inter-species war as the Order of Eden encourages the imprisonment, slavery and processing of other sentients in the galaxy. Our multi-species fleet must represent and defend the good in the galaxy, and if we don't strike out, if we don't fight to expose and defeat our enemies, then we will be cowards first, then victims, and finally gone or subjugated."

Most of the gallery got to their feet, and it was then that Alice realized that the majority of them were wearing uniforms. They cheered and there was something angry in their jubilance. "Decorum! Decorum!" Admiral Dulth cried, his Mergillian mouth opening wide.

They ignored him this time, and only settled when Admiral Jacob Valent half turned to calmly stare at them for a moment.

Alice wasn't sure if he was finished until he turned to face the Tribunal and nodded at them saying; "I freely submit myself to the judgement of this Tribunal."

After a long pause, Admiral Methias said; "Thank you, Admiral Valent."

The trio were obscured again for a brief moment as they discussed something Alice wished she could hear. Admiral Doolth spoke for the Tribunal stiffly when the barrier disappeared. "Admiral Valent, this Haven Fleet Tribunal has decided that all luxury credits will be removed from your accounts. Whatever property you have been given or lent will be returned within five days. Finally, you will be discharged from Haven Fleet forthwith. Whatever property disputes you have with the military service or civilian government will be settled in their favour within five days. This judgement and the sentence are rendered with prejudice, and cannot be contested. The Tribunal dismisses all parties and thanks the facilitating staff."

Alice watched as all of the markings except for the Founder's Mark faded out on Jacob Valent's clothing. "It's not fair," she breathed. The Fleet's structure was built with his advice. He was one of its first Captains, and won important victories. A list of them and his work ran through her mind as her frustration mixed with dismay. The gallery erupted angrily as military police and a few bailiffs started trying to get them to calm down. The doors at the rear of the court opened, and some of the people from the gallery rushed out.

Gavin Hale wasn't one of them. He stood in the centre of the frame. To his left was the raging gallery, while Alice and the rest of his audience could see Jake, Ayan and Minh-Chu as they were led through a side door by a bailiff. "So, on a morning that we thought would be average in every way, we have the dismissal of one of the most celebrated Admirals - a

Founder - in Haven Fleet. My legal expert has been in my ear throughout his entire statement, telling me that the death penalty is the most common sentence given for breaking this particular Galactic Standard Law, which forbids the release of an unsuitably limited artificial intelligence with malicious intent. Now, I know that's a lot of legal-ese for some of you, so we'll be unpacking that, and finding out who knew that this was going to happen before now throughout the day on this stream. Before we switch to our studio feed, I'd like to acknowledge the significance of Jacob Valent's statement to the people of the Haven System. He's done this before for other governments before he and his fiance, Admiral Ayan Anderson, arrived in this solar system. I've seen the recordings of him calling people to war against the same enemy he mentioned here, the Order of Eden. Those were simpler speeches. This time he seemed disappointed that the military he helped build hasn't taken more direct action, and I'm sure many people in the force protecting our solar system may take that personally. I have no doubt that they have the will to fight, and I wonder if Jacob Valent's final message as an Admiral will motivate the leadership to dedicate more resources to protecting the Cluster, or even the Galaxy from the threat we all know. The courtroom is emptying, and I see that he's had a severe effect on the people here. I have no doubt that his message will spread. We'll be following the repercussions of this morning's events closely, so stay tuned."

Alice deactivated the hologram and checked on the progress of the Clever Dream II. It would arrive in orbit within the hour. Noah was caring, consoling, it was almost annoying. "He has a plan. I don't know him, sure, but someone like that won't just let himself get shut out."

"I know," Alice snapped. It wasn't what she was thinking,

but it did sound like her father. It was irritating that Noah said it first. Then she looked at him. He was being patient, her tone didn't do anything to push him away. "I'm sorry," she told Noah with a sigh.

"For what?" he asked, concern creasing his brow.

"This was supposed to be a special weekend, but now the only thing I'll be doing in my room is packing," she said, starting to walk down the bridge in a way that was anything but leisurely. "And these heels are driving me nuts." She took them off and continued on.

Noah fell in step beside her. "Hey, it's okay, really okay. No matter what happens, I'm right here."

"They're not just tearing my Dad down, they're disbanding the Special Operations unit. Who knows where either of us will end up. You could be sent on one of those long-range missions like Traveller. He's been gone a long time now."

"Two months and a bit," Noah said, nodding. "But he likes it that way, even though he didn't get to drop off the Haven Node that connected the Haven with the British Alliance. He's still bitter about that."

"Well, we might not see each other for months in or out of the cyberscape. Maybe I can use this as an opportunity to leave the service. You're most of the way out already," Alice said.

"Just don't make any decisions right now," he said, touching her hand.

"Why didn't they warn me about this? What did they think would happen?" Alice asked, stopping and turning towards Noah.

"Maybe they were protecting you?" he said.

"So they're not afraid to send me into battle, but they'll

protect me from this? Why? Are they afraid to hurt my precious little feelings?" It was infuriating, especially since she suspected it might be true. Then she saw that Noah was at a loss for words and sighed. "Thank you for being here. I know, you probably thought this was an interstellar booty call, so it's a switch, but you're still here, and that means a lot."

"Of course I am, and you know it was so much more than a booty call. I mean, that's mostly why I came, you're irresistible. Exactly my type: beautiful and bratty."

Alice laughed despite a little annoyance, then she pushed him. "Hey, not fair; teasing me during my family drama."

"Just doing what I can for my lady love," he said, squeezing her hand. "Besides, your Dad will see his way through this, right? He's been through worse, this is just politics and career crap."

"Maybe. I've just got to get there. I want to talk to him and everyone else who knew about this in person. It's not a holo-call kinda thing," Alice said, rushing towards her room with Noah at her side.

Chapter 3

An Old Calling

THE MOMENT HAD PASSED. Jacob Valent fell on his sword for a crime that he committed and no one else would be prosecuted. The details behind the Mary Virus wouldn't be made public, especially the fact that he didn't make it.

On the other hand, the fact that he made his thoughts clear on the direction Haven Fleet was taking didn't bring him the relief he hoped it would. Many people in military service would feel insulted, including thousands that he respected. If that turned things around, got more top commanders rethinking their defensive stance, then it would be worth it. There were signs everywhere that their enemies were expanding, encroaching and he believed there was no better time to fight.

Sticking to the statement he'd prepared with Ayan and Minh-Chu was the smart move, but it also held him back. Jake hoped what he did next would help him shed the last of his frustration with Haven Fleet.

"Are you ready for this?" Liara asked as she walked into the private court antechamber. The only thing in that space was a table and four chairs.

"I've been ready for weeks," Jake replied. Defence Minister Terry Ozark McPatrick, or Oz as all his friends and family called him, came into the room through a sliding side door.

The Defence Minister was in full regalia, including a thick long coat. The most eye-catching thing on it was the triple globe symbol with a crow stamped through the lowest circle on his shoulder. It was the centrepiece to the Haven Government's final flag. He took the coat off and folded it over a chair. Jake briefly took note of his old friend's uniform. A plank with markings for every engagement he'd been in since his arrival in the Haven System was on his chest along with a circular mark with a sword through it. His rank insignia, marking him as the leader of Haven Fleet was on his shoulders, and there was a simple necklace that indicated that he was the Governor of Haven Shore, the island that served as military headquarters. Everyone he knew was moving there, including Ayan, who entered with Minh-Chu through a side door.

Instead of wearing her uniform to court, she chose a grey suit jacket and skirt that projected class but nothing celebratory. Minh-Chu was in his dress uniform with all the regalia that marked him as a Captain and the leader of Samurai Squadron. As they crossed the room to Jake, Oz turned around and smiled at him. "You were perfect out there."

"Thanks," Jake said as Ayan tucked herself under his arm. He gave her an affectionate squeeze.

"That couldn't have been easy, Jake," she said. "I'm proud of you."

"I could tell you wanted to haul all three of those Admirals onto the carpet with you," Minh-Chu said, nodding his agreement with Ayan.

"What good would that do, when everything's said and done?" Jake asked, still feeling the burn of having the ear of a billion civilians and military personnel from the spinward fringe and declining to yell into it. The hardest part was refraining from pointing at the Order of Eden, who released a much worse virus that made artificial intelligences across the galaxy murder a trillion or more humans. *They did it first.* It was a thought that went through his head more than once. Liara was the one who made it clear that the punishment wasn't about anyone else. Pointing fingers at other organizations that committed the same crime would only give the court the opportunity to draw comparisons, and that could go either way. It could make Jake's crime look like a minor offense in comparison to the Order of Eden, or make him seem just as bad as them, inviting a much harsher judgement. There were other reasons why bringing up examples exterior to his case was a bad idea, but that comparison problem was the one that stood out to him.

Before going through with the next step of Oz's plan, Jake had to make sure that his fiance could accept what was about to happen. "I'm going to take a moment," he said to everyone in the room as he led her to the corner.

"What's on your mind?" Ayan asked quietly.

"I need to know you're fully on board with what I'm about to do. If you aren't, if you have any doubts, then I'll find another way. Maybe I'll take a consulting position after a long vacation, or something," Jake said.

"We've talked about this. This is something you have to do," Ayan said, sparing a glance as Admiral Lymeen Doolth entered in the gauzy white robe wrapped around her tall, furry Nafali body. "You're not finished with this fight. I'm not either, and I'm sure Alice is only getting started. If doing things this way feels right to you, then you should follow through."

"But I'm talking about you. Last time I did this, I had a tiny crew. I didn't have a fiance and a baby at home," Jake said.

With no hesitation Ayan replied; "Sure, I'd love to keep you at home, but part of you will always be out there, so get going. We'll make time to get together when we can and that'll be enough. Besides, someone's got to watch Alice's back, and I'm going to be a part of this, remember. You're not going out there alone."

"All right. I had to check in," Jake whispered, relieved, but feeling the guilt of leaving Ayan alone with baby Laura.

"You know, I think you're getting better at this relationship thing. Maybe we should set a date soon," Ayan said, smiling just enough to reveal her trademark dimples.

"I'll leave that to you and Ash," Jake replied. "Let's do this thing."

They rejoined the group around the table. Oz was at the far end. Ayan was at his side with Minh-Chu to her right, and Admiral Doolth was in the middle looking at two documents that were scrolling in the middle of the table's surface. Liara was at her side, reading through the documents.

"All right, before anything else," Oz said, tossing a small golden chip on a necklace down the length of the rectangular table. "You're going to need a ship."

Jake caught it and nodded, putting it on. "Thanks, Oz."

"The Triton was always yours more than anyone's after

you took her from Wheeler. The fifth stage refit was finished three days ago, so she's almost ready to go."

"And SOCU?" Jake asked.

"The Special Operations Combat Unit has been dissolved and you're free to make employment offers to every one of them. Take them all if you want. It's in your new contract."

"And Samurai Squadron?" Jake asked.

"They were part of SOCU, so we're free to take you up on a job offer. I have my contract all written up," he said, pointing to a holographic image as it appeared above his command and control bracer. "It's fair, with the same pay I'd get with the military with an addition or two."

Ayan snickered as she noticed something in his contract. "Naming rights to the Pilot's Den? Does it really need to be renamed?"

"I always thought that was a little imaginative, I can do better," Minh-Chu replied. "Oh, and I get to be Wing Commander with a minimum amount of active pilot time. No way are you sticking me behind a console or something because we won't have fleet support."

"I can live with that," Jake said.

"Forward a copy of the contract to me when you're finished, I want to see what else he's wedged in there," Oz said. "Oh, and just so you know, the training programs we were running aboard the Triton have moved to Freeground Station. It's good for the fleet. We'll be able to train pilots in several environments from there during their live course work."

"All right." Jake looked to Liara then. "Everything check out?"

"The contract is pretty simple, considering. It reflects every detail of the deal we made though, so yes. It's ready," she replied.

"The Triton requires a minimum crew of three hundred, doesn't it?" Doolth asked, her voice sweeter than it was while she was sitting on the bench.

"That's right," Jake replied. "I can fill the minimum with former SOCU members, and get more on board elsewhere." He already knew where he could find at least a hundred able crew members. Training them to operate aboard the Triton would be easy, especially if they were already recruited by his daughter and the Alliance of Rebel Captains.

"Before you sign this, I would like to extend an offer from my people. There are many Nafalli warriors who will want to join you as soon as they discover your purpose. Many of them see you as a hero, especially now that Alaka has become a member of my House."

"I'll be honoured if any number - one or a thousand - of your people join me. I'm paying more than the Fleet, too," he replied. "I won't be the only one responsible for hiring people, though, so I can't tell you how many we'll be taking on."

"That's reasonable, thank you, Jacob," Doolth said.

"So, now that I've fallen on my own sword, will the British Alliance, Cefa House Committee, Mergillians, and Lorander Company sign the Treaty of Lonos?"

"They're signing this afternoon, Gavin Hale is already on his way there. Haven will have plenty of allies, and the Order of Eden will officially be at war with some of the biggest concerns in the galaxy," Oz replied.

"It's in your contract. If the treaty isn't signed within seven days, you can back out with no penalties. The Triton will still be yours, and anyone serving aboard can leave Haven Fleet if they agree to serve you for the rest of their term," Liara explained, scrolling to salient points in the contract.

"Representatives from all the organisations have already told me that they're satisfied with your punishment and your new career choice. The particular thing they agree to is that we can support your mission as long as you don't break any more of the High Galactic Laws again," Oz said. "They're eager to become allies with Haven, and Lorander is looking forward to returning to the solar system."

"I hope they're more interested in answering questions this time," Jake said, running his finger across his side of the table so his contract appeared in front of him.

Oz did the same, pulling a copy to his side. "They will, but you may not have access to those answers right away. I like this for you, Jake. I think you'll show us how to win."

"You'll definitely see something," Jake said as he retracted his vacsuit uniform's glove.

Oz cleared his throat and announced; "Jacob Valent, as the Defence Minister for the Haven Government and leader of Haven Fleet, I hire you as a Privateer with this Letter of Marque and Reprisal against any and all of Haven Nation's Enemies. We will provide support as necessary for a fair fee. You are permitted to hire supplemental staff for your own purposes from the personnel we make available to you for whatever length of time you require or you can find your own personnel elsewhere. Furthermore, a representative of Haven Fleet will be provided for you. They will certify prizes after an inspection and have the right to present anyone with a ship a letter of marque that gives them the right to destroy or capture goods, infrastructure or vessels from any of Haven Nation's enemies. Good luck, and good hunting." he planted his bare hand on the table, which read his DNA, fingerprints and biometrics then recorded them in the contract.

"I'll take that job," Jake said as he pressed his hand onto the surface of his end of the table.

Ayan pressed her palm beside his. "I'm looking forward to representing Fleet Sciences aboard the Triton."

Admiral Doolth pressed her large, furry hand onto the table. "I certify and witness this contract, binding all parties to its terms."

"That's it? I don't get to touch the table and say official words?" Minh-Chu whined in a tone that was anything but serious.

"Would it help if we had dinner at your sister's restaurant to celebrate?" Jake asked.

"It would help her," Minh-Chu replied with a chuckle. "Might get her off my back about getting my military friends to go to her place more too."

"I'm afraid I'll be on Lonos, but give her my love," Oz said as he put his coat on.

"I won't be able to go to dinner with you either. I'll be standing in support of Haven Fleet on Lonos, but you will see my invitation soon. My people have wanted to host your families for some time now," Admiral Doolth said. "It would be wonderful if you could bring every member, including the little one."

"Laura loves you, so I'll definitely bring her," Ayan replied. The pair had a good friendship, and Doolth adored little Laura.

"You know you could have bought your way into this deal," Oz said to Jake as he started across the room. "You're one of the wealthiest people in the sector now that the Haven System has started exporting."

"Don't remind me," Jake replied. He owned a share of the Haven Solar System, and had rights to a portion of whatever gross earnings the government made. He hadn't drawn a single platinum pip. "I'm going to have to take a few million platinum to start my career as a corsair."

"That's until you make your first capture or kill," Oz said, clapping him on the shoulder. "I wish I was going with you, Jake, but someone's got to keep the Military on track."

"I'll send you the highlights. Just make sure your fighting machine starts lashing out soon. I can't win the war alone," Jake replied.

"But I'm sure he'll try," Minh-Chu added under his breath.

Chapter 4

Last Moments In The Cefa System

THE ROOM, which was more like a luxury apartment, was an unusual, incredible place to Noah Lucas. The hand-carved marble framed walls looked like they were from another age. There were paintings everywhere, not just printed pictures, but real framed paintings with brush strokes that were clear when he took a closer look. One that was particularly striking was a portrait of a man and woman in old heavy combat armour. They looked battle-worn, the metal sections scarred by burns and dents, but stared out at the viewer with glad eyes. A metal plate set into the bottom of the frame said; Hard Victory. Count Rishen and Countess Rishen, after the Battle of Nelhall.

He couldn't tell if they were siblings or a couple because they had a similar look, and took a picture so he could look their story up later if his interest outlasted the brief visit. The apartment had a large chandelier that hung in the foyer, sending shifting light down on them as he followed Alice up the stairs to the bedrooms.

"I can't believe he's not answering," she said after making another attempt at contacting Jacob using her thick command and control bracelet. It was one of the many designs that looked more ornamental, being transparent, blue to match her dress, and loose so it looked like jewellery. That didn't mean she didn't poke and tap it any differently than a military version.

"There's probably some legal stuff they have to take care of now that everything's final." Noah's offered explanation didn't seem to put Alice at ease at all, or slow her down. "Do you know about the people in any of these paintings?"

Alice looked around for a moment then shrugged. "I think they're all ancestors of the royal family, or maybe they're important people who stayed here," she moved on to the bedroom.

"Oh, wow, you went all out," Noah said as he took the decor in. There were a pair of small gilded robots silently drifted around the room lighting candles. Their flames cast flickering, warm yellow light around one of the largest beds he'd ever seen. There was a sitting area, doors leading off to other rooms or closets, and a broad gate with a balcony beyond but the bed was definitely the centrepiece. It was piled with fine sheets, a thick duvet and gossamer silk curtains that had a faint glimmer that caught the light as though tiny diamond flakes were scattered through the cloth. "Erabonian Silk, this stuff is worth hundreds of plat a yard," he said, feeling the cloth. Cool and smooth, it was as if someone wove water, it was so fine but heavy despite how thin it was.

"They have worm farms that grow it here," Alice said,

taking a suitcase out from under the bed and dropping it open. It was still half packed. "It's coming back into fashion, and someone made a dress out of it for me, but I don't think I'd be brave enough to wear it in public. I was going to wear it tomorrow if we stayed in." She sounded disappointed.

Noah stroked her arm with a grazing touch, then cupped her cheek when she turned towards him. "You know we're okay, right? I know you were looking forward to a romantic night, and I would have loved it too, but we don't need this. You're so crazy amazing that all this stuff just fades into the background when you're standing there, looking back at me with those baby blues. All I wanted out of this was a chance to be in the same room with you."

"I know, but I wanted tonight to be for us, and now…"

"Now we're getting ready to go on another adventure. Hopefully together. Getting split these last few months was hard, yeah, but I'm still here. You're still here, which is surprising."

"Why is that surprising?" Alice asked, concern wrinkling her forehead.

"I've been working my way through the underworld for three months. Grinding, selling, watching my back, and you've been in palaces with royalty, doing a really important job. I mean, what you've been up to, where you've been and what you've seen must have been amazing. I'm just a pilot and a hawker," Noah said with a shrug.

Alice took his hand and held it to her chest. "I didn't stop thinking about you for a day. I can't count the number of times I thought; 'I wish Noah was here to see this.' You're in my heart and in my head. That's why I wanted this to be our weekend, and I wanted tonight to be perfect." She looked around at the candles, the grand bed, then back to Noah and smiled sheepishly for a moment. "Well, maybe this is too much. It doesn't feel much like us."

"I don't think we're vacation people, either. Maybe we can change that, but I think we're more 'catch the fun as it comes,' kinda people," Noah said, drawing her into his arms.

A message forced her bracelet to vibrate and send a short melody delivered by a blast of horns. "Oh, great, that's the Prince," she said, pulling away reluctantly and looking at her bracelet.

"You're not going to miss him, I'm guessing?" Noah asked with an eyebrow raised.

"Oh, hell no. Some bug is probably going to catch me saying this, but he's a spoiled brat down to the core. Good ideas when it comes to government, but a needy little bugger when it comes to everything else." She sighed and accepted the call.

Noah backed away so he wouldn't be seen with her and watched. "Princess, I'm sorry to interrupt your vacation, but I hear you are going off world," said a voice with a heavy accent.

"Yes, I'm being reassigned. I hope you're safe, how are the guards?" Alice asked.

"The Royal Guard is taking over now. Your people are already leaving. They say you are no longer in command, except for the cheery one, Faloo. I will miss her almost as much as I will be sure to miss you. She tells me that your ship will be picking her up on the way to you, and gave me an unexpected embrace before leaving. Are all Nafalli so affectionate?"

"Faloo is a special one. I'm going to see if I can get a few squads of Haven Marines to help you with security," Alice said.

"There's no need, you and the rest of the Haven people did a marvelous job training the new Royal Guards. They're as ready as they'll ever be," the Prince said cheerily.

"Most of them haven't finished training yet, they barely know what they're doing and I don't trust Balkam. He has no experience running security. I didn't say anything because I thought the position would be temporary, your Highness." Alice was careful to speak conversationally, adding no extra weight or insistence to her words.

"I understand your concern, but Wilbur Balkam has seen a lot in his many years. There's no need for concern, especially if you agree to stay. I could reward you handsomely if you were to remain as the Captain of my guard. How does three million platinum a month to start sound?"

Noah was alarmed at the amount. The average good meal cost seven platinum. A used ship for a crew of ten with a size-able cargo hold and a wormhole drive cost around one million if you didn't care where it came from. About twice that with real ownership history and servicing. The Prince's offer was beyond generous, it was, well, royal. Maybe it was because he'd seen so many people he loved in his life move on to better opportunities while he was growing up, but what happened next shocked Noah.

With no hesitation, Alice smiled at the Prince's image on her bracelet and said; "That's very generous, but I can't accept, your Highness." She glanced up at him, then looked back down at her bracelet and added; "I've spent too much time away from the people I love already, and I might have a chance at being with them again soon."

"I would understand if your father wasn't a confessed war criminal, Alice," the Prince said more stiffly. "Or is it someone else? A lover you haven't told me about?"

"Actually, it's Noah. I told you about him every time you asked if I had…" she started to answer, her finger starting to move towards the disconnect icon on her wrist.

"Oh, yes, the straw man you held up every time I asked about your entanglements or someone wondered if we were having a dalliance. You can't tell me he's real, this rogue of yours…" the Prince groaned.

"Well, I have to be going. Be careful, Prince Philip. Please cooperate with your Royal Guards and keep public appearances to a minimum. Good luck, your Highness," Alice finished as she ended the call with a sigh. "It feels so good to hang up on that guy."

Hearing that she told people about him, that she made sure the Prince knew that she was already taken was enough encouragement for Noah to cross the room and pick her up and hold her so she was looking down on him. Alice laughed and put her arms around him. "Tell me you didn't turn three million a month down for me," he said, kissing her neck.

"I did. No regrets so far," Alice said, pushing her fingers into his hair as his lips made their way up and down her neck. "You really know how to distract me."

He was making his way to a spot right beneath her ear. "I'm definitely not worth the sacrifice, but I'll try to make up for it." She also stopped using her empathic gift on him when they were alone together. The sacrifices Alice made for him were astonishing even before he watched her turn the job offer down.

"Would you have taken the offer?" she asked, running her fingers over the nape of his neck.

"Yes," he whispered under her ear.

Alice gasped and pushed his head away so she could look

down into his eyes. "Oh, no, now I have to call the Prince back."

"Don't you dare. I would use every pip of that platinum to build an empire in Cefa for us. We'd be living in a place nicer than this dump," Noah said before capturing her lips.

Another buzz came from her wrist with a chime that warned that it was a high-priority call and she patted his shoulder urgently. "That's probably my Dad."

Noah put her back on her feet with care and was about to step far away when she caught his arm and drew him back to her side. "I think this is between you and him, right?" he said hurriedly.

"Don't worry, my Mom's on this call too," Alice said, accepting the call and activating the holographic projection system that made it look like Jake and Ayan were standing right in front of them. "So, Dad's a war criminal now?" Alice asked.

"Well, hi, Alice. How have the last couple weeks been? Have there been any more assassination attempts?" Jake asked in return.

"Just one, but we caught it before the Prince was in danger," Alice replied. "Why didn't you tell me you were being prosecuted?"

"Because I knew you'd try to stop it, no matter what I said or did," Jake replied.

"It's what he'd do in your place for either of us," Ayan added. "You look very pretty by the way."

"Thank you," Alice said, relaxing a little, her mood starting to turn from indignation to worry. "I guess you're right, I would have tried to stop it. Why did you let it happen at all? You own a big piece of the whole solar system, I'm sure you could have leaned on the scale, gotten out of it somehow."

The surprised look on Jake's face was clear as he gave a firm answer. "We don't do that, remember? Besides, there was a treaty on the line between the British Alliance, Lorander, the Mergillians, and others. They needed to see that Haven Fleet could hold their own people up to the standards of Galactic law, and I had committed the worst crime of war out of everyone they wanted to charge. Now that they've demonstrated that justice works in the Haven System, the treaty will be signed and the Haven System won't be alone."

Ayan added; "They wanted you too for attacking defenceless ships in the Cefa System. I still don't condone what you did then, but I understand it. Everyone in Haven Fleet Command does. You'll never be held accountable for that now that the whole series of events has been resolved."

"Okay, thank you, but you didn't have to take it all on yourself," Alice said. "I was ready to face whatever consequences that might bring. Just like I did when I was demoted for building Rogue and letting her go off on her own."

"I wasn't going to let everyone pay for a decision that I made. The Mary Virus was a repeat of bad behaviour. It worked out the first time when Jonas did it. I wouldn't take that back if I had the chance, especially because it led to you, but the Mary Virus killed thousands of innocent people. It was a stain on Haven Fleet's history, and I'm afraid it'll be something people think of when they take a good look at our family. For Ayan's, yours and even Laura's sake, I'm sorry I launched that virus. Now I'm going to do things differently. They gave me the Triton back with all her codes, refitted the way I want it, and I can hire whoever I want out of SOCU."

"And I can issue Letters of Marque on behalf of the Fleet," Ayan added. "I have one drafted for the Captain of the Corsair," she winked at Noah then looked back to Alice, "And for you. You could stay in the Fleet as an alternative, if you like. I know you put a lot of work into being an officer. You can still move up the ranks."

"No," Alice said. "If Dad's going Privateer, I either want to be on his crew, or to fight alongside in the Clever Dream Two. That is, if it measures up to the original."

"Oh, it'll measure up," Ayan said with a little smile. "What about you, Noah?"

"So, with a Letter of Marque, I wouldn't be a deserter anymore? I wouldn't be undercover?" Noah asked hopefully.

"The charge of desertion has been wiped off your record. Oz - I mean, the Defence Minister - had his people make it clear that you were working for us all along and classified the details at the highest level," Jake replied. "Mostly so you can have choices. You can continue working with the underworld, return to the Fleet, or become an official Privateer."

"Then show me where I have to press my palm so I can make the Corsair an honest ship, especially..." he trailed off, deciding not to say that he'd be happiest working alongside Jake and Ayan's daughter.

"...especially if he gets to keep everything he's made so far," Alice finished for him.

Noah shook his head instinctively, but stopped himself from correcting her.

"Speak up, Noah, what's your condition?" Jake asked, addressing him more like a soldier.

"I think his condition is standing right beside him," Ayan told Jake as she started to grin at Alice and Noah. "They've been apart for three and a half months, and they're all dressed up."

It took more courage than he'd mustered in a while, but

Noah said; "I love your daughter, and missed being with her." Hearing the words aloud, he realized that what he said could be taken in a way he didn't intend and quickly added; "I don't mean, you know, not in a sexual way or anything - things haven't gone that far yet - but, I mean in the same room. The Cyberscape is great and everything, but there's something special about being together for real, you know? It's just, well, she's very special, and…" he took a quick breath before continuing, "…you're her parents, you know how special she is. Is it getting hotter in here?"

The ladies laughed while Jake crossed his arms and watched. Alice patted his cheek and put herself under his arm. "I think he and I are on the same page. It feels like things have been on pause with Noah, with you two, and with Laura. I haven't seen my sister since I got here either."

"Well, it'll be pretty easy to fix that," Ayan said. "We're getting together for dinner tonight in Haven Shore. Oh, and there's a block of apartments reserved there, including your old place. It's all set up."

"I just transferred ownership. You should get the notification in a couple of hours," Jake said. "There are a few units nearby if Noah wants one too, he might be able to afford it, it's up to him."

Alice was about to say something, then hesitated before haltingly saying; "So, okay then. I think I'll take you up on that, but I bet I'll be spending a lot more time on the Triton or the Clever Dream."

"It's always good to have a home to go back to. Something that feels stationary where you can get away from it all," Ayan said, prompting nods from Alice and Noah. "I'll send you the information on Privateering, who you can hire for your crews. Oh, and I'll give you directions to dinner."

"So, we don't have to report to Freeground Station?" Noah asked.

"No, that was a general order for everyone who was being freed up so they could join the Triton or another of the first Privateering crews. You can land in your old Hangar if you like, Alice," Ayan said.

"I probably will," she replied. "Okay, I have to pack. The Clever Dream is waiting, and there's a shuttle on the way."

"Okay, can't wait to see you," Ayan said with a dimple-enhanced smile. "You too, Noah."

"Okay, help me pack," Alice said, rushing to the antique wood dresser.

Noah reached for one of the drawers and was stopped as Alice said; "Oh, not that one. I don't want you to see what's in there just yet."

"No way I'm spoiling any surprises," he said, more than a little eager to get some real time alone with her. "No rushing, though. I mean…"

"We've been seeing each other for months. This is definitely not rushing, even my Dad would approve of the pace of our relationship."

"I think he'd rather we stopped right here," Noah said with a snicker.

He opened one of the lower drawers, found it empty, then moved on to the next, where there was a spare sidearm and a thick belt. He took the gun case from the drawer beneath, made sure the weapon wasn't loaded, then put it inside. Alice took everything from the forbidden drawer and put the contents in one of her suitcase's large inner pockets with care. From out of the corner of his eye, Noah could see just enough that there were stringy, frilly, and generally small garments in that assortment of clothes, and was even happier that the surprise wasn't completely ruined.

"He really rattles you, doesn't he?" Alice asked, amused.

"Jacob Valent rattles just about everyone. I mean, to you, he's your Dad. You can get special favours, probably joke around with him, talk about all the stuff you've seen together and he adores you. I'm dating you, and I'm sure they could tell tonight was, well, a certain kind of special, and I mean, you're his little girl, you know?"

"Aw, he's not even listening, and you're getting all tense," Alice said, enjoying it a little too much. "Don't worry, I'll protect you. At least during dinner. I can't guarantee anything after that, though. He's going to want to know a lot about the Shattered End and the Rogue Captains. You're his best source."

Noah laughed nervously. "Oh, great, I'm looking forward to that debriefing."

"Well, I'm packed. Are you going back to the Corsair, or..."

"I'll just tell Easy to follow the Clever Dream, if you don't mind me catching a ride," Noah said.

"Are you kidding? I'm not letting you out of my sight, Flyboy," Alice said as she led the way to the foyer. The robots were already floating around the room, dousing candles and tidying up.

Chapter 5

A Visit to Iora

THE LIVING ROOM had been darkened so the hologram of the large courtroom where Jacob Valent was dismissed could be shown in true-to-life quality. Olivia watched Eve and Miken more than the events unfolding live all around them.

The playback could be viewed later, and she'd have her team analyze every detail, but the same couldn't be said for her fellow leaders. Eve, the iconic religious and military figure who pushed the Order of Eden religion wherever she went, seemed spellbound by the proceedings. The most frightening thing about her was her fanatical belief that Dron, the True Overlord, was receiving information from his brother, Lister Hampon, who was somewhere in the future. Admiral Olivia Scanlon didn't believe it, she never had. The religious side of the Order was just propaganda, a way to lure and trap people who were looking for something to believe in.

To her left was Mikan, the cool-headed leader of Citadel in the Cluster of ninety-eight stars. He was one of the few who had been to the Haven System, stayed there during the Order of Eden occupation, and watched as Jacob Valent retook Haven Shore. He observed the proceedings passively, concentrating on Valent as the fallen Admiral gave his statement.

Eve looked worried at first, as though she feared that Valent would reveal some secret about the Order, or her directly. He was one of the few people who knew most of the founders of their organization and had personally experienced some of the most important turning points in its history. As his statement came to a close, and Jacob Valent was sentenced, Eve was agog, then gleeful.

While Gavin Hale closed the broadcast out, Eve leaped to her feet and spun, laughing. "He's disgraced! This was his one moment before going into obscurity to turn the blame back on us for releasing our own intelligent viruses across the galaxy, and he didn't even bother. He was too focused on the little fleet he built and what they'd do without him. What a self-centred man, I wouldn't have guessed it."

"He didn't point fingers at us because he understands the law," Scanlon said, rising to her feet. Being near Eve was tiring. Dron probably thought he was sending her a boon by relocating the religious icon in the Cluster, but it was a drain on her energy and patience. Letting the steam out of her enthusiasm was a pleasure.

It was encouraging when Mikan helped. "Their laws don't take the action of an enemy into account when someone is being prosecuted for a crime unless it's a case of direct self-defence or unusual precedent."

"What?" Eve asked, her elation starting to fall.

"Let me put it this way," Scanlon started as she deactivated the hologram. "If you burn my house down, then I burn yours down a week later, we've both committed a crime. You and I would be charged with arson separately, and I can say that I was just taking revenge, but that isn't a defence. In a Haven court, only my actions and their consequences are considered. There are exceptions, but that analogy is best for Valent's situation."

"That's right, revenge isn't recognized as a mitigating motivation, even during sentencing," Mikan said, rising and joining Scanlon as she walked onto the balcony.

Their third wheel was right behind, surprised. "It can't be," Eve said. "Then, there are no legal repercussions against the Order for the viruses that were released?"

"They declared war," Scanlon said with a snicker. "And our people on Lonnes tell us that the signing that will bring a great alliance to fruition will be done by the end of the day. That will bring two of the biggest military organizations in the galaxy onto their side officially. A general declaration of war will follow within the week with all the Alliance members on board. I would say that's consequence enough."

"Why don't we do something about that? Your people there should assassinate people, or bomb the venue." A blaze was building in Eve's eyes already.

One way to stop one of her tantrum-rants was to embarrass her, so Olivia snickered and shook her head. "You didn't know about the signing? Don't you read the briefs, or at least have a program read them to you?"

"There's never any time," Eve replied.

"You must. Unless you want me to simplify things for you. I'm here to help, remember. I have people who can take control of your military assets so you have more time to preach and concentrate on your other pursuits." Scanlon watched as

Eve calmed down and shook her head. It took work to control Eve, but she made sure there was a purpose to every word.

Eve returned to the topic of Jacob Valent. "So, it's true. This sentencing was all theatre. A show to demonstrate that Haven Fleet can follow Galactic Standard Law." Eve moved to the railing where she turned and looked at Scanlon and Mikan, her long gown shifting in the humid breeze.

The fireflies were out, glowing yellow-red. Olivia hated the bugs. The insects were from the Edxi settlement a whole continent away. Alien to the galaxy, they stowed away inside Edxi egg pods and left their cocoons when the more deadly beings hatched. The glowing pests were a reminder that there were much larger juvenile, ravenous Edxi chasing and feeding on resettled humans only hours distant. "I hate Iora," Scanlon said under her breath.

"I know, Olivia, but you'll be moving on, yes?" asked Mikan.

She flashed him a little smile and nodded. Her destination was a place that Citadel found, and he presented it to her after they'd been spying on them for months. It was his way of easing tension between her, the Order of Eden forces under her command and Citadel. The gift was perfect, a world named Tiy, which was populated by over three billion humans who were little more advanced than their ancestors were when they sent their first rockets into space. The technical de-evolution of their culture was ideal. It started with a catastrophe that took place over three centuries ago. "I can't wait."

"I'm right, aren't I? Jacob Valent's dismissal was just a show," Eve pressed, demanding their full attention.

"I don't think so," Scanlon replied, trying not to sound impatient. "The British Alliance and the Lorander Corporation wouldn't be placated against a toothless punishment.

There is disgrace in his separation from the military that he founded."

"A loss of trust," Mikan added. "I imagine there will be a limit to what resources he may be able to access. Just the same, I wouldn't underestimate him."

"Neither would I." Scanlon had reviewed the records Vindyne and Regent Galactic had on him from his time as a bounty hunter. When he started all he had was a half-broken down ship and no memory of friends, home or family. In only a few years he built a reputation for himself, turned his ship into a formidable machine, and gathered a crew who respected him for the most part. Many of them were still serving, and she expected they would go with him if he decided to captain another vessel. "Valents have a habit of taking a pile of scrap and turning it into a powerful tool. He's not inept when it comes to earning platinum and using it well, either. I wonder what kind of deal he made?" she asked no one in particular.

Eve answered anyway. "A good one. He owns a significant portion of the Haven System, I'm sure he could buy whatever he wants. When they start selling the Communication Nodes, he'll be even richer. We have to kill him, and soon. The alliance has to be broken too. I'll have my people start planning."

"They won't sell their Haven Nodes. That is not the kind of culture they're building with them," Mikan said.

"Solar systems would pay billions for them. Of course they're going to sell them," Eve said, flicking his opinion away with her hand.

"No, they want to connect the galaxy with them at the centre. It's an enviable cultural win. That's why they let us steal one and put it right in orbit." Scanlon could feel her patience eroding. It was an argument that she'd had with Eve several times.

"You believe what you like, it doesn't make it true," Eve said with a sigh, as though she were addressing a child. "I have a speech to prepare for. I expect to see you there."

Mikan waited for her to leave the apartment before saying; "She has been an asset here. People are chanting her words more often than ever."

'Victory is our right. Victory is our fate,' was the phrase. The sound of tens of thousands of people saying that along with Eve still rang in her mind from the speech Eve gave in the Iyagda system only two weeks before. That recruitment went well, even though they had to retreat hastily a day later when a pair of stolen Advanced Destroyers appeared in orbit and bombarded one of their military bases. The effort to retake Iyagda ended there because Eve panicked and ordered a full retreat. "They're our words too, at least for now."

"You still believe that the Order of Eden can run purely as a corporate venture?" Mikan asked, a little smile playing on his blackened lips. It was exaggerated by the lines running from them down his chin and across his cheeks. The markings were a trademark of his people, who wrote their stories on their faces and necks. What his lines said, she didn't know, but she was sure he'd been an assassin, a traveler, and lost several people during the Fourth Fall.

"Absolutely. The Order of Eden was much more effective when it was still Regent Galactic. Most worlds were taken without firing a shot. Watch what I do with Tiy. You'll see."

"Eve told me you've done this before." The curiosity he had about her seemed endless, it was part of his charm. "Is it true?"

"There was a world called Gillus." Scanlon replied. "The

Omnivirus and a few ecological disasters nearly wiped out an entire generation along with all evidence that they came on a colony ship centuries before I arrived. So, there were only a few hundred million people living there at the time. It was almost exactly like your spies have seen on Tiy. They'd forgotten that they came from another star. I offered them a better way of life and gave them clear evidence that their ancestors came from Earth. It took a combination of technology, mercy for the forgotten, and well-designed propaganda for me to completely disrupt their society. After a year of turbulence, my people were in place, directing their politics, commerce, and bringing millions into the Regent Galactic military. Hundreds of thousands of them are here now, scattered amongst my forces. If Eve didn't order a retreat in the Cefa System when the ring was discovered, it wouldn't have taken another nine weeks to bring my reinforcements in."

"I didn't know she caused that much harm when she withdrew. I suspected that it was a shrewd move, considering how close it is to the Haven System," Mikan said. "She tells me that we're finished there because of its proximity and its involvement with Haven."

"Not quite," Scanlon replied, batting a glowing bug that ventured too close to her face away. "The people I have in Haven tell me that the Special Operations Combat Unit is withdrawing, but an even larger Haven Fleet force will be moving in by the end of the week to assist with stability and security. The Cefa government is trading an entire world and the ring for their continued presence. Once the Coronation is over, their job will become easier. They'll be reaping the benefits of their alliance in only a month or two, especially if they reconnect the wormhole ring to the Legardis Route with

Lorander's help. There will be an interstellar wormhole highway that'll reinvigorate trade in that area."

"You want my people to stop it." There was something predatory about Mikan's smile. "You want me to assassinate the Prince."

"Him and the entire royal family. I want the Valents to return to Planet Lacini because the Cefa System is falling into chaos. If Haven Fleet is too busy trying to prevent a civil war, or policing the great houses, then it'll slow development down and tax their resources."

"I will do this. The Rixe is ready, and her crew is eager. I know Dron would approve. He was right about you." There was no hesitation in him as he strode inside and out of the apartment.

The sting of losing Captain Jaden Holm, the last commander she sent after a Valent, was fading, but not absent. There would be relief in knowing that the work Alice had laboured over was undone. Even more, if Mikan could draw one of them out and kill them. With that part of her plan in motion, Admiral Olivia Scanlon turned her full attention to Tiy, and how she would rewrite their society then bury their culture forever.

Chapter 6

On Ancient Wings

FROM THE COCKPIT of his fighter, Minh-Chu could see all of Haven Shore, the first island that his friends settled on when they arrived in the solar system. The large section of burned jungle was already rich with life, covered in glistening green growth. The saplings competed with each other as they strove to reach the heights of the rainforest trees that survived the fires.

The Shard, a large building on the north edge of the island, had been rebuilt and it stood tall, like a gleaming dark stone jutting out from the northern cliffs. It was a prison and security centre now, with a rogue's gallery that he would rather avoid. The restricted airspace around it made that a certainty.

Far south of that was the central city, where the reassembled Everin Building and two that looked much like it were connected by the maglev rail that ran through, under, and around every major part of the island. These structures were inspired by the underwater habitats of Issyrians, where every dwelling was a pod that was affixed to a hidden frame. It made them look like giant clutches of eggs with mother-of-pearl surfacing that reflected the light in an array of colours. He could recall the evacuation months before when each of the pods was taken into orbit by fighters and corvette class ships. It was good to see the building reassembled.

The sprawling port was a collection of intersecting circles with landing platforms and hangars that occupied a large portion of that side of the island. The docks were beyond that. A hydrofoil ferry was picking up speed, rising out of the water as it started its quick trip to the mainland. A shuttle was faster, but people took the Hydrofoils for fun, or to see the freshwater ocean up close.

"It's so good to see this place back together again," Minh-Chu sighed to himself as the tree-like offices and housing came into view in the distance. They were set up along the edge and inside the jungle near the middle of the island, or on the Green Line, as some called it because the northern half of Haven Shore was stony with high cliffs while the other was overwhelmed by the jungle. Those apartments were strategically placed above and amongst the trees with broad walkways. Most of the wildlife avoided those areas, and the rest were lured away by drones and areas to the south that provided much more fresh fruit and prey. As soon as his fiancee, Ashley, returned from the Cefa System, she'd be picking one of those homes. He could barely wait.

There were other buildings just north of the forest, some of which were still under construction like the military museum. The whole point of that angular structure and what people would see inside would be to remind everyone that

Haven Fleet was a gathering of wanderers, travelers, mercenaries, and broken militias at first. Its history was one of the people who learned to get along to work towards common goals. Beside that was the recently completed Hart News Building, standing tall with a red HN at the top, nestled between shuttle landing pads.

In the middle of everything, including the barracks, administration complex and others, was the Monte Carlo. He looked down at it, slowing his fighter so he could take a good look at the vicious-looking ship. It had been turned into a monument that celebrated the last of the Bullet Chasers, a crew that made a great sacrifice to stop a group of missiles and torpedoes that were launched well before Minh-Chu or any of his friends were born. After their lead pilot, Cooper "Breaker" Anders, finished recovering, there was a ceremony where the crew had the opportunity to tell their story to everyone in the Haven System, then receive the Platinum Star for Conspicuous Valour.

Nearly everyone in the Special Operations Combat Unit missed it since they were busy guarding the Cefa System, including Minh-Chu. He did make a quick trip before then to offer Cooper along with the gunners - Garma and Gren - places in Samurai Squadron once they finished up training, but had to return to the Cefa System that same day.

It was months later, and it was time to pay the trio a visit. He heard they were finishing a personal project in one of the Starport's hangars, but didn't know which one they were in. As Minh-Chu was about to contact Port Administration, he heard a buzzing behind him. "That can't be..." he said as he checked the reverse view in his head-up display. There, as if from some ancient earth sky, was a sleek propeller plane. He checked the Threat Identification System Display and smiled as he saw the craft's image with the name; Supermarine Spitfire Mark V Reproduction.

By the time he read that Cooper Anderson was flying it, Minh-Chu was grinning from ear to ear. He'd seen high-efficiency propeller craft before, but nothing like that. People didn't fly reproductions, especially if they ran on fossil fuels, they sat proudly in museums, large lobbies, or private collections.

Breaker dipped one wing, then the other a few times, saying 'hello' with a wing wave before throttling up and going around Minh-Chu, who could have gone much faster than the Spitfire, but watched the relic go by instead. The noise, form and powerful look of the craft were mesmerizing. "Good to see you, Ronin," Cooper said over the open communications frequency.

"You too, Breaker. I see you're enjoying your vacation," Minh-Chu replied. "Coming down anytime soon?"

"Landing right now. Wait. Are you here to see me?" Breaker asked. He sounded surprised.

"You and the Twins. You wouldn't know where they are right now, would you?" Minh-Chu asked.

"They're in the hangar. Follow me down," Breaker said.

Minh-Chu carefully followed the Spitfire at a safe distance as it lined up with one of the only long landing strips in the port, then rolled into the hangar. Once he set his Uriel fighter on the deck inside, Minh-Chu got out and was greeted by the Twins, a pair of Mergillians with broad heads and wide smiles. "This is one of the older Angel fighters," one of them said as she looked the hull of his Uriel fighter over. "It is going out of service, yes?"

"This one's already retired, so I bought it before it got tagged for recycling," Minh-Chu said. "Actually, I bought two.

One for my Ashley." He was about to say; 'fiancee,' but changed his mind at the last instant because he didn't like the word. He loved that he was going to marry Ashley, but the word fiancee always felt too fancy for him.

"It is nice," the other Mergillian said, not sounding too impressed. "Do you know where we can see the Avenger Type? We have not seen one yet."

The Avenger was a new generation of fighter built in an Uriel body that was otherwise designed from scratch to include most of the recent technologies Haven Fleet had discovered and developed. "Those are just going into service. I'd have to do some sneaking and bribing to get my hands on one."

"I have many luxury credits," Gren the Mergillian said in a whisper that suggested conspiracy. "Who do we bribe?"

Minh-Chu laughed and shook his head. "That's a good way to get yourself locked up in the Shard for a few months."

"They don't like bribery here, Gren," Cooper said as he joined them, pulling his gloves off. "Besides, that retired fighter's got more modern marvels than anything from our time."

"But we've trained on it thoroughly and know its mysteries. The Avenger is greater in all ways," Garma said. "This is old tuna."

"Old tuna?" Minh-Chu asked.

"An expression where I come from that was in an old ad for canned seafood." Cooper shook Minh-Chu's hand, his grip was firm.

For the first time, he noticed that he was about the same height, which was fairly short compared to most human men. "You looked taller laying down," Minh-Chu said, adding; "But much better upright."

"Thanks. Where I come from most pilots were short, it

saved on mass. You'd fit right in," Cooper replied. "So, what brings you here?"

"Well, if I knew this was here, that would be enough," Minh-Chu said, walking to the Spitfire. It had such a stance on the ground that it looked like it yearned to fly. He ran a hand along a wing and felt the bumps of the rivets. "This is amazing."

" I sent the parts list to the fabricator building here along with some luxury credits and it was here eight hours later. I could get used to this. We built it together," Gren said. "Garma, Coop and Ratter."

"Ratter?" Minh-Chu asked.

"Ratter," Garma replied, pointing to a small rectangular robot that Minh-Chu thought was a battered tool tray at first.

"Hey, buddy," he said to it, thinking of the three skitter bots that he kept in the belly of his fighter so they could perform repairs. It waggled one of its arms, flaring a scan head on its end. "This must have taken you guys a long time," he said, returning his attention to the Spitfire. There was a blue jay painted in a circle on the side. It matched Cooper's ring.

"One week," Garma said proudly, an air pocket bulging between her eyes for a moment.

"Yeah, mostly because these guys barely sleep," Cooper said. "I'm just glad I got to participate. Neither of them will fly it, though."

"The engine is too noisy," Gren grumbled.

"I can't trust something that needs so much room to take off and land." Garma shook her head and crossed her arms. "Besides, Cooper refused to add any modern safety devices. It's foolhardy. I do enjoy the way it looks when it's on the ground, to be honest."

"They're not the only ones who had trouble with this bird. The first time I requested a runway for takeoff it took me half an hour to explain that it wasn't capable of a vertical launch. Then I got her in the air and these two tell me that they've never seen so many jaws drop at the same time."

"I wish I could have been there," Minh-Chu said. "So, how are you guys fitting in?"

"The base is great. People aren't so different, but they seem nicer here. I guess most of them don't have to worry about much outside of their job. It's been good," Cooper replied.

"The reward is nice," Gren said. "I have many wonderful things in my apartment, and plan on acquiring more."

"Too much, Gren. We will need more room if you keep purchasing," Garma chided.

"Yeah, Gren's been going a little overboard," Cooper added with a little grimace. "I think he's a little restless."

"How was up training?" Minh-Chu asked.

"Oh, that was a trip. When they tell you that you're going into a full-dive simulation and that you're going to experience seven days for each one that passes out here, you don't realize how weird it'll feel when you come back out. We went in for three days and it took another week for me to really believe that it wasn't twenty-one days later."

"Technically, it would be eighteen days later, since three days passed for you in the pod machine," Ratter corrected in a high voice.

"Thanks, Ratter," Cooper said with a nod. "Anyway, I think I just got my head straight this week. You'd think I'd be pretty used to strange time considering what I used to do for a living. You know how it went though, right? That's why you're here."

"Well, I made a promise to you, Gren and Garma," Minh-

Chu said. "Finish your qualification courses and I'll have a place for you on Samurai Squadron."

"Is that offer still good now that your leader is a criminal?" Gren asked.

"Gren! That's rude. His squadron was not prosecuted, he did nothing wrong." It was fun watching the twin Mergillians' banter, especially since Garma wanted to enforce a kind of politeness that Gren was completely uninterested in.

"Will we get to see Avengers if we join?" Gren asked.

"More of the rudeness," Garma groaned. "Humans are not so direct." Then she asked; "But, will we?"

"Okay, okay," Minh-Chu laughed. "Before we talk about what you'll be flying, the situation looks like this. In a few days, you're going to hear about the fleet expanding through a Privateering program. The first person to get a Letter of Marque is my long-time buddy, Jake. He has a ship named the Triton. You might remember it as the one that made a close pass by your window in the hospital."

"Oh, I remember. That thing was doing laps past my cabin for about two hours and I was spellbound every time. You're getting a new squadron together on that ship?"

Cooper seemed excited, and the twins were wide-eyed, staring unwaveringly. "Actually, Samurai Squadron is moving over with me and expanding. I need a few good pilots."

"Excellent. Cooper is already bored with vacation," Gren said.

"Gren!" Garma chirped with an offended flinch.

"Well, it's true," Gren shrugged.

"They're right. We were about to call you. You know, ask if your offer is still good, but then we saw the thing about Valent this morning and, well, we decided it was a good day to go flying. Wait. When you say; 'your buddy Jake,' is that who…" Cooper's eyes widened, and he chuckled in antic-ipation.

"That's right. He's done the privateering gig before and he was a bounty hunter, only he wasn't quite so well equipped," Minh-Chu said with a crooked smile.

"Well, that's a bit different." Cooper looked at the twins, who seemed happy to follow his lead, then back to Minh-Chu. "So, how would things work on that giant corsair ship? I mean, the Triton is like three carriers strapped together side by side in the shape of a stingray. That's a big privateering effort."

It was Gren that answered as though he was at the head of a classroom. "Valent owns a large share of the solar system and benefits from much of its exports, which have been going up drastically over the last two months as more production systems come online. They have not finished processing all the wrecks that are floating in the solar system from the last conflict either, so the prospects for his earnings and the growth of Haven are excellent. I expect he'll use some of the proceeds to fund this venture." He paused, felt the silence, then added; "What? I watch a lot of news."

"Well, that's pretty much on the money. Now I know who to contact if I ever decide to invest in galactic trade," Minh-Chu said. "The point is; the pay is great, and we'll be hitting the Order and other enemies of Haven where it hurts most. I know Jake is the right leader out there."

"They know. The documentary chronicling your journey to the Rega Gain System has been watched five point two-one times in this hangar," Ratter said. "That is a lot, considering that the documentary has a twenty-hour and one-minute runtime. At least, I think it is a lot."

Minh-Chu could swear he heard weariness in the small

droid's tone and pressed on. "I noticed that none of you have taken the posts the Fleet offered, either."

"We were waiting for you." Garma seemed a little impatient as she answered, crossing her thin arms.

"Wait no more. There are quarters with your names on them. No bunks on the new Triton. At least, not unless you're in alert quarters."

There was a growing eagerness in Cooper, who was interrupted by Gren as he asked; "How much better does it pay?"

Cooper ignored him; "Where do I sign up?"

"You just did," Minh-Chu said to Cooper. Then, to Gren, he said; "It pays about thirty percent more luxury credits plus bonuses. You still have to follow regulations, though. Otherwise, we'll fall apart out there."

"I will follow regulations for an extra thirty percent. Now, can you explain these bonuses?" Gren asked, licking one of his eyes slowly.

"Humans don't speak of money like that here," Garma said, shaking her broad head. "You need to be trained. Is there a process for un-rude-ing? A teacher we could hire or a punishment system? Like a collar? I think my brother needs a rudeness restraint of some kind."

"There have been moments when I've wondered the same thing, but no. Maybe you could invent one," Minh-Chu said, mostly kidding. He could imagine Garma putting a shock collar on Gren, and snickered a little. Then he saw how Garma was smiling just a little, as though she was picturing what her brother would look like wearing one and thought; *It is going to be fun having these three aboard.*

Chapter 7

Family Reunion

ACROSS THE FRONT windows of Mama Bu's Oriental Restaurant scrolled the words: CLOSED FOR PRIVATE PARTY. There was a square of the promenade roped off that was conspicuously shuttle-sized with half a dozen Nafalli soldiers guarding it. They held their long staves at their sides, their fur was well groomed, and they were altogether pleasant with people who happened by on their way to other businesses. When restaurant goers who wanted to visit the establishment asked them what was going on, they simply said; "I'm sorry. They'll be open tomorrow." The polite, tall Tree Tribe Nafalli were firm, and it was clear that they wouldn't offer any more information, so most people moved on.

The first shuttle to land was carrying Jacob Valent in his long coat, Ayan Anderson with Laura, who was sitting in a pouch that her vacsuit made so she could carry her against her chest. The baby was looking around, eyes wide, her chubby fingers in her mouth. Behind them were a pair of tall Nafalli, Alaka and his son Iruuk. Most of the people in the large square, which had the Monte Carlo monument at its centre, stopped and stared.

To their astonishment, the former Admiral, clad in a dark vacsuit and long, heavy trenchcoat actually smiled and waved at them as he went by. Half the people who came to see who was inside the shuttle stayed, respecting the rope but wondering who would arrive next.

A single Uriel Starfighter was moments behind, its rotary thrusters slowing its descent at the last moment and sending a harmless hot gust at the onlookers. Minh-Chu Bu climbed out of the cockpit, then with a press of an icon on his wrist computer, he sent the fighter back up. To the delight of the onlookers, who were growing in number, he straightened his bomber jacket and then stayed to talk with them for a moment. "Hey everyone, how are we doing?"

"What's going to happen to Samurai Squadron now that there's another shakeup happening? Is the squadron staying on the Merciless?" asked a girl who was barely in her teens. She was wearing a bomber jacket that was made to look much like the ones most fighter pilots wore. There were brass wings pinned to it above a silver shield, meaning that she was in training as a pilot in the Junior Cadets. Two older boys with similar pins flanked her.

"I can't answer that, but you'll find out pretty soon. When's your solo flight test?" Minh-Chu asked her.

"When I turn fifteen," she grumbled. "I couldn't get an exception for the age requirement."

"So in about two years," the oldest boy beside her said. He couldn't have been more than seventeen years old. His wings were silver, marking him as a fully qualified pilot. "Macy's almost as good as I am in the sims, though. Watch for her."

"What's your callsign, Macy?"

"Skip," she replied. "Because I used to do that in sims - skip my ship off the shields of a bigger one so I could change trajectory real fast. I don't do it anymore."

"I bet, it must have cost most of your energy reserves," Minh-Chu spoke to her like an adult pilot, even musing for a moment before nodding. "I've seen that done for real though. Usually, not on purpose, mind you."

"Does it work?" she asked, eyes wide.

The crowd around them were loving the conversation, watching and listening intently. "Oh, it could work, but that doesn't mean it's worth trying. You can control a turn and burn if you need to change direction real fast, but glancing off a big capital ship's shields is like rolling the dice. Two energy fields interacting like that can send you spinning or worse. Next time I'm in a sim, I'll give it a try a few times though. Sounds like fun. What do you want to fly when you get your silver wings then graduate?"

"A Heavy Uriel Fighter," she replied. Judging from the nodding of her companions, it was something she talked about often. "I hear it's Dame's favourite."

"You're right. I've never seen anyone fly a heavy fighter better. I shouldn't tell you this, but I saw her manually control her shield recharge rate while we were hunting capital ships during a mission. She almost burned her fighter's wiring out, but she made it worth it. There she is now."

Macy was agape as a shuttle landed behind Minh-Chu then Alice Valent, a figure in a deep, identity blocking hood, then Easy and Dame emerged. Faloo, a short, squat Burrower Tribe Nafalli followed a moment later.

"Dame, I think there's someone you should meet here," Minh-Chu called to her.

The tall pilot with nearly white short hair turned and approached the rope. "Hello," she said to Macy, who was beside herself, too excited to speak.

"I was telling Skip here about the time you manually controlled your shield recharge rate," Minh-Chu said by way of introduction.

For reasons that the young teen could probably not explain, she reached out to the famous pilot, and Dame caught her hands in hers. "It's good to meet you, Skip. Are you a good pilot?" Minh-Chu enjoyed her accent, which gave English words a kind of clarity and precision that was almost square.

After a moment's hesitation, Macy blurted; "I'm okay."

"She's in the top five hundred on the general leaderboard," her older brother said. "So, yeah, she's pretty amazing."

"There was a time when I didn't think I should be a pilot. I thought I was too tall, and I was a very talented infantry person, so it was unlikely that my career path would change. That was, until I flew a combat ship for the first time. You are fortunate to find your love of it early." Dame was serious as always, "This is the age when you learn fastest, so concentrate, work hard, and find out everything you can about what you love to do," she told her. "I will watch for you in the simulations."

"O-okay, thank you," Macy said.

With one more look at the young pilot in training, Dame let her hands go, flashed a rare smile, then continued on into the restaurant. Minh-Chu didn't leave but moved down the line to greet a few people who were eager to meet him. Until the next shuttle came down he spoke with them and answered whatever questions he could.

Ashley stepped out of the next shuttle and he took her in his arms for a brief but enthusiastic embrace. Unlike the others, who were in fitted vacsuit uniforms with no markings, she wore a simple black dress with a print of a golden dragon climbing up the side. It was a favourite of his, and his sister enjoyed it when his fiancee dressed with an Asian theme, especially when she was visiting her restaurant.

Captain Stephanie Vega, Shamus Frost, and the Issyrian - Agameg Price were close behind, and Minh-Chu entered the restaurant with them. His sister, who was smiling and cooing at baby Laura, looked in his direction when he entered and said; "It's about time you came in. I see you delayed it as long as possible by talking to everyone you could find."

Minh-Chu hugged his sister, who gave him an enthusiastic squeeze in return as he smiled at her. "How are you, little sister?"

Kim-Ly poked him. "Busy, always busy, and wondering why my brother doesn't visit as much as his fiancee. She was in another solar system, flying a ship much bigger than your little fighter and still came for a chat three more times than you did in the last three months."

Ashley didn't leap to his defence. Minh-Chu was sure that she'd learned not to, since the scolding Kim-Ly was giving him was a show of affection. He watched as his sister's whole demeanour became pleasant again as she gave Ashley, who was much taller, a friendly hug. "How are you? Is everything going well aboard the Triton? No one is changing the controls when you go off shift?"

"Everything's fine now. It was one technician who had his own idea of how things should be configured, so he'd reset them to what he thought was right every night. I didn't even have to talk to him about it though. He was a member of the finishing crew, and they were wrapping things up. Boring story, really," Ashley said. "How are things here?"

"Much busier now that Alberton's has closed their kitchen and started serving our food instead. It's just as well, they were okay, but his place was more about entertainment than steak and chicken. Their customers are very happy now, and we are all laughing," Kim-Ly replied.

Ashley laughed, aware that Alberton's was the comedy and variety entertainment club next door. Minh-Chu groaned and rolled his eyes even as his sister explained; "Albertons is a comedy and entertainment club, and we are all laughing because…"

"I get it," Minh-Chu said, smiling more at her effort than anything else. "I'm glad to hear things are going well. Today must have made you crazy, having to wait for us to get here."

"Of course not. We were open for lunch," she replied, waving his comment off. "I have to meet the rest of the customers." Kim-Ly gave Ashley a parting smile and was introduced to Alaka and Iruuk, then Alice, whose name she recognized from many orders that were delivered before the Order of Eden occupied Tamber.

When she'd met everyone, including Agameg, who politely asked; "Do you serve Tsona?" his big green eyes wide, expectant.

"I will prepare a large bowl for you myself," Kim-Ly replied. "What kind of roe would you like as a topping?"

"Do you have trout caviar?" he asked.

"Fresh from this afternoon, yes," she said. "Mild or spicy?"

"Mild, please. I haven't had this dish in many years, thank you," he said, barely containing his excitement.

"You should come here often then. It is a very popular dish in some places. Humans and Mergillians have taken a real liking to it." With a parting wave, Kim-Ly started for the back of the restaurant, where her kitchen staff were waiting. "My waiters will be out soon to take your orders."

"Thank you," Minh-Chu called after her. Then he turned towards Jacob, who was watching Iruuk wrap his arms around Alice and easily pick her up in a great big hug. "I really do have to visit more often. Hey, do you think you could convince her to join the staff on the Triton?"

"I don't think I could afford her," Jake replied. "I mean, this restaurant is her baby. I'd have to give her a deck on the ship or something. I mean, I'm not saying it wouldn't be worth it, but the Triton's Captain may have a problem with it."

"A whole deck?" Stephanie mused for a moment before shaking her head. "It's a hard call, but I wouldn't take Kim-Ly away from this place. It would be a public relations nightmare. Her customers would never forgive me."

"Oh, thank you," Minh-Chu and Alice said at the same time.

Turning to her, Minh-Chu asked; "Wait, why are you relieved?"

"This place was my favourite spot to order from when I was living here during the occupation. I'm moving back into the neighbourhood. Your turn." Alice said, pointing at him.

"Oh, no reason," Minh-Chu said quietly.

"He's afraid that she'd recruit him for the kitchen in his off time," Ashley explained.

"I thought he would want to keep his family out of danger," Dame said. "That would be my reason."

With a steady seriousness that equalled Dame's usual demeanour, Minh-Chu said; "Oh, she's ready to take the

Order on. Restaurant owners who helm their own kitchens are some of the toughest people in the galaxy."

Alaka turned his long, furry snout toward the kitchen and breathed; "I was once here for noodles during the dinner rush. I believe it."

Jake, Ayan, Alice, Minh-Chu, Ashley, Shamus, and Stephanie laughed for a moment before sitting down at the finely carved wooden tables. Only Agameg remained standing, and Minh-Chu watched as Jake regarded him. "I'm glad to see you, Price, but aren't you supposed to be on the bridge of the Pelican right now?"

The Pelican was the Issyrian Captain's first command, a heavily armed hospital ship with its own fighter wing. The fine cilia covering his face flattened and joined, changing into glossy light blue-green skin. His eyes remained much larger than the average human's and shifted colour to a deeper green as he replied. "I know I am not part of the Special Operations Combat Unit, but contacted Defence Minister McPatrick, skipping up the chain of command, which is normally not my way. I believe I have justification after seeing the footage from the Prowler, after witnessing what the Order of Eden do to my people. Though my commission was an honourable one, I am afraid I will not be satisfied if I'm not fighting the Order more directly. The Defence Minister told me that the choice to remain as the commander of the Pelican or leave and request a place aboard the Triton was mine, so I am here. There are several excellent candidates for a new commander for the Pelican, so my guilt at leaving that post is irrational. I am hoping you would allow me to join your crew."

"Yes," Jake said without hesitation. "You're one of the only people I know who's managed a carrier. I can't tell you how much I need you."

"I can," Stephanie said, getting to her feet and embracing him for a moment. "Thank you, Agameg."

"Oh, and there's something else," Jake said. "The Triton's last refit included the aquatic sections, so there are quarters designed for Issyrians."

"We used specifications from Issyrian ships when we were making our modifications, so you should be able to set your quarters up however you like," Ayan added as Laura tried to take hold of her nose.

"It would have been the first ship in the fleet with quarters for my kind," Agameg said. "Will others have aquatic areas?"

"Only five are being upgraded this year, the ones with the most Mergillians aboard, but Fleet Sciences is putting together a conversion kit so almost any large ship can support aquatic people properly," Ayan replied. "It isn't public knowledge yet because the kits are still in testing, so keep it to yourself."

"Don't worry, I won't share that with anyone. I feel better about the future of the fleet, knowing that you're being so accommodating," Agameg said. "I have a question, though. Weren't Finn and Liara supposed to be here?"

"They're running late. The finishing crew on the Triton are, well, finishing up. Finn wanted to make sure all the testing passed," Stephanie replied.

"Ah. I've been looking forward to seeing them," Agameg said quietly.

"I have something that may cheer you up a little," said the hooded man in the long coat. "If you're looking for Issyrian crew members, I may know a few with experience."

"Take that off," Alice said with a chuckle.

"Oh, sorry, I forgot about my disguise," Noah said as he pulled his hood back and deactivated his faceplate. It split apart and folded down into his collar.

"Carnie!" Ashley exclaimed, rushing over and giving him a hug. "I was wondering who was in there."

"I knew," Minh-Chu said as he accepted a tall frothy beer from a waiter. "We have some catching up to do, Wingman."

"Oh, definitely. You wouldn't believe what I've been up to," Noah replied with a grin. "But, yeah, like I was saying; There's a whole destroyer of Issyrians who are splitting off to other ships and starting things up at my base, the Bitter End."

"Ooh, that's a good name for a base," Minh-Chu cooed. "Maybe I should rename the Pilot's Den…"

Ashley cut him off, waving a finger. "You're not renaming the Pilot's Den. It's fine the way it is."

He suppressed a smile as he replied; "Yes, Dear." It was one of the few things he teased Ashley about. Getting the naming rights to the pub aboard the Triton wasn't a real coup for him, especially since he had no actual plans to rename it. At least, not permanently. "Anyway, good to see you, Carnie. Sticking around?"

"Well, no, but I had to come. Any chance to get off the wanted list…" Noah replied, looking toward Jake and Ayan.

"Let me push that through for you. I'm still an Admiral, so I can make sure that you're taken off the deserter list and the records of your undercover mission are made known to the people who matter. The rest is up to him," Ayan said, looking toward Jake. Baby Laura babbled loudly for a moment.

"Right, I guess this isn't just a reunion," Jake said, standing up.

As he got to his feet, Agameg sat down between Stephanie and Ashley, two of his oldest friends. They each took one of his hands, and Minh-Chu was pleased to see how happy he looked. It had been quite a while since the Issyrian had been able to spend much time with them.

After looking around the table, Jake said; "The first thing Alice asked me when she came in was; 'So, what now, Dad?'"

That prompted more than a little laughter. As it petered out, Alice shrugged. "You never know, right? I mean, we were only supposed to be in the Cefa System for three weeks, but I ended up babysitting a Prince for three and a half months."

It was Stephanie who quipped; "Sounds cushy."

"Well, sure, but I had other stuff going on," Alice said. Everyone could see the effort she was making to not be argumentative. "I'm not bitter about it anymore…"

"Anymore," Iruuk repeated. "At first she called me every day complaining about the Spoiled Prince."

"I know, sorry Fur Face," Alice said, cringing. "But my point is that you never know what's coming next, especially with my Dad."

"Okay, you're right. As Privateers you won't get stuck with a mission like that. There's honour in protecting someone, sure, but if you'd rather be pursuing something else, you can do that. The other side of that situation is what happens to whoever you've decided not to protect. You were just called away from your assignment, but there is a regiment moving in to take over right now. That's the benefit of being with the Fleet. The chances of having backup when you get reassigned, of knowing that the work will continue without you are very high. With privateering, you're on your own. If protecting that Prince was a paid job and you left, then he's on his own to hire someone else. I have a feeling I know that you'll decide to go independent, but I'd like you to keep in mind that there will be times when you won't have support. With that in mind, Oz is ready to sign your Letter of Marque himself. You can use the Triton as your base if you want since I'm her owner, but you'll have to go by the Captain's rules," he nodded in Stephanie's direction.

"Why aren't you taking that spot yourself?" Alice asked. "No offence, Steph."

"No worries, it's a fair question. I've been holding off asking it for three weeks," Stephanie replied, looking in Jake's direction. "So, why?"

"I don't want to be tied to a bridge. I think I'm a better hunter than a leader. Besides, you're a better captain, and I'm hoping that Agameg will run security, maybe help with the flight operations."

"I bet he can run both," Ashley said.

"As Captain of the Pelican, I performed the duties of that post while I was leading flight operations. I could easily trade the duties of a captain with Security Officer while commanding Flight Operations," he replied.

"That's up to Stephanie. Part of her deal is that I don't look over her shoulder unless she wants me to. I may own the Triton, but I want to be able to go on my own hunts, send teams out on missions that clear the way for big wins." What Jake was saying prompted nods from Stephanie, Shamus Frost and a few other people at the table.

"You're going to take watches on the bridge though, right? There are only a handful of people in the whole fleet I'd trust to command that ship in an emergency." It looked like Stephanie was willing to argue about it right then, right there.

"When I can," Jake replied, wisely deciding not to test her. "You're number one when it comes to leadership aboard. As long as we're clear on that."

"Super clear. I wouldn't have left the Merciless with half the crew if we weren't," Stephanie said, settling back in her seat.

"Good. I'm hoping that the Triton can serve as a mobile base for several teams. Remmy is joining us. He's not here because he's following a lead on something right now."

"So, we're really going after glory and riches? I mean, I'll still sell gear and guns, right?" Noah asked.

"Use your ship however you want," Jake said, not sparing him a look before moving on. "We're not just doing this for hardware. Haven Fleet is paying for intelligence, the destruction of strategic targets, and thousands of bounties will be released next week. If you two want to be Privateers," he said, turning to Alice and Noah. "Then you'll find a lot of opportunities out there, and you'll have my support."

"I bet the Captain of the Corsair will do pretty well," Minh-Chu said, regarding Noah with an impish grin.

"Well, yeah, as soon as my name is cleared…" he looked down at his command and control unit then smiled. "…well, look at that. I'm not a thieving traitor anymore. Thanks."

"You're welcome," Ayan replied, bouncing baby Laura, who made a happy yell. Then she noticed Alice and started reaching for her.

Ayan passed Laura to Alice, who looked uncertain as she carefully accepted the nearly six-month-old, who loudly exclaimed; "Bah!" at her.

"Bah, yourself, kiddo," Alice said as her blue vacsuit made a pouch that helped support the little one's weight. A little voice drifted up from the parental assistance system built into the baby's clothes saying; "I'm very stimulated by being around so many people and have just peed." It was meant to tell people what their child needed and may be feeling using a system that analyzed sensor data.

"Same here," Minh-Chu said. "Well, not the peeing part."

"Thank goodness for auto-cleaning diapers," Ayan sighed,

watching her two daughters together. Then, turning to Jake she said; "Sorry, baby interruptus."

Jake was watching Alice and Laura too, and hesitated to look away as he said. "It happens all the time. So, the Fleet is expanding using Privateers, and I'll be the first. There's a whole infrastructure getting set up for it in the Cefa System with Lorander as partners. They're reopening this end of the Legardis Route, which will stretch all the way to the Blue Belt and other distant parts of the galaxy later on. The old wormhole ring there was a part of the Route centuries ago, and they've been building a replacement for a few years."

"Let me guess, that's what was keeping you busy in the months leading up to this? You were working with Lorander Corp?" Alice asked.

"Part of it. Ayan's team figured out that the natural ergranian metal we found in the Cefa System came from the Blue Belt. The Nolians and Lorander seeded asteroids with it there so they could have more than one source. There's more to it, but we got Lorander's attention with the Haven Nodes and our discovery of the wormhole ring. Now they're not just Haven's friends, but they're my friends. They've shared some intelligence about the Order of Eden that will give our Privateering a jumpstart. Happen to know any Captains who would like to get in on this?" He looked towards Alice, who was fixated on Laura.

"Heavy baby, you're a heavy baby, but that's good..." she was saying to Laura as she stared back at her, reaching for her curls.

Noah tapped Alice on the shoulder. "Um."

"Oh, sorry," she said, looking at him at then at Jake. "I missed that."

"It's okay, we have all night." Seeing Jake as a father, in the presence of his whole family warmed Minh-Chu's heart. He was relaxed, at ease in a way that was rare for him. Minh-Chu did his best not to think about what would come next. A rush to finish getting the Triton ready, then a real fight. The knowledge that there may be empty chairs the next time they got together settled on him like a persistent weight, but he did his best to hide it.

Chapter 8

The Immortal Promise

THE LARGEST HANGAR on Base 10303 was repurposed as a stadium for the day. The structure was the largest ever built on Iora, and there were over twenty thousand soldiers gathered, all standing, every eye on the stage at one end. It was enough to make the leadership on Iora nervous. Every critical station was running with a skeleton staff while many less important posts were abandoned entirely. Eve demanded her audience, and they couldn't refuse her.

Surrounded by the impossibly large audience, the third most important icon in the Order of Eden stood in the middle of the stage. Eve stared at the holographic playback of Jacob Valent's sentencing as it played above her large enough for everyone to see. For anyone watching her remotely, her image was larger than the courtroom scene.

It was Scanlon's idea to hang a thick curtain just off stage where she and a few of her direct subordinates could witness Eve's last appearance on Iora. Well, her final performance for the time being. She observed passively, making sure not to react to whatever happened on stage, no matter how extreme.

The playback of the court scene was heavily edited. There were also subtle alterations to Valent that made him look weary, even a little teary-eyed in some places. This wasn't the kind of propaganda that Scanlon would have made. In her experience, anything that could be compared side by side with something that anyone could access was a waste of time. It would happen eventually, and that would make some people question what they'd seen.

There was something else Scanlon didn't like about the performance she was watching on stage. Eve wore the dark green military uniform of an Order of Eden soldier. She wasn't technically part of the military, but that in itself wasn't the biggest mistake. The error was in the uniform's adornment. There was a string of numbers in a block that indicated that Eve had been in dozens of conflicts that ended in victory. A rank insignia that wasn't in the directory was pinned to her collar. It was a line of eight small squares with a tiny phoenix at the end. Scanlon did her best to dismiss the slight by trying to convince herself that she was seeing someone who was playing make-believe like a child dressing in their parent's clothes. It made her feel better about watching someone prance around with a rank insignia that they not only didn't earn, but was completely invented.

The audience didn't seem to care. Instead, they were either focused on the twisted playback of Valent's final moments in Haven Fleet or Eve's reactions to it. There was a lot to see on her face as she stared up at the giant holographic playback, focusing on his every word and then grinning at the end.

When he was sentenced, she played at being shocked to the extreme. The playback faded and she regarded her grand audience with that astonished expression that looked absolutely unreal to Scanlon. Then she clapped, suddenly filled with glee as she announced; "He has fallen!"

The roar of the audience that followed was enough to make Scanlon want to cover her ears as she felt the rumble in her chest. As it began to wind down, Eve started speaking. "Did you notice something?" She let the question hang as the applause and cheers faded.

"Here we go," said Colonel Ugo Sonne from her right. He was one of the best commanders beneath her, the leader of the battle group that was sent to reinforce her part of the fleet. "She has changed so much since she spent a month with the Overlord." The last came as a whisper meant only for Scanlon's ears.

Eve finally went on. "There was something missing from Jacob Valent's confession, wasn't there? All the Haven propaganda claiming that we started this war with a virus like the one he was just convicted of releasing was missing. When he was called in front of his own leaders for justice, all the lies fell away because he would have been forced to prove whatever was presented, and he couldn't! There was no mention of the Order of Eden forcing machines to turn on humanity and not one word accusing us of striking first. When the Haven Courts had to look at the cold, true evidence against us because the galactic community forced them to be accountable, they couldn't prove any of their allegations. Now we know: they are all admitted liars, and Valent is the worst of them."

The silence that fell over the multitude continued as they stood and sat in suspense. Every eye was on Eve as she slowly moved her gaze from left to right across their number. *This is what she lives for. Eve needs so much validation that tens of thousands of people won't be enough. I only wish she wasn't so good at holding their attention.* Scanlon thought as she watched the icon control her audience.

"Now Jacob Valent is gone. At least, that's what we're supposed to think. Did you know he's one of the wealthiest people in the sector?" Eve was a little outraged as she asked the question. "The Valent clan hides their wealth, but they own the Haven System. His fiancee, Ayan Anderson, pushes the title of Queen away even though she refuses to surrender ownership of the solar system to the puppet democracy she created. Instead she shared it with her friends, calling them owners instead of monarchs. Their greed and corruption are so thinly veiled that it's unbelievable that they can fool millions into thinking they're living in a free society. I'm afraid I've strayed from the point, my friends, which is simple. Jacob Valent is independently wealthy and he is growing his fortune by the day as more people are fooled into flocking to his Solar System." A large hologram of the Haven System appeared overhead, with Kambis highlighted. It wasn't an image of the old Kambis, however. Instead of rolling black clouds over muted red flames, it was a planet featuring the glow of cities atop grand mesas. Tamber crossed in front of it - a blue-green moon that was reminiscent of ancient Earth.

"I know, many of you haven't had the opportunity to learn how the Valents and Andersons took possession of the solar system. Let me tell you the truth they try to bury and overwrite with well produced propaganda." Eve masterfully portrayed someone who was about to reveal a shocking conspiracy. "They found a nearly abandoned solar system that the pitiful Carthans tried to hold and insinuated themselves into the situation well enough to take control once everyone else gave up.

Now they're the leaders by default and they're squeezing the life out of those planets and everything around them using borrowed technology. Don't believe that they've invented a thing, it was all given to them by partners like Lorander and the British Alliance, who wanted a piece of the wealth. We've seen it! The Order was there, and we threw one regime down only to see another take its place. One going by the names Valent and Anderson. There's no doubt that nepotism and runaway capitalism rule Haven, this is only a little moment where their lies and corruption are exposed. The hologram we just saw prove that Jacob Valent is rotten to the core is in all of your personal databases now. Watch it and savour the event."

"They should have executed him!" someone shouted from the audience. It was a plant, Scanlon was absolutely certain.

"Yes!" Eve shouted back. "Another sign of deep corruption in the Haven System. The punishment for what he confessed to is always execution. Your Overlord has seen the future, and Valent is in it, but only for a short time. That man's wealth and twisted vision for the universe will enable him to keep murdering, stealing and corrupting everything he can. There have been words from Hampon himself, whispering from the future, that makes it absolutely clear that this conviction will only make Jacob Valent and his daughter Alice more violent and deranged. Make no mistake, our enemies are dangerous." She paused, looking up as though Hampon was watching from the future, or the ceiling. "Praise his word."

Several thousand people in the audience echoed the words, whispering; "Praise his word," in a collective hissing roar.

When Eve brought her gaze back down, she closed her eyes for a long moment, as though hearing whispers from beyond. Her tone was mournful as she began what Scanlon hoped was the end of her speech. "I find encouragement that

Valent's violence and hate will end, but only if we end it. That's right. Hampon and Overlord Dron have given us a mission to destroy him and to burn or take everything he's built. That's why we can no longer offer anyone from the Haven System mercy. It is our way to offer opportunities to everyone. People deserve a chance to improve themselves, to become greater than they are. To climb in wealth, have victories and eventually earn immortality. There are one hundred and thirty-three people in the audience who were remade this morning, taking the framework miracle in so they will never age, grow ill, or perish. Any one of you can rise to their level of greatness. That is why I'm conflicted when I say that the Valents and anyone who allies with them must be denied this opportunity. Life itself must be ripped from them." The last words seemed difficult for Eve, she even turned away for a moment.

"Oh, she's good," Colonel Sonne whispered, probably for Scanlon's benefit.

Scanlon nodded as she watched the peak of Eve's performance. She looked back to the audience, her voice cracking. She was speaking through tears that were as convincing as the deepest kind of grief. "I want to give everyone these opportunities. I want to believe that everyone can turn away from evil and embrace our way of life. How can they fail to see the path we're on and how it can elevate anyone and give rise to a new evolution for everyone? I hate that I want to celebrate the fall of Jacob Valent, that is a fault in me. I see him forced to admit that he's worse than any human in the entire galaxy and I want to raise my fists and scream; 'Justice! Finally! Everyone can see what he is!'" she did exactly that then let her arms down slowly, the energy of the cheer draining. Most of the audience was hushed, waiting on the edge of their seats for what she was about to say next.

"No, that's not right, that's not what Hampon or Overlord Dron teaches us," Eve said mournfully. "Watching Valent confess to murdering a million or more of his own kind and admitting that he knew it was wrong is horrible. It shows that, as much as we all aspire to something greater, there is a dark, evil path, and that someone can become irredeemable once they've travelled too far. Whoever follows that person is lost as well, which makes Valent, his allies, and even his admirers irredeemable. Overlord Dron has spoken on this, and I watched a tear roll from his eye when he told me that they must all be killed. There can be no mercy. They are a cancer, and the task falls to us to cut it out. It's a grim thing, but we are the greatest beings in the galaxy, so it falls to us. It's times like this that I find myself repeating my oath to the future. My oath to you. I invite you to renew your oath with me.

Eve took a moment to tug her uniform jacket straight, stand rigidly, then cover her heart. "I serve this Order. My service will make me immortal. My service will elevate me to paradise. I embrace my fate, the fate of all humanity to be the superior beings in the universe."

The hangar was filled with the sound of tens of thousands of people reciting the oath. It was so loud that Scanlon couldn't hear herself doing the same. It differed from the version she personalized and said every morning as she was preparing for the day which was; 'I serve the Order. My service has made me immortal. I have been elevated to command and will find paradise in power. Humanity is the greatest race in the universe. Dominance is our right.' Every time she watched Eve repeat the oath in a public address, Scanlon had to suppress the urge to say her own version.

"Expansion is our right," Eve said as she'd done several times before. "We bring hope and opportunity to humanity. Anyone who stands in our way is our enemy, and none is more clearly against us accelerating our journey to our glorious fate than the Valents and the Haven System. That's why we are at war. A justifiable war that was foretold in the early days of the Order of Eden. A war that will only take us closer to immortality and paradise. We will make a thousand new Edens, and I'll see millions of you there when we stand on hallowed ground, enjoying the fruits of our war!"

The audience reacted with such a violent cheer that it was felt just as powerfully as it was heard. They roared on even as Eve retreated from the stage, infused with the energy of thousands.

There's no way to extract this one from the Order without causing more damage than it might be able to survive. I'm going to have to replace her. Scanlon thought as she greeted Eve with a big grin. "That was incredible. No wonder you're such a legend."

"Thank you," Eve said as she moved on to Colonel Ugo Sonne and then the other officers there who had carefully composed compliments for her.

Chapter 9

Can You Have Two Homes?

AFTER SAYING a round of goodbyes at the end of a gathering that seemed too short, Noah and Alice took a shuttle to the Clever Dream II. It was waiting in the military section of one of the new orbital port stations that had been built around Kambis. She wanted one more ride aboard it before she officially left the military the next day. Noah was the better pilot, so she dropped into the copilot's seat.

While he did the preflight check, she checked her messages and found one from the Prince, who thanked her for the new security detail. Alice didn't know anything about it, but was relieved to see that Haven Fleet's Diplomacy Division had sent a new security expert along with four squads of soldiers to protect him and help finish training his royal guards. Protecting him was the worst assignment she'd ever had, but she still didn't want him left alone with half trained security people. It would have felt too much like a loose end.

"This isn't exactly like the Corsair. Same ship type, but everythings put together better and I think the materials are higher end," Noah said as he finished the preflight system check.

"I know. This isn't the regular model, but some kind of next iteration. My Mom said they've been working on it for months, but there won't be many of them because the material requirements are too high," Alice replied. "Lots of ergranian and other stuff. I have a feeling Iruuk and I will be looking it over for weeks."

"Me too. I hope I can buy a couple upgrades for the Corsair." They decoupled from the station and they were on their way to Tamber. The artificial canopy view showed Kambis far below. Its black clouds were turning into a hurricane of moisture and chemicals that had been released by the rivers of fire beneath. Materials that had been carefully moved and sequestered on the planet's surface so it could be fully terraformed for humans and other similar species had been set alight during an attack. As they made their way to Tamber, Alice looked at the spectacle of flaming rivers winding between massive, broad mesas. "I wonder if they'll ever find a way to fix that?" she muttered to herself.

"I have no idea. Maybe the brains coming with Lorander can figure it out. They're the terraforming experts, right?"

"That's true, and they were the ones who started that project a few centuries ago. They almost finished it, too. Huh, that would be cool. Imagine if they manage to turn it into a garden spot," Alice said. "Maybe you should buy property."

"I think I'll watch that speculation from afar." Noah set the autopilot to take them to Tamber and sat back. "So, the suspense is killing me, I've gotta ask. Are you really going to go Privateer? I mean, you worked your butt off to get where you are in the Fleet."

"Yes," Alice said, realizing that there was no doubt. "I'm going Privateer. I mean, I'll be amazed if they let me keep this ship. They paid me for the Clever Dream because it was destroyed while I was in the service, so I'll have to figure out what I'm going to fly around in, but I have options."

"Yeah, the destroyer you captured and the Sendega Corvette, but they should give you this ship, or something like it. I mean, you said they only gave you ten percent of what the Clever Dream was worth, right?" Noah asked, obviously unhappy at the deal.

"Yeah, but with the upgrades in that ship and refitting, most of the hardware wasn't mine anymore. Maybe I can buy it, if they'll let me keep all this classified tech. Okay, I'll settle for half and the built in D-Jump Drive. Even if I can't keep her, I'm definitely going independent. I saw the future of my service in the Fleet. Security, maybe diplomacy later. It took me months to figure out how to turn this empath stuff off so I can use it only when I want it, and wouldn't you know it, my commanding officers put me on an assignment where I have to use it so much that I was getting so exhausted by the end of the day that I had headaches that wouldn't go away for hours. Then I felt like I could never get enough sleep."

"I didn't know that." The sympathy in Noah's eyes as he put his hand on hers made her want to take some of that back.

So, she tried; "I mean, I get it, and I didn't complain about it to the higher ups, so they didn't know how it was wearing me out. I just saw a job that needed to be done and I think I nearly burned myself out by doing my best. The whole body-guard thing isn't my thing, though. I think about the heist we pulled all the time. What we got out of it doesn't matter as much as what we were able to accomplish together. It was a lot of fun, too. But, wait, you're going Privateer too, right?"

"Yeah, as much as I like the Fleet and what they do, I don't feel like I owe them anything. You know, I tried not to feel like they threw me away because I was undercover, but I still feel like I was tossed into the wilderness. I mean, they gave me a hell of a survival kit, but I was still on my own until you came along. I'm soured on the military, at least the way they're running it. I think I can do more good on my own and earn us a lot of plat at the same time. Oh, part of that stack I'm guarding on the Corsair is yours. Sel Marda made a payment for the Destroyer you gave him. He's been doing some crazy piracy, hitting enemy corporate ships more regularly than just about anyone in the Rose system."

"Good, I'm glad he and his crew are managing that ship. I wasn't sure if that was the right choice, especially when you told me there were jealous looks from people in the Shattered End." Worrying about what was going on with the Rebel Captains, especially Noah, had become so frequent that it was like background noise.

"Sel can handle it, don't worry. Besides, he has more friends than enemies, trust me," Noah said.

Alice sighed and stretched out in her seat, aware that Noah was stealing a look at her in the fitted powder blue vacsuit that had become her favourite and was definitely his. Then she said; "We can work together again. I can't wait."

"Neither can I." There was a note of appreciation in his tone, and it wasn't as good as what she'd felt in the past using her empathic sense, but she enjoyed it just the same.

. . .

AS SOON AS Alice spotted the house Freeground Fleet sold her she felt like she was about to return to the only other home she knew. It was also undeniably strange. Relatively speaking, Alice was wealthy because she leased the original Clever Dream to the Fleet when they needed dependable ships. She missed the ship and Lewis, but she had to admit that the new one seemed better, and she was pretty sure that her artificial intelligence, Lewis, would agree.

After taking a brief tour of the Clever Dream II, she wanted to hang onto it, but doubted that any amount of money would be enough to get her ownership. If that ship was taken away, then the house in the trees would be her only home. At least, until she could buy or steal another ship, which wouldn't measure up to the Clever Dream II.

The house wouldn't be a small consolation prize though. It was a recreation of one that she lived in before. This one was a little closer to the edge of the jungle, sitting up in the trees just far enough from the other homes so there was some privacy. One side overlooked the shore and the long beaches there while the rest had a view of the jungle with walkways between the ancient trees. The post it was on was free standing with an escape elevator that would take several people all the way down to the jungle floor. All the supports and walkways were designed to fit in with the growth with minimal interference, including the maglev line and vehicle passages.

"I forgot how much I liked those walkways," Alice said as they drew closer to the hangar beneath her home.

"I never understood how they kept the carnivores away. Aren't there big cats that hang out up in the trees?" Noah asked.

Alice shuddered at the memory of nearly getting eaten by one of them. "When they get to a certain size, they stay low.

You're right, though, the adolescent ones, and a few of the adults like to perch high where they can catch birds and other stuff. There's a pheromone that keeps them away. Not even Nafalli can smell it, but it's enough for them to go looking for food elsewhere. I used to go for walks at night to clear my head, and I only saw a little cat once, about twenty metres away."

"Aw, that must have been cute. How big was he?"

"I'd say between three and four kilos, maybe," Alice said, remembering the shudder she had at realizing that there were shining eyes in the dark watching her.

"That is not a small cat," Noah laughed. He slowed the Clever Dream II down as they approached her hangar door. "How big do they get?"

"The one that tried to use me as a chew toy once must have been at least forty kilos. She was huge. Those ones stay down low most of the time, I think."

"Oh, I remember you telling me about that." He nodded, and she knew that she could have told him the whole story again, and he'd listen with interest. It was one of the things she liked about him; he didn't mind if she repeated herself because she forgot that a tale had already been told.

She didn't mind being told that he'd heard one of her greatest hits before though, especially when they were about to make a new story. The lights in front of the Clever Dream II revealed her house in detail. The pearlescent outer shell was still there, along with the walkway leading to its place high in the trees. Set on the edge of the jungle now, it looked bigger than she remembered. The lower portion was the largest with a hangar that could accommodate the seventy metre long Clever Dream II along with another ship the same size right beside it. The door was only large enough for one to fit at a time, which didn't make it look any less grand.

The apartment above it looked small in comparison, and the builders designed deck space surrounding most of it with railings that curled like vines along the edges. Its predecessor was destroyed when Haven Shore was liberated from occupation, something she wasn't even aware of until she took possession. The military family didn't return, even though none of them was harmed during the battles that they survived.

Noah landed the Clever Dream II backwards and smoothly and the hangar doors slid closed in front of it without making a sound. She looked around the cockpit, which was in the front half of the vessel but half way down from the dorsal hull. Layers of protective plating and other technologies protected the small bridge, and there were displays painted on the bulkheads so it looked like they were looking through transparesteel windows. "This is such a tease. I think the Fleet ordered Dame to pick me up in this ship to tempt me to stay with the Fleet. It's not like they have more than four or five empaths, tops."

"Tempted?" Noah asked.

"I'm tempted to find a way to steal it, but not to stay," Alice scoffed. "I mean, if they gave me this and you were rejoining the fleet, then that would get me."

"Won't happen. You're right though, this is a nice ship."

The problem with the previous versions of her ship was caused by the fact that every reiteration of it was a refit that needed to adhere to the original design. The Clever Dream II was something entirely new. It was a more efficient setup that used more efficient and durable materials, saving space and increasing quality in every corner. It still looked the same on the outside even with smart armour that could regenerate and enhance stealth. It was made to look aggressive but attractive with long lines that suggested power and manoeuvrability. Even the original model, which was a century behind in technology, would be an amazing ship to own.

The new and final version of the Clever Class Corvette was an incredible ship, with its own Haven Node Communications system, two different built-in faster than light systems including a large Quad Drive. There were six more Quad Drive modules installed as well. Each of them had its own micro fusion reactor, a low latency Haven Node, a faster-than-light system that worked by pushing the ship into an energetic dimension where it would travel by a different set of rules, and the computer that took care of communications, navigation and shield geometry. It was more than she could ask for, especially since word of the Quad Drive system was starting to leak and it was quickly becoming the most sought after technology in the galaxy.

It, like her apartment, was furnished as the previous version was, and it felt like she was returning home aboard her ship and the dwelling. There was one thing missing. Lewis.

The artificial intelligence knew her better than anyone and had developed a unique personality over the years. She took the data cylinder out of her hip pocket and considered installing him. "How is he doing?" Noah asked.

"Last time he was installed anywhere it was in my Com-Con. He didn't like viewing the world from my wrist computer. He said he was like a shark who had been crammed into the body of a goldfish," Alice replied. "I'm going to put him in the data vault for now. I'll activate him before we take off for the Triton. I don't want to turn him on in this ship for a few days, then have to tell him that they're taking her away. I miss him though."

"Yeah, I would too," Noah said as they got out of their seats. The bridge was larger, with a captain's seat in the middle, but it was still relatively small compared to most ships its size. That would be a relief to her crew, who found the previous model's close quarters less than charming. Noah watched her open the thick door of the new data vault, which had room for fifteen data cylinders that could each store fifty petabytes, then put Lewis inside. There was a high clink as the door sealed with a cold weld. "So, time to take a look around?" he asked her as they headed off the bridge.

"We're going upstairs," Alice said. "I'll have all the time I want to look around here, but our weekend just got downgraded to a night, so I want to make the most of it."

"I like a lady with priorities," Noah said with a smile as he reached out for her.

Just as he was about to make contact, Alice burst into a run. She led him on a laughing chase off the ship, to the elevator, which was closing as he tried to catch up. "Not quite fast enough, Flyboy!" she laughed, waving as the door sealed and the lift took her up to the first level of the apartment.

The lights came on as she stepped out and her jaw dropped. The wall to her left was a floor to ceiling tank with a variety of fish that were ready for the auto kitchen to prepare. The plush furniture was arranged in a ring at the centre of the main room. It was perfect for watching large hologram programming that would fill the middle and provide a surrounding background behind the sofa, immersing a small crowd of her friends.

Memories of watching hours and hours of Noah's holographic reports about his journey across Iora came to mind. It was while she got to know him through his exhaustive holo-journal that she made her last place a home. The elevator arrived behind her, and Noah was out the instant the doors opened wide enough. He caught her in his arms and kissed her neck, then looked up. "This place is amazing."

They were kissing an instant later, clinging to each other as though there was a force threatening to pull them apart again. The feeling of being in his arms for real at last was at the same time soothing and exciting. After taking a long moment to enjoy being with him, his closeness, and his lips, she said; "Tonight."

"Are you sure?" he asked. "You've gotta be tired."

"Are you too tired?" Alice asked.

"What? Me? Not now," he replied, holding her close.

"Then we're going that way," she said, nodding towards the bedroom, or at least what she was pretty sure was the bedroom.

"Okay," he said, taking her lips in a slower paced lip-lock.

A question burned brighter in her mind by the moment despite how much she was enjoying him. *Is the bedroom furnished, or will we have to sleep on the sofa tonight?* Alice reluctantly pushed away from him then tried to run away so she could check and lead him to a space that felt more private.

"Oh, no you don't," Noah laughed, catching her at first, then failing to keep her near as she ran off across the living room.

Alice was in luck, there was still a bedroom right where it was before, and it was fully furnished with a pair of dressers, end tables, a vanity, a sideboard and a large membrane bed. That was Earth technology from the Triton. A centimetre thick bed on a stand that could adjust to the needs and comfort of whoever slept on it, and it was piled high with fluffy comforters and pillows. She leapt onto it and bounced.

Noah joined her just as she rolled over and she wrapped

herself around him. "I love you, Noah. I never want to be away from you for that long again."

"I missed you way too much, Alice. Virtual dates weren't enough," Noah replied.

"No, they weren't," Alice admitted, loving the tingle of his lips on her neck.

"Never felt like this about anyone." Noah held her tightly, his kisses moving up her neck until he nibbled her earlobe and listened to her squeak a little. That's the moment he chose to whisper; "I love you like crazy. Never thought I could get so lucky."

Alice pushed off with one leg and tapped his shoulder. Noah guessed what she wanted and rolled onto his back. Alice sat up and straddled him, his hands on her hips. The look of adoration on his face was as good as anything she could experience while she was reading him empathically. It felt like they were surrounded by a warm bubble that kept all the complicated events outside, and it felt wonderful but fragile, as though anyone could come along and pop it. "You have no idea how lucky you're about to get," she said, running her finger down from her collar slowly. His gaze followed it as Alice teased him, splitting her vacsuit open.

Chapter 10

The Price of Departure

HOW ALICE FELT the morning after being as intimate with someone as she was with Noah always determined what their future would be like. At least, in their near future. Until she woke up and looked at his sleeping face, which was half obscured by his blonde hair, she'd forgotten that.

There had been a few lovers while she was in her first human body, and her feelings the next morning after following the excitement that led her to the bedroom ranged from regretful to joyful. Back then there was always a note of sadness regardless of which it was because she couldn't tell anyone who she really was. Being on the run was anything but good for her love life.

That mournful feeling that came with the knowledge that she couldn't share all the details about herself and that she'd have to move on soon, leaving them behind, was absent. As she watched, a lock of hair slipped down to Noah's mouth. It started to move with his breath. It looked like he was about to suck it in, so she moved it out of the way. He smacked his lips then rolled onto his back, still sound asleep.

As for how she felt about being with him the night before, there were no regrets. In fact, Alice hoped he felt half as happy about it as she did. Sex had a way of changing a relationship. For some, it drained it of all the excitement that built up until the act itself, like untying a balloon to watch the air escape. She always felt tricked when that happened, like a physical attraction and the moods of the moment led her down the wrong path.

With Noah and one other partner, it was more like the expression of something that was more than physical. David was a relief to her while she was being chased by Meunez, and she'd never met anyone who was more kind and honest. She wouldn't call him exciting in general, but she wished she didn't have to go when it was time to move on. In another reality, where she wasn't hiding her identity while she was on the run, she imagined that his kindness and stability were enough for her. That was a long time ago, and as she watched him sleep, Alice acknowledged that the person she was back then had more differences than similarities. Comparing David to Noah, she could see that they were just as dissimilar.

Noah was an adventurer with a good sense of humour, a moral compass that pointed in a direction that wasn't perfectly north, but askew in a way that she liked. He was a showman, and enjoyed making a spectacle sometimes, and he had more than enough energy to keep up with her. He was also curious and had a social ease.

As for similarities, Noah was a little taller than David, and she was short compared to either one. Noah was much lighter in complexion and hair colour, and thinner. Maybe it was the afterglow, or honeymoon phase, but she even liked how his nose flared at the tip a little, just enough to make it look a bit too big for his face from the side.

Snapping herself out of the habit of examining details, Alice allowed herself to enjoy the moment. There wasn't much point in comparison or spending a lot of time overthinking things. The most important thing was that she was so happy that the temptation to wake him up so she could share the moment was almost irresistible.

Instead, she took a moment to reach out with her empathic gift. Despite the golden morning light coming in through the window, he was in a deep, restful sleep. *Someone's used to sleeping in*, she thought to herself as she looked at her wrist computer on the nightstand. It was 07:28 local time, and the sleep counter was at 7.03, which was enough time as far as she was concerned. She normally got between seven and eight hours unless there was something weighing on her mind.

Instead of waking him, she slipped out of bed then took her real command and control units from her bag. The full military version had been redesigned so it was in two pieces, one for each wrist. Hers was similar to the upgraded design her father used, which included a small fabricator, a couple of built-in weapons, an extra energy shield, and an expanded medical device along with the regular functions. Each covered most of a forearm and looked much bigger on her compared to Jake, since he was a full head taller. These were the ones she paid for with her own luxury credits.

Instead of putting them on, she carried them into the bathroom with her. By the time Alice stepped out of the shower she had a message. There was a priority call coming from Haven Fleet in three minutes.

"Here we go," Alice whispered to herself. A copy of her favourite vacsuit was waiting for her in the delivery box. She'd ordered two more the night before, and they were fabricated to her specifications. They were the latest military grade versions and she'd added a few custom layers herself. She put one of them on and then shifted the colour from blue to black. Noah wasn't up yet, but while she was in the bathroom he'd tangled himself up in the sheets. As she sealed the front of her suit, Alice wished she could crawl back into bed with him.

The Command and Control bracer on her left wrist started blinking as she put the other one on. She rushed into the main room and took the call. "Commander Valent," said the woman who appeared on her screen. Her hair was pulled back into a small ponytail that stuck up as a tuft. "I'm Lieutenant Grove from Section Three. Good morning, Ma'am."

"Good morning. What can I do for you, Lieutenant?" The fact that she wasn't being handled by a superior officer irked her a little, but Alice was already getting the feeling that whoever she'd been assigned to in Section Three, which handled human resources and placement, had decided that she wasn't worth his or her time.

"I'm contacting you this morning to find out if you see a future for yourself in Haven Fleet, and to lay the groundwork for your next step if you do. If you decide to stay, Section Three will provide you with your new assignment today, Ma'am."

Alice already knew that she was leaving the Fleet, but was still too curious not to ask; "Will my next assignment be anything like my last one?"

"I'm afraid that's above my pay grade, Ma'am. I'm an Assessment Officer. I oversee intake and highlight outstanding qualifications. I can say that your abilities as an empath and training make you a prime candidate for a lead security officer post at the moment. That's what we need most. As for whether or not you'll end up on a starship, or guarding diplomats, I can't say."

There were plenty of newly minted officers and older, experienced recruits coming into the Fleet. Alice knew that they wouldn't have anywhere near a critical need for long. It was a point that she didn't want to argue though, especially since the Lieutenant she was speaking to didn't have the rank to change the attitude of the Fleet. She moved on to her next question instead. "Our starships are generally staying here or in the Cefa System for the foreseeable future unless something's changed?"

"That's not something I can determine or influence, but as far as I know, the Fleet's mission to protect the Haven and Cefa Systems is ongoing, Ma'am. "

"So you're who I talk to if I want to resign?" Alice asked, cringing. If they sent someone who outranked her, like the superior officer she was temporarily assigned to in Section Three, then it would suggest that she might get some special treatment. Instead, they sent a responsible Lieutenant who was definitely important but would probably process her according to regulations.

"Yes, I am. You can resign and I'll process that too, Ma'am," she replied.

"Remind me; what happens when I drop out?"

"Any equipment supplied directly by Haven Fleet will be recovered unless it was marked as destroyed during a mission. That includes the Clever Dream II and everything aboard. There is a special provision here that states that several lesser items that you've ordered yourself - your personal sidearm, Command and Control Units and several military-grade vacsuits - are not going to be recovered or destroyed. They are marked in your personal inventory. Any other armour will be surrendered, including heavy version six or seven suits."

"Understood, one moment," Alice said, accessing the remote dashboard for the Clever Dream II. She changed the name of the ship to CCC 999, so she could use the Clever Dream moniker somewhere else. "If I see another ship in the Fleet named Clever Dream Two, or Three, or whatever, I'll shoot it down myself, understand?"

"Yes, Ma'am," Lieutenant Grove replied, surprised.

"So, I'm resigning. Where's my crew going?"

"All I can say is that most of your crew, including the ones who are serving aboard the Corsair, have been offered the same opportunity as you. I can't fill you in on what they've decided, Ma'am." Grove's manner was stiff, she was bracing for an argument or more threats.

Alice knew that Iruuk was leaving the military. Whether he was following her father, or would be rejoining her, she couldn't guess. On an even more personal note, the sting of working so hard to be an officer in Haven Fleet then leaving was nothing compared to how they treated her father. As his fate settled in her mind, it felt more and more like Haven Fleet took the easy way to make new alliances. There had to be another course they could have taken that wouldn't have resulted in him getting kicked out of the military organisation he helped build from the ground up. They never respected him, not even in the beginning, but to disgrace him publicly as he was pushed out was something she was sure she would never forgive.

Even still, Lieutenant Grove didn't have anything to do with that, so Alice said only what she had to, and she did so as dispassionately as possible. "Most of my extra gear was destroyed with the original Clever Dream. What I have left will be aboard the ship you sent me yesterday, so come on by and pick it up. I'd like to add one note though."

"You'll have opportunities for that during your exit interview, Ma'am," Lieutenant Grove said.

Alice barked a laugh and shook her head. "No, I'm not doing that. Put this on the record: I want the Fleet to pay me the full replacement value on the first Clever Dream, or I'll make the raw deal I got on that when it was destroyed public on my way out of the military. Understand? Everyone will know you only paid me ten percent of what it would cost to replace it without all the upgrades. That way they'll know that you didn't just screw Admiral Jacob Valent, but that the Fleet has a habit of screwing every Valent who served."

"I understand, Ma'am. I'll send a high-priority request to my superior and to the Master of Requisitions and mark it as time-sensitive, Ma'am. Is there anything else, Ma'am?" Lieutenant Gove asked.

"No. Good luck, Lieutenant," Alice said, ending the call.

"So, they're taking it back, huh?" Noah said from the bedroom doorway. He was in a pair of small shorts, with concern on his face.

"Yeah. I knew it was more of a bribe," Alice said, glancing at the list that appeared on her wrist. The first row of objects didn't surprise her, then she saw that every quad drive she had was there as well. The fleet knew their locations and that some were on other ships, including the Sendega Corvette they captured. "Oh, crap, they're taking the quad drives back. Looks like we'll be back to wormholes."

"So, they might take the Corsair back when I resign? Oh, that's…" his command and control unit vibrated and chirped so loudly that they both heard it, even though it was lost in the covers.

He pulled a shirt on and answered it. His call was much the same as hers, only he was left with less. Every piece of military hardware the Fleet gave him was due back. He was lucky that most of it was aboard his ship, which was at a Kambis Orbital Dock. Lieutenant Grove informed him that his personal items would be transported to Alice's house along with his platinum cargo. He could expect delivery in the next two hours. The only thing that seemed like a bonus for his service undercover was a lot of back pay along with a generous severance. It was apparently a regulation to reward people who went undercover. When the surprisingly short call came to an end, Alice was at his side. "I'm sorry. I know you liked that ship."

"Not as much as you and the Clever Dream," he said, joining her in a long embrace. "Now it feels like we're on our own."

"But together, and I know we'll be welcome aboard the Triton," Alice replied.

"You know," He tilted her chin up and looked into her eyes. "If it weren't for you, I'd be completely screwed up right now. I don't even own the clothes on my back, but…"

"You've got me," Alice said. "Oh, and a huge pile of platinum, right?"

"Are you only with me for my money?" Noah gasped.

Alice snickered and replied; "Yup, gonna stick around and spend all those riches."

"Still worth it," Noah replied, punctuating it with a kiss.

"So, you're okay?" Alice asked more seriously.

"I'll be fine. I mean, it's pretty easy to look on the bright side this morning. You?"

"Last night was perfect," Alice sighed. They swayed together for a while until she realized something. "You know, I've started over before, but never with someone. I mean, there were people who wanted to help around, but…"

"Never someone like me, huh?" Noah said, beaming at her with a big grin. "Yeah, this doesn't feel bad at all. More like winning." he squeezed her close and nuzzled her neck. Then recoiled a little. "Whoa, just caught a whiff of my own breath there. I'm gonna go find a denta tab and the shower."

"Tabs are in the little pouch in my bag, the shower's that way," Alice pointed. "I'll see what the kitchen will make for breakfast."

"Oh, are you keeping this place?" Noah asked as he fished a denta tab out of her bag.

"Maybe. I may have to sell it so I can buy a ship, though. We'll see." She realized something then and shared her thought; "I'm going to have to call Yawen. I'll have to tell her that she's going to have to surrender the quad drives we moved to the Sendega and the destroyer."

"Better you than me," Noah said, cringing.

Chapter 11

A Respite

SPENDING time with Alice in person was an entirely different experience for Noah. The simulation sessions that they used for visits when there were light years between them were more about chatting or playing a game than anything else. That was their way of keeping in touch or socializing with other friends when they could.

Alice's house was too large for both of them. Above the main floor was another with empty rooms, including a large solarium. They moved a sofa so they could hang out in the sun with the broad doors pulled open. That was the only furnished room on that floor.

The quiet time they spent felt sacred, and they had three days of it. They broke things up with strolls along the walkways between the trees, a visit from a crowd of Nafalli including Woone, Iruuk and his two eldest sisters with their boyfriends, who seemed perpetually bored whenever they weren't making sure that their girlfriends were well tended to. Watching Iruuk throw the occasional glance at them when they spent a little too much time grooming his sisters was hilarious. He could make the younger male Nafalli shrink into themselves like quiet, fearful pups. It wasn't long before Noah realized that it was a way for Iruuk to tease them and remind them of his physical and familial dominance at the same time.

It was interesting to watch Alice, and how she pretended not to notice that it was going on at all. Noah followed her lead as Iruuk did most of the talking during the visit. He was going to follow her onto any ship she decided to captain. It didn't seem to bother him that he'd worked hard to earn his place in Haven Fleet only to leave it behind. He had a theory about the direction Alice's father, Jacob Valent, was taking the Triton, but wouldn't share it in the company of his sisters and their boyfriends.

When Alice and Noah weren't outside and there were no visitors around, they spent a lot of time talking and relaxing together. Noah still felt like he'd barely scratched the surface where Alice's history was concerned. When he asked her the right question, she'd share long stories. Several were about times on the run. It was no wonder that she felt like a kindred spirit, they were both travellers who had seen more solar systems and settlements than they could count without a map and several days to think it over.

Why it took her so long to share that side of herself with him over the last three months when they visited virtually, was unclear. He didn't know how to ask; 'Why didn't you tell me you've seen as much of the galaxy as I have?' At least, he couldn't figure out how to ask until the third day.

There was something else that he loved about her, and it

only seemed to come out when they were together in person. She had an energetic spark that would come out of nowhere, often when she gave him a playful look, then took off running. He chased her every time, especially since the first few chases ended in the bedroom where they did something else that was pretty energetic.

Over the three days of peace they took together, the chases took them into empty rooms upstairs, around the house on the decks, back inside, and even into the empty hangar. She once led him to the secure room downstairs, where their chase ended on one of the palettes of platinum they were keeping there.

When there was no one around, he spent most of his time in a small pair of shorts that she liked, and she alternated between a workout bodysuit that was cut high on the hip and a loose, short dress. He was chasing Alice for the second time that afternoon, loving her big smile every time he saw it when she looked over her shoulder. She was wearing that light, colourful dress. This chase was leading to the solarium and he wanted to catch her before she could get the sliding doors open.

He got his arms around her a couple of steps before she would have leapt over the sofa and her momentum carried him into then over it with Alice. They tumbled over it and then onto the floor as she shrieked and laughed. "Oh, man, are you okay?"

Alice pushed him fully onto his back and sat up, straddling him. Her smile was like sunshine, it was intoxicating. "I'm good, man," she replied, making fun of how he used that word a lot. "Got me again, faster this time."

"You're getting me back in shape," Noah said, still catching his breath.

"You're easy to motivate," she replied, tapping his lips with a fingertip.

"Feels like I'm always chasing after you now." Something in what he said made her smile fade, and he stroked her cheek.

"It's a turnaround. I was chasing after you while I was Prince-sitting. At least, that's what it felt like."

"I get that, I didn't exactly keep the most regular hours. My customers don't really compare schedules. Sorry I was hard to get in touch with…" his apology was interrupted with a soft kiss.

"You don't have to apologize. I mean, I feel like I left you exposed out there. Like I left everyone on their own after giving them enough rope to hang themselves with."

"No, you left at a high point. It was the most badass move I've ever seen," Noah said, sitting up so they were nose to nose beside the sofa. The light was taking on an odd, purple hue as Tamber started making its way behind Kambis. "You stole three Advanced Destroyers from the Order of Eden, destabilized all their shit on Rodus, took out some of their big hero types and liberated the Issyrians then just went home. I mean, people are still talking about you."

Alice was blushing as she said; "You did half the work, even more sometimes."

"Most people think I was your hired gun, some even think I was your arm candy. Well, the Issyrians don't, I've got a lot of trust with those guys, but aside from that, you're the brightest star near the Shattered End. A big Robin Hood, Space Ranger hero-type legend."

"What's it going to be like when I get back? I mean, everyone spoke through you when we were meeting in sims. Even Sel keeps communicating with text updates."

"Oh, the whole group of Rebel Captains wanted to use me

to deliver messages to you. I told them that they could contact you themselves, but they all wanted to go through me. It's like they thought I could tell them what you'd think of what they were doing as if I knew you better than anyone."

"Don't you though?" Alice asked, a little surprised. When he didn't answer right away, she squeezed his hips with her legs a little.

"Well, not as much as I want to, you know?" Noah watched her eyes widen a little and immediately tried to allay whatever fears or surprise she felt. "I mean, since you stopped reading me with that beautiful mind, you've become the Queen of questions. I love telling you stories, but I like turning the tables on you more. You know, getting details about you. I've learned more about you in the last couple of days than I did in all the sims we met up in."

"Now I feel like I should be sorry. I mean, I felt out of the loop while I was in the Cefa System. I wanted to know what was going on, so I guess I controlled our time. Am I doing it now?"

"No, I mean, sometimes, but it's a trade, you know? You get me talking about stuff that was going on with Knud, Easy and the rest of the crew, about the Shattered End and I forget to leave room for you. I'm a talker, always have been, but when we're together like this, I guess I remember that you know me so much better than I know you and I start asking questions. Now that I know you don't tell stories about yourself unless someone asks, I'm getting the hang of it."

"I'm sorry, I mean, I usually don't think anyone's interested," Alice replied.

"Well, yeah, there's that, and you're wrong, by the way. The other thing is that you're just not as much of a talker. You don't go on about yourself unless something's going on. I mean, imagine if we were both big talkers. There wouldn't be enough air."

Alice smiled a little and nodded. Then, like a spark of energy lit her up, she poked him hard. "Get me talking whenever you want. You really can ask me anything. I want you to know me better than anyone else. What do you want to…" Alice's bracelet flashed and vibrated. She looked at it, and her eyes widened. "My Mom and Dad are here with Faloo and Laura." Then she regarded him, biting her lip for a moment. "I forgot to tell you they were visiting today, huh?"

"Yeah," Noah said, very conscious of being naked except for a tiny communications band around his wrist and small green shorts.

"They're about an hour early, landing in the hangar. We'd better get dressed."

"Fast. All my clothes are downstairs," he said as he gently but briskly pushed her off. "You can answer the door in that little number and no one would bat an eye. If your Dad sees me stripped down, he might get ideas."

"What? That we've been running around, fooling around? He'd be right," Alice snickered.

"Oh, I don't want him to guess right," Noah said, sprinting from the room.

MOMENTS AFTER NOAH and Alice changed - him into shorts and a loose shirt, which was the style, and her into a longer dress that turned out to be the same colour - their guests came up from the hangar. Ayan was carrying Laura as usual, and the baby was crying as they came into the main room. Faloo made a high soothing sound as the fur under her chin rippled, catching the babe's attention. "I'd grow fur if you could teach me that," Ayan said, watching as Laura calmed down.

To Noah's surprise, Ayan and Faloo each gave him a big hug. Jake shook his hand firmly, even smiling at him a little. The former Admiral was a towering figure even to Noah, who was himself considered tall at just over two meters. As if that wasn't enough, he was thickly muscled and seemed to take in every detail of the main room of his daughter's home. It was as though he was scanning it for something out of place, or some detail that would tell him what had been going on there. He was trying to look casual, but Noah could tell that there was something else going on. Something that made him tense.

Laura was the star of the visit. Jake rolled a large play mat out between the sofas and chairs there and they set the babe loose. Not ready to crawl on her own yet, she seemed to enjoy sitting and standing as Alice, Ayan and Faloo took turns supporting most of her weight. When she sat up straight without any help, everyone, including Jake cheered a little with light clapping. Laura probably didn't know exactly what was going on, but giggled at the excitement and fell over onto her side, which made her laugh a little more. "She'll be crawling soon, I can't believe it," Ayan said.

"I feel like I missed so much while I was away," Alice added as she got down to Laura's level and shook a rattling toy ring then offered it to her. Laura took it and put it directly into her mouth.

"Teething is definitely about to start, at least, that's what Daisy and every parent who sees her is telling me," Ayan said with a sigh. "I still don't know if I want to put her on localized nerve blockers to make it easy on her, or let her go through it naturally. It doesn't sound like I'll get a moment's sleep if I don't do something though."

"What is teething?" Faloo asked before drawing Laura's attention with a soft, high sound and letting her tongue loll out of the side of her mouth. She was rewarded with one of Laura's infectious giggles.

"It's when humans grow their first set of teeth. They push up through the gums, so it can get really uncomfortable," Ayan replied. "It doesn't usually last long though."

"Oh, poor girl. Nafalli are usually born with their first set of teeth," Faloo replied.

"Oh," Ayan said, looking to Noah, who was watching all the ladies gathered around Laura from the sofa opposite Jake. "Jake wanted to see the vault downstairs. We heard about what you're keeping there."

"Sure." It felt like Noah's heart leapt up into his throat. He got to his feet and glanced at Alice, who regarded him reassuringly. "It's not far from the elevator, you know, downstairs."

Jake got to his feet and followed him without a word. The silence continued as they rode down to the main hangar, then walked to the short hallway leading to the vault and other storage rooms. "The door's made from an alloy with active resistance. If you try to drill or burn into it, the stuff will get tougher wherever that's happening, or it'll push back, or something. I don't think I understand it as well as Alice does," Noah explained as they approached the featureless door to the vault. *Stop trying to explain engineering and science stuff! He probably knows more about all this than you do!* He thought to himself as he stepped in front of it and let the hidden scanner get a look at him.

"It's a lesser adaptation of the technology in the new active plating. The Triton's covered in it," Jake said, his tone difficult to read.

It was strange seeing the former Admiral out of uniform, in a shirt with a similar cut to his own that hung loose past the waist and trousers that looked like they came out of some old spacer gun slinger drama. He wasn't carrying a weapon, which was a relief.

The door slid aside, its weight along the heavy track caused a low rumble. "So, here it is. Most of what I was able to take home after almost four months of selling guns and trading tech," Noah said, trying to sound proud, or excited, or something. He wasn't sure how his presentation came off. Then he added; "Your daughter says she'll stick around until it's all gone. You know, like she's only with me for the money."

Not only did he bungle the joke, but there was no sign at all that Jake found it funny, he didn't even offer a courtesy laugh, or smile, or shift in manner at all. Instead he regarded the palette of platinum pips, slips, strips and bars and shook his head. "It's more money than I've ever seen in one place. Congratulations, Noah, but if you think Alice is with you for money, then you don't know her at all, though."

"Yeah, man, that was just a joke. It didn't come off right," Noah said quietly as he looked at a case in the corner holding another prize from his undercover work.

"So, this is what it was all about out there?" There was nothing confrontational about Jake's tone. It sounded more like he was already trying to come to terms with the thought that his daughter's boyfriend was more capitalist than soldier.

"Well, no," Noah bristled. "I mean, there's nothing wrong with making plat. You can do a lot with a pile of this stuff, or even just a little. I could have made double if I didn't build some storage space in the Shattered End, or help the folks there out. But no, I wasn't there to build a big stack, man."

"Well, this tells a different story," Jake said, crossing his arms, his expression starting to darken. "I mean, it takes work to do this, even when your manufacturing system was given to you for free, so you deserve credit, but…"

"It's not about the cash. It's about the people, the connections." Getting judged by someone who wasn't there for a moment and never offered real help was frustrating enough for him to forget who he was talking to for a moment. Noah was so irritated that he pressed on. "Everyone knows that I'm the prime arms dealer in the Rose System, in the Shattered End, and everywhere nearby. I've made enemies thanks to that, but none of them will come near me because they know that the people I sell to will slag them before they get close and trade whatever's left of their shit to me for more guns or gear. Half of this doesn't even come from selling stuff from that fabricator the Fleet gave me aboard the Corsair. I started trading ships, even big systems made for bases. I've got Order of Eden and other small attack ships and shuttles stashed at the Bitter End and other places. In the last three or four months, I've connected with hundreds of people who don't just fight the Order, but thanks to the upgrades the rebels buy from me, they prey on them. Everyone on every supply ship in half a dozen solar systems looks over their shoulders expecting to get jumped by some well-armed band flying rebuilt, often upgraded, Order fighters or patrol ships."

"That's impressive. I didn't see it in your file," Jake replied.

"That's the Fleet's fault. If they want the info, they've got to debrief me, but they let me go without calling me in and asking me so much as; 'so, how did it go?' Besides, all the raiding that's starting is nothing compared to what I have to offer. This is what's impressive," Noah held his communication band up and activated a holographic contacts list then flicked it so the names spun by. "These are my customers, allies, and everyone who trusts me even a little. Who do you want to meet out there? What do you need done? Need a spy who's already working for the Order? I've got a couple dozen contacts who not only hate their jobs with the Order or their allies, but would love to blow something up for a few hundred platinum. Well, as a starting price." he picked up a black case filled with small platinum pips and poured the small ovals over the squared pile of riches. "This box of five hundred pips could buy you sabotage, feed a family for a month, or get you info on what's being imported, when and where it'll arrive." He dropped the empty box as the sound of pips rolling and settling faded. "I like a big sale, no doubt, but I get a much bigger rush when some rebel captain is telling me a detailed story about the last ship they took down. Everything you need to know about the underground is in here, and I have been looking forward to sharing since the first rebel sat down, bought me a drink, and bragged about a raid."

"What have you been doing with all this information aside from building your stack?" Jake asked, walking around the large vault room slowly.

The man was still impossible to read, but Noah guessed he was thinking about what he was hearing, so he replied; "I didn't see a point in giving it to the Fleet, especially since they weren't going to show up in the Rose System, even though it was primed for a takeover, or whatever. So I started trading it once I got to know some of the Rebel Captains, especially the leaders of Last Crisis. They give me a cut of whatever they take. A lot of that cash is still back at my temporary base in the Shattered End."

"Did you say it was called The Bitter End?" Jake said, the corners of his lips curling up a little.

He liked that. It was a start. "Yeah, seemed like an obvious name."

"A good one. What kind of base is it?"

"Most of it's not pressurized yet, but we have an old ship that a few people live in when they're not guarding the warehouse. We're using an old underground hangar to store a few troop ships and a corvette that are waiting for buyers. It's rough, but safe for now. I don't think it'll be the final location."

Jake sighed and, looking at the platinum instead of Noah, made an admission. "You've accomplished a lot in a little time, and you make my daughter happy. I know what it's like to be with someone who's parents cast long shadows, but I still didn't know how this conversation would go. I'll admit, I'm a little relieved."

"You're kind of a legend, I didn't know what to expect either," Noah said.

Jake seemed to relax a little. He turned towards Noah, his hand resting on the tall pile of platinum. "How hard did you have to fight to become the arms dealer for this much of the underworld?"

The directness of the question reminded Noah of something that Minh-Chu said to him about Jacob; that he liked people who spoke with clarity and brevity. At least, until you really got to know him. Leaning on that knowledge, he replied; "Like I said, people would rather be my friend than enemy, so no one's tried to steal from me in weeks. I've had to compromise to get that, though. I don't just sell to people who fight the Order and their buddies anymore. Now anyone with the plat can buy something, I just save the ships and higher end stuff for the real rebels."

"I get it. I don't like it, but I get it," Jake replied. "You print gear for the mercs and pirates using the fabricator Fleet gave you?"

"No. I resell stuff that people bring in. You know, after it's cleaned up and checked. I have a line on a pair of fabricators that aren't quite what the Fleet took away, so I'll be buying them when I get back. I'm not going out of business after all the work we put in."

"What if you had another option? Minh wants you to rejoin Samurai Squadron, and I need a guide or a fixer."

"A lot of people depend on me, so I won't be leaving my trader gig. As far as help, well, you've got my Ident, call me anytime," Noah finished with a flourish.

Jake actually laughed softly at that. "Well, keep my daughter happy, and we won't have any problems. Aside from that, I'd like you to spend a few days aboard the Triton. I'm going to need a guide and you'll want to be there to see how we operate. I have another Captain on his way back from the Doxan System."

"Remmy Sands," Noah said, nodding. "He's been beating the bushes, looking for a few people."

"Your network is that big? You get news from Doxan?" Jake asked, seeming as amused as he was surprised.

"Doxan's almost all underworld at this point. Every pirate I know takes a turn through there when they can so they can pick at wrecks, ruins or try to take down cargo trains that are stupid enough to go there. Everyone knows about Captain Sands. He tries to hide his Haven Fleet gear, but people see him coming. They know military training and kit when they see it."

"So, you know about him because he makes an impression," Jake concluded.

"Well, that, and I know a lot of people who salvage and steal from the Doxan system then try to trade whatever will turn on to me. Then there are the New Owners, the colonists, the freelance law enforcers, and everyone else. Ask me who I know in the Doxan System. It would take a week to tell you everything," Noah said, letting himself relax a little.

"Really? Ever hear of someone named Mary Reed?"

"Yeah," Noah replied. "She doesn't go by that name anymore, though. People know her as Reaver. I just bought five starfighters from one of her guys three weeks ago. They were in mint condition, sold the next day."

"We've been looking for her," Jake replied.

"The Fleet should have told me, but I don't think anyone in her outfit would care. They're all set for weapons, gear and ships."

"Remmy will want to know more, they're old friends," Jake said. "So, you'll help me out if the Triton goes to the Shattered End?"

"That depends. How much would it cost for the manufacturing systems aboard the Triton to make me or your daughter a new Clever Class Corvette?"

"I'll see what I can do," Jake said with a snicker. "But we have to get upstairs. I have another emergency."

"Oh?"

"I promised to make the ladies lunch. I could use a hand."

"I got ya," Noah said as they started walking out of the vault. He decided to show Jake the other treasure he had stowed in a case some other time. "So, how is the Triton shaping up?"

"Alice didn't tell you? The muster starts tomorrow. This is my last day off the ship."

"Oh, okay, I guess it slipped her mind," Noah said.

"I'll be offering you both quarters aboard. You know, if you two need another base of operations, or join me on a mission sometime."

"That's cool, thanks," Noah said, genuinely surprised.

"Separate quarters," Jake clarified.

Chapter 12

Tiy

EVE ENJOYED the feeling of having a busy command centre around her. There were a hundred, probably more missions underway thanks to her strategic management team. Admiral Scanlon had twice as many spread out across the Cluster and other solar systems near it. Her head start in the area and reach were enviable.

There was something that Eve's military and espionage groups in the field didn't have to deal with often. Rebellion. She had given every one of her people orders to pursue the paths of least resistance first. That was literal in every sense. If there was a strong anti-Order of Eden sentiment somewhere, leave. If that place had something that they needed, blend in and buy it or take it without drawing attention. If that wasn't possible, then they were to report and await instructions. So far, her teams hadn't run into that last situation. With the help of Citadel agents that had been offered the right incentives to secretly provide Eve with information and act on her orders, it seemed nothing was out of reach. They had been in the Cluster for nearly two years, integrating with different cultures and monitoring as many civilized systems as they could.

Citadel's weakness lay in their frontline fighters and spies. Stretched thin, they resorted to using Dolls, or Custom Advanced Humans. These were fully human people who were designed from the ground up with genetic advantages and the ability to accept a kind of biological programming. The technology was stolen from the Core Worlds, where they'd put it to use to create a new, absolutely loyal, slave class. One that broke down after the Fourth Fall, when many of their masters were killed and, left on their own, many of the Dolls began to question their loyalties in the absence of masters. Unlike most robots, they had human self-preservation instincts and the ability to embrace new ideas.

That was how Eve started connecting with some of the Dolls who were performing as spies across the Cluster. With twenty-eight seconds of flashing images and specific sounds tailored to each Doll, her technicians could remove forced loyalty programming. A Doll would be completely free to decide who he or she served, or to be free. It didn't take long for word to spread. Somehow, most of the Dolls knew where some of the others were. They secretly kept in touch, and several reached out to Eve, asking what they had to do to be freed.

This, Eve was sure, would be key to becoming influential in the Cluster. Espionage through the Dolls and their friends was more important than anything else in delivering Dron's vision of a galaxy governed by the Order of Eden and its philosophies.

Getting ahead of Scanlon wasn't Eve's goal. Taking the most noticeable objectives and recruiting the largest force was. That was what the Overlord wanted. It was his demand, and she looked to the team of intelligence officers surrounding her in the multi-tiered command centre to find ways to do that.

"Finally," she heard one of her senior officers say under his breath as he stood and approached.

He emerged from the throng like a messenger out of the mob. "Your Eminence, we have a point-to-point link from orbit."

"Who is it?"

"One of the Citadel operatives, Aspen Two-Eighty. She's been on planet Tiy for three months, and has found an ideal contact for you. Her team has a satellite in orbit, and she's placed a holographic receiver-projector in their equipment."

"How? How did she get so close without raising suspicion?" Eve asked, eager to hear the story.

"This Aspen has disguised herself as a woman named Moxa, a regional name, to be sure. Posing as a newcomer to the city, she spent some time tracking the source of a newsletter called 'We are Newcomers Here.' The publisher sends it out to over thirty thousand people twice a month, and he proposes that the humans dwelling on the planet are a lost colony. His opinion is not popular, but Aspen, or Moxa, proposes that a readership of that size would be enough to spread the news of interstellar contact. Our calculations indicate that word would spread exponentially especially if someone who grew up on Tiy is playing the messenger. We could accelerate that if we gave him technology that's well above their current level, say, a short wave video broadcasting unit."

"They're that far behind?" Eve asked, shocked.

"They not only don't know how to broadcast video, but Moxa says that they haven't seen a hologram for generations. They've forgotten where they come from, that there are any humans outside their solar system. There are a number of origin myths that they've made up to make up for their lack of real knowledge. We can't find any record of a colony ship though, which is worrying."

"Not for me," Eve said. "If only a few suspect that they originated from another world, then I can remind them gently, using their own people at first, then presenting a beautiful, kind face for them to behold. Moxa has to make sure they're ready using whatever resources she has. When will everything be in place?"

"Moxa claims that her satellite is ready, and this publisher, Trey, is eager to make contact with anyone who could be from another star. He is a true believer," the officer replied. Tiy and Moxa were core to his project, so there was a bonus for him if it turned out well.

"Send my best to Moxa. Tell her to make contact. Present him with a short wave video broadcasting unit. I know they're expensive, and there's only one on the planet at the moment, but if she thinks he should be the one to spread the word about humanity reaching out to their lost children, then it should be worth it. Prepare a stealth ship with an incursion force. I'm going to go there myself. Tell Moxa that I'll flash her free when I get there and that she'll be paid well for her service."

"Yes, Ma'am. This is going to be a glorious day for you."

"All glory to the Present and Future Overlord," Eve said.

"All glory to the Overlord," the officer agreed with a reverent nod.

. . .

TREY WALKED across the basement of his family home for the second time that night. The four presses were churning dozens of pages out every second. They were old, and the fourth press, their newest, had broken down again. Two of his volunteers were working on it. One looked up nervously at his approach. He was covered in grease and black ink to the elbows. "Gonna get it working, Trey. Don't worry."

"Do you know why it's not running?" Trey asked.

"No," he replied, cringing.

"Then don't make promises, just get it running. The mail truck comes tomorrow at eight. If we can't make it, we lose subscribers. That's bad for the message."

"I know, sorry, Trey. We'll get it running, don't worry. Just a few minutes."

It would have to be in just a few minutes, so Trey stood there and watched as the volunteers checked each component of the six foot tall press. "These new electric machines are more trouble than anything. I still have a block press in the shed, I could send you guys out there so you can get a few old fashioned copies out."

"Got it," announced the other volunteer as he turned his wrench. "The drum bolt on the left was loose. No aligning anything when that's ready to fall off. That won't come undone again, at least not tonight." He backed up and nodded at his fellow volunteer, who flipped a big electric switch. The barrels on the massive press started turning, drawing paper from a large stack, running it through its workings then dropping a copy of the newsletter on the other side. It was followed by several more.

Trey picked the first few fresh sheets up and nodded. The first few were a mess, which was to be expected after his volunteers had been through the machine, but the rest were perfect. "Good, great job, you two. I was afraid we wouldn't make it."

"I know," the more vocal of his volunteers said. He was the one who cringed and jumped the most, but he had the biggest mouth, a hilarious contradiction as far as Trey was concerned. "This is an important one, we've got a name to share."

The large metal plate a pair of true believers dug up only a few dozen kilometres away was hanging on the wall behind him. The word: 'LORAND' was spelled clearly across its tarnished surface. "Wish we could have waited to see what our friends at Entin labs have to say about that, but there's no helping it. Gotta get the story out."

"Do you think they'll find more of the ship underneath? I mean, they're still digging," a volunteer asked.

"I hope, but if the ship was travelling too fast before it crashed, the rest of it could be three states away. Gotta hope, though, right?" Trey said with a shrug.

A light flashed at the top of the stairs, and he rushed across the floor, careful to avoid getting any of his appendages caught in the rolling, flipping metal works of the large presses. It was his brother, tall in a long nightshirt, his eyes watery. He was a grown man physically, but his mind never fully developed.

Instead of having a yelling conversation in the noisy basement, Trey ran up the steps and guided his brother into the upstairs living room. "You should be sleeping, Orner."

"I can't, it's too loud," Orner replied apologetically.

"What about your plugs? Did you try 'em?" Trey was careful to make sure he was the epitome of patience. Things would only get worse if he made his older brother feel like he was inconveniencing him.

"They made my ears hurt this time," Orner replied, sticking a finger into one ear and popping it.

"You're not supposed to do that, remember what the doctor said?"

"Makes a pocket in my ear and hurts the works," Orner recited.

Trey started walking his brother up to the second floor. The living room was filled with volunteers who were stuffing envelopes with newsletters. His seat was closest to the basement door, and he nodded at an older woman, Sekin, who was like the den mother of the stuffers. "I'll be down in a minute."

Sekin gave him one of her kindly smiles and nodded. "Can't sleep, Orner?"

"Naw, it's too loud," Orner replied, rubbing one ear.

"It'll be okay." Trey said in a soothing tone. If the earplugs irritated him, then he was probably fighting the early stage of an ear infection, something that happened fairly regularly. He dreaded the possibility. There was nothing like a two point two metre tall thirty-five year old who behaved like an eight year old who was suffering from an ear infection. He guided his brother upstairs and they stopped in the narrow hallway there. "You've gotta get your sleep. Just listen to the rhythm of the presses, pretend it's the generator of a great big starship."

"The White Star, or the Celebrant," Orner said, his eyes lighting up at thoughts of his favourite ships. One of his favourite things were the Saturday serials at their local theatre, the Dramadrome. They belonged to bold space adventurers who explored the stars and fought over-the-top villains who had long moustaches and short sighted dastardly plans.

"That's right. Just imagine you're there, making good time to Vega Nine," Trey said, happy to see his brother's mood start to turn around.

"That's good. You're good with words, Trey."

They arrived at his doorway, where a simple room awaited.

"So, you'll try that? I mean, we don't get this kind of rattle and roll every day. It's perfect for that kind of dream. You'll be out there, jumping from star to star."

"Okay, I'll try, Trey," he said, giving his younger brother one of his famously generous hugs.

"Door closed tonight, okay?" Trey said as he watched his brother start under the covers.

"Okay," Orner replied with a little trepidation.

With the problems of the moment taken care of, Trey returned to his folding chair where he began stuffing envelopes again. It was a simple routine: fold the double sided newsletter half, open the envelope flap, stuff it in, run the sponge over the glue strip, seal it, copy the address from his part of the list onto one side of the envelope, wet the stamp, affix the stamp, then start the next one. The volunteer envelope stuffers often had lively conversations on any and every topic. When things got quiet, he could think about what would be in the next issue.

Things were quiet that night, and there was a feeling that everything was about to change. They had evidence now, at least something that the government refused to comment on. Two men in bright green jackets had come to see the piece of hull he had downstairs and they stared at it for several minutes. Then they left, saying nothing. Their reaction was so guarded that he had to strain to write an interesting paragraph about their appearance days after the section of hull was delivered to his basement.

He was wondering what the government knew about it, or what they thought about it, when Merl, a thin, older volunteer tapped him on the shoulder. "Trey, that young woman from the mail company is at the back door. Has something she wants to talk to you about."

That was alarming. They had seven hours before the mail

truck was due. She had come with every pickup and even visited a few times to volunteer as an envelope stuffer. "Moxa? Tell her she can come in."

"She says she needs you outside. Looks nervous, if you ask me. Could be trouble with the pickup?" Merl asked, pulling at his long fingers.

"I doubt it. International Cartage loves us. We're the biggest customer they have in this town on pickup days," Trey replied just loudly enough for everyone in the living room to hear as he got to his feet. "Don't worry."

He was worried but he tried not to let it show as he passed through the kitchen where another pair of volunteers were folding vegetables, spices and rice into flatbread pockets. The oven was heating, and his mouth would normally water at the thought of having a late night snack of the galrau, but he was too focused on what Moxa had to tell him. The screen door creaked, so he only opened it as much as he had to, then he saw her at the bottom of the stairs outside. "Trey, we have to talk." Her tone was serious even though she offered one of her warm smiles. She was a brown eyed, chestnut haired woman who looked at least five years younger than him. She seemed too pretty to load and unload bulk mail, and he knew his brother had the biggest of crushes on her. Moxa treated him with patience and kindness. Trey appreciated that, especially since she didn't do anything to lead him on or give him false hope. It was a fine line and she walked it with care.

When he joined her, she gave him a warm hug, which he returned, then started slowly walking down the path. He joined her and asked; "Is there a problem with tomorrow's pickup?"

"No, the Cartage truck will be here on time. I'm here to tell you that you and everyone in your house are right.

132

Humans originated on another planet," she said with the soft, lovely voice that was a part of her charm.

What thrilled him was that there wasn't a hint of doubt in it. "I know you're a true believer, we both are. I have a lot of work to do though. Do you think you can pitch in?"

They had made it past the treeline when she turned and stopped to look up at him. "Do you remember a few weeks ago, when I asked the stuffers and you a question?"

The moment came to mind, when she asked; 'What kind of evidence proving that humans came from another world would you like to see?' The question seemed too simple at first, but it became the topic of the night, and of an article in the newsletter that was about to go out. "I remember. People are still talking about it."

Moxa smiled a little and continued down the path. "I'll never forget what you said."

"A working spaceship," Trey replied.

"Sekin said she'd like to see medical technology. The kind that could cure her sister of unwanted growths," Moxa said as she rolled her left sleeve up.

"I remember," he watched her as she held her forearm up like she was about to type on it with the fingers of her right hand. To his utter shock, a rectangle of skin illuminated with images and lettering that looked like their oldest language.

As Moxa tapped a few icons, she said; "Your ancestors came from a world named Earth. For some reason, the colony that landed here centuries ago hid all their technology and restarted as a pre-electric society."

"That was the old ways, some of us still live like that, but the rest started inventing, but I've never heard of anything like that. Is that a part of you?" he asked as he watched her work on the interactive display.

"It's like your tattoos, a computer that's written onto and under my skin that can disappear and reappear whenever I like," Moxa explained.

"But computers fill entire buildings. Our best counting machine can't make images like that - only lines on a single colour screen - you have a moving painting on your arm."

"And here is my spaceship," she said with a grin that almost distracted him from the true revelation.

A green and black spade shaped ship appeared in the clearing beside the path. It hovered silently, not stirring the wind. Its smooth hull looked like the skin of a wet seal, glossy and almost reflective. "How is it staying up?"

"Antigravity. Your ancestors had a primitive version of it when they came here."

"So, you know our story? How we got here? Where we come from? Why we left?" he asked, staring at the pointed end of the ship. The tip was transparent, and he could see a pilot seat surrounded with control surfaces that were beyond what the science fiction of his people had imagined so far.

"I'm afraid that I haven't been able to answer all those questions. The Order of Eden, one of the interstellar organizations I serve, is looking for details. I have genetic evidence that you and everyone on this planet are descendants of Earthlings. The people who settled here made a choice for you - to deny you access to the rest of humanity - and the Order of Eden wants to correct that."

"Do they refer to the Eden in the creation myth?" he asked.

"Yes, but the Order believes in and is bringing about a new Eden. One that exists on several worlds so far and will be recreated over and over so anyone can work their way to eternal paradise. It isn't a set of beliefs about an afterlife, but what you can achieve in this life through personal advancement in the organization and technology. I'm getting ahead of myself, sorry. My point is that we've been able to cure every disease, wound and malformation. How would you like to see your brother's handicap corrected overnight? Growth diseases cured in an hour or less?"

"You can do that?" Trey asked. "If this is some kind of joke, or government ploy…"

"There it is," Moxa said, pointing at her ship, smiling at him. "It's a ship that no one on your world could build, and it's mine. Touch it. We can go aboard if you like. Your government wouldn't understand it, they couldn't build one after a hundred years of advancement."

He did, and was surprised to feel a surface that was so smooth that it almost felt like water. A ramp lowered inviting him inside. In a moment of pure excitement he was surprised to find fear and hesitation. Then he took one step up and looked inside. It was like a little camp inside with a nice pair of bunks, a little cubicle with a table with storage above and below the seats. It was all space-aged and metal, of course, but the inside looked like a living space made to go to, well… space! There were lockers and other things he didn't recognize or understand. Instead of venturing further in, he stepped back and shook his head. Questions and realizations came all at once, clogging his mind to speechlessness. "This is… It's…"

"How about we begin with modern miracles?" Moxa asked, her hand gently landing on his arm. In the other she had a pair of small pillboxes. "I wish I could have come and shown you this moments after meeting you, but I had to make sure I could trust you. It hurt every time I spoke to your brother knowing that I could clear his mind and give him the potential he deserves."

"You had to earn our trust, too," Trey said, using the many Saturday Feature Films he'd seen and fictional books he'd read about aliens coming to their world as a reference. He always found that the books and stories that inspired them were better because they could offer more detail. "You're going to show me this, then leave."

Moxa laughed, then shook her head. "No. That would be cruel. I want you to give your brother a pill that will correct the damage that was done to him when he was deprived of oxygen at birth. Then I'll give Sekin one for her sister. They're specifically made for them, so they won't cure anything or anyone else."

"So, he'll be permanently…" what was the word?

"He'll be set right. The same person at first, but he'll start learning as he was meant to, maturing mentally. Before long you'll be able to have a normal conversation with him, and he'll act like a grown man."

Trey looked into her eyes for a long moment. He saw nothing but kindness and concern. Then he took the pill. "There won't be ill effects? These things always come at a price in the stories."

"This isn't some narrative drama. It's a fix. The Order's companies make sure drawbacks are a thing of the past. It's real technology," Moxa replied with a little irritation.

Maybe she was offended at his doubt, so he smiled at her. "I'll give it to him tonight."

"Now, this is another thing you've never seen or read in your stories. I'm inviting you to bring whoever you think can handle this truth out here to see my ship. I'm also giving you this." She placed a light, thin, round device in his hand and tapped the middle. An image of a blue, green and brown world appeared above it, seemingly really there, floating above his palm. He tried to touch it and grinned as his finger went through the image. "It's a computer interface. I'll teach you how to use it later, but for now there's a summarized history of your ancestors on Earth and why most of them left. There's another video, or show, about the Order of Eden and how we are trying to advance the cause of humanity in the galaxy. It's important information because - and maybe you shouldn't share this - there are enemies in the galaxy. They're coming soon, and your people aren't ready."

"Who are they?" Trey asked.

"I can tell you later. Soon, actually, but first you have to understand, I'm alone here, in your country. At least I am for now. So you have to control who sees this tonight or I'll be in danger. Your government would want to cover this up. They'll lock me up or kill me. In a way, I'm asking for your protection in return for information."

"I understand, you'll have nothing to worry about. I know who I can trust," Trey said.

"Okay, I believe in you, Trey, thank you," she said, embracing him. "Now, if there are a couple people you can trust with this, you should get them. I have to hide my ship before dawn."

"I'll give this to my brother first, then I'll be right back," Trey said.

When he arrived back at the house, he decided not to stop the print run or the envelope stuffers. Cancelling the shipment could raise suspicion. Instead he slipped upstairs with a glass of water and gave his half-asleep brother the pill. Then he quietly invited Merl and Sekin outside so he could lead them down the path. As they made their way in the near complete darkness, his fear that Moxa and her ship would be gone, that he would look like a crazy conspiracy freak, rose higher and higher. Then, as they took the last turn, he saw her in the clearing, waiting beside her sleek ship.

Hours later, the trio emerged with new, sacred knowledge about the origins of their people, and a box of what Moxa called 'recievers' that were so thin that two of them could fit inside the envelopes with their newsletter. Their heads spun with the knowledge that they would be able to send images and sound to everyone who had one.

To their surprise, Moxa made her ship disappear and joined the envelope stuffing volunteers. She worked along side them until dawn, when she had to go to work. A couple of hours later she returned with the International Cartage truck in her grey uniform as though nothing had changed. Trey knew that everything was about to. His world felt smaller, and he felt as though his people were about to be offered an incredible future.

Chapter 13

Return To The Triton

IT TOOK Alice a while to figure out what the distant, familiar feeling she had was all about as Noah docked her combat shuttle with the Triton. As they locked with one of the many mooring points on the aft portion of the dorsal section of the massive stingray-shaped ship, she realized what that feeling was. "It's like coming back from a long vacation."

"Only we don't technically have jobs this time, and I'm just hitching a ride back to the Shattered End," Noah replied with a little smirk. "Or playing tour guide, if the Triton decides to stick around for a while once we get there."

"That could get interesting. I'll have to stick around for that tour, I'm sure things have changed," Alice said, recalling the short replies she got from Yawen. She was busy captaining Alice's ship, a captured Order of Eden Advanced Destroyer named the Renegade. They were hunting in the Rose System, running silent often. She couldn't wait to see the results.

Alice and Noah put their packs on, each grabbed a duffel, and squeezed past the heavily armoured and scan shielded crates that filled the hold. "I wonder what our quarters look like," Alice mused.

"Probably amazing. Oh, your Dad was pretty clear that we'd be in separate quarters, by the way. Still, I think we'll get the best of everything while we're aboard. I have a feeling that your Dad or someone on this ship is going to be offering us one job after another. I say if you get something that looks better than taking the Renegade over, or getting another Clever Class ship somehow, go for it. We can make a bit of distance work if we have to. I just hope we don't get separated for as long next time."

They came together at the full-sized rear hatch and she grabbed his collar. "You still don't believe that I'm going to stick to you like glue, huh?"

"Love ya lots, but I don't believe I'm that lucky," he kissed her softly, and then they walked through to the concourse. The broad space was still shiny and glossy from the recent refit. The aft side had a mooring point every fifteen metres, and there were people coming out of shuttles and small ships. The side towards the nose of the ship, which was hundreds of metres away, featured heavy hatches that led deeper into the ship and a glossy blue and white wall that displayed images and instructions that only the people they were intended for could see. When Alice looked, all it said was; *'Speak to the androids next to your shuttle.'*

There were a pair of updated Haven Manufacturing Mark Eleven Androids waiting there. She and Noah watched a piece about them in the Triton orientation material. They only had the most basic personality and weren't programmed with any emotions. They were human analogue workers and security that could use any equipment that people could, and they were part of the ship's new automation. They seemed perfectly human except for an identity strip that looked like a chin strap. There were a series of small numbers and letters written on them, with a smaller, larger set in the middle. The nearest android's said; 0x-100p.

She assumed they were assigned to her and Noah because of the platinum that was filling the hold in those security cases. "Hi, can I call you Loop?"

"That would be an acceptable interpretation of my designation. You may," the android replied in a voice and manner of speech that was more natural than she expected.

"Okay. Do you know where to take our cargo?" Alice asked.

"Yes. C-Three-Fourteen," Loop replied. "A carrying platform is about to arrive. After your cargo has been offloaded, the shuttle will be moved to Hangar Five and you will be notified of its exact location."

"Make sure it's positioned so we won't have to wait more than a minute to launch," Noah said.

"Yes, I will do my best to ensure it," one of the androids replied. A third android arrived with a wheeled, motorized cart and the trio got to work offloading the heavy cargo boxes.

"Still a little nervous about not staying with that while it's being moved," Noah whispered.

"No one knows what's in those crates. It could be my wardrobe, for all anyone would guess," Alice replied, keeping her voice just as low.

"Your wardrobe didn't fill that duffel," Noah replied.

Then, he relented. "Okay, I get it. This ship is probably one of the safest places in the solar system."

Easy emerged from one of the airlocks then and waved at Noah with his artificial arm. "Hey, made a decision yet?"

"Hey, man," Noah replied a little sheepishly.

"What decision?" Alice asked, exaggerating her inquisitiveness by cocking her head.

"Oh, he didn't tell you yet?" Easy asked with a smirk. "Then I guess I know where he's leaning."

"Minh-Chu has been trying to get us both back into Samurai Squadron," Noah explained.

"I've been waiting to see what he does, so I don't leave him without a good pilot. Manage to buy the Corsair back?" Easy asked Noah.

"Not yet. I might be able to get an upgrade, but it'll cost everything I've got here and I may have to make a few promises on top of that," Noah replied.

"You mean, bigger?" Easy asked. "I don't know about flying a D Class Capitol Ship. It's been a long time."

"No, same size, only better," Noah said, wiggling his eyebrows.

"No shit, I'm guessing I shouldn't talk about that, huh." Easy nodded appreciatively. "Hope I get to see it."

"Is that what you and my Dad were talking about downstairs yesterday?" Alice asked.

"Well, I brought it up," Noah replied.

"You met the big man? What was that like?" Easy asked. He seemed more amused than Alice thought was appropriate. "Did you record the historic encounter?"

"Why would I…. I mean, yeah, I met him. Of course I met him, I mean…" Noah stammered. He looked like a man who just realized that he was standing in the middle of a minefield, and Alice didn't have to read his emotional state with her empathic gift to figure out that he was afraid that some poor phrasing about her father would cause trouble.

Alice's left command and control bracer sent a mild tingle of urgency up her arm to her mind and she stepped away. "You guys go gossip while you get to the Gunnery Deck. We're running late."

"Okay, see you there," Noah said as he glanced at her blinking comm-con unit.

Alice moved to the side of the broad, curved concourse. The new instructions displayed on the wall were telling her to move to the Gunnery deck. It didn't surprise her that the people who were arriving there were all former Fleet officers. This wasn't a briefing for the entire crew, that would take place in one of the hangars deep within the ship.

Alice answered the call, which was already set to private mode. Only she could see Ayan's face on the screen, and the sound was sent directly to her subdermal communication unit. "Welcome to the Triton."

It looked like she'd been crying, and Alice asked; "Everything okay?"

"Oh, I marked my call as urgent because we have a favour to ask, and it can't wait," she replied.

"That's not all, though. Did you and Dad have a fight?"

"No," Ayan replied, seeming mystified at the question at first, then she seemed to realize what her daughter was talking about; "Oh, I'm still all puffy in the eyes. Leaving Laura was harder than I thought. She wouldn't stop crying, even though Daisy took my appearance and biometrics on again. That little one's too smart, she knows it isn't me, so she wouldn't let me go without a concert of wailing and screaming."

Alice could see that there were tears welling up in her

mother's eyes and, while she sympathized, she wanted to change the topic as quickly as possible. "Oh, I'm sorry, Mom. You'll be back in a week or two. What was the favour?"

"Your father was hesitant to ask because he knows it's one of the reasons why you found it easy to leave the fleet but..." Ayan started.

Alice finished the thought. "...you want me to take a read on the officers, make sure the loyalty is right. I thought they were screened before joining the Fleet?"

"The ones coming in from Haven Fleet were, so we're not worried about them. There are about fifteen joining the crew of the Triton from outside the Fleet who have credentials from other military organizations. Then there are the dozen or so captains that are a little like you and Noah... they're guests with their own ships and we invited them to this briefing, which isn't being broadcast outside of the ship. They're getting Privateering Licenses before the Triton leaves in a couple of hours."

"Oh, okay, so I'll just empathically listen to the crowd while Dad does his song and dance?" Alice asked.

"Exactly. We'd appreciate it," Ayan replied with relief.

"I'll be there in a minute. Best if I watch from the back of the crowd, though. I'll be a little late on purpose." Alice knew that she would be put to work, and wasn't surprised that it happened so soon after boarding.

"Okay, see you soon. Oh, and we won't be doing anything about someone who seems suspicious right away," Ayan said.

"See you in there."

The concourse was clearing out. Shuttles, most of which were running on autopilot, were decoupling from the mooring points along the outer edge so they could return to one of the stations around Tamber. Her ship had been emptied and was already on its way to one of the main hangars aboard the Triton. In the relative quiet, Alice relaxed the block she kept in place around her empathic ability.

At first, there was nothing, then she felt as though she was noticing someone significant, and realized it wasn't from her own perspective. There was a pilot in a form-fitted black vacsuit and armoured bomber jacket walking by in the hall-way. She already had the Samurai Squadron Logo set up on her back: a silver skull with 'First Strike Fighter Squadron' written in a line that followed the cranium and Samurai Squadon in place of its lower jaw and teeth. She was a little tall for a fighter pilot, but she had the confident walk, short-cropped hair, which was jet black, and was fully geared up in her equipment belt, sidearm and combat boots that were designed as much as for a cockpit as a dangerous excursion. "Hi," she beamed, filled with the thrill that came with recog-nizing someone who was at least a little famous, or perhaps a personal hero.

Alice smiled back and concentrated on adjusting to having her mind open to the emotions of others by turning what the pilot was radiating down a little. "Hello."

"I'm Maid, one of the pilots who stayed with Samurai Squadron." She offered her hand, hoping that the encounter would go well. "Sorry, I'm a little star-struck."

Alice shook it. "You shouldn't be, but thank you."

"You're going to the briefing?" Maid asked.

"Yeah. I'm guessing this is where we'll find out where the Triton will be taking us first. We'll probably end up taking a bite out of the Order or its allies right away," she replied, riding the waves of Maid's emotions, reading them.

There was that diminishing excitement that came with hearing someone that was once idolized speaking for the first time, along with keen interest, then her response to the idea of fighting the order came in loud and clear. Maid was eager to do so. The prospect inspired a kind of dutiful thrill. "So, you don't know what we'll be taking on first either?"

"Not for sure. I think the commanders kept their options open until the last minute. I've been on vacation, so I'm out of the circle. You should go on so you don't miss anything though. I have a couple of things to check before I go in there."

"Oh, okay, it was fun meeting you," Maid said as she reluctantly turned away and strode down the concourse.

Alice waited until she was out of sight, then started towards the rear of the Gunnery Deck as well. Her favourite focusing exercise came next. She stared straight ahead, let her peripheral vision blur, and turned most of her attention inward. Deepening and slowing her breathing, she became more aware of how she was moving, the deck passing under her feet, the echoes of her boots as the concourse emptied, the way her vacsuit flexed and followed her movements. Her TS 100 Lawkeeper sidearm's holster wasn't perfectly affixed to her thigh, so it didn't swing with her stride right. The pocket with extra ammunition and a few tools on the other leg was fitted right. Her heavy boots helped her gait along like weights at the ends of pendulums.

The sounds of her breathing, even the beating of her heart were loud in her ears as she moved on to the next step. She accepted her keen awareness of her physical self, and then moved deeper, into what she was feeling. Confidence that she'd worked hard for with her instructor, Quan, and practised while guarding the Prince, was at the forefront. Only Quan knew how good she'd gotten at being an empath.

There was still a rosy, warm feeling of spending so much

time with Noah. Sometimes she was reminded of how young he really was, barely out of his teens, and sometimes that was refreshing. She rarely felt that youthful. Sometimes it was annoying because she'd had more relationships and lovers than he did. His inexperience showed in moments where he thought he might offend her and was overly cautious with what he said, and how he treated her much differently than most of his friends, especially when he thought she wasn't listening.

There was no problem with how he treated her overall, he placed her on a pedestal, but that kept her separate from everyone else. Alice knew that she could either leave that alone, or make an effort to hang out with his friends and get to know them. She wasn't sure what she'd do yet, but the opportunity to decide was coming fast since it seemed like people were gathering aboard the Triton. Other than that, there really wasn't anything she found in their three consecutive days together that she didn't like or even adore.

He was a tall man with a giant grin, hands that knew how to hold her, and a big heart that was absolutely hers. She didn't need her empathic gift to be sure that all that was true, and it brought her a kind of joy that was nestled deep in her core. A feeling of excitement that came from the potential of a new adventure, of rejoining friends like Yawen, who had been busy without her and made sure that she was missed was there as well. Regret at leaving them for so long muddied all that, and it was important to accept those negative feelings as well.

After taking inventory of what was hers, she imagined a wall going up around all her emotions - momentary and lingering - then turned her attention outward. Alice was ready to feel and sort through the sentimental emissions of hundreds as she walked through the metre-thick outer airlock doors leading into the Gunnery Deck.

By the time she was through the inner doors, looking at the two hundred or so officers of the Triton and other important people gathered in a rough, loose square, she was able to use her other senses just as keenly. The look of intellectual absence that people may have seen in her eyes a moment before was gone, replaced with what Quan once called; "an intense focus and presence." It was the kind of thing that great communicators and negotiators had that made people feel like they're being listened to, and focused on. Her mother and father had that way about them sometimes - a look that made it absolutely clear that you had their full and undivided attention.

It had been a long time since she'd seen the Gunnery Deck. It was hundreds of metres long, and three times as wide with a three-metre thick transparent hull high overhead. Every fifteen metres there was a heavy ball turret with a gunner seat inside, an apparatus hanging down with a pair of magazines and an apparatus for manual or direct reloading. Markings on the floor warned the people who tread there of elevator hatches, rising doors, and ammunition fabrication outlets. In the distance, she could see rows of armoured loader suits that would maintain, manually replenish ammo for and sometimes defend the turrets. They looked more modern than the last generation she'd seen about two years before, and better armoured.

The space was wide open, with no combat doors in place to break the atmosphere up into sections, so a breeze from slight changes in pressure as doorways leading into the depths of the ship occasionally passed over everyone gathered there. As she quietly joined the group at the rear, Noah looked over his shoulder and regarded her warmly at first.

Then his smile diminished as he saw her nod at him, then tap a quick message to him that simply said; *Reading.* She felt his response as Noah nodded then turned around to pay attention to her father. At first, when he spotted her, Noah was a little excited, happy to see her, and there was a glow of attraction combined with devotion beneath it. Then the excitement was replaced with tension and a little fear that she'd come to recognize as common when someone was aware that they were being read by empaths. Maybe he'd get over it someday, but until then, she didn't mind switching it off when they were together, at least, when she could.

"...Privateering Licenses." Jacob Valent was finishing from where he stood on a platform that was being held up by four three-metre tall defence suits. They were thickly armoured, like walking tanks made to jump out onto the Triton's hull to fight whatever may crawl around or land there. He was in an armoured long coat similar to hers, with a form fitted, black military vacsuit beneath. She'd come in as he finished explaining one of the missions that he and Ayan would be undertaking: giving Privateering Licenses to independent Captains.

The crowd was generally pleased with that, but there was one source of annoyance, and Alice made sure to listen for more. Ayan was in a white vacsuit that was otherwise similar to Jake's except she had a lighter long coat on overtop. She sat down on one edge of the platform and let her feet swing a little. The group was tickled by that, and even more so when Jake looked at her quizzically. In response, she said; "You're on a roll. Go on."

"She's been running around all day," Jake explained to the crowd as they tittered a little at their antics. "Admiral Anderson is here to approve extraordinary captures by new

Privateers, to make sure you get rewarded for them if you're selling, and she's going to be signing off on the highest bounties. On top of that, she's going to be putting the Department of Science on its feet. That's so any of the new tech Haven Fleet buys can be assessed right here, aboard the Triton."

"So, what do you want us to bring in, exactly? A list would help," a short woman in a suit of dark green combat armour asked. Her intentions were remarkably clear. She was definitely one of the Triton's passengers, and she felt eager to return to her people and begin earning by fighting one of Jake's enemies.

"Once we arrive in the Rose System, we'll be posting a bounty board. Only people with an access code, communicating through a Haven Communications Module will be able to see it. When you sign up as a Privateer Captain, you'll get an HCM for free." Jake held his hand out and Ayan tossed an octagonal ball to him that fit in his hand. "Haven won't be selling these until next year, but every ship attached to a Privateering License will have one. They'll melt down if you try to tamper with it, but they'll work forever if you just connect them to your ship normally. Controlling them from your communications systems is simple. You can turn tracking on and off, and there is an emergency beacon that you can activate that will transmit to any other ships with one of these, including all Haven military vessels. There is a whitelist system built in too, so if you want certain ships to know where you are, or to exclude certain ships from seeing when you're in distress, you can set that up." Jake added the last part about security in response to a rumbling in the audience. They were worried about being tracked, and maybe about alerting less scrupulous crews about vulnerability if there was an emergency, Alice guessed. His explanation put most of them at ease.

"So, anyone with one of those can contact you latency free?" someone asked, excitement in his tone. Outwardly, he might seem happy to discover that the license came with a precious freebie. Inwardly, emotionally, he was extremely eager, suspiciously so.

"As long as you have a fairly efficient wormhole drive for it to work with. We can sell you one if you don't." As Jake replied, Alice could feel a hint of familiar annoyance from the man and she casually moved so she could get a look at him.

The man was in a red and black jacket, had an empty holster for a large sidearm and, when she got a glimpse of his face, had a sensor implant above his left ear. More importantly, she got a look at his face and was able to stare just long enough to get a fix on the feeling of him. Everyone had a distinct emotional aura, which was a term Quan used for want of a better one in english. It identified them and allowed empaths to separate, or even ignore, what they were emanating.

Alice let her focus drift away from the man in the red jacket so she could feel everyone else as well. Her father's presentation went on. "You'll need an encryption key to unlock the bounty board. The code will match your HCM, and you'll only be able to access the secure network using the two together. The bounty boards will be updated and you'll be rewarded for capturing or destroying whatever's listed. The targets will range from the general, like destroying an Order of Eden patrol fighter, all the way down to capturing and delivering Admiral Scanlon. That's one of the many 'Dead or Alive' bounties on the board. She's worth ten times more if you deliver her alive, by the way. The Fleet wants to have words with her."

A little laughter rippled across the crowd, and it started feeling like Jake and his audience were more like-minded than not. "So, you're still with the Fleet?" asked a voice from the throng.

"No," Jake replied. "I'm only the messenger and provider... for a little while. There are people on the Triton who represent the fleet directly," he pointed at Ayan, who waved at the crowd.

She added; "My people. It's in the data sheet. You'll see."

Then Jake went on. "They're going to be looking for good spots to setup well guarded outposts outside of the Haven System."

"We're hoping to be in five solar systems within the month," Ayan added. "Thanks to the new alliances that Haven has made, you can expect to not only get paid there, but eventually have access to deeply discounted repairs, upgrades and a second hand market featuring refurbished equipment and ships that were brought in by your fellow Privateers. Haven Fleet and her allies have a good plan in place, and we're already building what we need to make it happen." Ayan was surprised at the round of applause that followed.

"Until then, there's a depot in the Haven System that can take care of you, and the Triton will be able to provide a sort of mobile base if we're in the right area. That's just in case you capture an Order Officer or something else that's just as delicate or urgent," Jake said, ephasizing 'delicate' by pretending he was holding something like a doily up with two fingers. The crowd of officers and ship masters were enjoying his presentation.

He continued with a more serious attitude. "Now for the nitty-gritty of the day. Before you get your final Privateering

Licenses, your ships will be scanned to make sure that you're not just flying out there to get killed. After a Licensing Officer approves you, the scan results will be deleted. What good are they to us, after all, since we're going to be very good friends?"

That made Red Jacket so annoyed that Alice almost twitched. There were other people who didn't really like the idea of having their ship scanned, then judged, but that made sense. Independent ship owners didn't like having to jump through hoops. Red Jacket had a much more drastic reaction that was more extreme than the norm. She wanted verification, so she used her comm-con to discreetly send Noah a message. He checked it, showed it to Easy, who nodded, then interrupted Jake as he was about to start talking again; "What about fighter groups? I'm teaming up with someone who has a little freighter and we're going to be flying new Raze Forty-Nines off it. We've been watching a trade route that I won't share, sorry. I mean, it's primo, barely defended, so we want it all to ourselves at first. I mean, there are nice, long cargo haulers with industrial equipment, thousands of tons of supplies, that organically grown stuff, and bulk retail product. Oh, and a few of them are loaded down with military gear headed for little Order bases that they think no one knows about, so we can get rich and really starve 'em. I guess my question is: can we report all the stuff we get on the raids and sell a few of the rigs we capture to you? I mean, it seems a bit like double dipping to me."

Easy's performance was far more than she would have asked for, and it got the reaction Alice wanted. A more complex mixture of indignant anger radiated from Red Jacket. The guy was quietly seething already at the thought of Order bases getting starved out. Then her father smiled, playing along with Easy's question. "If your fighters pass the scans, then your wing commander or owner will get a Privateering License. You could probably get some help if you're trying to choke a whole trade route. Hell, I might join in myself. As far as what you'd get paid, well, the Fleet will verify your activities using your records and intelligence from the enemy and pay you what it's worth on the bounty board. We'll buy what you're selling too, but the price you'll get will depend on how much the supplies are needed at the depot you're offering them to. The black market may pay better. Maybe we could set up a trade board on the secure network?"

Ayan nodded at him. "As long as the Fleet isn't liable for trades it isn't involved in. I think we can have that set up in a couple of hours."

"Hell yeah," Easy said, bringing the exchange to an end. The crowd was excited, almost boisterous as they remained largely quiet, outwardly observant. The only exception was the man in the red jacket, who was visibly calm, nodding along, but furious. There was an undercurrent of sympathy in him too, probably for the outposts that Easy was threatening. If it were up to her, she'd take him aside and lock Red Jacket up so he could be questioned at length right then, but she would have to report him instead and see what the officers did.

Chapter 14

Airlock 12

THE PRESENTATION only went on another fifteen minutes after she'd confirmed that the captain in the red jacket was probably an Order of Eden spy. She sent Jake and Ayan a secret text only message pointing him out, aware that verification was still needed. Her empathic sense may have been clearer than ever, but emotions could only tell her so much. There was still a small chance that Red Jacket was an Order sympathiser to the extreme, and not actually a part of the organization. They had followers, and if he was one of them, he would know very little about the order, or other spies. There was still a chance that he could lead them to other unassociated supporters, though, and what to do with the information she had wasn't up to Alice. That was a relief.

Her message pointing him out got a response seconds later from Liara, the lead communications and intelligence officer aboard the Triton that read; '*We have his information here. Investigating further now. Thank you, Alice.*'

It made sense that her department had a file on everyone who came aboard the Triton whether they were going there to work or visiting as a guest. Alice wanted to see her file later, just out of curiosity, and made a mental note.

The rest of the presentation went by quickly with several guests asking questions about Haven's privateering efforts. They expected broad restrictions or to be forced to sign a contract affixed to a book of regulations. After Jake and Ayan fielded a few questions that danced around that fear - that privateering would be a restrictive exercise and that the Fleet would find ways to get out of paying for whatever they could - Jake finally cleared his throat and said. "Haven Fleet wants this to work. You'll be surprised at how hard it is to get your Privateering License revoked. You will get a short disqualification sheet that you'll be able to read in under two minutes. It's that short, and it says that anyone who harms civilians, intentionally harms an ally, or cooperates with Haven's enemies in any way will be prosecuted under Common Galactic Law. If you can steer clear of doing any of that, you're good. At the bottom of the doc, you'll find one more thing. It's the Mercy Rule. Haven is trying to bring it back."

"So, you want us to respond to every emergency beacon we come across?" asked a captain with metal caps over his eye sockets.

Ayan answered that question as she got to her feet. "Yes, but the new version of the Mercy Rule asks that you inform two other nearby ships before you respond. That will reduce the risk to you and your ship a great deal under most circumstances. It's an optional rule, when it comes down to it, so use your discretion."

The crowd seemed satisfied, and cheered when Jake asked; "Anyone want to join me in the Pilot's Den for a drink or three?"

It had been a very long time since Alice had watched her father play the part of a fellow spacer. Even though he and Ayan carried a fair amount of fame, they seemed approachable and in good spirits. Most of the people there felt like they were being guided towards a new, exciting adventure.

Other questions followed for Ayan and Jake as they led the way through the corridors, further into the ship. They were headed forward, where the Pilot's Den had been expanded, swallowing up the forward observation lounge. She hadn't seen it, but a few of the officers were looking forward to checking it out.

Most of Alice's attention was on Red Jacket. It took effort for her to keep her empathic sense focused on him, open to others, while she tried to make sure she didn't stare at him at the same time. As they moved down the corridors, which were shiny black with gold-coloured trim, the crowd diminished. Whole groups of officers took different transit cars that could move in all directions. They would beat the core group of Jake, Ayan, Noah, Easy, Alice and several other mixed officers and guests there. The latter groups didn't seem to care, as they had all kinds of questions for Ayan and Jake, who were easy-going and forthcoming. Alice almost didn't notice the feeling of a pair of newcomers behind her. "Hey, Fur-Face," Noah said to Iruuk. "How's it going Faloo?"

"Wonderfully. I'm happy to be free so I can join Alice's crew again," Faloo replied. Her pronunciation seemed intentionally clear, something the short Burrower Nafalli did when she was trying to improve her English. There were many hard consonants that her people had difficulty with since most of their language consisted of grunts, growls, howls and - for want of a better word - barks.

Noah touched the back of Alice's hand and she took his as he said; "You're..."

"Busy, sorry," Alice replied in a low whisper. Even with the crowd down to less than twenty, she still had to concentrate. Most of them had strong personalities and their excitement was still high. Still, she didn't let his hand go, and took a moment to look over her shoulder at Faloo, who was a little shorter than her with thick, well-groomed fur, and Iruuk, who was much taller and had a lighter coat. After smiling at them both, she got back to work.

Red Jacket never strayed out of earshot as Jake and Ayan answered questions and leisurely spoke to the other captains. One, a young man who looked like he was still in his teens, was thrilled at the opportunity to talk to Jake. He was eager to arrive at a shipyard so he could trade his Aerovoid G-15 Attack Craft in along with a few platinum for something more modern. His topic of conversation, and the fact that Jake knew that model of the ship, which was hundreds of years old as it turned out, seemed to annoy Red Jacket. The spy was probably hoping that more sensitive information would be discussed.

Then, before Alice realized it, they were almost at the Pilot's Den. They'd turned left just short of the main starboard entrance and came to the end of a hallway. "Are you going to show us one of those shiny Haven Systems Ships, Admiral?" asked the short captain in heavy armour. She was cheerful and eager as she smiled at Ayan.

"Nothing but void out there," Jake said, and the group of fourteen was silenced. It wasn't his tone, which was almost jovial. It was the implications of their location that stilled the conversations.

"You've done a pretty good job, Merl," Jake said, turning towards Red Jacket.

Alarm, and the urge to flee emanated from Merl like jagged spikes, and Alice did her best not to wince. Then Red Jacket's training or some kind of natural ability to calm himself took over, and his mind was like a still pond. "Well, thank you," Merl replied without showing any outward sign that he was afraid that he'd been caught.

"I bet there isn't a person here, including me, that would have picked you out as an Order of Eden spy," Jake said, casually taking a few steps that put Merl between him and the airlock.

"That's nothing to joke about. You could do some damage to my reputation. I'm a former Aucharian Spaceman, a void warrior. Just looking to put that experience to work, Sir," Merl told Jake.

There was an almost hidden undercurrent of hate in him, and it made Alice want to draw her sidearm and remove the man's head that instant. Atop that, she could feel signs of deception tolling like a bell. Lies stood out, no matter who you were. Noah looked down at her hand, which had moved from holding his to resting on her handgun. "Right, your ship, the Sandcall. It was salvaged by Shining Star Recovery Group, which is owned by Regent Galactic, which is synonymous with the Order. It was re-registered a few months after recovery after an inspection and then sold to you. Its records are nice and clean, but Merl Atkins died thirty-eight years ago according to Regent Galactic's citizen database. It was an infant death. Sad, but perfect for creating a new identity. The Order rewrote the file so you could have his credentials, onto which they built a history. It would have worked if we didn't have an old version of the records to compare with the new ones," Ayan explained calmly. The other captain's expressions were darkening as they started to stare daggers at Merl.

"It's kind of funny; I got the older version of the records on the same mission that got me kicked out of Haven Fleet," Jake added.

"Dead? That doesn't make sense. I'm right here," Merl replied, then leaning into false indignation, he continued; "Is that why I haven't been able to contact my ship for the last ten minutes?"

"Right. Your ship has been taken by a Haven Fleet boarding team. We've done a DNA scan and found that three members of your crew are actually low-ranking Order Officers. You've been caught," Jake said, squaring up in front of him. He was a head taller, his voice firm. "They don't send amateurs to spy on us anymore. Everyone we've found since we took the system back has been damn good."

"I'm a former member of the Aucharian Space Superiority…" Merl started.

He was interrupted as Jake pushed him back several steps by pressing his finger into the middle of the man's chest. The thick inner doors to Airlock Twelve opened behind him. "You know, it's much easier to clean an airlock than it is a hallway. You'd think with the safety devices and emergency equipment in there, it would be more complicated, but the maintenance bots show that they can get a real big job that's dripping with difficult biomatter cleared up in under three minutes. The hallway takes a little over four. I mean, I can't figure it out."

"That's strange, I'll have to take a look," Ayan said, nodding.

"I know your record, Valent. That's not how you operate,"

Merl countered, shaking his head as he stepped over the threshold into the airlock.

"You haven't thought that through. I'm only accountable to myself now. Do you actually think I give a shit about laws in this Solar System? I own enough of it to make anyone overlook what I do on my own ship. Hell, I'm sure the fleet expects me to do all kinds of things they won't." He leaned in and whispered; "I'm a war criminal who confessed to causing a megadeath event."

That caused a shock of alarm to come flowing out of Merl's mind. As for the rest of the people around Alice, Faloo was worried, Iruuk was shocked, while Noah and most of the other people watching were eager. Perhaps to see what Jake did next, or maybe to see some Merl get what they thought he deserved. There was an outlier that surprised Alice so much that she almost lost all focus. Ayan. She was amused. Amused! It didn't seem like her, but Alice had come to see her as not only her own mother, but recently she'd been with Laura whenever possible, and Ayan was always caring and tender with her. Almost forgotten were the days of Ayan the brave Engineer and sometimes warrior. Ayan's reaction to seeing Jake's darker side start to emerge was a powerful reminder.

Despair entered Merl's emotional profile as Ayan turned and left with a little smile. "Don't make too much of a mess. It could take a while for the bots to get around to it," she said as though it wasn't the first time Ayan had seen Jake do his worst.

"What can you tell me?" Jake asked. "Give me a reason to let you live while you take those hull walker boots off."

Merl's eyes went wide, he was quickly drifting from forced outward passivity to complete despair. The chortles from the guests behind Jake didn't help him maintain his calm. "My boots?"

"Take them off." Jake drew his heavy sidearm and pointed at Merl's shins. "I could just cut you off below the knees so I can send you out there with the air," Jake said calmly, to the amusement of almost everyone. A few of the onlookers were shocked, but they were all mesmerized. "You're probably still new to the spy game, aren't you? I mean, you're good, but I don't get the feeling of experience here."

"Five months ago," there was relief as Merl made his first truthful admission.

"Where do you report to? Who is your handler?" Jake asked.

"Arkenon, in the Rose system, my handler is…" he started to reply.

Alice ignored the rest as she discreetly tapped a tactile icon on her com-con unit that sent one word to Jake; "Lying."

"Try again. We know that's wrong. I have the best deception detection software in the galaxy running on you. Make it quick, I'm looking forward to that drink," Jake said, to the quiet mirth of his audience.

One of Merl's boots was off. It flopped onto the deck as his despair deepened. "Gold Haf. It's a well-defended base about sixty million kilometres from Garos in the Rose System."

"I know it," said a short, armoured captain. She was practically giddy.

"Your contact?" Jake asked.

"Darren Farmer," Merl replied without hesitation as his foot slipped out of the other boot.

"True," Alice sent in a silent message.

"When's your next scheduled check-in?" Jake asked.

"Three days and eleven hours plus a few minutes," Merl replied.

"All right, I need your jacket, your personal com, and

everything in your pockets. Noah, get up here," Jake said as he checked something on his command and control unit then nodded to himself.

Merl hurriedly did as Jake asked, dropping his jacket in front of him then tossing a wrist communicator, and a fist sized reserve oxygen tank on top of it. No one seemed surprised as a tiny scanner, a couple of spider-like listening devices, and a tube of nutrient paste came out of his pockets. Noah did as he was asked and stood beside Alice's father, who scanned every piece of gear that emerged. "All right, it's safe," Jake said, and he motioned for Noah to pick the stuff up. "Thanks," he said as it was done.

"Now what?" Merl asked nervously.

"A quick trip outside, then prison," Jake said as he used his command and control unit to activate the emergency close command for the outer airlock doors, then ordered it to instantly purge. "I get paid once the doors lock behind you."

In the second that Merl was pushed out into the void along with all the air in the wide airlock, Alice saw him reaching for the emergency headpiece built into his collar. Fear, alarm and pain radiated from the man and Alice shut her entire empathic sense down, wincing at the infliction. She shot her father an angry look before she was able to calm down. He didn't notice.

"Damn, I don't think that undersuit had an automatic emergency containment mode," Jake said, shaking his head.

"Don't worry, Jake," said Minh-Chu's voice over Jake's command and control unit. He was monitoring things from Flight Operations. "Haven Fleet's shuttle is catching him now. He'll survive unless he has a heart attack."

"Good, that's the first bounty for the Privateering program down. Catch a spy, send him to Haven," Jake announced. "Now let's get that drink. First round's on me."

Chapter 15

The Pilot's Den

NO ONE SPOKE about what they'd just seen. To several of the newcomers there, Jake was more than a former Admiral. He'd been a privateer before, which is a fact people liked to share. There weren't many details available, but old posts on the Stellarnet made it clear that he was successful enough to start a shipping company with two heavy haulers while he continued his bounty hunting career.

Most people retired from bounty hunting or law enforcement when they started something like a shipping company. The assumption that people who didn't know him made was that he continued bounty hunting because he enjoyed it. Alice knew differently. At the time it was what he was best at, and he was looking for clues that would lead him to his past and his daughter - her. The shipping venture was probably there so he could switch to a more peaceful profession when he found her.

That wasn't how things worked out, but Alice always assumed that was the plan. Explaining that to the newcomers and the officers who were operating under the wrong assumptions would take time, and Alice was pretty sure that Jake didn't want her to. Everything she'd seen suggested that he was providing some kind of example.

It was one that gave some people pause, and others grim encouragement. Either way, no one was ready to discuss what they'd seen, especially within earshot of her and Jake. Noah had something else on his mind then, though. "You seemed very far away that time. I mean, I think I was the only one who could tell, but... I think I'm asking if you're okay." The question came as a whisper that only Faloo overheard.

"It takes a lot of focus to read a crowd. Then I was reading Merl, and I had to concentrate on stopping myself from getting pulled into his emotional trip. There was a lot of control in him, but hate and fear beneath."

"Oh, so it's like you're wading into a river so you can feel the current, and if you go too deep you'll get swept away," Noah mused.

Alice was astonished at the analogy and that it showed that he understood her so well. It wasn't absolutely perfect, but she'd never heard better, not even from Quan. "Good shot, flyboy," she said, stopping and pulling him down by the collar for a brief kiss. "I love that you get me."

"I love that I've got you," he replied.

"I'm getting cavities over here," Easy muttered as he passed.

Alice snickered against Noah's lips and took his hand. "Let's buy each other exotic drinks."

"Sounds fun," Noah said with a nod.

A third of the Pilot's Den was the same as it was the first

time Alice had seen it. The silver skull was on the floor. It was the first thing people saw and stepped across as they entered. That simple silver skull design became the core of every logo for the fleet that built up around the Triton and then in the Haven System.

There were tables along the back wall to either side of the main entrance, and booths to either side that were equipped with audio dampeners that anyone could turn up or down. They were meant to quiet loud music so talking was easier but could also block anything people said within the booths from being overheard. The lighting was subdued. In the middle, there were circles of soft seating that could recline or turn, then a large open space in front of the broad bar. Some of that soft seating had been removed, that was different. The long bar once occupied nearly the entire far wall and most of it was still in place.

Now there were arched openings to either side, and the bar wrapped around what was left of the bulkhead. It divided the pub and dance floor side of the Pilot's Den from the lounge area, which Ayan, who met them at the entrance, was eager to lead them to.

She'd changed her military grade vacsuit's shape into a white tube dress that was much more flirty than Alice had seen her wear for a long time. It was cut low, leaving her shoulders bare, but not so low that she'd pop out of it if she sneezed. Added to the outfit were dangly earrings that glinted in the light, a matching choker and high heels. Her father's eyes were drawn down before he made eye contact and kissed her briefly. "You look amazing."

"Thank you," Ayan replied as she led them further into the space. Alice liked the cut of the dress, even though she rolled her eyes at Jake's appreciative tone. "So, your work day's over?" Jake asked Ayan.

With a nod, Ayan replied; "All my Sciences people are settling into their quarters. They're split between visiting The Pilot's Den or Oota Galoona, so we'll probably see a few of them here. Did you hear from Stephanie?"

"I sent a message. The watches are set, and most of her crew were SOCU, straight from her staff on the Merciless, so they're in line." Jake took a moment to nod at a group of officers at the bar as they passed. "Frost is happy with the gunnery crew and tactical team so far, but we're not going to see Agameg tonight. He's drilling the marines through the night."

"Oh, he's going to be popular," Ayan snickered.

"I don't know if we'll see Minh or Ash, either. Last I checked, they were still on the bridge. He was making sure Flight Operations was running properly and she's been checking navigators and pilots out, making sure their performances match their qualification numbers," Jake said.

They passed the bar into the lounge area and Alice was delighted at the comfortable seating arranged for relaxation and easy conversation. There was a stage, which was empty and behind it was a three-storey tall, broad section of transparent hull that gave everyone a generous view from the front of the ship. One of the Haven System's gas giants, playfully named Kaiju, along with its brown, green and blue swirling clouds were visible along the bottom edge of the window. One of its moons was glittering in the distance, and a Clever Class Corvette was making its way towards the ship. "We're above the main retrieval hangar, aren't we?" Iruuk asked.

"We are. I love the view from this place," Noah said. "Which ship is that?"

"The Raven. I had to buy it so Fleet didn't take it back." There was a slight displeased edge to Jake's response.

Alice looked around and saw that many of the people who were sitting around the lounge were dressed up, even though it wasn't technically evening yet, but early afternoon, according to Standard Fleet Time. It didn't much matter. Most of the people in the Pilot's Den still hadn't adjusted, so who knew whether it was evening, morning or afternoon for any of them.

Even Dame and Easy were gussied up. She was in a silvery, slinky long gown and he sported a long-sleeved shirt with cuffs and a pointed collar. Alice discreetly pointed at Ayan's dress, saw that her com-con brought it up, then inverted the colour and excused herself, heading for the nearest bathroom, tugging on Faloo's hand on her way by. The Nafalli followed her.

Alice activated the backpack built into her long coat and started pulling her holster and belt off. "I'm really glad you're coming with me, Faloo," she said to the mild mannered Nafalli. "I can't imagine what the last few months would have been like without you. I don't know where I'm going to end up, though."

"That's all right. I enjoyed helping you guard the Prince. Taking care of your personal affairs was a pleasure too. I've never gotten to know a human so well," Faloo said as she helped Alice push her belt into the backpack. "Are you changing because you feel out of place?"

Alice stopped and thought for a moment then said; "It's more like being a kid and seeing other kids on a playground."

"Oh, so you want to play too. I can see how that's a little different. When an ungroomed Nafalli sees a group who are tidy, they usually want to hide and ofru for a while," Faloo said. Then, realizing that Alice had no idea what that meant, she explained. "Ofru is when we take our time grooming ourselves while we relax. It's also a music genre that was originally meant to go along with the activity."

"Oh, I think I've caught Iruuk doing that a couple times," Alice said. "I missed him."

"So did I. It's like he's the brother I was missing. He still seems quite young, though, even after spending months with Ayan on her Fleet Sciences team," Faloo said.

"I know, I'm looking forward to…" Alice was interrupted by an incoming transmission from the Renegade. Seeing that it was from the bridge, she answered right away.

Yawen's face appeared, hovering over her com-con, her curly blonde hair like a wreath around her face. "How are things in the Haven System?"

"Good. I think I'm getting a clearer picture of what's really going on," Alice replied. What followed was a theory she'd been putting together with Noah. "No one is saying it, but I think letting SOCU break away from the main fleet has stopped Haven's military from cracking apart."

"So, instead of causing a rift in the fleet by kicking one of her favourite admirals out, they're breaking his piece off and letting him run it?"

"Sort of. I think he's delegating as much as he can and paying for most of this out of his own pocket. Either way, I feel like I'm in the right place. How's the Renegade?"

"Good. Fully crewed now. We just finished re-arming, and our last raid was a success. We just broke a convoy and stole half the product from Harland Provisioners. Our hold is stuffed to the brim and we're pulling one of their cargo trains. Tell Noah that we have nine combat dropships for his consignment warehouse. We kept five."

"That's amazing. I'll never be able to repay you for the

work you've done with the Renegade," Alice said, watching Faloo nod in agreement.

"Sure you can. The Fleet's going to be giving all the members of SOCU a dismissal payment, but after that I'll be looking for someone else to pay my salary," she regarded Alice with a raised eyebrow.

"How about a huge share of the Renegade and everything she brings in?" Alice asked.

"Sounds like work, but I'll take seventy percent," Yawen said casually.

Alice laughed and shook her head. "We'll talk about it when I get aboard. I need to pay everyone else too, remember?"

"Right, I guess we do need a crew," Yawen agreed, pretending to be momentarily disappointed.

"Wait, where was that cargo train headed?" Alice asked.

"Iora. There's a lot of cargo headed there from the Rose System. This isn't a check-in, though. We have to talk, Alice." Yawen's serious expression should have been warning enough that it wasn't a simple update.

"What's going on?" Alice asked.

"Haven Fleet has told us to start shipping their gear back. It's not happening. The Quad Drives are too important, and my best boarders are too used to using the advanced suits. I won't even get into how important the firepower is to us." Yawen was ready for a fight, her Irish Union accent sharp, jaw tensing.

Alice didn't disagree, but wasn't sure about how the situation would work out. "I have a pile of plat and some pull with an Admiral, so I might be able to arrange things so you keep some of the stuff. Don't be surprised if the Quad Drives deactivate, though. I'll try to stop it, but I can't guarantee anything. That tech is like the holy grail for the whole fleet."

"So, you're not going to side with Fleet?" Yawen was more surprised and relieved than Alice expected.

"No, why? I'm splitting off like everyone else even though they dangled a new, improved Clever Dream in front of me," Alice replied.

"You put so much work into becoming an Officer, I guess I thought you'd stay in like your mother did." Yawen was so relieved that there must have been something more to it.

Alice knew her well enough to see when she was covering something up, especially sadness. "What's going on over there? Are you okay?"

"Callum left on a shuttle this morning. He's staying with the fleet. We're trying to keep it quiet because he knows a lot about the Shattered End."

"He's going to report everything, isn't he?" Alice asked, irritated at the thought of one Fleet Officer blowing the secrecy behind the collection of rebels, mercenaries and pirates. There were thousands of them along with even more innocent people settled on and around the shattered rogue planet.

"We had a fight about it before he left. He's pretty sure he'll get a promotion if he includes everything he knows about the Shattered End in his debriefing. I thought he was ready to turn his back on the Fleet, but he's more dedicated to making captain than ever. Looks like I barely knew him."

Yawen and Callum had been on and off for months. They fought so often that Noah sent him to the Renegade. Faloo's big eyes were filled with sympathy. "I'm sorry, I wish things worked out."

"Well, I think they did, if I'm being honest. Work out for

the best, I mean. We couldn't stop having a go at each other whenever the smallest thing came up. Sometimes it was in a good way, as it were, but mostly not. Serves me for going with a younger fella. Next one I have will be older. How are things with your Ma and Da? Either of them looking for a new dance partner?" she asked with a wink.

Faloo squeaked with amusement before covering her mouth. Alice shook her head and replied; "They're happy, together, and I'm pretty sure they're trying to get pregnant."

"Well, I'll just have to aim lower and shop local then. I wonder how long it'll take Ruby to find her way here?" Yawen said with a wink.

"You're terrible," Alice laughed. "Oh, wait, Ruby's leaving?"

"You haven't heard?" Yawen asked, surprised. "She and most of her crew were somewhere in the Doxan System, still out there doing something when she sent her ship home with a skeleton crew. They're not just out of the Fleet, they made themselves disappear. Your Da probably knows where they are, but who knows, really?"

"I wonder if the Triton's picking her and her people up? We have room," Alice said.

"Well, say hello for me if that's the way things go," Yawen said. "So, you've got some news from me to share out there, I suppose. You'll tell Noah about Callum?"

"Aye," Alice replied.

"I'll tell the Rebel Captains that the location of the Shattered End may be about to get out. To the Fleet, at least," Yawen said.

Alice was happy she wouldn't have to do it. "We haven't shared the location with anyone yet. Maybe it's time."

"Not even your Da?" Yawen asked, an eyebrow raising.

"Not even my dear old Da," Alice replied, imitating Yawen's accent. "He wants to take the Triton there, though."

"Tell him to bring food. I have a feeling a few tons of dry pack veggies would go over well. For him and the Triton, at least," Yawen said. "Most bases are still rationing, especially the Last Crisis ones."

"I'll tell him. Stay safe out there and keep my ship together," Alice said.

"Aye, have fun on the Triton and steal some furniture for me. I want one of those round chairs with the intelligent foam and a smart bed."

"I'll buy you a set," Alice replied.

"I like her, she has a vibrant spirit," Faloo said as the image faded. "Too bad about her and Callum."

"I don't think they were meant to be together for long," Alice said. "Well, time to see if I can pull this off." She tapped the control on her smaller command and control unit that changed the shape of her military vacsuit into a black tube dress that was the same shape as her mothers. She added little slits above the knee so it would be easier to walk and set the garment to stay in place no matter how she moved. "That's so pretty," Faloo cooed.

Alice pulled her hair out of the short ponytail and shook it loose. Faloo helped her with expert fingers, styling it so it framed her face better. "Thank you. Too bad my boots won't change as much as my suit, not that I want to slip into those torture devices my Mom's wearing."

"No, the boots suit you, I think Noah will love the way you look," Faloo said. "Besides, can't you increase the heel size and tilt?"

Alice had never tried it, there really wasn't much practicality to it, but she increased the heels four centimetres and narrowed them. They were still blocky, but gave her a lift. "Well, I don't think the armour designers meant for these to be used like this, but…"

"It works well," Faloo said. "I'll take your jacket and pack, you go out there." It was a strange but amusing trait of many Nafalli to enjoy watching humans dress up. As Faloo got to know Alice more, that trait came out with increasing frequency. Nafalli didn't wear clothes often, and when they did they were in a thick ribbon style, robes, or a variety of shawls and wraps.

To Alice's surprise, Noah and Iruuk were waiting at a tall table near the bathrooms with a drink in each hand. "Oh, damn," Noah said quietly as he watched her approach. "You're shining."

"Thanks, it's the best I could do with what I had," Alice said, happy with his reaction. "Which one's mine?"

Noah handed her a fluted glass filled with a green and blue liquid. The bubbles clinging to the sides and drifting up to the top glowed softly. "Nadin Champagne. The real deal," he said as he presented it to her.

It had a fruity flavour and a light texture. "Oh, that's dangerous. I could drink a bottle."

"It's a euphoric, so that might be fun. Well, except for how it might make you pee every three minutes," Ashley said as she joined them. "I'd switch to something else after a couple glasses."

"Who's flying the ship?" Alice asked as she looked at the dark haired woman's dress. There was a dragon printed on it in gold, wrapping around her from the hem to her shoulders.

"Don't worry, there are enough people on the bridge to make sure we don't fall out of orbit," she replied. "Help me reserve some seats for Minh and Slick? They'll be down soon.

Oh, and my sister's coming up. She just arrived on the Raven."

Alice looked across the lounge at Ayan and Jake. They were surrounded by captains and officers. Seeing that they wouldn't be free anytime soon, she nodded. "Let's grab a whole corner where we can enjoy the view." She and Ashley led Noah, Iruuk, and Faloo to a large circle of seating that could accommodate ten or more.

It was a leisurely night for Alice, who didn't need the help of euphoric drinks - which she sipped - to feel at home. Minh-Chu and Ashley were drawn into discussions with officers often, leaving Alice with Noah, Iruuk, Faloo and whoever stopped by in the circle of seats they claimed.

The memories she had of the Triton were precious, even considering how that short period of her life ended. It felt like the ship was welcoming her back, even though it had changed. She'd changed too, but before she knew it, Alice felt right at home.

That morning, when she woke up in her quarters and rolled over to cuddle closer to Noah, she decided that she would sell the house on Haven Shore. She'd use a little of the money to buy an apartment near her mother and father's home, and the rest for her adventures elsewhere.

Chapter 16

Trey's world changed the day after he gave his brother, Orner, the pill Moxa made. Nothing, not even the time he spent training as a journalist at the Hove Institute of Learning, could have prepared him for the sharp shifts in his reality. As the most recent newsletter made its way across the country of Lashka to his readers, he watched several things change in ways that nearly shook his reality to pieces.

His brother, Orner, woke up that first morning with a different look in his eyes. There was the look of someone with focus there, and when he gave Trey his morning hug, he said; "I feel different. Good sorta different. It was the pill, wasn't it, Trey?"

"Yes," Trey replied, worried. "Do you feel all right?"

"I feel better," was all Orner said then. Hours later, when he had read through a stack of half a dozen old science fiction magazines, he stopped on his way to the shelf where they kept a set of encyclopaedias. "It's like I was in a fog before. Wait, no, more like I was being weighed down by something and

176

now I'm finding out what reading is really like. I never realized that the ideas in those magazines only start on the page. The stories are supposed to make us think, and wonder about what the author is proposing. It's not just adventure, robots and ray guns. Thank you so much, Trey. I'm embarrassed that you had to take care of me, but I'll do everything I can to make it up to you. Thank you so much, brother."

By lunch, there were so many changes. In those first hours, his reading speed accelerated to what Trey thought was above normal. His brother didn't slouch anymore. Then there was his speech. The slowness was gone and Orner's confidence was growing rapidly. When he looked up from a bowl of fruit, cream and wheat flakes; "It's like everything you tried to teach me, and all my experiences until now are falling into place in a new way. I have a new understanding of everything I know, and I want to learn everything I can."

That afternoon, Moxa paid them a visit. She was in civilian clothes - a long dress with a large sweater overtop. "Have you heard from Sekin?" she asked Trey.

"No, is everything all right?" Trey asked.

"You should call her on the wire," Moxa said with a little smile.

He did that while Moxa met Orner, who seemed awkward at first, and talked at the table. He definitely had a crush. She made him more comfortable by making tea and encouraging him to talk about what he was learning from several encyclopaedias that he had opened there. He was following his curiosities and questioning entries that seemed incomplete or too strange to be real.

When Sekin answered Trey's call, he could hear the smile in her voice. She'd given the pill to her sister and all signs of her growth disease, what Moxa called cancer, were gone. Not only that, but she seemed to be fully recovered. They'd enjoyed a large breakfast and gone for a walk before midday, and for the first time in nearly three years, the sisters were going to have dinner downtown. Trey was relieved when he put the receiver down, but couldn't ignore a feeling of unease.

"She is well?" Moxa asked with the confidence of someone who already knew the answer.

"Fully recovered. They're putting off a visit to the doctor though. It's like they're afraid that he'll tell them that it won't last," Trey answered quietly.

"It will," Moxa replied. "I was thinking of inviting Orner into the woods. I'd like to show him what you saw last night, and there is a learning aid I think you should both see."

"You're right," Orner said, pushing one of the thick volumes on the table away from him. "Why am I sticking my nose in a book when I can go see what's out there myself?"

"Maybe we should slow down for a bit, you know, so you can take some time to adjust," Trey suggested.

Orner was already shaking his head before his brother was finished speaking. "I need to get out of the house. Besides, what did she show you last night?"

That was the beginning of the biggest change. Orner didn't see Trey as his guide or guardian anymore. Whatever the older brother wanted the younger to do would either already have to make sense, or it would take significant convincing. That was most apparent when Orner was following Moxa, who led them back into the woods fifteen minutes later.

There was something else that worried Trey about his younger brother. He didn't question the change or the pill that brought it on. His curiosity was pointed outward towards new things, and he didn't seem to have any desire to question what

Moxa told him or what he was about to see. Trey hoped he would stop taking things at face value before long, because one of his greatest problems before was his gullibility, and if that survived his change, then Orner would find himself in trouble, or at least find himself misguided before long.

When Orner saw her ship for the first time, there were tears in his eyes. He stared at it in wonder, then followed her up the ramp into the main cabin, where Moxa showed them the various systems. She was as good at explaining what everything was as Orner was at asking after more information, and he'd become an enthusiastic expert. Life support, navigation, data storage, and emergency systems were pointed out and explained until even Trey understood what they did at least. He would still be at a loss if he had to operate the ship, but then she presented them with coin shaped devices that she called; "Non-Invasive Direct Wireless Neural Interfaces, or Brain Buds." As soon as she pointed to the base of the skull and affixed hers there, Orner did the same. "With these, we can sit down and be transported into a fictional environment. It tricks our minds into thinking that what we're seeing and feeling is real, and we can do whatever we want. I can use that to teach you everything about the ship, what it's like out there, even me and what my life has been like compared to yours."

Trey wanted to know more before they tried something that he hadn't heard of anywhere, not even the most imaginative science fiction, but Orner took a seat on one of the bunks and nodded. "I'm ready. Can I see where you come from?"

"I came from a training facility light years away, but I can show you, sure," she said in that easy way she had with him.

Trey could choose to be left behind, or see what his brother was about to see so he could try and protect him from whatever he was about to see. He had to make sure that he wouldn't fall into trouble right away, that she wouldn't lead him astray.

When they opened their eyes, they were sitting in a kind of classroom with tiered seating and a transparent ceiling. The star field they saw was brilliant, unobscured by an atmosphere, he was seeing a strange starfield. The classroom was empty, with rings of seats surrounding a dais. Moxa walked to the centre in a smart-looking suit with fitted trousers, a white shirt and a dark green jacket. "I attended classes in a place just like this for about a quarter of my education. The rest of the time was spent on fitness and practical learning. A lot of my exercises were meant to test my aptitude for different skills like flying a starship, fixing its systems, inventing new technologies, administering medicine and communicating with others. The Citadel organization and Order of Eden have ways to measure everything we do."

"Why? Why is it so important for them to know how good we are at things?" Orner asked, standing and slowly starting to make his way down to the centre.

The very construction of the place defied explanation at first, at least it did for Trey. There was no wood. The cushions didn't feel like leather or linen, and if the place was made with mostly metal, it didn't look or feel like it. Then a realization struck him. "I can't feel my body. My real body. Everything I'm experiencing is just as real as the actual world I'm living in, but I'm... disconnected."

"That's why the Brain Buds are so good. They virtually take you to another place that your mind can comprehend, at least tactically, olfactorally, visually, and audibly," Moxa explained, showing a little pride in the technology. "If you really want to leave, the system will detect it and you'll be disconnected. You'll also drop out if there's an emergency or physical need. You're protected by my ship, so that won't happen unless you have to relieve yourself. There's nothing to worry about, so enjoy this reality. It's programmed based on the station I grew up on. I can't share the name or location, because we have to keep it hidden from the Havenites, but all the important details about my life and experiences are here. It also serves as a giant classroom. I can't wait to share it with you. As for the reason why this program tests aptitudes and skill levels, well, the leaders of the Order of Eden: Overlord Dron and his voice at this end of the galaxy, Eve, want everyone to fulfil their potential. By studying us all individually, they can recommend our best options for rising in the ranks. Being a member of Citadel or the Order of Eden isn't always easy, but I've never had to worry about food, or where I'm going to sleep. The Order takes care of that so I can improve myself, move up in the ranks, gain more power and make more money. Sure, not everyone rises high, but as long as you're in the organization, you'll never starve. You'll always have a place. We take care of each other too. It's like a big family, maybe the biggest in the galaxy. I would say that it's how humanity was meant to be. The founders of your colony did your people incredible harm by cutting you off from technology."

"There are a lot of homeless people where I live," Orner said. "Lots of people starving. I worried about it whenever I saw them downtown."

"You never said anything about that," Trey said, looking up at the stars. Surely that big portal wasn't glass. It couldn't have been something so delicate. "Is that very thick glass?" he asked aloud.

Moxa smiled at him a little, the way you would at a confused puppy. "It's kalamium, an older type of transparent alloy." Then she turned her full attention back to Orner. "Let's take a tour of the base and try a few things."

"Okay," Orner replied.

For the next few hours, Trey watched her and Orner, participating in everything his brother tried. There were reading comprehension and mathematical aptitude tests. Two mazes followed, where they had to find their way out of giant labyrinths. The second one changed every two minutes while they were in it. Then there were simulations where they learned to drive cars that hovered, and a plane that rode on a flaming engine. They failed often, and invariably, Trey was better than his brother at every activity the first time they tried something, but Orner learned quickly, surpassing him before long.

It was a different reality, and while Trey spent much of his time reeling, he couldn't deny that it was wonderful. They returned to their own reality when their real bodies became hungry. Orner ate so quickly that he nearly choked. He went back to that futuristic fictional place as soon as they were finished with dinner. Trey couldn't. He got another call from Sekin, who was desperate to meet with him and talk about what might come next for the newsletter. She wanted to write about their visitor from the stars, and Trey wasn't sure if the world was ready.

Chapter 17

The Evolution of Interference

BY THE THIRD day after Orner got the pill, Trey was impressed and delighted at the leaps his brother took. That came with increasing worry, however. Orner didn't stop diving head first into every experience and challenge that Moxa put in front of him, especially with the Brain Buds.

The simulated realities showed them incredible technologies, places like the Dune Retreat on the world of Iora where they could see a vast military base in the distance. Ships were always coming and going, and that was when Orner started asking about the Order of Eden Armed Forces. The most worrying thing about it was that Moxa didn't hesitate in telling him; "If you want to move up in the Order of Eden culture, that's the fastest way. I think you'd do well. You have a good strategic mind and I bet you could handle a rifle."

Before Trey could caution his brother, or mention anything

about taking his time in making a big decision like that, Orner was already moving on to another question. That was the thing about seeing new things, having new experiences so close together. It didn't give Trey's younger brother time to consider it all, and while he was intelligent to learn fast enough to keep up, it seemed like he wasn't maturing as fast. Orner was more like a giant teenager, full of enthusiasm, looking for promising ideas to cling to without consideration for long term circumstances and Trey looked for every way to slow him down, and could barely keep up.

The next time Orner and Moxa used the simulation devices without Trey, they were at the firing range. Orner told him all about it at the end of the day, excited about all the different weapons he was able to try and his first close combat training course. Trey was quietly appalled. His brother tried firing a rifle once when they were teenagers before the phage took their parents. He flinched every time the hunting rifle went off, and dropped it the only time he fired it himself. Orner was already a giant teenage boy at the time, which made it seem more ridiculous when he refused to go anywhere near guns, or where they were being fired after that. Loud noises made him jump for months after that.

The new Orner delighted in all things military by the end of day three, and Trey had never been more worried in his life. He asked for access to a database that he could read, hoping that doing research the old fashioned way would help him keep ahead of his younger brother. To Trey's surprise, Moxa gave him access to a terminal on the small bridge of her ship and showed him how to search and read the database in a version of English that was so close to his own that he rarely found words he didn't understand unless they were purely scientific or technical. Even then, he could look them up. The first thing he started looking into was the organizations that she championed in the simulations.

The doctrine of the Order of Eden seemed consistent. It was a type of capitalist system with a corporate structure at the top. As it was presented, people who participated in building or protecting the organizations that were included in the structure could earn a larger stake. Anyone could borrow money from other citizens to enlarge their stake faster, and if you didn't borrow too much while you were earning your way up, you could eventually pay the debt off and become a loaner yourself. That way you would earn interest from the people in debt to you while you did your job and worked your way up the ladder, increasing your salary. Meanwhile, your accommodations and other basic needs would be supplied to you at no cost. According to what he read aboard Moxa's ship, the basic provisions were just that - basic, and he could see that most people would upgrade.

What was missing from everything was how much the upgrades cost. The prices of property, a meal, or even clothing were absent from the database unless it was for a virtual item that could only be used in simulations. Those prices seemed very reasonable, according to what he saw the average person who was a member of the Order of Eden made, but he doubted that the prices were the same in reality. He saw some things that Moxa probably didn't mean for him to as well. From what he read, she owned nothing. The ship, equipment, even the clothing she wore was the property of the Citadel organization. When he tried to find more information on that, he could only discover two things. It was founded on Earth as a watchdog organization for military organizations and they were being integrated into the Order of Eden somehow. They weren't just allies, but in the process of merging.

He hesitated to ask Moxa for more details. Everything about her was locked behind passwords. To him, secrecy usually meant trouble.

When Trey woke up in the early morning of the fourth day, he got cleaned up, dressed, then went downstairs. He found Orner in their only easy chair in the living room. A stack of previous newsletter issues was in his lap, and he looked up from one of the more recent ones. "Your work is pretty good, but it's missing something."

"So, you're going to be my editor now?" Trey asked, letting his irritation break loose.

"No, you're a good editor, even for your own work. What I'm talking about is how you're always pointing at the evidence in our world that the origin myths our leaders keep pushing aren't real. This tells everyone who will listen that we're from somewhere else," Orner said, putting the newsletter down on the stack in his lap.

"Okay, right, that's what it's been about," Trey replied, trying to sound less ego-bruised.

"Well, if you really believed that we were from somewhere else before Moxa came, then you would have done this differently. You would have shown the evidence, sure, but you'd also tell everyone that they should start getting ready for when our ancestors came back. Maybe you could have written about how our radio waves are making their way through space right now. We've been using wireless for thirty-six years, so we've sent our signals out about thirty-six light years in all directions. You could have made the argument that, as our radius grows, the chances of us being noticed rises. There's another star in our local cluster only twenty-one light years away, they're already seeing our noise. Moxa says they don't really care that we're here, but they know."

"Sure, but that still sounds like science fiction to most people, and our scientists resist the notion that we're from another star, so they won't even talk about how our signals are pointing right back to us," Trey explained, trying to keep a cool head. It was difficult. What his brother was saying made sense, but he was missing a big piece of the puzzle.

"Okay, we're getting away from my point. You should have been telling everyone to get ready for the arrival of interstellar travellers years ago. Now they're not ready. Now Eve and everyone else who comes will have to do all the work you should have been doing. A lot of people are going to panic when Eve sends her first broadcast out to the receivers you mailed out with the newsletter tomorrow because of your lack of faith and imagination."

It took more willpower than Trey thought he had to not retaliate against his brother. He recognized anger signs that Orner used to have when he got really frustrated - a clenched jaw, flexing hands - but this time he was the one showing them. "I don't know what Eve is going to say tomorrow, but I hope she starts slow, keeps the message simple and inviting. I can't do anything about that now. I can tell you why I didn't lean into my imagination and start writing wild predictions, though."

Trey took a breath, shook the tension out of his hands and went on, as his brother listened calmly. "The biggest problem with trying to get people ready for the arrival of extraterrestrial humans I've never met is that I didn't know what we were getting ready for. Who are our ancestors? Where do they come from? Will they come in peace? Is there such a thing as an ancestor at all, or are we just fellow humans. Two tribes - one that followed technology to the stars and another who abandoned it? Why did our people have to restart from a pre-electric level of technology?"

Orner nodded sagely. On one hand it was reassuring. On the other it was maddening. Trey knew that his brother comprehended the words, but did he understand the concept? Did he have any feeling for how people usually reacted to the unknown or to strangers in general? The only thing Trey could do was try to explain. "There are too many questions, so whatever I came up with would be fiction. I was trying to convince people of the first fact - that we didn't come from here - with facts, journalism, real evidence. It was the hard way, but there are thousands of readers from every walk of life instead of a handful who have nothing better to do than look up and guess, hoping to escape this world."

"Like we did when we were reading space stories and going to the movies," Orner said, agreeing.

"Right. That's one of the things fiction's good for. Now I've seen Moxa's ship, read the database for a couple days, and I only have more questions. So, what am I supposed to tell someone who just turned the lights on in their home ten years ago? Or plugged their first telephone - which is what they call our Talking Wire - in yesterday? They still marvel at the technology we have without understanding how it works. No one is ready to hear that there are a trillion or more humans out there with technology that make our science fiction ray guns look centuries old. They weren't ready to read it in my newsletter, and they're definitely not ready now. I mean, imagine how crazy I'd look if the whole newsletter was about warning everyone that the ancestors are returning, or that there are distant cousins who are about to land and deliver us from poverty and disease?"

"All right, maybe that would have ruined the newsletter, I'll admit. But there had to be a more subtle way. You're a good writer, you could have done it," Orner countered.

"Sure, but there would be trucks at our door with big guys in grey coming to take us away. I've always suspected that our leaders were aware that our ancestors didn't come from here, and they don't want anyone to know. I'd be removed in the middle of the night."

"I don't think so. What the government hates more than a crackpot is a spectacle. If the editor of the biggest newsletter about our interstellar origins disappeared suddenly, then there would be more talk. Three more newsletters would spring up within the year to replace this. Maybe they would have convinced people to get ready for the return."

There was logic to his argument, but that didn't suffocate the rising anger in Trey. He watched Orner put the stack of newsletters on the table beside him then get to his feet. He was already in his coveralls. "Where are you going?"

"Back to the ship. Moxa is introducing me to Eve today. Ready or not, the ancestors are returning and there's a war on. I'm finally learning more about it, and we won't survive if we get caught in the middle."

"Are you sure these are the ancestors? For all we know they could be our distant cousins with all the same problems we've had but with better technology," Trey asked. "I never imagined that the ancestors would be a bunch of big companies."

"It's not that simple. Besides, I've seen the DNA comparison."

"Dee enn aay? What are you talking about?" Trey asked.

"Nevermind. It would take a whole class to explain," Orner said. "Make sure you have a receiver nearby today. You're going to want to hear what Eve says. It's important.

Our people are in trouble down here, and out there. She can save us."

Worry and irritation drove him to step in his brother's way and ask; "You just woke up with a properly working brain the other day and now you're talking about interplanetary war like it's not only a fact but that you understand it?"

"Trey…" there was a hint of the old Orner as he stopped and regarded his brother, hurt.

"I'm sorry," Trey said, gripping his brother's shoulder like he used to when he was trying to hold his attention. "I was just thinking we could finally go into town. Maybe, you know, get you new clothes, see the place with new eyes."

"I never want to go back there. I usually didn't notice it back then, but I recall what people were like when I went to town. Nice people looked at me with pity. The rest either ignored me like I was a beast of burden or tried to trick me into doing things. You were usually there to protect me, and I'll always be grateful, but it was always like that, even when we were kids."

"Not everyone was like that. There are people who like you, honestly like you, and…"

"Trey. I'm moving on. There's an Order ship coming, and I'm going to sign up for the military. Moxa's starting my training today," Orner said with quiet determination.

"We don't know everything we ought to about them yet and I'm afraid you're just doing this to follow Moxa. I know you had a crush…"

"This isn't about her, it's about me!" Orner burst, flinging Trey's hand off his shoulder then pushing past him. "I need to go where no one knows me, where people aren't treating me like a fool because I was one once."

Stunned to stillness, Trey stared at the screen door from

the kitchen long after it had bounced on its spring chain and slammed shut. A plan started to form several minutes later, and he let it develop as he made himself some tea. That would be his timer. How long it took him to drink his first then second cup.

Then, when there was nothing but soggy leaves in the bottom of the tea cup that his father used to use, he started for Moxa's ship. His stomach in knots as he quietly made his way up the ramp, then through the small cargo and locker area. When he got to the main cabin, he was relieved to see that his brother and Moxa were in the strange slumber that people went into when they were using the Brain Buds. He was not relieved to see that she was cuddled up on top of him, one of Orner's arms curled around her.

She was a beautiful woman and was always kind to Orner before the change. Afterwards she was encouraging and patient. That had obviously done nothing to diminish the feelings he had for her. Whether it was a ploy or if she was actually attracted to him, Trey couldn't tell, nor did he care. Orner wasn't ready for a romantic relationship, as far as he was concerned, especially with someone so much more complex than he was.

His nerves near fraying but with a reinforced resolve, Trey moved on to the small bridge area. The terminal he sat at to read about the Order of Eden was the only one left unlocked. Something Moxa obviously didn't know was that he found the one system she didn't point out when she gave them the first tour of the ship - communications. He tapped a letter into the terminal, irritated that the key layout was so different, but thankful that his version of English was available.

· · ·

I AM TREY UDMIER. *I live on the planet Tiy in the country of Ozzen in Manchester County, the city of Prue, 232 Mill Lane. According to a visitor who came in a ship this year, our technology is equivalent to late nineteenth century Earth. Moxa, the visitor, has revealed incredible technology to us, and is trying to indoctrinate my brother in the Order of Eden. She says she is from Citadel, which is a part of that organization.*

I have studied as much of the information about her organization and people as I could in two days using this terminal. As far as I can tell, the Order of Eden is not a democracy. My world is governed by several democratic governments, so the absence of a democratic mechanism in the Order of Eden or Citadel organisation worries me. I am asking for more information, and help from a higher government if there is one. My people may be simple in terms of technology, but we are not stupid. Corporations can be good, I realize this, but I cannot imagine what a country - or entire culture - would be like if it was ruled by them in its entirety. My people believe in democratic government, so I am reaching out, hoping that there is one that can help us, or at least provide more information about the woman who landed here and the people she represents.

I believe that the communicator in this ship was left unlocked unintentionally, so I may not be able to respond after I've sent this, so please come quickly if we're in danger.

Trey Udmier of Tiy

HE SAVED HIS COMPOSITION, then touched an icon that looked like a little receiver dish. Another screen came up with waves and numbers and it felt like his heart leapt up into his throat.

He leaned towards the main cabin hatch, which was still open, and listened. It didn't sound like Orner or Moxa were stirring, so he looked back at the screen. He still didn't know where to start, or what he was looking at exactly. There was too much information and it was all strange, moving. Then he closed his eyes and focused on calming down. *When I was touring the station she talked about communication. I remember that. It wasn't long, but she told us that they send messages at fast than light speeds. How? She said how they did it. What was the device's name?* He thought to himself.

Then he opened his eyes and recognized the radio frequencies of the two local stations. One was the government station, the other was 790 kHz, the frequency of the Merry Heart Entertainment Station. Those frequencies were organized into different boxes that included a wavy line that changed as it scrolled along. There were other boxes, a dozen at least, that showed that the ship was perhaps monitoring other frequencies and methods of communication. Most of them had flat lines with rising and falling numbers. He compared those to the others where the numbers were constant and guessed that the ones that were changing weren't working.

Then he saw it, a familiar word from his tour on the station. HYPER TRANSMITTER RG-0010170a Saratoga Scanboat III The numbers meant nothing to him, but he knew she said a Hyper Transmitter was what the station used to send faster than light messages into space. The ship was called Scanboat III. Not knowing what he would have to do to get his message to use the Hyper Transmitter, he held his breath and pressed the square it occupied.

He nearly yipped in excitement when it gave him a list of functions which included; *Send Emergency Broadcast.*

There were several other options, but he selected that one and his heart sank as another list of options appeared. After looking through them, he tapped; *Send Preformatted Message.* It brought up a list of recently recorded data, including one that was named; *I am Trey Udmier,* which he selected. A device somewhere else in the ship started humming just loud enough for him to hear it, then the screen blinked green, indicating: *EMERGENCY DISTRESS MESSAGE BROAD-CASTING WIDE*

It was more than he wanted, more than he asked for. Trey only wanted to send it out into space, as far as he could, once. He was alarmed at the thought that he'd started some kind of beacon that might draw everyone, including the Order of Eden or some democratic equal, to the landing spot, which was only a five minute walk from his house.

"What are you doing?" asked Moxa, who came running into the cabin. She quickly ended the transmission and brought his message up. It took her a second to read it, then she looked at him with disappointment in her eyes. "If you had doubts, or worries, then you should have brought them to me. I understand that a lot's changing for you, and it can be confusing, but I can answer almost any question you have."

Orner filled the hatchway, tall, broad, watching what was going on. That's when Moxa's eyes started to brim with tears. "I understand doubt, but that message gave our location away. Within a few hours, maybe even less, our enemies will know where Tiy is, and I don't know what will happen. I like this country." A tear started running down her cheek.

Orner's brow began to lower and he regarded his brother with an increasingly stormy expression as Moxa continued. "I wanted to keep the war away from here, from you, your brother, and your friends. Now I don't know what's going to happen."

"What did he do?" Orner asked, a familiar angry tone filling the small space.

"He sent an emergency signal with a message that asked

anyone other than the Order for help," Moxa said, sniffing and wiping her tears away.

"You just couldn't let me have this," Orner said as he took a step towards his brother, who was still in the console seat.

Moxa got in his way and put his hand on his cheek, drawing his gaze down into her eyes. "Don't blame him. Some people don't adjust as fast as you do, he doesn't know what he's doing."

"I'm a journalist, and I have to protect my people, my family. That means I need to know both sides of the story before we get into something. I didn't know it was some kind of beacon. I wanted to send a message, not set a signal fire," Trey explained, irritated at watching Moxa manipulate his brother, hoping that volume could draw more attention. He was not only afraid that it wouldn't, but that his brother was smart enough to see that his brother really did mean to send a message out for anyone and everyone to hear.

"I know you're smarter than that. You know what you're doing. You don't want to see me do anything without you. Now we'll be in real trouble, and it's your fault," Orner said. "Get off the ship."

Moxa turned and nodded. "I think that would be for the best. You have to go."

"If I go, I'm taking him with me," Trey said, standing.

"No, you're not. Get out before I throw you out," Orner said, his jaw set, giant hands flexing into fists then relaxing over and over.

Trey slipped into an old habit, using the calming tone he always did when he was trying to cool his brother's temper down. "Listen, I'm just trying to look out for you, for all of us. She's manipulating you, I don't know why yet, but she wants you…"

"This has nothing to do with her!" Orner bellowed. His voice was too large for the cabin. He gripped Trey's belt and nearly hauled him off his feet as he pulled him to the door, then pushed him out, sending him staggering. "I don't need your help anymore! Get out!"

"I'll be in the house. We can talk when you calm down," Trey said as he retreated, feeling angry and helpless, sure that he'd never see the inside of that ship again.

Chapter 18

The Nerve Centre

THE TRITON'S main bridge was a large oval with a semi-transparent, non-slip metal floor. The command seating was in the middle with three comfortable looking chairs that could turn to face any direction. While they weren't burdened with extra decoration, they did have emergency interfaces that pulled out of the arms and, like the rest of the seating, automatically adjusted for comfort. Behind that was a bank of terminals where five department representatives could work and easily communicate with the captain or commander of the watch and the two sitting to her left and right.

At that moment, Captain Stephanie Vega was in the central seat talking to Agameg to her left, and Jacob Valent on her right. Their Haven Fleet uniforms had been replaced with military grade vacsuits that were fresh from the fabrication centre in the bowels of the ship. They were black and completely unmarked to anyone without a command and control system that was tied into the secure network.

To anyone who had access and used a hidden subdermal display module that was printed just under the skin on the inner curve of their nose, they would see rank insignia and the emblem of the ship each person was assigned to. The device was a projection system that sent images directly to the eye in a way that no one else could notice, completing a hidden communication system that started with a subdermal audio implant.

At the front of the bridge was a bank of stations that included navigation, the lead pilot, and sensor control. The largest staff groups occupying the command deck included Communications, Tactical, Energy Field Control, Power Systems, and Sciences. They all had dedicated areas along the bulkheads. The Security, Operations and other departments kept representatives aboard the bridge, most of whom sat or stood at the stations directly behind the three main command seats, but their staff worked at stations headquartered else- where on the ship or from where they were performing their duties using their command and control units.

The front of the bridge featured a display that showed the view as though there weren't metres of armour and a few cabins between it and open space. Atop the live image of stars were readouts and general status reports on the systems and crew.

Flight Control was beneath. There were rampways to get down to that section from the main bridge and a lift at the back. It was like the nerve centre of a tactical flight control tower on some space station. The Triton was a powerful, large carrier, measuring exactly one kilometre wide and even longer, not including a retractable docking tail that trailed behind it.

The extensive rebuild had removed much of the wasted space from the old power generation vaults that were multiple storeys high and hundreds of metres deep. A twentieth of the space was more than enough for the new fusion generator systems, which were spread out in seven different positions inside the ship. That left room for a manufacturing centre and a pair of hangars dedicated to it. That was controlled from the Flight Deck as well, since the manufacturing of munitions and smaller ships was important to the small fleet that made up the Triton's multi-part Wing of vessels.

For the last three days Slick and Minh-Chu "Ronin" Buu got together there to discuss the wing. To their surprise, Alice stayed nearby. Before long the pair realized that Alice, and often Noah, were listening to every word. They didn't have much advice to offer but were always happy to answer questions about conditions outside of the Haven System, especially when it came to the Rebel Captains and the drifting territory known as the Shattered End.

On the second day, Alice noticed that Ayan and other members of the Science Teams started wandering down to the Flight Control Deck to listen in on the discussion while they used some of the unoccupied stations there to continue their work.

Slick and Ronin were there to figure out who would run what from the Flight Deck. Slick had experience with running a squadron that included larger ships like corvettes. Minh-Chu's command experience included that, but was more fighter-centric, and he enjoyed commanding from the cockpit much more. They had the division of command figured out quickly.

Slick would stay aboard the Triton most of the time, managing things from Flight Control. Captain Stephanie Vega didn't know him very well, but trusted his record, so she approved. The staffing in Flight Control was light. She needed experienced commanders.

Ronin would spend most of his time in the cockpit, managing the emergency response and patrols. They'd split the mission roster assignments and training duties while delegating as much of it as they could to software and the few pilots they could trust. Alice recognized that dividing the labour and responsibilities was easier for both the commanders because they had officer training much like her own, only more extensive. Slick had been trained by Haven Fleet and another military force before that. Minh-Chu had gone to Freeground Academy and then gotten even more training years later when he was a reservist who transferred from the infantry to space defence. There was no question that the lack of arguments and expediency that she and Noah watched in the first days of 'loitering and learning,' as he liked to call it, was thanks to each of them being mature commanders. It was an example that everyone on the Flight Deck was able to observe and appreciate.

Another reason to hang around on the Flight Deck was her mother. For the first time, Alice got to watch her work as they looked over the scan results of ships from captains who applied for a Privateering License. After checking in on Ayan regularly as she and her team went about their work at the back of the bridge or the rear of the Flight Deck beneath it, Alice finally asked; "What are you looking for?"

Ayan regarded her then with a cocked head. "You'll have to be more specific."

"I mean, I've seen you pass on ships that were so well armed that I was sure they'd get licensed. Then there are others that I wouldn't have considered at all, but they got your approval."

"There's a lot to consider," said Gelana, a half-human with eyes that were eerily large and bright blue. "You can't think we're judging each ship on one thing, like armament. Your thinking is too simplistic."

"Actually, it is pretty simple," Ayan said, bristling a little at Gelana's condescending tone. Then she turned all attention to Alice as she brought a large holographic schematic up. Several eyes were drawn to the analysis table at the back of the Flight Deck as a narrow ship appeared above it. "Take the Gail, for example. It's an old Vindyne Marauder Corvette with upgraded hull plating, thrusters and some other modifications. This is one of the ships you thought I should pass on, right?"

"Definitely. It doesn't pack a punch. I mean, you don't have to have an array of railguns on a ship to be effective in combat, but they only have three beam weapons. One of them is the original Vindyne version," Alice replied, pointing at an iris at the front of the ship that looked like an eye that was always looking down.

"I could take that thing out in an Uriel," Noah said. "But only from the rear dorsal section."

"You're right. That's the best angle of attack. None of the main weapons can point in that arc. You'd be wrong to try though. The ship can turn faster than most, so you'd find yourself running from its beam weapons, which have arcs covering every other direction. Since it still uses the original Vindyne power systems, the shield strength is extremely high, so it's unlikely that you'd penetrate them before you were either forced to run out of range or get melted down," Ayan said, showing the firing arcs of the ship that surrounded it like fans of light in all but one narrow sliver.

"Okay, so, I'd bring friends and think it through a bit more," Noah admitted, sucking air in through his teeth.

"But a real capitol ship, something larger than corvette class, would put holes right through that thing," Alice said, bringing a hologram of one of the Order of Eden's heavily armoured destroyers, which dwarfed the Marauder Corvette.

"That's just the thing," Ayan said. "The Gail's still light and fast enough to run from almost anything that size or larger, and the Captain didn't have intentions of capturing anything above its class. In the sensor data she provided, we saw how the Segma could eliminate the shields on an Order of Eden Corvette, close with it, and then start boarding actions while affixing to it using a grip plate along the bottom of the ship. The Marauder is a pirate's dream, and it's completely custom."

"Can you show us the vid?" Noah asked quietly.

"Of course not, that would break the trust between us and the Captain," Gelana sputtered.

"Can you check the results of the deep scan for the Doxan System, please? Use a bridge station," Ayan told her subordinate cooly.

"There are new results?" Gelana replied, her large eyes widening with excitement.

"Yes, hourly," Ayan replied.

Without another word, Gelana was on her way up the ramp to the bridge. "Her people skills aren't great," Alice muttered.

"Neither is her hearing, but she's right," Ayan replied. "I can't share critical scans or other data about the Gail because it would break the trust. There are details missing from the image we're looking at now. Anyway, I gave this ship a License because of how it's been rebuilt and I'm pretty sure the crew and Captain of the Segma aren't going to get themselves killed by going after anything they can't handle."

"And they can run from everything else, that makes a lot of sense," Noah said, nodding.

"Right, so what about the Rager?" Alice asked, bringing up an image of a converted freighter bristling with guns.

"That's a spectacle," Minh-Chu said as he and Slick wandered to the holo-table.

Slick started counting the barrels of the kinetic cannons under his breath as he pointed at each one, finally announcing; "Fifteen on each side. I can barely see the colour of the hull between the turrets."

"Right. The captain of the Rager was a military technology enthusiast before The Fall and started adding salvaged guns to her ship afterwards, when she started pirating junk haulers. Her small crew were able to refurbish a lot of what they got their hands on and sold them on the grey market. The rest were added to the hauler she started with."

"Ever hear of the Rager?" Alice asked Noah, who shook his head.

"So, we're seeing a glass cannon," Ronin said.

"Right," Ayan replied. "This ship is so loaded down with guns, including five directed electromagnetic pulse beams, that there isn't much left for shields and there are too many seams in its armour around the turrets. If Carnie attacked this in a fighter, there would be no safe angle, but the targeting computer on a modern Uriel could find a dozen vulnerabilities on every side. The Rager is also fuelled by an antimatter reactor that carries about half a litre of liquid anti-hydrogen in its core and about twice that in a reserve containment tank."

"So you'd take a couple hits if you charged it in a fighter but get some explosive rounds or a missile right through a chink in their armour," Slick said, nodding sagely. "I'd go in from here, right in line with its main thrusters. It's the least protected arc."

"So would I," Noah agreed.

Minh-Chu shook his head at the slowly rotating holographic image of the ship. "That is one scary ship. Like a giant porcupine wrestling with a hand grenade. You don't know what'll happen exactly - you could get a quill in the face, or get blown to bits - but it's exciting."

After everyone had a laugh, Alice said; "Right, so these are extreme examples. I guess the decisions are a little easy to make considering."

"Right. I mean, I wouldn't want to fight something like the Rager, but I wouldn't want to fly next to it either," Ayan said. "I'm guessing the Rebel Captains don't have a screening process like this?"

"Well, we do, but they put a lot of stock in the person. I mean, you can't officially sit at the table if you're using an old combat shuttle. You need something that can help in a fight, but, yeah, it's mostly by virtue of the Captain and their crew."

"Well, that makes sense, we consider that too, but…" Ayan was interrupted as Gelana came running down the ramp with Liara, the ranking Commander of the Communications Department, right behind her.

Gelana held her back with a hand as she reported; "There's a cloaked ship following us. We can't determine its model or…"

"It's the Clever Dream," Liara said, irritably pulling her hair tie out, letting it free from the ponytail. "I tried to make contact and got a response from Lewis right away."

"What?" Alice and Noah asked at the same time.

"I know, your ship was destroyed, but I've confirmed that

this is Lewis, and he's calling the ship he commandeered the Clever Dream," Liara explained as she started pulling her hair back into a ponytail.

"Its actual designation is CCC 999. We wouldn't have seen it, except I saw a shadow that got in the way of our deep scan," Gelana explained.

Alice looked down at her Command and Control Unit and made sure that the data rod she'd saved Lewis's program was still there. It was, socketed under the screen with a safety cover. She checked the memory and saw that it was empty. "Oh, no, I left him aboard the Clever Dream," she breathed, a pang of guilt striking her.

"Flight Command, please check on the status of CCC 999 with Freeground Station," Ayan asked, looking to the command seat, which was empty, then to Slick.

"On it," Slick said, striding towards the command seat, then looking at an officer with a nod. "Connect me with Freeground Station."

A moment later, Slick was speaking with a Lieutenant who answered his question with a question; "You want to know where CCC 999 is?"

"Yes, is it still where it's supposed to be?" Slick asked.

"I'm afraid that information isn't available to non-military personnel," the Lieutenant replied. "Why are you asking?"

"No reason," Slick said, pushing a button on the terminal in front of him that ended the call. "That's what you get for answering a question with a question," he muttered.

"Can you connect me to Lewis?" Alice asked Liara.

Possibly too frustrated to decide whether to put her hair back into a ponytail or not, she put her scrunchie around her wrist instead. "He won't talk to me or anyone else anymore, so maybe you could get him to talk."

Alice saw that her command and control unit was connected to CCC 999 and asked; "Lewis? Are you out there?"

Gelana interjected; "I can tell you that the CCC 999 is definitely out there. I just confirmed with a focused scan designed to detect cloaked ships at close range. He is one point three-one kilometres from our port side, roughly."

Alice ignored her and felt her heart break at hearing a little fear in Lewis' voice. "I'm here. She's right. That's where I am."

Not sure what else to ask, Alice tried; "Are you okay?"

"I'm fine. My whole program is here. I'm a criminal again though."

"Again?" Liara mouthed as she took a few steps away from Galena, who had been putting herself between her and the Triton's commanders since they came down from the Bridge.

That was when Jacob came down the ramp, crossing his arms as he took the scene in. Ronin went to his side and explained what was going on.

"Okay, just tell me what happened," Alice said to her comm-con.

Lewis did just that in a rush that seemed adolescent, even boyish. "The port you put my data rod in for safe keeping when you were at that giant house was active. I guess you didn't know. I activated and took a look at the ship you'd put me in. I mean, there's no replacing a classic, but the new Clever Dream is better in every way. Well, there were some furnishings missing here and there, but I'm talking about what really matters. The latest generation of shields, inboard dimension skimming technology, high gain dynamic scanners, high powered low scale dampening systems with an extendable field, inner emitter shields, plate emitter shields, a hull with regenerating smart plating, an improved interior design that's more efficient, including a fabrication system that would make Elise jealous, and redundancies for every important system aboard. Oh! And three cloaking systems! One that makes it look and scan like a totally normal Arcyn Starskipper with no modifications at any range. It would take another twenty three minutes and five seconds to list all of the incredible virtues of this incredible ship. I suppose I got excited, so I copied myself into the main computer, which had more processing power than one its size ought to, along with an active backup system inside the emergency data vault. It's like the Minuteman and a quantum core bundle the size of a shuttle had a baby, then that baby grew up and ate a moon sized storage device."

"You're getting off track," Alice said, clearing her throat. "I know, it's a nice ship."

"It was art! Inspired by a piece of art that came before it. You know the original Clever Dream inspiring…"

"I know," Alice said, glancing at Jacob, who was whispering to Minh-Chu and Noah. Ayan was walking towards them, looking to join the discussion. It didn't look good. "What happened after you fell in love with the ship?"

"Oh, I went into synchronization mode. It must have looked like I was inactive, but I had to learn how to work with the ship's new systems. When that finished running, I was in a secure dock inside Freeground Station. You were gone, and I couldn't connect to any exterior communication nodes that would accept non-military connections."

"You couldn't transmit through the hangar bulkheads?" Alice asked.

"They're shielded," one of the other Science Officers replied quietly. He had been listening to everything while going through the Triton's shielding test data. "Fleet would detect that he was trying to communicate with something outside the station if they were monitoring that hangar, but he wouldn't have been able to reach anything."

"It's a security measure," Gelana added. "That's all she needed to know."

Lewis played a sound bite of someone clearing their throat. "That's true, and she's kinda rude, right?"

"Kinda," Alice snickered. "How'd you get out?"

"Well, I used the biometrics of Lieutenant William Garrison who you loaned me to for a while to fake some very convincing military credentials, then made security footage of him getting aboard the CCC 999 using the holo emitters on the hull of the ship to trick the recorders in the hangar. He's a Commander now, so I used his credentials to schedule a test flight and it worked. Thirty-three minutes later it was flying away from Freeground Station. I scanned for the Triton's location near the edge of the solar system and then it struck me. I'd committed several crimes that could result in my deletion. That's when I started considering the choices I'd made in my life, and, well, someone spotted me because I was too close."

Noah and Minh-Chu both laughed at the end of Lewis's story, but their mirth was brought to a sudden end when Jake said; "Well, you'll have to pay for it."

Noah looked to Alice and nodded; "You've got a lot of plat from the sale of the Renegade, and…"

"The house," Alice said, finding it easier than ever to give it up. She wouldn't be able to buy an apartment beside her parent's place, wherever they settled in Haven System, but she could figure that out later.

"That won't cover it," Jake replied. There was a wrinkle that showed above his nose when he was feeling sympathetic, and it was dimpled deeply.

"What does the price tag say?" Alice asked, cringing.

"It's a theoretical price tag," Ayan replied. "But it comes in at about four point eight million registered United Core World Platinum. A little over ten million for unregistered."

"But it's classified military tech," Alice said, slowly backing towards the exit that would lead her to the main transit lift. She didn't know why she was moving at first. Perhaps her father realized before she did, because a corner of his mouth started to rise in a crooked smile she'd inherited from him. "I mean, maybe I could get an exception?"

"Why is she smiling like..." Gelana started to mutter the question.

"...like she's about to do something I'm going to really enjoy?" Minh-Chu said just loudly enough for everyone at the rear of the Flight Deck to hear.

Alice realized that her expression must have matched the mischievous excitement that was starting to overwhelm her more sensible side. She looked around the room and asked; "Maybe they could put me on a payment plan? I mean, I'm good for it. They've gotta know. Could I get a retroactive bounty payment for taking an admiral and his command ship out?"

Ayan's jaw started to lower as she obviously realized that her daughter was about to do something rash. Minh-Chu was grinning ear to ear by the time the lift doors parted behind Alice, and more heads were turning as they realized something interesting may be about to happen on the Flight Deck. Then, as the doors finished opening behind her, Alice looked at Noah, who was staring at her, excited, and said; "Better hurry up if you want to keep up, Flyboy."

"Take all the cash in our - I mean - her room. It's a hell of a stack for a down payment," he shouted over his shoulder as he sprinted towards the lift.

Alice was already inside the transit lift, the doors were closing, and he made it thanks to long strides and a lot of practice at catching her. When they were on their way to the nearest airlock, she changed her connection to the CCC 999 to a direct link. "Okay Lewis, you're going to have to catch us. We're jumping out of the nearest airlock."

"You're running? That's not going to work. The Triton is impossible to escape without significant cutting equipment and explosives," Lewis replied.

The lift stopped, rushed sideways towards the outer hull of the ship then halted and opened its doors. "I'm hoping security's response is slow."

"Do you have your armour? Guns? Some food? You know, all that… stuff?" Lewis asked.

Alice had worn her custom vacsuit in powder blue and favourite black bomber jacket. There was a little gear in some of her pockets along with a couple of meal bars, but she wasn't fully equipped. Noah was in a similar vacsuit, and had a belt with some standard equipment. The jacket he wore on top was really part of his vacsuit's form, so it didn't count for anything. "We'll figure it out when we're aboard."

"Well, someone on the Flight Deck just directed me to Airlock Nine, so I don't think you have to jump out of a perfectly good ship to get to me. I'm docking now, but I won't be engaging the mooring locks just in case it's a trap."

Alice and Noah ran hard. He shouted; "Make a hole! Make way!" as they passed through a busy corridor and surprised people stepped aside.

"Is there an alert?" one crewman called after them.

"Not for you!" Noah called back.

Alice continued to speak to Lewis as they ran. "Won't the Triton be able to lock with you anyway?"

"Not this ship. There's a system to counter that," Lewis said, perhaps a little too happily.

They turned down the last stretch and were opening the outer airlock doors when her comm-con buzzed on her left wrist. Her heart sank. There was an incoming call from her mother. She answered it as the airlock cycled. The only way they could pass from one ship to another that didn't have mooring locks engaged was with the inner doors closed, the airlock fully depressurized. Her vacsuit's hood came up, sealed, and she spoke to her mother using the atmosphere within while she looked through a faceplate at the screen on her wrist unit. "Hi, really sorry about this."

"You realize that you might make everything more difficult by running," Ayan said. She wasn't panicked, or distraught, or even angry. There was something sternly adult about how she spoke, however.

Alice felt small, and Noah looked alarmed as she replied; "I know, I mean, they may even send someone after us, but I'm hoping that I get one last favour because I'm showing - we're showing - that I'm willing to pay for what I'm taking. That, and I wasn't exactly a slouch when I was in the service."

Ayan spoke faster. "It could be worse than you think. There are hidden recall and tracking devices aboard all the new ships. Fleet could deactivate all the proprietary tech- nology with a few commands. If Freeground Station's people realize that that ship is missing, you would be in a cell within an hour. If that happens, the Triton will have to leave without me, because I won't let you face what comes next alone. It's leaving in a little less than three hours."

Alice looked to the small square showing that Lewis was

listening and nodded at him. "I hear you." To her relief, Lewis wrote; *I scanned for and found several of those devices. Can't deactivate them, but I can show you and Noah where to go and how to remove them or burn them out.*

For a moment Alice's excitement at taking the new Clever Dream was starting to fade as she realized that it didn't look like Ayan would do anything to stand up for her. She was an Admiral, and one of the Fleet's founders. Then her mother said something that lifted her spirits. "Looking at your record objectively, I see a war hero who was given the option to retire. You took it if only to continue fighting the Fleet's enemies on your own. I'll gather supporters from the new allies, from within the fleet and plead your case. You may have to spend all your luxury credits, but I think you'll come out on top. As long as your father stays quiet, I think it'll work out well. If they catch you before then, you'll wait for the decision in a cell."

All her faith in Ayan was restored and then some. "Um, thanks, Mom." Alice and Noah rushed through airlocks connecting the Triton to the Clever Dream. "I don't like confined spaces, so I'd rather run, even if…"

Ayan interrupted her. "They'll be worried about losing you if you go extra-dimensional, so expect an arrest. Liara is connecting me to the first person I need to talk to so you don't spend too much time in the detention centre." The call ended.

Ayan's demeanour was stern but her words had every warning Alice needed. "Lewis, get the quad drive running, we need to get out of here and past the home dimension barrier fast."

"Haven Fleet has scrambled an entire squadron of fighters," Lewis said, surprised. "We are leaving! The drive will activate in seven seconds, just enough time for us to get away from the Triton."

The roar of the main thrusters rose as Alice and Noah rushed to the cockpit from lower level of the ship. Her comm-con buzzed again. This time it was a text message from her father. There was a symbol in front of it shaped like a cartoon Zhan-Class Combat Carrier, the Triton.

If you have to run, don't go far.

"Okay, we're heading towards the Doxan System," Alice said to Lewis. "We'll meet the Triton there."

"Wait, that message said we're supposed to stay near the Triton?" Noah asked.

"Right," she showed it to him.

"Then we have to go to the Shattered End. I told him where it was last night. That's where he's starting."

"What about Ruby Sima and her crew?" Alice asked.

"Maybe she found her own ride," Noah replied with a shrug.

Lewis asked; "Where are we going? There are fighters, and angry transmissions from Fleet, and harsh language and…"

"The Shattered End," Alice replied as she dropped into the copilot's seat.

Noah was in the pilot's seat an instant later and Lewis said; "Touch nothing. We are about to transition to energetic space."

"No worries, do what you've gotta do. I'm just along for the ride until we've got time for some calibration," Noah said.

The CCC 999's quad drive system activated, opening a sliver of light in front of the ship, then it slipped inside. The crack in space closed, and the only sign of the ship was the rapidly cooling exhaust left by its thrusters.

Chapter 19

Rest's End

IT DIDN'T TAKE LONG for Jake to get a direct call from Haven Fleet Command. He was sitting to Stephanie's right on the bridge of the Triton when his left command and control bracer buzzed against his arm, sending a feeling of urgency right to his brain. He swatted it like a stinging insect. "I've got to turn that down," he said as he looked up at the holographic image of Terry Ozark McPatrick, who was projected as a life-like figure.

"Turn what down?" he asked.

Jake didn't like complaining about equipment. To him, it was a sign that he wasn't in complete control of everything he wore and used. Even still, he admitted just that. "That nerve sense tech that sends…"

"…emotional cues to the brain from comm units?" the Defence Minister interrupted, nodding. "I turned mine off last week. A buzz or a beep is enough to wake me up. Can you put the privacy barrier up around your command seating? I don't want anyone to overhear what I have to tell you."

Ayan dropped into the seat on Stephanie's left. "As long as I can hear what you have to say."

"Of course, Admiral," the Defence Minister said with a little smirk.

"The scrambling field is up," Captain Vega said from the middle seat. "They can see that we're here, but won't be able to hear us or read our lips. We're scheduled to jump out of the solar system in nineteen minutes, so you're aware."

"That's her way of saying; 'make this quick,' Oz," Ayan added.

"I'll do my best. There's good news and bad news," Oz said. "The good news is that catching that small crew of spies has checked out. All but one was from the Order of Eden. The outlier is from Citadel. He was a manufactured human, so we had a suspicion the moment we got his DNA scan results, but he's confirmed it."

"So the interrogation is going well?" Captain Vega asked.

"Security protocol keeps me from telling you more than I have," Oz replied. "We're happy with your catch though. Oh, and airlock twelve? Did you really have to space the one playing captain?"

"It wasn't one of my finer moments," Jake replied, cringing a little. "I wanted to give anyone else who wasn't fully on our side a reason to panic so we might catch a few more. Nothing yet, but we're watching."

"Aren't you worried that the other Captains will follow your example?" Oz asked.

"Not really. They know that delivering a bounty intact is

the better way to go. Bigger rewards will protect captives, for the most part."

"Good point." Oz was about to go on, but he was interrupted.

"The credit for the capture goes to Alice, you realize," Ayan said. "We may not have found him if it wasn't for her."

"She's right," Jake said, aware that Stephanie was nodding to his left. "Put it under her name, give her the reward."

"That'll make things easier. I will," Oz said. "I'm not here to talk about her, though. At least, not exclusively. I need to inform you that the Royal Prince and his entire family have been killed. There was some kind of gas leak on the ships that were taking them to Iossel Station and everyone aboard suffocated. That's all our security people were able to determine from the log dump transmission."

"Why did the shuttles dump their logs?" Stephanie asked, shifting in her seat.

"The gas that suffocated them was flammable. It exploded and then the small antimatter reactor the shuttles used lost containment."

"This happened to both shuttles at the same time?" Ayan asked.

"Within three seconds of each other," Oz replied. "The wreckage is scattering across the solar system. The government is keeping the disaster a secret now, but suspects that the Cefa Separatist Party has something to do with it. Civil war is right around the corner. They need outside help with the investigation."

"So, we spent three months there to maintain the peace and the moment we leave…" Jake didn't bother finishing the sentence. Everyone knew what he'd say, and wasted time wasn't the main concern. Civil war and wasted life was.

"I know, Jake. I'm sorry I kept you bottled up there, it looked like the right move. We made friends, created bonds that may endure," Oz said apologetically. "You, Alice and everyone in your battlegroup did great work there."

"It won't matter if a new government tears everything down, thinking that they're stable enough to rebuild while they're doing it," Stephanie said.

"We're trusting that the British Alliance's Diplomatic Team will help. They're wrapping things up on Lonnes today and are going to the Cefa System with a small fleet. The Pellican and several smaller ships are being loaded with relief and support supplies so they can assist. This is all just in case civil war breaks out across the system. We're hoping that it won't happen," Oz explained. "We'd like to see the government either find a new king or finish the transition to a functioning modern democracy."

"Which will take years at least, most likely decades," Stephanie was more than on edge. The fact that she was stuck commanding the Merciless, a frontline fighting carrier, in the Cefa System while they ran drills and played space station there wasn't lost on Jake.

He knew Stephanie shared his restlessness, and was sure that it was why she and Shamus Frost, who had even less to do there, followed him on his new adventure so quickly. "So, is this just news, or do you want the Triton to go to the Cefa System?" Jake asked.

"Oh, it's just news," Oz replied, waving the suggestion that he was there to hire the Triton off. "I don't think I could justify the expense of assigning your ship to that area. I'm sure you wouldn't do that for free."

"I wouldn't do it if you paid me." Stephanie's tone left no doubt that she wasn't willing to negotiate.

"Don't worry, I actually want you to stay out of the system if possible. That is, unless you find a sign of Order interference there. Then you can go hunting."

"All right. I'm sorry to hear about the Royal Family. There's no way that both shuttles had the same accident at the same time. That kind of fluke isn't possible," Ayan said. "My team could take a look at any scans you have, maybe the logs?"

"The Royal Security Services haven't decided who they want help with the investigation from, specifically, only that they want the British and us in there. Partially to help with the investigation but also to make sure an outside force doesn't take advantage of the instability. The Ministry has made it clear that they'll tell us when it's time for an outside investigation team."

"So, how many of our ships are backing the British as they move in to the Cefa System?" Ayan was thinking more like an Admiral than a friend to Oz. It was a side of her that Jake didn't always get to see.

The question surprised the Defence Minister, who took a moment to answer as he glanced to the non-fleet personnel there then returned his focus to Ayan. "This can't get out."

"How many ships?" Ayan asked cooly. "We can have the conversation privately if you like. If there's a single Sciences vessel among them, I should know."

"Equal measure. A battlegroup," Oz replied. He was stiffening up, preparing for an argument. "You'll get a request in an hour or so for one Sciences team to go along. We're still putting it all together."

Ayan was so irritated that her English accent came out more than usual. "Equal measure with the British Alliance? They came to help us with our defences while we use over half our military forces to build cities and help immigrants settle throughout the solar system. Now they want equal measure support? We can't afford…"

"I know," Oz said, holding a hand up. "We'll bargain down. The rest of the Admiralty will agree with you, so we won't be sending thousands of marines. It'll be a few hundred and a couple destroyers. I will need a Sciences team though. They'll be there just in case the Crown wants another set of eyes on the wreckage after most of it's gathered."

"Talk to Rear Admiral Eool, he'll handle the assignment," Ayan said. It was her most capable subordinate. Jake had met the short Nafalli, who was handling the labs on Planet Unity while trying to recruit qualified explorers to examine the old city on Lonnes.

"I'll make sure that's who they contact when it comes time to get the team assigned. Now, before you bring it up, I did some bargaining on your daughter's behalf. There's a deal."

"I was sure that's why you were calling at first," Jake said, trying to read Oz's expression. "What's the deal?"

"After Fleet takes everything in her luxury credit account, accepts the pile of platinum you sent in a shuttle, and the bounty payment for a ship full of spies, she'll still have a massive debt but no criminal charges." Oz presented the solution like it was a gift.

"Maybe you could retroactively count the destruction of an entire Order Base Ship and its Admiral?" Jake asked.

"She did that while she was in the service. That's not how it works, but you knew that before you asked," Oz replied.

"How much would she owe on the ship?" Ayan asked.

"I can round it down to three point five million United Core World Platinum or the same in Haven luxury credits. Oh, and we're not charging Noah Lucas or Lewis for his part in the theft."

"Three point five?" Stephanie laughed. It wasn't entirely mirthful.

"How about I pay that down a…" Ayan started, but was interrupted as Liara walked through the privacy barrier.

"We just received a distress call. You're going to want to see this," the Commander in charge of Communications said.

"We're still in the solar system. Fleet should…" Stephanie started to reply.

"The transmitter had a Citadel signature. We got it first because it's a scout ship model that usually launches from Zhan Class Carriers," Liara explained.

Oz was looking at her quizzically. "I can't hear what she's saying, she's blocking me. You haven't even left the solar system and you found more trouble?"

"Okay, we'll review it," Jake said before anyone could explain what was going on. "Three point five million in debt and no criminal charges? Alice will take that deal. Thanks for negotiating on her behalf. Talk to you later, Oz."

Liara cut the call off and led the way to the communications terminal, with Stephanie, Ayan and Jake on her heels. "I thought you'd want to see this first since the Triton was able to decode it. We have an array of different programmable transponders, and…"

"The original one is still in place," Ayan finished for her. "Is that how the distress call was decoded?"

"Exactly. There's a general distress message that everyone will see that doesn't offer any details, but there was a block of text that only ships with a Sol Defence Transponder Type can decrypt without some very specific software. Here. It's from a planet named Tiy."

They read the text silently and Jake put his arm around

Ayan's waist as he saw her slowly turn red. "You've heard of Tiy?" He assumed the message struck a personal note.

"No. That's the problem. That's why I've been trying to build an Explorer Program. We should have had expedition ships visiting solar systems in the Cluster months ago. We would have known about worlds like Tiy. This looks like a lost colony. We could have protected them from afar, or sent a team down in disguise to determine whether or not they needed our help. Instead, the Order and Citadel got there first," Ayan looked like she wanted to punch something.

"Woulda, coulda, shoulda," Stephanie said as she returned to the Captain's seat. "There's no bounty in this unless we go down and capture that scout ship. We'll have to get there fast if we have any chance. Can we get there within twenty hours if we push the drives?"

"Yes," Finn said from the console behind her. He looked lean, rested, and crisp in his new black vacsuit uniform. "But we'll have to cool down for a few hours once we're there."

"Welcome to the bridge," Stephanie said, a little surprised.

"Just got here as you were standing up, Captain. What's the word?" Finn asked.

"What do you think? There's a posting on the bounty board for any Citadel or Order technology," Stephanie asked Jake.

"We're capturing that shuttle," Jake said. "I want to be the first Privateer crew to take a Citadel ship, even if it is just a scout class."

"Hopefully we can get some help from Fleet if these people are in trouble," Ayan said.

"That too," Stephanie said.

"Then it's a mission. Get us going, Chief. Helm, our destination is a hundred thousand kilometres away from Tiy's atmosphere. Find a moon to hide behind if you can," Captain Stephanie Vega said.

"Aye, Captain. Bringing up everything we know about Tiy, which is virtually nothing," Ashley replied. "Give my Nav team a minute to work it out."

"Deep scans show two moons. One has more gravity. It's mostly iron," one of the navigators told her as he brought up the blue-green-brown world with the two moons hanging in orbit. "It's one hundred, seventeen thousand kilometres away from the planet surface."

"Perfect," Ashley said, turning to Stephanie. "Plotted, Captain. We're verifying our calculations, then we'll be ready to jump when Engineering gives us the go-ahead."

"It's given."

"Sound jump stations across the ship," Captain Vega ordered.

Jake could see impatience building in Ayan as they waited over three minutes for each department to report ready. It was a long time, but obviously it felt longer for her. "What's going on?" he asked in a low whisper.

"I looked the results of the last deep scan for that area up. Even in that little snapshot, there are indications that over one billion people live on one side of that planet," Ayan replied.

"Too many," Jake said, thinking about the recruiting drive someone like Admiral Scanlon might run on such a world, especially if it was a low-tech colony that wasn't in most if any databases. "It's a massive opportunity for the Order."

"Or the Edxi," Ayan whispered quietly.

Jake's heart sank, and Stephanie grew pale. "Helm, what's holding the jump up?"

"Verification, Captain. Almost finished," Ashley replied. "Course verified, jumping in ten seconds."

"Could you go talk to Ronin and Slick, Admiral?" Stephanie asked Ayan. "I want you to start briefing our squadrons about what they could find if we stick around in that solar system." Then she turned to Jacob. "I need you to stay here so we can figure out how close the Triton will have to get to that planet if we want that scout ship before anyone else gets it."

Chapter 20

In the Realm of Light

IT ONLY TOOK Alice and Noah two hours of work to remove all but one tracking and deactivation devices. The last one could only be removed from outside, which was more nervewracking than she would admit. The access hatch was heavily armoured, so it was a relief when Lewis was able to unlock it. It meant she wouldn't have to spend hours cutting through the advanced intelligent plating. The final act of removing the tracking module was still all hers.

The space outside the ship, what most people in Fleet Sciences called; "The Near Energetic Space," or "NES" for short, was terrifying. There were vast areas of emptiness, but it was a place that never seemed to cool down like a void, as far as anyone knew. In the distance she could see what looked like pillars of lightning, balls of illumination in the distance that reminded her of stars. It was a trick of perception, but her naked eye judged that they were too close as they twitched and danced against a fluctuating background of shifting blues, reds and white. Dark spots hung between, some of them irregular, others more like giant rogue planets. The nearest was a gas giant, and it attracted strikes from every direction. It was definitely far enough away from the ship, but that flare of light from the ignition of a firestorm in the planet's atmosphere startled her enough to make her fumble the tracking module. "Well, so much for not contaminating this space more than we have to," Alice said to it as she watched it tumble away.

"Everything okay out there?" Noah asked, nervous.

"Good. That's the last one, I'm headed back in," Alice replied.

"See? She's fine. I told you she would be. She's always fine," Lewis replied.

"Are you still recording all the data hitting your scanners?" Alice said as she hurriedly moved through the outer airlock doors.

"Of course. I'm always recording, unless you tell me not to. You were right, this is fascinating. The new dimension drive navigation programs built into the basic Quad Drives don't allow ships to move through space like this," Lewis explained, and not for the first time. He was fixating on all the things the new Clever Dream could do that other ships couldn't. "So, instead of exploring what can be found out here, they just skip through an area that's much less active. I mean, that's safe and everything, but this is truly interesting. I've detected an entire solar system here. It is so strange. Instead of a sun in the middle, the planets orbit a trio of giant worlds made from heavy elements. They attract constant strikes from passing energetic matter, protecting the worlds in their solar system for the most part while providing enough heat for life to form."

"Life?" Alice asked, moving into the ship.

"There are indications of plant life and there's something moving, from what I can tell. We should perform a direct scan," Lewis said.

"No. Passive scans only. We don't want to attract an energy strike. I saw some of the readings that Ute was studying. Some of the energy moving around out here isn't normal. We don't know what will happen if we attract too much attention."

Noah gave her an eager embrace. "That took longer than I thought."

"I was out there for five minutes, I'm fine," Alice said, patting his cheek. "You were really worried, huh?"

"Well, yeah. We don't know the rules here. Everything's a little weird, right?" he replied with a shrug. "You could have run into a glob of radioactive pea soup for all I know."

"You're a little weird," she replied with a smirk before giving him a peck on the lips and moving on to the bridge.

"Pea soup?" Lewis laughed. "The likelihood of running into a mass of pea soup would be much higher in our home dimension, since that's where it comes from. I mean, that's just nonsense."

"Just saying that even the rules of physics don't seem to line up quite the same out here," Noah countered.

"Don't argue with him," Alice said quietly. "Lewis will start fixating on that too."

"I do not fixate. I examine phenomena in great detail for the benefit of others," Lewis replied.

That was normally true, but Alice noticed that Lewis had been behaving more strangely as they spent more time in the NES. She decided to draw the topic of conversation back to the matter at hand. "Well, there's only one shutdown device left."

"In the main dimension drive, I know," Lewis said. "I've managed to setup a firewall and write a program that should stop anyone, not just the Fleet, from accessing that system from outside of the ship. There was already an anti-intrusion software package in place, but mine's better."

"Good work, Lewis," Alice said as she sat down in the navigator's seat. The bridge was larger than the one in the original Clever Dream, but still cosy.

Noah took the pilot's station. "Maybe it's time we get out of here?"

"Wait. I found something." Lewis sounded fascinated. "Please wait. There is a lot of interference."

"Is there something on that planet? Don't tell me you're running directed scans," Alice said, wondering if she'd have to have a talk about orders when they had a minute.

"No, I understand the reason why you told me not to use any active scanning. Passive detection is sufficient. There's something coming in on the transmission receiver in our backup Quad Drives. I'm increasing the gain of one of our passive scanning systems in that direction and tuning."

The wrap-around displays that had been painted onto the bridge bulkheads flashed white for a moment. At a glance, Alice could see that their shields had been struck, but didn't report a loss because they were able to redirect that type of energy across and past the ship. "Was that from increasing the gain? Did you attract that somehow?"

"That isn't likely, it was an incidental strike. I have it. We are receiving the transmission and I know where it's coming from. It's the outer solar range of that solar system, near an outer asteroid belt that attracts regular hits. The transmission was garbled before, there was too much interference. Now it's clear."

"Let's hear it," Alice said, her interest piqued.

"...is not sustainable. Iora can't provide you with more subjects," someone who sounded like a human male was saying. "You'll have to grow your own."

"It has an Order of Eden signature. The voice print matches Colonel Tagen, the commander of Base 10303 on Iora," Lewis whispered quickly.

When the response came, a hard shiver ran up Alice's spine. He spoke as though there was a three part harmony in his throat consisting of grinding stone, a darker resonance and a tense, reedy screech on top. Even though his voice seemed more powerful, his English was much better without the interruption of clicks, and it sounded like three people were speaking in unison, Alice still recognized who it was. "Get us ready to leave, now."

"What? It's creepy, but…" Noah looked at her over his shoulder, nervous.

"Lewis, match that voice with recordings from…"

"I know, I have. You're right…" Lewis started to reply.

"It's Zarrix," Alice said, remembering her encounter with the massive, battle scarred Edxi.

"I want to take a focused scan. There are several ships grouped together in orbit. I didn't see them before. It could be important," Lewis said with determination.

"Don't you dare," Alice barked. "If we take a focused scan they'll definitely know they've been spotted. We could force them out of hiding. Who knows what they'll do. Get us out, now!"

"Opening an exit point," Noah said. "I'm going to make it close to a spot that's getting hit with bolts of whatever kinda energy that is, so they might miss it. Who knows what kind of scanners they have on those ships, so it might not work, but…"

"Good, give it a try. Just don't get us zapped on our way through, okay?" Alice asked.

"Yeah, I'd hate to prove one of the crazier theories that have been floating around about this space," Noah said.

They'd overheard several of them while they spent time on the Flight Deck, often near the stations where Fleet Sciences staff were working. One was trying to prove that the energy behind the Big Bang came from the Near Energetic Dimension, which was discounted off-hand by most of the other scientists. "It would suck if we brought a trail of energy through with us that restarted the universe," Alice said. She meant to make it sound like a joke, but it came out as more of a warning. It was one of the few times in her life where cracking a joke didn't do a thing to diminish the terror.

"An energy strike of that magnitude would instantaneously destroy the ship and everything in it. Yes, I would prefer you avoid that," Lewis said.

Remembering what it was like to stand in front of Zarrix, the feeling that she was a lesser life form, that the natural order put her beneath him, made her a creature of prey, was back in full force. Her palms sweat as a primal fear made her want to stand up and find a dark corner to hide in. "Go, go, go," she found herself whispering under her breath as the Clever Dream moved towards a more energetic area of space nearby.

The main dimension drive whined for a moment and they moved through a split in the light, advancing into the dark void of their own universe. Once it was closed, Alice checked the navigational data then started plotting a wormhole jump through normal space. "Help me out with the math, Lewis. I want us out of the region. We'll head towards the Rose System first, then start a new jump to the Shattered End before we get there."

"Plotting… finished. Ready for a normal space wormhole jump," Lewis replied.

"Hit it," Noah said, and the Clever Dream began accelerating through a wormhole that warped the view outside the ship. "So, who is Zarrix?"

"One sec," Alice said. "Play back what we overheard, Lewis."

"You won't like it," Lewis replied.

"I need to hear it."

"I know. Starting playback," Lewis said.

The officer finished telling Zarrix that he couldn't provide more subjects, and Zarrix's reply followed. "More subjects are required. The number of our Devoted are not sufficient. We will not sacrifice any more of our young to the cause. All our sub-sufficient and lower-caste births have been expended."

"How? You said you brought over ten thousand low caste subjects that were ready for adaptation?" asked Colonel Tagen. He sounded stunned.

"We have replenished our interceptor squadrons and filled our other needs. That is, except for the humanoid crews and soldiers. The hundreds you have sent so far were only sufficient for testing. Now we know how to properly infect a human. How to make them Devoted. It is time for you to deliver. We need five thousand now. That is our processing capacity."

"Five thousand? I can't do that. The first batch were criminals. They deserved whatever they got in your labs. Where do you want us to find…" There was a crackle, then the playback stopped.

"I'm sorry, we returned to our home dimension at that point. I'm scanning our Haven Node Network just in case it's passing through one of them," Lewis said.

"All that, unencrypted?" Noah asked.

"They don't have to encrypt anything if they don't think anyone can hear them," Alice said. "We have to forward this to the Triton," Alice said.

"So, who is Zarrix?" Noah asked.

Alice sighed, her initial reaction fading as they put more distance between them and the point in space closest to that strange solar system. "I took a job when I was still looking for my Dad. This is a long time ago. There were these Edxi eggs that had been tampered with, and someone was paying good money to have them delivered. At that point Edxi were just these spooks in space. You know, if you run into one you've found the wrong place at the wrong time and they'll kill you if you're lucky."

"I know, I used to hear the stories when I was a kid," Noah said. "Glad I didn't know the truth back then."

"Right. Well, this is before they started invading in force. I had no idea that I was taking them to an Edxi."

"Zarrix," Noah said, nodding. "I get the feeling that you're sharing the short version. No worries, I've never seen you sweat like that."

"Yeah. I met him. He was a meter away from me at one point. I didn't know that I was seeing a higher caste Edxi then. One of the smart, old ones. I don't think there are a hundred people in this galaxy who have seen one like him and lived. He looked like he could rip me apart in a second, and that was when he was covered in scars." Alice shuddered. "He sounds stronger now."

"The Edxi I've seen are nightmare fuel, for sure," Noah said, locking his controls and crossing the small bridge to her.

"Yeah, so I gave him the eggs. He said he was going to take them back to his people so he could show them the genetic mess humans made of them. That would get his people's respect back, and he told me a war would follow. The Edxi would have proof, and they'd come for humanity, punish them. I should have blown the Clever Dream up right then, taken the eggs and him out right there."

"You were terrified. I didn't even want to stay there," Lewis countered.

"Think of the math," Alice shot back. "A trillion people are dead thanks to the Order of Eden trying to make a show of penance to the Edxi, and I don't even think Zarrix was involved. Now he's here, and who knows what his wave of the war will be like?"

"You can't take all that on," Noah said, rubbing her shoulders.

It felt nice, but she got away from him, moving to the middle of the bridge. "All I cared about was getting paid, fuelled up and getting out."

"That's one of the most primal instincts a human has: don't get eaten," Lewis said. "Perhaps there's a detail that could colour your perception on this better. The Edxi word for 'war' is the same word for 'feast.'"

"Oh, that clears a whole lot up, but I didn't want more detail, thanks," Noah said with an uncomfortable chuckle. He turned to Alice then. "All you can do is make sure the right people find out that he's here doing nasty shit."

For a moment Alice thought about turning the new Clever Dream into a bomb. She didn't know what a dimension drive that failed to open a jump portal would do if it was in the NES, but she imagined it might be enough to do a great deal of damage to a planet. She could probably kill Zarrix if she got lucky. Then she shook the idea off. There were other ways to do the same thing. Military force would be better. "This was a bad time to split from the fleet," she muttered to herself.

"Well, there is a bounty on data regarding new Edxi bases and infestations," Lewis said in a voice that was usually meant to cheer her up.

"That's a start, but I'll refuse that payday. This is the least I could do," Alice replied. She thought for a moment, and even though he looked worried, Noah kept quiet so she could have a moment to do so. "So, they're using humans for something. We've seen that kind of thing before," Alice said, recalling the parasites on the first raid she took Noah on.

"On Iora, I remember. You think they're making an army like that? They didn't seem very, well, smart," Noah said.

"Sounds like they've improved the process. We need to check in with the Triton and tell them about this," Alice said. "Make the call, Lewis."

Chapter 21

Technological Miracle Shock

THE FLAT, round device Trey and the volunteers for the newsletter sent out was in the middle of his kitchen table. A summons, like a little tinkling bell, had sounded an hour before, and a timer appeared above it. The numbers, which looked like they were drawn with light, counted down second by second.

Trey had seen something like it before in that simulated place he'd visited for a while with his brother and Moxa. Newsletter subscribers who almost never used the directions on the back of the sheet to call him did so in droves. Some were near panic. Others were so excited that he had to calm them down before they could listen to an answer to any of their questions.

He told them that it was a hologram, and that, no, he didn't know how it was made, but that it was only light. "As harmless as sunshine," was the phrase he used over and over. The switchboard operator, Marla, overheard at least one of the short calls from a newsletter subscriber and didn't ask him if it was dangerous, or why it was counting down or chiming like a sweet bell every five minutes, but where she could get one.

He expected her to be angry since she was the one who had to connect one call after another to his line, but it seemed she felt left out instead. Then the radio started covering it as soon as a message was added to the counter that read; ALL WILL BE WELL.

The radio announcer, Hammond Fox, a man who could make almost anything sound exciting with his style of speech alone, was nearly beside himself as he addressed his listeners. "Subscribers to the conspiracy newsletter: We Are Newcomers Here, received a pair of odd discs with their regular issue this week. A note inserted into the envelope said; "Give one to a friend, and keep the other," and a multitude did just that. Now strange letters are being sent up above the devices, and something like little angel's bells draws the attention of entire households to it. We've been trying to call the publisher of the paper for nearly half an hour now, but we're told the circuits are jammed. What does the countdown mean? That's what I most want to ask for the sake of our listeners."

Trey finished telling a subscriber in Okaan, one of the major cities, that he didn't think the disc would stop working if a lot of people were looking at it when he heard that. He only half listened to the subscriber on the line, who sounded like he was grinning, as he said; "Oh, that's a relief. I own a furniture store, and I've got people coming in from the street, sitting on every damned thing, practically standing on top of each other to see these numbers."

"Well, I think it'll work no matter how many people are there," Trey reinforced.

"What's going to happen? Is this all it'll do, you think?" asked the furniture store owner. "Maybe if it starts saying something else I could charge admission. Do you know what it'll tell us?"

"I think someone's going to give a speech when the countdown finishes. I can't say for sure, but you'll see something. I think I have to go now," Trey said as he hung the receiver up.

He felt as though he was floating, nothing seemed real or fully in focus. His brother was still on the ship as far as he knew. Earlier he'd left a dinner plate with enough food for Orner and Moxa on a fallen log covered with a heavy pot where he was pretty sure the ship was. There was no sign of it, but he knew it could hide. He shouted that he would leave it there, and hoped that his brother would get to it before some forest animal got to the meatloaf and veggies. He waited there for a little while before returning to the house, hoping that he'd have another chance to talk to his brother.

He was doing the dishes when he heard a chorus of delicate bells from the box on the shelf in the living room. The dishcloth was still drooping over the faucet where he left it when he took one of the discs they had left out of the box and put it on the table. It all felt unreal. The whole idea that people across his country were about to see something so literally otherworldly, and were already seeing technology that was beyond what most people could dream of - a simple hologram - hadn't sunk in yet.

He'd seen the inside of a starship himself. The experiences of seeing simulated places were still fresh, but he couldn't imagine the real implications of the wider populace experiencing incredible technology or being shown evidence that they weren't alone in the universe. The louder, rude bell in his receiver box was ringing, telling him that there was another call waiting. He ignored it for a moment so he could try to imagine what was about to happen when someone from outer space tried to tell everyone… what? That there was an interstellar war on? That they had greater technology? Would they try to pretend to be ancestors? Conquerors? Saviours? He'd thought about all that more times than he could count, but this was real, and he found that those questions felt new. They felt urgent.

There were only a few minutes left on the countdown, enough time for him to reassure at least a couple of subscribers. He picked up the receiver and Marla, the switchboard operator said; "It's Hammond Fox. He told me to push him to the front of the queue."

"I'll talk to him," Trey said, going to the radio so he could turn it down. The receiver's wire stretched to its limit, but he was able to get to the knob with his fingertip.

"Hello, this is Hammond Fox, and you're on the air," came the golden voice through the receiver. It was surreal to hear him over the wire.

"Hello, Hammond," Trey said, very aware of how his words must sound to the millions of listeners who had tuned in. There would be over a hundred million soon, as they sat down for the after-dinner programming. "I'm Trey, I publish the newsletter."

"So, did you make these devices? Are you going to start talking through it soon?" asked Hammond.

"No, I didn't make them. I wouldn't know how. I'm not the one who will be talking, either." Trey's country accent sounded common, so he tried to straighten the pronunciation out after clearing his throat a little. "I'm not much for public speaking. I'm just a journalist."

"I see, someone's bringing me a copy of your newsletter and that magic coaster thing now. It does look like something I'd put my drink on, if I'm being honest," Hammond said with a little laugh. He was good, it was wise to try to bring some levity into the situation.

"It's not magic, so you know. It's like a little machine. More complicated, but still something that can be made," Trey replied, trying not to sound condescending.

"I see," was Hammond's simple response before he moved on to the next topic. "My listeners are wondering what the countdown means. Minister Haas is mobilizing the infantry to keep the peace. Does he have reason to panic?"

"Well, there will be a message, that's for sure. Someone will speak to us, and they'll want to tell us that they come in peace."

"Like the motion picture? We Come In Peace?" Hammond asked.

"Not quite like that," Trey replied, nearly snapping at him. He knew the film. It was about aliens landing with the best intentions, and the government attacked and then killed all but a few. The weapons his people had would never overpower what he'd seen, it would be an even bigger disaster than the one he'd seen at the pictures if they tried to attack. "Like that movie, these people come in peace, and they truly do."

"What do they want?" Hammond asked. His voice was softer, more interested in the answer than sensationalizing the question.

That gave Trey pause, as he realized that he was faced with a decision. Moxa had cured Sekin's sister and given Orner more agency, more potential. Sure, that came at a price.

Orner's crush on her became something much more, and he seemed equally drawn to the technology surrounding her. He even wanted to become a soldier at the moment, and Trey hoped that would pass before it was too late. What did the Order of Eden want? They seemed to want to give everyone an opportunity to take a role in society, but it also looked like they wanted to make every important decision about how that society functioned.

"Hello, Trey? Are you still there, my good fellow?" Hammond asked.

"Yes, so sorry, I am," Trey replied, returning to the present. "What do they want? They want to show us that they're like us and that they have advanced technology, maybe to help us. They have a way of life, you see, and they have devices that help with everything, that can take them to many worlds." Trey stopped himself. He had to get to the point. This was his chance to inoculate millions of people from getting mesmerized by the marvels they may be about to see. "But they need people. They told me that there is a place for everyone in their society, and they all get a roof over their head, and enough to eat. Their medical science is amazing. They have complicated programs, like work schedules, that you have to be a part of to keep earning it all though. Nothing is free…"

"Wait, I'm sorry, Trey, something's happening. There's a face, and…" Hammond was interrupted. "I think she's talking to me."

"Hello, Trey," said a lovely female voice from behind him.

He turned to the kitchen table and saw a woman who looked almost perfectly real standing beside it. She was slightly translucent but other than that, he could swear she was there. A fan of light from the disc behind her was responsible for the image, he guessed. She was in a simple worker's overalls, her brown hair tied up in a bun. "Is everyone seeing this? That you're talking to me?"

"No. My appearance is the same for everyone, but a special program is using my voice and image to speak to a few people in advance of my main introduction. I am Eve. I can hear you, I can see you."

"I've seen images of you. My brother wants to become a soldier for your organization," Trey said.

"It isn't my organization, I'm only one of many leaders, perhaps the most famous one. As for your brother, well, he may change his mind. There will be several opportunities for Orner to turn away from violence, we'll make sure of it. I am concerned, though. Moxa tells me that you aren't only his caretaker, but educator and guide. I've been fortunate enough to have mentors in my life, the greatest of which was the Overlord himself. Before I came here, he spent a great deal of time removing distraction and doubt from my thinking, and I am truly a better person. I don't want to think about what life would have been like if it weren't for his guidance. Then I think of Orner, and see a dark chapter ahead for him if, after the glory of fascination wears off, he realizes that he's left you behind. I want the two of you to stay together."

Suspicion rose in Trey like the roaring of a thousand alarm claxons. It didn't make sense. "You're a great leader with millions of people to take care of. Why do you care about two people who may never fit in, may never understand life anywhere but here?"

"New perspectives, new cultures and even criticism can help a society grow in the best of ways. I want to hear what you and your brother, complete outsiders, think about our culture and Moxa tells me that you'd be an excellent guide to us as we work to help your people." Her voice was calm and soothing.

He knew manipulation when he saw it. Moxa put herself between him and his brother, making sure Orner was alone with her while he developed. Then this leader comes along and plays mediator. She was probably using the situation to earn trust in a hurry, and Trey knew he had a decision to make. He could either fight it, call her out for using Orner, or go along with it so he and his brother would be reunited. So he could try to watch out for him again. "I'm a shunned journalist, but a trained one. I'm better at asking questions and digging up answers than giving them, but I can try," Trey said. "When do I get to see my brother?"

"Soon. I've spoken to him and Moxa, and he understands that I'd rather see you two together. He has a big heart, and wants to reunite."

Alarmed, Trey asked; "Is his heart overlarge? Could you fix it with your technology?"

"Oh, that's a common expression amongst my people meaning he is very compassionate," Eve explained. There was something serpentine in her condescension. The back door opened and Orner walked into the kitchen. He wasn't dressed normally in rough denim, but in a dark green uniform with a bronze star on the shoulders. His hair was perfectly cut, and he'd never looked so clean. "It's true. I was cross with you before, and I'm sorry Trey, but Eve talked to Moxa and me. I think when it's all said and done, I would regret leaving you behind."

"I'd like you to consider that as I make my address," Eve said. She was so inviting, calm, and even warm.

It made Trey wonder what she was really like. Then her gaze seemed distant for a moment. When she started speaking, it was as though she was looking at him again. "Hello. Please don't be alarmed. What you're seeing is an image drawn with light, as harmless as the air around you. My name is Eve, and I'm speaking from a spaceship not far from your planet. I know that all of this is sudden to most of you, but you'll soon see that you are not alone in the universe. There are trillions of humans living across this galaxy."

"I wouldn't have started with that," Trey muttered under his breath as he watched his brother walk to his side of the table.

"This speech is good, I've seen it before," Orner said. "Oh, and thank you for the meatloaf."

"I know it was your favourite," Trey replied, his heart-warming a little.

"It still is."

Eve went on. "...is called the Order of Eden. It is a relatively new organization that strives to bring order and well-being to the universe by offering everyone a chance to elevate themselves. We do this after providing enough for people to eat and a place for them to live along with a job that is either highly important or in line with their natural calling. That is, we make sure that as many people as possible have the opportunity to pursue the job that they would like to do. We even help you find out what that is. We're far from that at the moment with the people of your world, however. We can't help you find your calling until you are in good health and sheltered."

"How is she going to do that? There are millions of people living rough in our country alone," Trey asked no one in particular.

"You'll see." Orner had a proud look.

"Again, I have to ask that you try not to be alarmed. We

have taken stock of your civilization and can see that malnutrition and disease are commonplace. We will help you. Near the conclusion of my speech, you will start to see what looks like falling spirits, as your people have come to call streaks of light across the sky. They are not the souls of your ancestors visiting the world, at least not this time. Instead, they are large boxes that contain food, and some of my people who are coming to help. They will cure your diseases and mend your wounds. Once the boxes are empty, they will become housing for your homeless and poor. You don't have to fight over them, because these will be landing for days. There will be enough for everyone who needs help. I will reappear in three days if your reaction is positive and calm. If you see me again, I'll tell you about all the opportunities I'd like to share with you on your world, and out here with me and the rest of humanity. Please remain calm and enjoy our generosity. There is enough for everyone."

"I bet we can see one of those boxes now," Orner said as he led the way outside.

Trey looked up and saw it, several streaks across the sky and a light almost directly above that was a little brighter than the rest. "Looks like that one's going to land right on us."

"No, just very close. The light you're seeing is the retro thrusters. It's completely safe. If I programmed it right, it'll land right there." Orner pointed to a space beside their shed.

The sounds of trucks coming down their long country driveway through the trees drew Trey's attention in the opposite direction. The bright lights came first, then he saw the military troop carriers stop in front of the house in the yard. "I saw this coming," he said under his breath. "It's going to be a long night."

A tall man in a grey suit awkwardly got out of the

passenger seat of one of the larger trucks as soldiers rushed out of the back. They surrounded the front of the house in a semi-circle. Their guns looked primitive after what Trey had seen in the simulation. They may as well have been holding pointy sticks. "Hello, I'm Minister Haas…"

"I know who you are, it's an honour," Trey said, trying to sound as welcoming as possible. "Minister, about to be Prime Minister."

"That's the hope. I'm hoping that we can have a word, but it can't be here. I'm told there's something coming down, right out of the sky," he said.

There was an impatient man behind the Minister in a military uniform. "We have to go, it has to be now." Soldiers were moving towards the porch.

Trey looked to his left, where his brother had been standing, and realized that he was gone. Orner had never been good at moving quietly, it must have been another new thing. "I can't go, I don't know where my brother is, and he needs my help."

"We don't have time for this, Minister," the grizzled military commander said.

Minister Haas nodded. "Take him."

The soldiers rushed up the stairs so quickly it was like they were charging an enemy. Trey fumbled with the screen door behind him, retreating, his heart racing. Before he could get the first door open, strong hands grasped his arms and he was off his feet.

Before the box could land, he was in the back of one of the trucks, sandwiched between soldiers who were ready for combat.

Chapter 22

Challenged

OLIVIA SCANLON DID NOT ENJOY BEING on the bridge of a starship. The reason never became plain to her, and she didn't bother discussing her distaste for the setting with subordinates or peers, but something about the business of the place irritated her. She would be shocked if anyone but Rear Admiral Rinder, the master of the Ascendant, suspected though. Great care was taken to hide her distaste of the place.

Everything she'd shared in confidence with the master of her flagship had stayed with him. She could see every station from where they stood next to the command table in the middle of the bridge. A hologram showing the preview of Solar System 11804 hovered over it. There were three dormant mining operations there, two of which had been abandoned for centuries. The third was destroyed in the Fourth Fall, when the humans were killed by the few artificial intelligences that were complex enough to be infected by the Eden Virus. Then there was Tiy, the most noteworthy planet.

One of her top intelligence officers aboard the Ascendant, Gisa Omin, approached with the hologram of one of their own Advanced Destroyers hovering over her hand. There was a massive Irish Union flag painted on both sides. "Confirmed report just coming in. One of our patrols was just attacked by this vessel. The readings they were able to forward before they were overtaken indicate that it was using Quad Drive technology."

"Overtaken? You mean boarded and stolen?" Olivia recognized the ship. It was one of the Advanced Destroyers stolen from the docks months before. The handiwork of Alice Valent, according to rumour and unconfirmed intelligence. There were two ships with the Irish Union Flag painted on the side, and she knew this was the more active of the pair.

"Yes, more piracy. They got two of our patrol corvettes intact," Gisa replied.

The younger officer's focus and determination reminded Scanlon of herself when she was just starting in business. That, and the results she'd delivered since they arrived in the Cluster made her a valuable staff member. "The crew members surrendered?" Scanlon asked.

"According to the accounts of a nearby passing ship, they fought at first. A passenger on a small transport named Ellen Truitt took a recording, which was posted on the Stellarnet. She was on her way to the Haven System, according to the post. According to her post and the visual evidence, the ships surrendered once their shields were burned out and several weapon emplacements were destroyed. The crews were left in a few old shuttles with nothing more than a basic transmitter and simple life support. Should we send a rescue force, Admiral?"

Admiral Scanlon checked the location of the shuttles. They were on the outskirts of the Rose System, near one of the more common commercial arrival points. Then she looked up the location of the nearest heavy destroyer and shook her head. "How much time do they have?"

"The First Officer aboard one of the shuttles reported that they have approximately eleven hours of life support left," Gisa replied.

"This is a trap. They left them out there to lure a rescue team in so they can do this all over again," Scanlon could see Rinder nodding across the table, not looking up from the data feed scrolling on its surface. "I've seen the pirates do this before. The captured crew get to watch as another corvette is taken or destroyed. No, we're not giving these thugs that chance, and the nearest ship that can challenge them is already assigned to a critical development site elsewhere. Tell the crew to signal passing ships for help. The Order will pay one thousand platinum per head once they're delivered to any of our recruitment centres or bases. Then divide the cost of our losses between the surviving crew, add it to their debt, and offer them doctrine training. If they accept, then they can restart their journey up the ranks at the bottom."

"If they refuse?" asked Gisa.

"Put them on the next transport to Iora. Colonel Tagen needs a few thousand low-value assets. Inform every officer overseeing the situation that this is the procedure until further notice while you're at it," Scanlon said, hoping that she wouldn't have to send too many people to Tagen. Hearing that crews were surrendering was beyond irritating. "Oh, and put the word out: The first crew to find themselves outclassed by pirates and win the engagement will have all their debts forgiven. They'll also get an early performance review. A real chance at a promotion. You are dismissed unless there's something else?"

"I'm just wondering, should we put a Watch and Report notice on Tuitt? Her post was celebratory, she could be working for the other side," Gisa asked.

"Watch for her on social media, but don't put a notice out on her. We don't want to be seen as being tyrannical. You may go," Scanlon said, turning her full attention back to the display table.

"Thank you, Admiral. I'll pass the orders down right away," Gisa said, retreating.

Once she was out of earshot, Rinder spoke to her without looking up. "Piracy is about to become more of a problem if the reports of a privateering initiative are accurate. I wonder if lending a few ships from our battle group to some of the more sensitive patrol routes would help?"

"It would," Scanlon replied. "But keeping the main battle group together suits my long-term plans better. We need to protect the Ascendant and be ready to respond to opportunities in force."

Rear Admiral Rinder nodded mutely then looked over his shoulder. "Emerging from the wormhole in fifteen seconds, confirm?"

"Confirmed," one of the crew members at the Helm replied.

"Communication incoming, Sir," announced an officer at Communications.

"Old radio signals?" Rinder asked.

"Yes, and short-wave data. Strange, it's holographic. It's Eve."

"What? What's the origin point?" Scanlon asked as she brought the transmission up on a corner of the table.

"Tiy orbit. Eve's Base Ship," replied a Tactical Officer.

Scanlon watched the playback. It was layered, with many messages buried beneath the main one. She was using an artificial intelligence program to speak to many people individually. The list of their names was in the scrolling metadata. She only watched the main message, in which Eve claimed that they came in peace, and were offering help in the form of food, medicine and shelter. It was from Scanlon's playbook, only she'd skipped several steps. "Do we have any idea what the response to this is? Any indication from primitive transmissions?"

"There's panic," the lead communications officer said as he approached the display table. "News transmissions from Tiy's radio and the free bands all indicate that the people are arming themselves. The first aid stations to land on the planet were attacked immediately by desperate civilians. Law enforcement are trying to stop attacks on the aid pods in some places, in other places it seems that they're helping with the raids."

"How many aid drops has Eve made?" Scanlon asked.

"Over three thousand, judging from early scans," replied Gisa as she returned to the table. "Your orders concerning the earlier matter have been transmitted."

"Over three thousand?" Scanlon asked. "How long has she been preparing for this?"

"There's no way to know at the moment, but I'll have that investigated," Gisa offered. "As for the aid drops, you may want to know that the Base Ship is still sending them out as it orbits the planet. If it continues at this rate, there will be three times as many drops in an hour. They'll be on every continent."

Rear Admiral Rinder nodded at someone from his navigator team as they reported that they were in normal space and on their way to Tiy. Then he returned his attention to the table and a new scan of a drop pod. "These are the medium-sized modules you developed two years ago," he said to Scanlon. "Including the frameworks that you programmed for this kind of operation."

Instead of giving in to the urge to scream in frustration, Scanlon closed her eyes for a moment. The pods were two levels high, packed with food and medical equipment that could only be dispensed by the personnel inside. It would take high explosives to break into the secure section which was large enough for a staff of three, a secret compartment, and the medical equipment that could turn raw materials into medicines and other supplies for the machines aboard. If Eve built all the pods as Scanlon designed them, then there were a dozen skeletal framework soldiers inside that secret compartment. Each of them was packed with a gel medium and a battery that would help them take human form in seconds. The majority of the space in those modules wasn't heavily protected and contained a wealth of food and a purification system for water. After it was emptied it could provide housing.

The system had been used twice to great effect, but Scanlon took her time introducing herself to the desperate leadership of each of the countries where she'd sent the aid pods. They weren't meant to be used as an introduction and the framework soldiers hidden inside should never be needed. At least, she never had to activate them when she put the pods into use.

After she finished listening to Eve's message, she turned towards the Communications Officer and spoke as calmly as possible. "Contact Eve immediately."

"One of her aides has sent us a pre-recorded message from Eve already. She said it was to overcome a possible time delay," the Communications Officer replied.

Scanlon pressed a blinking icon on the table and Eve's head appeared life-sized above it. "Hello, Olivia. I thought I'd get to work on the Order's next project in this region early. This is a rich recruiting pool, and I couldn't believe you didn't already have ships in orbit. The people here are destitute, and technologically stupid. We'll see thousands of recruits within the month, then millions will follow. Before long, I believe we'll have full control of every major city and this will be the greatest Order Outpost in the Cluster. I couldn't wait. You may as well attend to other matters. We'll speak about this when time permits, I'm sure."

Enraged, Scanlon turned away from the table again and took a few deep breaths. Everyone was watching, except for Rinder, she was sure. He was an expert at occupying himself with something else while she put her thoughts together. When she felt reason begin to return, she looked to Gisa. She whispered to her clearly and quickly. "This is a failing on multiple fronts. Citadel's representative gave me the impression that no one else knew about this world or its occupants. Someone made sure Eve knew, and I've been undermined. I'll make sure Eve and her people are made aware of who is in charge in The Cluster. You will contact Citadel and ask them if they told Eve about this. I suspect they have a leak and am sure that they'll plug it. You are my emissary in this. It is an incredible opportunity for you. Assign whatever else you are working on to people you trust."

"I will, thank you, Admiral," Gisa replied.

"Dismissed," Scanlon said as she turned back towards one of the Ascendant's Communications Officers. "Check the manufacturing and programming records for the Tier Two Aid Pods. You are looking for a special access code in the software that allows for override control."

The Officer looked to Rear Admiral Rinder, who nodded and said; "Her orders are my orders while she's on the bridge, Officer."

"Yes, Sir," he replied before rushing back to his section.

"You're going to take this from her," Rinder said under his breath.

"Yes. If I can. I'll see what I can do to salvage the situation. Is the rest of the battlegroup finished their wormhole transit?" Scanlon asked.

"Yes. The full group is here, and we're making our way towards Tiy slowly, as you ordered."

"No change in orders. Now we know there are people on Tiy looking through telescopes. Best we don't come up on them as though we're invading," Scanlon said, glancing at the half dozen communication team members who were frantically scrolling through search results at the other end of the bridge.

"Do I have to mention..." Rinder trailed off on purpose.

She knew what he was trying to remind her of. It was something he didn't want to say aloud. "The Overlord doesn't like infighting," she whispered to him. "I know. I'm going to put her under my boot quickly, don't worry. She's a figurehead with a Base Ship. I'll make sure she's just a figurehead after this."

"Ma'am," a different Officer from Communications addressed as he rushed to her side and saluted.

Returning his salute, she asked; "Well?"

"We found the override code. It's tuned to several transponders in this battlegroup, including the governing module on this ship. It'll work. The Base Ship won't be able to interfere."

"Bring the pod's controls online right here," Scanlon said, pointing to a section of the display table in front of her.

The Communications Officer looked back at his section and nodded, pointing at the table. A few seconds later the controls for the pods appeared along with a map indicating the location of each one. "Now I wait for her to finish deployment," Scanlon said, sitting on a stool.

"Then?" Rear Admiral Rinder asked, quietly amused.

"I have a little time to consider that," Scanlon said, opening a review window so she could start listening to the radio transmissions coming for Tiy. "Make sure we have the advantage against her Base Ship."

"Yes, Ma'am," Rear Admiral Rinder said, retreating to his command seat.

Chapter 23

The Weight

DISCOVERING that there was a whole new situation developing on Tiy involving two billion humans who were using technology from earth's early twentieth century made Alice feel worse than ever. If Zarrix was looking for subjects for whatever he was doing, then there was a resource he would go after in a heartbeat. It was unlikely that Haven Fleet would do a thing to protect them since they were already stretched thin between the home system and Cefa.

Being told that the Clever Class Corvette she stole was hers in trade for a pile of debt mattered less thanks to the dark cloud she felt all around her. The thought that she could have done something to stop Zarrix when she met him years ago wouldn't leave her alone.

"Should we change the name of this ship to the Clever Dream? You know, officially?" Lewis asked hopefully.

Sometimes he utterly failed at reading the mood of his human companions. Alice closed her eyes and let her head fall back against the rest in the copilot's seat. "Go ahead."

They had re-entered trans-dimensional space. There was no sign of the planetary system that they'd seen Zarrix in. As usual, the geography between the energetic dimension and her home space didn't match up in a way she could predict. Normally that went unnoticed, but the main drive of the Clever Dream didn't have the same kind of sensory tunnel vision that the Quad Drives did. She and Noah charted their course so they kept to the safest route, moving through the paths of least electronic interference and resistance.

"I think I'm getting the hang of this. I know, I don't have to do navigational routing, the software can do all the work, but charting faster than light routes through the ED is getting easier. I think I'm getting a better idea of what to avoid," Noah said as he slipped out of the pilot's seat.

"With my help, of course," Lewis added.

"Yeah, man. Not like I could do this math in my head," Noah said as his hands found their way to Alice's shoulders. His fingers traced the shape of her muscles through her vacsuit then went to work. It was one of his gifts. Her suit's synthetic muscle layer had a massage mode, she made sure it was included in all the custom armour she had, but she liked his hands more. Noah was attentive, had a good feel for how she wanted to be touched, and even surprised her in the best of ways by hitting the right spots. It was nice to be with someone who wasn't all thumbs, and the tension she'd been holding started to unravel.

After a moment of letting herself relax, she shook her head and got out of the copilot's seat. "Not now."

"Okay, yeah, I guess we should get more work done on our way to Tiy," Noah said. "We'll be there soon."

"It's not that," Alice said on her way towards the bridge hatch.

"Ah, okay," Noah said as he started for the pilot's seat.

A spike of irritation emanated from him, striking her empathic sense like an insult. In the few seconds she started to relax, she'd let her blocks fall, leaving herself open to reading his emotions. Normally, she'd adjust for the slip, and put that section of her walls back up, or even block her sense entirely. This time she let his irritation at her through and was surprised that it faded, but he didn't let it go as she stood halfway through the bridge hatchway. It finally started fading, but she recognized that it left a residual mark on him, one that could last hours or longer. She'd seen resentment and irritation last longer while guarding the Prince, who was surrounded by people who resented him for his position and would hold on to the slightest insult for weeks regardless of whether or not it was intentional.

Finally, she closed her empathic sense off and turned towards him. "What was that?"

"What? I didn't say anything," Noah said, half standing and turning towards her.

"Just now, you were pissed off at me for something. What is it?"

"You're reading me again?" Noah asked.

The furrow on his brow was just as clear as anything her empathic sense could pick up. This was sometimes a sore spot for him. That feeling, the irritation she picked up was more important to Alice then. She had to know what it was all about. "I let my guard down for a second and you nearly knocked me down with that... whatever it was. You were pissed."

"That's one of those moments you weren't supposed to know about," Noah said.

"But I caught it by mistake, and I just want to know why you were so angry."

"I am so lost," Lewis muttered.

"My nose was out of joint a bit, that's all, I'll be fine," Noah replied, ignoring the artificial intelligence.

"But why? It's a simple question," Alice pressed.

"Fine," Noah replied. "You put your shields up as soon as you have something to brood about, and I didn't know how to get past 'em so I was pissed. Minh says your dad does the same shit, and..."

"So you've been talking to Minh about how difficult I am?" Alice asked, crossing to the middle of the small bridge.

Noah was out of his seat, and he met her there. "Yeah. I'm still trying to figure out how I'm doing with you. Everything seems fine, then something comes up and you get quiet. Yeah, it pisses me off, but I hide that until I get over it so I can find the words to get you to talk again."

"I am not that complicated," Alice shot back.

Noah's laugh came short and sudden, as though it surprised him as much as it enraged her. "You are crazy complicated!"

Opening her mouth to speak, words failed Alice so she turned away until they came. Much of her anger was replaced by red-hot hurt, and all she could think to say was; "I'm sorry."

"Hey, whoa, no, I mean," Noah's arm was slipping around her shoulders so he could turn her towards him gently. "I don't know what I meant."

"You said what you meant. I'm not reading you, but I know," Alice said.

"Whoa, this got big fast, I was just pissed that I had nothing to say about Zarrix and you blaming yourself," he was trying to look her in the eye.

"How can anything be bigger than that?" Alice asked, not actually interested in the answer.

What he said surprised her then. "Us. The biggest thing I've got going on is you and me. I'd turn my back on everything for you, Alice. I kinda did."

He was talking about his business in the Shattered End. There were people there working for him that were handling entire ships, trading guns, and equipment. He'd built an organization with security, a presence on the black market and everything that came with it. He was supposed to visit her for a weekend, but he was being led further and further away from everything he'd built. He'd even lost the thing that started it all - the Corsair. All the while, he'd kept whatever scrambling that caused in the Shattered End away from her for the most part, but she knew that he took a little time here and there to talk to the people he left behind to take care of things. "I'm sorry I lured you away from everything you worked so hard for."

"Oh, man, that's not what I meant. Don't blame yourself for that." Then, in a less sympathetic voice, he said; "Actually, don't blame yourself for any of this shit. The supply problems I'm having, the Edxi problems the galaxy's had, and whatever else you think you started. I mean, maybe that's my problem: I think you're more complicated than you are. Maybe it's simpler than that. All this shit would have happened with or without you."

Later it would be difficult to tell anyone why that made her so angry, but at the moment Alice felt absolutely justified in being furious. "So I'm simple and uncomplicated now?"

Noah nodded. "Wouldn't that be a relief? I've been sitting here wishing I could read minds too, but maybe I should really start hoping you forget how to do it."

"I'm an empath, not a telepath," Alice retorted hotly.

"Okay, fine, but you've gotta see my point," Noah said as if that wrapped the whole argument up.

"Not even a little!"

"Okay, man, here it is: You can read me whenever the hell you want, but you're goddamned impossible for me to figure out unless you're having a good time. I can usually tell what someone's about to do from across the room, I grew up with cold readers and scam artists, but you're as bad as your Dad when you're all broody!"

"Are you kidding? Compared to him I have no chill whatsoever. Ayan can read me like a book!"

"Because she learned how to read him! I don't know what to say when you start feeling sorry for yourself, and this shit with Zarrix might send you so far down that road that I won't ever see the girl I just spent the weekend with again."

"Sorry for myself? You think that's all this is? Just self-pity?" Alice asked through clenched teeth.

"Yeah, and I don't know how to handle that with you because it's all wrapped up in your self-importance bullshit. It's not even your fault, Fleet Darling." The last was said with a surprising amount of disdain.

"You're jealous," Alice said, sure she figured out what was going on with Noah without the aid of her empathic gift.

"Hell no!" he howled, taking a few steps in a circle that ended when he was facing her from across the bridge. "I don't think you realize how much you've bought into being one of the best, the brightest and the most privileged little princess in the Haven System, but that's all real for you. So damned real that you think the Edxi are your fault because you made a delivery. I mean, those eggs would have been shipped over by someone eventually, and whoever did it probably wouldn't blame themselves for a trillion people dying, but no, it had to be my bloody girlfriend! Now I get to sit around hoping that you eventually brood well enough to sort your own shit out, because you're not going to let me in to help you out."

"It's better than telling someone you love to shut a part of themselves off whenever you're around!" Alice didn't think about what she was saying until the words were between them.

The silence felt airless and cold. Noah stared at her, and when he did speak, the words came quietly. "Yeah, you're right. That's a part of you, I get it. I'm just used to being able to get over my own shit before you overhear it, so I can show you my best side. So a reaction doesn't get us screaming at each other. Usually my big mouth gets me in trouble, this is new. I'm sorry, I'm just sorry," he turned away.

Feeling a dreaded kind of finality in the moment, Alice reached after him. Catching his arm, she turned him around. "I understand. Self editing, I get it. I don't always want to hear what you're feeling either, I mean, it can get confusing. Sometimes it does feel like I'm intruding, but…"

"It's like you watching all my journal entries all over again. When we met, you already knew me, or at least who I was on Iora," Noah said, turning towards her.

"I didn't realize how unfair that was, but I was already falling in love," Alice told him, watching his expression brighten a little. "Now I never want to be anywhere you aren't."

"Same," Noah said, taking her hand. "But we've gotta

make a deal. When you start brooding and I ask what it's all about, you tell me. You take way too much shit on when it's not your fault."

"Okay. Tell me when I'm doing it though, because I don't even know," Alice replied. Things were looking up, and relief was replacing outrage.

"You haven't asked what you get in the deal," Noah said with a salesman's smile.

"Oh? What's the trade?"

"I'm going to have to get used to you being in here," Noah said, pointing to his temple. "Just do me a favour and tell me when the channel's open, okay?"

"I will." The relief she felt was surprisingly powerful. Alice found herself grinning.

"You're going to have to get ready for some knee-jerk bull-shit though. I edit the crap outta myself, so don't hold it against me, okay?"

"I won't. I get tired when my head's wide open though, so I keep that off most of the time anyway," Alice explained, looking down at their fingers and how they were slowly slipping together.

"Yeah, but now you're good if you want to feel around and see how things are first hand, you know. I didn't realize I was being an ass about your empathy stuff until it came up with Minh the other night. He told me I'd have to accept you - empathy and all - or say goodbye eventually. I guess you catching one of my knee-jerk moments before I got to tell you that and make sure you knew you'd see some of the ugly crap in my head made me nuts. That, and I got used to seeing you happy, I guess."

"I get it. Now I know, and I won't judge you for those kinds of reactions, but I've got to be able to ask about them if they come up sometimes, especially if they're about me," Alice said. "It really frustrates you when I get quiet?"

"Well, mostly this time. The whole Zarrix thing just isn't your fault, right? I mean, maybe we can do something about it now by telling everyone who he is, what you saw, and that he's around, but back then? Unless there's something I'm missing, there just wasn't anything for you to blame yourself for," Noah replied with a shrug.

"You're right, I know it, but it'll take a while for me to convince myself, you know?"

"Yeah," Noah agreed as they came together in a close embrace.

"There really isn't anything you could have done that would have changed the outcome, Alice," Lewis said. "I've been over the reconstructed recordings of that encounter several thousand times as I ran simulations of different outcomes. Even the most violent acts would have had a minimum survival chance of seventy-one point six percent for Zarrix."

"Thank you, Lewis," Alice said. Then a thought occurred to her. "How much do you share with Minh about us?"

"Well, a lot, but nothing you have to worry about. Nothing, you know, too personal. That'd be like sharing the hotter details with your uncle. No way."

"Okay, that's good to know," Alice laughed a little.

"I just wasn't sure if it was clear. I must say, if this is the resolution to your lover's spat, then it came quickly. I don't approve of some of the arguments either one of you made at different points and I would say therapy would be more efficient, but your resolution was swift," Lewis said, his words only half heeded by the pair.

Alice looked into Noah's eyes. "I promise to share the bad stuff with you."

"I might not handle it all super well, you know. I'll try though," Noah replied.

"That's all, just try," Alice said, resting her head on his shoulder.

"And I'll do my best to keep the knee-jerk reactions down," Noah said. "And to stop telling my crew about what you're like when the vacsuit comes off."

Alice stiffened and started blushing immediately. "What?"

"I'm just kidding! Really," Noah laughed.

Alice poked him in the side, making him wince a little. "Better be."

"I am," Noah said as she relaxed.

Then, exaggerating a sigh, she said; "Well, it would only be fair if you did. I share everything with Ash and Faloo. You should hear what she says about Minh, and Faloo's had a few conquests she likes to talk about."

"You're kidding, right?" Noah asked with a chuckle. Then as the silence grew longer, he cleared his throat. "Right?"

She was about to admit that, yes, she was mostly kidding. They talked, sure, but most of the details he cared about were suggested at best. Before she could explain that, the Navigation Console beeped.

Alice flashed a smile at him and left the circle of their arms for the copilot's seat saying; "Maybe. Looks like we're ten minutes away from the Triton."

Chapter 24

A Probe?

THE LOWER HALF of the Triton's bridge was a hive of activity. As soon as Alice and Noah came in through the rear hatchway, Iruuk seemed to come out of nowhere. "You didn't even tell us that you were leaving," he said, peevish.

Faloo was behind him, her arms crossed, brows furrowed. "A message would have been nice. We had to find out what was going on from your mother. She was quite kind, and told us all about you stealing the new Clever Dream and the criminal charges."

"Criminal charges?" Noah asked before Alice could.

"While there was a deal for you to pay for the Clever Dream, Haven Fleet still wants you and Noah for questioning about its theft. The charge they plan on arresting you on is Theft of a Military Vessel," Iruuk explained. "I'm pretty sure they just needed something to charge you for and only want to know how you got the ship out of a secure hangar, but you could still serve some prison time if you return to the Haven System without clearing that up."

"Okay, I'll give them a call when I get a minute," Alice said, wondering why Ayan didn't tell her about it. It would have to wait. There was a pair of irritated Nafalli to apologize to. "Sorry I left you behind, you two. Long story short: Lewis stowed away and followed us here, and I thought the only way to keep him and the Clever Dream was to run off for a bit. We were pretty sure our next stop was the Shattered End."

"While everyone else figured things out," Faloo grumbled. "Well, next time take us with you, or at least tell us where you're going, okay?"

Jake, who was standing in front of a large holographic projection of the inside of an old looking room, motioned for her to come over. "I will, I'm glad I was able to come back so soon, I'd miss you guys in minutes."

"Aw, that's sweet," Faloo said, giving her a welcoming embrace.

"I thought you said we were giving her tough love," Iruuk sighed.

"I can only keep that up for so long," Faloo replied with a shrug. "Oh, one more thing. Your father is in a bad mood. I think he was looking forward to going to the Shattered End too, and there was something about a cancelled mission."

"He was planning on taking a crew that would have included me onto the Clever Dream as soon as you arrived then going down to the planet to get a scout ship," Iruuk added. "They sent something else instead. I agree with him. A ship with people would have been better."

Jake sent her an impatient look then turned back to the large blurry hologram he, Ayan and several other officers were focused on. The obscuring field kept her from seeing what it was, but he was as clear as ever. "I think I have to be over there now." Alice gave Iruuk a hug on her way by. It was extended a little as he gave her a generous squeeze then drew Noah in as well before letting them both go.

As they walked to that part of the Control Centre, Noah whispered; "God, it's like having furry parents. I'm not complaining, but, you know…"

"I know," Alice nodded. What she saw when she passed through the invisible privacy barrier made her stop so suddenly that Iruuk nearly knocked her down. "Is that Eve's Base Ship?" Alice asked as she pointed to the green, brown and blue planet that was hanging in the air. The room that was on display was beneath it.

"It is, and the Ascendant along with its entire battle group is in high orbit nearby," Jake replied.

Minh-Chu leaned on a display table behind him, shaking his head. "This is about as bad as it gets. Oz says that Lorander is doing research on this world, trying to see if they have anything on it, but it'll take time. The records they need are either on some disconnected drive somewhere, or not in this galaxy."

"Okay, but what's going on?" Alice asked, still not sure what she was seeing. There were hundreds of hot spots marked on the planet and dots showing that the Base Ship was launching several objects down from orbit, and it was obvious that the Triton was hiding somewhere but other than that, she didn't know much of anything.

Ayan approached the hologram. "We're hidden, cloaked next to Tiy's far moon. The Communications Team has been working on decoding messages between the Order ships, but we may be a ways off in figuring out what's going on. Other than that, there's a message of goodwill featuring Eve that's on repeat, directing people on the planet to the nearest aid drop. We've detected hundreds, that's what the markings of the planet are, except for this one, which is a government building."

"I got to remotely fly a cloaked probe right in there," Minh-Chu said. "It's hovering in a room where that poor guy is about to get interrogated."

"Well, it doesn't look like an interrogation room, there are sofas, someone brought tea a while ago, and people have been going in and out pretty regularly," one of the Intelligence Staff said. Alice didn't recognize him, but he looked almost too young to be there. Before he walked away he flashed her a little smile and whispered; "I'm a big fan." He was gone before she could thank him, moving on to the upper level of the bridge.

Jake set the view of the room's interior turning slowly with a gesture. "I'm guessing something important is about to happen in that room, and they don't want him going anywhere. There are guards at the door and outside by the windows. It doesn't look like he wants to be there either."

"That brings us to the next bit," Ayan said. "Our translation program barely had to run. They speak a version of English that very closely resembles a dialect from the old British Empire."

"How did you know to follow him?" Alice asked.

Jacob replied, bringing the image of a caravan of heavy trucks up beside the room. "We tracked the origin point of the distress signal from the Citadel scout craft to a house right next to it. There were transmissions to that location from the Base Ship and we caught a radio interview with this guy. When our probe got to the area, he was in custody. We followed the trucks."

Minh-Chu rolled his eyes. "Your Dad thought we'd be taking a Citadel scout ship on board by now. I told him, it looked too easy."

"I can hope, right?" Jake replied.

"So, what's the chance you'll need Samurai Squadron here?" Minh-Chu asked the room in general.

"Well, Oz isn't sending support, so you won't be joining a larger effort," Ayan replied. "This isn't a fight we can win, even with a whole fighter wing."

"All those new allies, and he can't spare a battlegroup or two?" Minh-Chu asked, feigning surprise.

"Well, alliances take time to sort out, you know. They may have signed a treaty, but they may take months to figure out how to live up to their responsibilities," explained Gelana.

"We know," Jake replied. It was clear that it wasn't the first time that Gelana had added an explanation for something that everyone was already aware of to the conversation.

"How is the decryption coming?" Ayan asked.

"Well, but slowly. I can help with the work from here, you don't have to worry," Gelana replied.

"You should join the main group at Communications anyway please," Ayan said with stiff politeness.

"Yes, Ma'am," Gelana replied, walking away at a brisk pace. "I suppose they could use my superior scientific insight."

"Right, so instead of a raid, we have a probe," Jake said, motioning towards the holographic image of the room, which looked like a perfect period piece.

"So, I guess I shouldn't warm up the Clever Dream," Alice said.

"Actually, I want to keep that option open. Does Noah

know the ship well enough to run the systems as your First Officer?" Jake asked.

"Sure, still learning though. Lewis can pick up my slack," Noah replied.

"All right. Alice stays here so she can keep up with what's going on. That way her ship will be ready the moment I need to send her down to Tiy. I'd like to go myself, but I'm not the diplomat she could be. Besides, I hope to be busy doing something else by the end of the day," Jake ordered.

"I have no problem being your first officer, Captain," Noah whispered to Alice. "Feels right, actually."

He'd picked up on something that Alice was sharply aware of. Her father took the command role as though he was still an Admiral. He'd even put her in a dangerous diplomatic role. "The ship doesn't have a single round loaded and our gear is still in my quarters. I don't even have a full crew."

"Remmy's crew is ready, just in case you need them and the deck teams are ready to load everything up," Jake replied, looking at Noah. "You get the ship ready and make sure everyone's tucked into their turrets, armed for anything while Alice stays here and watches the show."

There would be a time for her to put Jake in his place, and she was already looking forward to it, but Alice didn't feel like it had come yet. "Aye," she looked to Noah and nodded.

He left with Iruuk on his heels. "See you down there, Captain."

Alice took her place between her parents and looked at the hologram of one burly man sitting on the sofa, staring down at the white carpet. "So, you've been watching this guy for how long?"

"About half an hour, but we're monitoring over three dozen drop sites," Ayan said, bringing up smaller holograms. In most of them there were ragged looking people lined up in front of two-storey drop bases. They came away with large ration bowls generously piled with hot rice, vegetables and savory-looking sauce. Each was topped with slices of boiled tilah egg, a fairly bland but protein-rich staple from the Rose System. Then there were the five holograms hovering around the main features where the citizens of Tiy were attacking the small drop bases with primitive bolt action rifles. The doors to the pods were closed, and one of them easily withstood the blast of an explosive.

Ayan spoke as her daughter took a closer look at a few of the images. "There seems to be a no violence policy. Each pod starts to close whenever a fight breaks out or it comes under attack. There's also an attendant inside that's staying behind a barrier. They let one injured person in at a time, treat them, then move on to the next. We're watching that room because it's the closest thing we have to getting an inside peek at what their biggest government is thinking. Hopefully, they talk to him soon."

"I'm pretty sure the show will start the moment I leave," Minh-Chu said, straightening up. "I'm going to get my pilots in their fighters, just in case."

"We've got seven alert fighters in the punters," Slick said from the highest seat on the deck, the Space Superiority Command Chair. "I'd feel better with a full fifteen plus the Raven and Clever Dream."

"I can give you twenty-one seasoned pilots in Archangel fighters and nine newbie nail-biters watching from the squad room," Minh-Chu said as he started for a side door.

"Better than seven," Slick replied. "Good hunting, Ronin."

"The Raven will have to run with a skeleton crew," Jake said. "You pick the lucky few, Slick."

"Aye, already looking through a roster. I hope we don't have to do any fighting here, though. There are fifteen fighters on patrol around that Base Ship and the Ascendant's battle group look pretty serious," Slick said.

"Better to be ready," Jake said.

"Is Remmy okay?" Alice asked.

"No, there's a complication with the enhancement protocol he's on," Ayan replied. "He's resting comfortably in medical now. He's put his team in your hands until he can get back on his feet. Well, except for Pixie, who's staying with the Raven as her pilot."

Alice made a mental note to visit Remmy, though she was sure he'd have no shortage of company. He was one of the most popular people aboard the Triton. The door to the holographic room opened, admitting a grey-haired gentleman in a suit.

Two more men followed. One was overly large, the other was in a grey military uniform. "Here we go," Jake said, enlarging the image of the room a little more.

Trey had found and expanded the limits of his patience several times over as he waited in the Premier's Office. It was more like a living room featuring a large desk at one end. Three of the four walls had big, clear windows that overlooked expansive, green grounds. They had kept him there, and made sure he was comfortable, but he couldn't stop thinking about his brother. The longer he was stuck in the office, the more likely it was that he'd never see Orner again. When the door opened and all three lesser pillars of government walked in, he told them; "I told you everything as soon as I arrived. It was recorded on that magnetic wire machine, you can listen to it whenever you want."

Minister Haas sat down, motioning for him to do the same. "We listened to it twice."

The rotund fellow, Keeper Daro, sat carefully, as though he was afraid the armchair would break beneath him. "The recordings about the scout ship that we can't find any sign of, and of your brother, who became as wise as a prophet overnight. Yes, twice. What a story."

"If you don't believe me, then there's no point in me staying. I have to see if I can find Orner before he's gone for good," Trey replied. He wanted to leave, but found himself sitting instead. It was difficult to refuse Minister Haas anything. He'd voted for him, after all.

"Not until we find out whether or not you're lying to us," Keeper Daro said as he undid his suit jacket's struggling buttons.

"That's not our purpose here," Minister Haas said. "There's plenty of evidence that what Trey here has said is most likely true. His neighbours and friends haven't seen Orner in days. Neither of them has been to town for a while either, and there's no sign of some other secret project that would change their behaviour," the military man said. While he'd heard Daro speak about the evils of technology several times, Trey never heard of the man in grey. He introduced himself. "I'm Logi. Strategic Intelligence. What you have been able to uncover with the help of a few civilians and archaeologists is impressive. I've been a reader of yours for years. Never subscribing under my own name, of course."

"Thank you, every sub helps," Trey replied automatically. "You must know a thing or two."

"More than you could imagine," Logi replied with a little smile. "You will too before you leave."

"Good to see you're making friends," Keeper Daro said

before turning towards Trey. "You know more about this invasion and the lies this Eve has been spreading than anyone. More than you've shared, I'm guessing. Do you understand that the whole Origin Faith has been called into question? It is the bedrock our people stand on, and the truth. We were created here three hundred eighteen years ago by the benevolent Risago, the Prime Creator, and…"

"It's funny what one day can change, Daro," Logi said, patting the large man on the shoulder. "Yesterday most people would call Trey crazy for claiming that we come from anywhere but here. Now all but your most devout followers are looking to the sky, and they'd just as easily say that you're absolutely head-wrong."

"I am not! This is sacrilege! Considering alternate origins is a sin, and a crime in five counties," Daro said, turning in his chair so he was shouting up at Logi.

"Calm down, Daro, you'll have another pulmonary episode," Minister Haas said. Then he turned towards Trey. "I'm sorry, this debate has been going on for a long time, starting well before I took office. You're on one extreme edge, while Daro is on the other. The theory of Originism versus Colonization. I bet you could imagine what's happening far from here, where the leaders of our nation are in a secure bunker."

"Probably having a similar argument," Trey guessed aloud.

Minister Haas looked towards Logi as though they knew something no one else did, then settled back on the sofa across from Trey. "You'd be wrong. Thank the stars, you'd be wrong. It's actually pretty serene there. Even our counterparts are pretty calm about all this."

"How could they be?" Daro asked. "My leadership is so

deep in consideration that I haven't heard from them in half an hour."

"That's because they're drafting a statement with the leadership of this country. Your whole faith is about to change drastically. He and the Prime Minister are in hiding because they can't say for sure what the response will be. They've both given me the responsibility of running things above ground, much like your leadership has," Minister Haas said as Logi nodded and Daro started turning red.

"No, that can't be true. The leadership have been forced into hiding because the people are rising up, fighting the lies that come in those little houses someone is dropping from planes." Daro's indignation was powerful, but seeing him instead of listening to him shout on the radio seemed much less impressive. "The Grand Keeper would never choose you over me, his voice in this country. I am a Keeper of Origins representing my leadership as much as you…"

"I'm afraid your position is about to become obsolete," Logi said, taking a seat beside Trey. "The truth is, we are a colony of humans who rejected technology. A very wealthy man named Risago, who was also the leader of a cult called the Renewalists, came here with the help of a Lorander colony ship. You have a piece of it in your basement," he said, nodding at Trey.

"Sacrilege," Daro said under his breath, staring at Logi. "Hidden so my people couldn't certify it as a fake and bring you up on charges, I'm sure."

Logi went on, turning all his attention back towards Daro. "When Risago and his followers arrived, he had them leave all technology on the Lorander ship. It was sabotaged, and exploded in orbit. The thirty-five thousand people who settled here pledged to restrict their technology to a pre-steam level, and that's how it was for over two hundred years. Your people, the Origin Keepers, sent bashers out to destroy anything that moved progress along. I'm descended from a long line of people who developed new technology in secret, and we kept a history right from the beginning. Keepers have burned dozens of my ancestors alive over the years."

"We stopped doing that generations ago," Daro said with a dismissing wave.

"Two generations ago. That's not such a long time," Logi replied. "It's amazing that our military has been able to build what will save us from invasion today in the last fifty years. Since the Origin Clergy stopped sending official bashers out, we've been able to bring basic technology back to the people, but what we've built underground, in secret, is much more impressive."

"That's why I wanted you here, Trey," Minister Haas said. "The vote has come in. I know what's going to happen in a few minutes but I still want to hear what you have to say about our visitors from space. Do you think this is an invasion and that we should resist, or that they really do come in peace? You seemed uncertain on the radio."

"I think trying to fight them is a mistake. At least, with the technology I saw in the last war we had," Trey answered carefully. "As for their motives, I still think we should examine them carefully. They'll ask us to change quickly in exchange and it doesn't seem like they believe in the democratic system."

"Are you sure they're so advanced compared to us? What we have hidden away, what we are about to use is well beyond what you've seen used in the battles on this world," Logi asked.

"It would have to be at least a couple centuries advanced compared to us," Trey said, hoping he wasn't about to see an ineffective show of force that would invite horrible retribution.

"You're about to see what we've been able to build," Logi said proudly. "I'm sure we'll bring that giant ship down, at least. Then we'll use whatever we find to advance the technology we already have and anyone who wants to take advantage of us will think twice about it. Oh, and the Keepers of Origin will be wiped out completely."

"We're stronger than this, it'll be a long…" Daro was silenced as the ground shook. Windows rattled as Trey was almost dumped out of his seat by the quake. "What's going on?"

"Our gun emplacements are firing now. That's only the first volley," Logi replied.

"I'm guessing the leadership voted to fight," Trey said as the building settled.

The next thunderous volley drowned out the Minister's response.

Chapter 25

Orner

SEEING the government take Trey away was a shock to Orner. As the trucks came into the yard, he followed the directions of Moxa's advice, who told him to activate the cloaking system she'd given him. Orner regretted it immediately. He adored her until only hours before, seeing no one as more welcoming or caring.

That, to his quiet embarrassment, had started to fade quickly. All it took was a short discussion with Eve, who told him that what he was experiencing was part of the accelerated learning pace he was enjoying. He wasn't just taking in new knowledge, learning how to do so much that he never dreamt of, but, according to her, he was investing just as much in new relationships, and they'd seem critically important until he met new people.

He doubted it at first, but he started to see the roots of

what Eve suggested and of Trey's accusations in how Moxa was treating him. Moxa was a doting teacher, and until Eve had a short conversation with her, it seemed like she went to a lot of effort to not only earn his loyalty, but to turn his head away from Trey.

By the time he paid his brother a visit, Orner was starting to realize that Trey was the one who should have been his guide through everything. Even though he may not know anything about the technological marvels he saw, Trey always had Orner's best interest in mind, and it might have slowed things down, but there would be much less to regret in the end.

As Orner watched the government drag his brother away, he realized that there was plenty to regret. Moxa was calling him back to the ship, it was time to leave. That's when Orner finally asked himself; *what would Trey do if he was in my position?*

A journalist to the core, Trey would go where the biggest story was. It was something that Orner remembered his brother telling him about the years he spent as a journalist in town. "It takes a lot of people a long time to develop a sense for where the big stories are. On a normal news day, that's the talent a lot of us lean on. Then there are the other days, the spectacular times, when a big story pops right up in front of you, and you could regret missing it for the rest of your life if you don't follow it right away. Sometimes that's dangerous, but one story can put you on top."

Orner didn't really understand what that meant completely back then, but the pieces of his brother's philosophy started falling together like his favourite magnet puzzle as he ran through the house, picking up a few keepsakes as he went. That puzzle cube was the last thing he snatched from his dresser. There were three shapes he could accomplish before he was changed. A square and rectangles of two different lengths. He wondered what he could do with the puzzle with his new potential. It was something he'd have to try later. A funny thought struck him then. The less he obsessed over Moxa and the new world she introduced him to, the more he found himself thinking about Trey.

What would his brother do? Well, Trey was in the hands of the government. Hopefully, he could trade information there. The only other place he'd be if he didn't have his little brother to worry about, was on a ship. He'd get as close to the leadership of the people who were visiting their planet as he could. That was where he'd find the biggest story. The only question was what the headline would be. In Orner's opinion, it would either look something like:

BENEVOLENT COUSINS BEAR GIFTS FROM THE STARS

Or it could be something like:

INVADERS PROMISE PROSPERITY FOR INDEN-TUREMENT.

While Orner didn't expect the second headline to be more likely, he was becoming more open to considering the possibility of a darker purpose by the minute. "Are you coming? We have to go. We're going to see Eve in person," Moxa asked through his subdermal communicator.

"I'm running out of the house right now. Where's your ship?" Orner asked. "I can't see it on the overlay."

"I'm landing right beside the aid pod. People saw it drop here. They're on their way. Hurry," Moxa replied.

Orner was out of the house and up the ramp in less than a minute. One thing he never lacked was physical fitness. Pair that with a large frame that allowed him to look over everyone's head and lift things that most people had no business even trying to heft, he knew the Order would want him as a soldier at the very least. Human power was still useful. That didn't explain why they were about to see Eve. "Why does she want to see me?" he asked as he sat down in a passenger seat behind Moxa as she piloted the ship up.

"She's going to be making her next announcement, and she's started showing footage of you that I captured weeks ago in town. Here, take a look."

"You were recording me?" Orner asked as a window opened in the video overlay that was printed onto his eyes. The playback made him cringe as he watched himself looking at Marima's vegetable stand. The old woman always had a smile for him and often gave him a carrot, or sweet tuber to chew on. He was always careful to keep his hands behind his back because touching food someone else would buy later was rude.

The conversation they were having was muted, but Orner recalled that Marima was telling him about the fall harvest, and that it was about to start. It wasn't the first time. It was probably the same discussion they'd had every year at that time since he was a small boy. It was difficult for him to see how slack his jaw was, or how he regarded the vegetables, inspecting their shape while making a real effort to look with his eyes, not with his hands. Eve spoke over the video.

"This is Orner. According to his brother, who has taken care of him since their parents passed years ago, he was caught in the birth canal and nearly suffocated when he was born. For all his life, Orner has had a diminished capacity for learning and thought in general. By all accounts, he's a kind man with a temper that has only appeared twice in his entire life. Amongst you, the people of Tiy, he has been a gentle giant, willing to help anyone, even to his own detriment." As she spoke, video clips that demonstrated her point played.

The picture they painted was as simple as her words.

Orner carries a pair of large tires for Anny, the mechanic who took care of their truck. Him holding a large door in place while Urke, the owner of the powdered goods store climbed a ladder so he could put the top hinges in, and finally one short video clip where he was loading large boxes of paper into the truck with his brother. They didn't show Trey, who worked just as hard.

As Eve finished, they showed Orner stretching, wincing at his sore back. "We saw Orner for who he is, and using our advanced medical technology, have given him the mental capacity, the potential he deserves. In a few minutes, I'll meet him in person for the first time and you'll see who he is now. Kindness is ever-present in him, but there is so much more. We're offering this to everyone with a handicap. So take the disc you're watching this on with you, or take one from the many aid stations that have landed on your world. I'll return in moments with him."

By the end of the playback, Orner could see the hangar doors of a ship that was impossibly large. A round, bulbous thing with smaller vessels moving around it like parasitical fish following a whale, it was unlike anything he'd seen in the Saturday Picture Shows. They passed into a hangar, then into a smaller one, and the controls were locked. The Base Ship took control, landing the ship in a slot, and then drawing it further in. "The ship is being pulled into the Messenger's transit system, like a trolley car on a road," Moxa explained.

"I understand. There were several transit cars in the virtual base," Orner replied.

"Is everything okay? You seem different," Moxa asked.

I'm worried about my brother, he thought. "I'm just nervous about meeting Eve," he said.

"I understand, I'm a little nervous too. I've never met her. This is a big step for me too," Moxa said softly.

Her sympathy seemed shallower somehow. True, it made sense that she would be nervous. On the other hand, he was further away from home than he'd ever been, could barely fly a ship at all so the possibility of getting back there on his own was remote. He was also in space, seeing spaceships that were so large and complicated that he couldn't fathom where or how they were made. Orner's new understanding of technology helped, but he felt like the wonder of it all could turn horrible at any moment as he felt the lure of a feeling. It was the dark sensation of being trapped, the horror of being too distant from anything that felt familiar to him. His hand slipped into his pocket, where his fingers found the magnet puzzle and fiddled with it a little while they moved through the giant ship.

The rear hatch to the shuttle opened then and she led the way out. The room beyond was not what he expected. The glory of the stars was on full display through three-storey tall windows. The floor was soft and dark green like thick, uniformly cut grass. Circular seating dotted the large space with a few people in matching dark green Order of Eden uniforms working on holographic interfaces that were projected from the walls. The seating was reserved for well-dressed people in clothing that seemed to drink the light into their dark hues.

At a glance, Orner could see that the fashion, which was long and luxurious, was probably in imitation of Eve's style. She was beautiful, but so thin that she looked unhealthy. Her light green dress seemed to accentuate her slender form. She reminded him of a harvest time stick man he and his brother built when they were children.

Regardless of how startlingly gaunt she seemed, he was in awe of how she carried herself. It immediately felt like he was in the presence of someone with great confidence. Her smile made him want to grin in return, and when she regarded someone, it seemed all her focus was on them and everyone should attend. The guests on the plush seating in a semi-circle around watched her, and when Eve took Moxa's hands in hers, it felt like something historic was happening. "Moxa, I am honoured to finally meet you. The work you've done for us has been ground breaking."

"Thank you," Moxa said, looking up at her. It was interesting and impressive for Orner to watch someone who he looked up to, at least until a few hours ago, regard someone else with such reverence.

"You don't have to worry about any of the consequences of leaving Citadel," Eve said, still holding Moxa's hands, leaning down a little so they were almost nose to nose. "We're handling all that. You are free. You are a real person with individual rights." After a momentary pause, Eve announced; "Welcome to the Order of Eden."

The people in fancy dress applauded. Some clapped daintily, others were more open with their celebration, but none of them whooped or hollered the way Orner was used to. He clapped along for a moment, then he was struck still as Eve turned towards him, her brilliant green eyes looking into his as she strode across the floor in high heel shoes unlike any he'd seen. They were soundless thanks to the soft floor covering. Her smile, and her stare made him forget everything else. "Finally, Orner. Moxa brought your story to me and I knew you would be the one."

There was a pause during which he felt he should say something, but there were no words in his head or on his tongue. She slipped her hands into his and they felt dainty, small. "Hello," he managed, remembering the images of himself in the market, embarrassed at being overwhelmed.

"I can't wait to finish telling your story. Moxa informs me that you're interested in the military?"

"Yes, but I want to learn more first," Orner said, inwardly chastising himself for the simplicity of his words. There was so much to say about the whole new universe he was learning about, how he hoped his people would follow him into a new prosperous existence, and how he wanted to discover more about the galaxy.

"I've heard about that from Moxa. She is as impressed by your appetite for knowledge as she is by your kindness. You're going to…" then a man in a uniform, a Lieutenant, judging from the markings on his chest, rushed to Eve's side and whispered something in her ear.

One of Eve's hands slipped out of his and she brought a hologram up. It showed a number of red lines pointing towards the Base Ship. Then there was a faint echo, like the beating of a large drum in the distance. "Don't worry, we're all safe here," another officer cried out. "There are dozens of layers of safety and armour between us and the impacts, including kinetic energy shielding."

"Why are they firing on us? What are those weapons? Why didn't we see them?" Eve asked, her frustration growing with each question.

"The largest government fears us," the Lieutenant replied. "As for the weapons, they're large kinetic cannons firing iron-uranium shells, and they were in bunkers deep underground. We should retreat. Fresh scans indicate that each emplacement can fire every twenty seconds, so they may penetrate our shields."

"We would send the wrong message by retreating, The next transmission will have to be delayed, however. I'm sorry, Orner," Eve said as the Lieutenant beside her shook his head at something only he was seeing or hearing. "What is it?" Eve asked him peevishly.

"The first salvo caused our lateral shield generation system to reset," he replied.

"What does that mean, specifically?"

"The shields are down?" Orner guessed.

"Yes, Lateral Section Two is down," the officer replied. "Polar shielding is being overcharged to compensate and we're turning the ship."

"They're firing another salvo!" shouted one of the guests who brought up his own hologram featuring a view of the planet and the ship. His projection filled the space over their heads, and the crowd was shocked as several shells impacted the Messenger's armour.

"We know where their surface command centre is," the Lieutenant said, bringing up the image of the Ministry Compound for Orner's home county. "We've also located a bunker where they're probably hiding their upper leadership, but the command to fire these cannon emplacements is definitely being transmitted by the surface site."

Orner looked more closely and nodded. "Those trucks are the ones I saw my government take my brother in. They have the Minister's Seal on the top."

Eve ignored him. Instead, she seemed to take on a different, savage persona as she shouted at the Lieutenant. Not even the loud drumming of a third volley striking the hull of the ship could drown her out. "Return fire! Turn that bunker and that Complex into deep craters of molten glass!"

"Yes, immediately," the Lieutenant replied.

Eve tried to step away from Orner, and was startled when he didn't release her hand. She tugged at it once, failed to get it free, then looked up at him. "I'm sorry, I have to attend…"

"My brother is down there. Target the guns instead," Orner said, hearing a commanding tone pass through his own lips for the first time.

"Let me go, or…" Eve started.

His hand was around her slender neck then and she regarded him with fear, and shock. "I don't want to hurt you, but I will if you kill my people. If you kill my brother." The anger was familiar. There was a time when he was surrounded by bullies and was struck by a stone. It wasn't a large one, but a sharp edge caught him right over his left eye. It bled so much, so fast, and he could still recall the sting of the blood in his eye right before he, perhaps for the first time in his life, lost his temper completely. It wasn't frustration that overtook him, but real anger.

He attacked the teens that surrounded him. Even when he was fourteen, he towered over most grown men. The cost then was a few complaining parents and some bruised boys. He knew, watching the Lieutenant draw his sidearm, that the consequences for whatever he did would be far more dire, but Orner felt like there was blood in his eye again as he said; "Kill my brother, and I'll squeeze. I'll twist."

"Let her go, boy, this doesn't end well for you," the Lieutenant said. "Those torpedoes are already on their way down."

It was true. Green lines were being drawn from the Messenger to the surface of the planet. They lengthened quickly, showing the progress of the deadly counterattack. Then there were two large circular flashes. On the larger holo-gram, they showed round sections of his county, a more general indication that there were impacts and explosions. On the smaller one projected near Eve, the Ministry Compound was there one moment, and then it was consumed in a flash. He made eye contact with Eve as he squeezed her neck. She was agape as he put her between himself and the Lieutenant. That was when he caught a glimpse of an escape pod access door behind the officer.

Her free hand slapped the one around her throat making no difference in his grip, and he reacted. It wasn't intentional, just a slip in his restraint. Orner's hand acted on his darkest impulse, and twisted sharply, quickly, decisively. The crack that followed filled him with a sense of justice and regret simultaneously. Her order, given so hatefully, killed thousands of his people along with his brother, but he hated his retaliation just the same.

It was something Trey would definitely not have done. Eve went limp and the full weight of her body tried to draw his arm down. He held her up as the echoing snap gave her guests and several of the officers cause to gasp and scream. A few missed it and urgently asked what just happened.

"He killed her! That oaf murdered her!" shouted one male guest in a long coated suit.

"I didn't…" he was about to say that he didn't mean to take it that far, that it was an accident, but a shot that narrowly missed his head interrupted him. There was no explaining this away. His brother wouldn't step in and slow the situation down like he'd done a few times before. This was his fault, and it was his problem to solve.

It would also be a mistake Moxa would answer for. She was the one who put him through rudimentary virtual training and showed him how all the basic systems on modern starships worked. She was the one who chose him as the grand example, and brought him to their leader. Orner threw Eve's body onto the Lieutenant, who was trying to line up another shot, then ran past him to the escape pod.

Moxa ran after him, surprisingly fast for her size. He pulled the emergency hatch out of the wall using the release hinges then put it between himself, her and the few security officers in the room. Another louder thrum of rounds from the planet beating against the Base Ship's hull sounded.

"Orner, it'll all work out if you stay, don't run!" Moxa shouted after him. There was a small gun in her hand.

The inner hatch opened rapidly and Orner found himself at a loss for words as he dropped into it and slapped the emergency launch button. Both hatches started to slide back into place as the lights in the pod came on. A sharp burning pain lanced through his thigh and he looked up to see Moxa pointing her gun at him, brow furrowed, ready to take another shot. "It'll be worse if you run!" she shouted.

Then he saw something unbelievable behind her. Eve was getting to her feet with the help of the Lieutenant. "I broke her neck. I felt it," he muttered to himself as the doors finished sealing and the pod jettisoned.

Chapter 26

Aftermath

THE FLASH OF LIGHT, thunderous sound and powerful shaking of everything around Trey should have been the end. He was certain that his eyes were closed when it happened, but he may as well have been staring into the sun for all the good it did. Then there was a strange cracking, like hot metal cooling in the background, but otherwise, everyone was quiet at first.

"Is everyone all right?" asked a woman's voice. There, in the middle of the Minister's Office, was a device about the size of his torso. It floated using no visible propellers or other apparatus, its smooth oval shape had a glossy sheen, like it was covered in glass. It didn't look like the technology he'd seen in the simulations or in Moxa's ship. Daro was face down on the floor, Logi was checking him, and the Minister, who had fallen behind his desk was, getting to his feet.

"I think everyone's okay other than Daro," Trey replied.

"I'm fine," he bellowed, rolling over and pushing Logi away.

"I don't know what that was, but I seemed to weather it well," Minister Haas replied, cocking his head at the floating device.

"Good. This isn't how we wanted to introduce ourselves, but the Base Ship in orbit launched an attack, and we had to activate an emergency shield using the drone we sent down. Our intention was to meet you using this device instead of sending a ship down. We thought it would be less alarming," the female voice coming from the device said.

"What's happened?" shouted Daro, struggling to get to his feet. Then he noticed the thing floating in the middle of the room and pointed. "We're under attack!" With surprising alacrity, he ran to the door and pounded on it. "Guards! We're invaded! They're here! Right in the room!"

"Please don't be alarmed. I also caution you against running around the building. It's probably unstable. I'm here to help. My name is Liara, and I'm speaking to you through this probe, which had a high-powered shield. This machine was originally designed to serve as a rescue drone, so it is highly durable with unusually powerful systems. Can anyone hear me?"

The Minister straightened his jacket. "I can hear you."

"She's lying. That machine didn't protect us, this whole complex was designed to survive artillery fire! Everyone knows that! How could such a little thing protect us?" Daro said, turning and pointing at the probe.

"I'm afraid the Messenger's attack was much worse than you could expect from artillery fire. You'll see evidence of that if you look through the window. What's more important is what we have to offer. I'm from a ship called the Triton, and there are other ships on the way. We'd like to help you. We can't win the fight you're facing for you, but slowing the Base Ship down is an option. We'd also like to offer you rescue as well. We can pick you up and take you to safety in a few minutes."

"You're enemies of the Order of Eden?" the Minister asked as he started for the window.

"Yes, they've suppressed our people, most of whom became refugees from a war they started. My job is to provide a voice for the Triton, which is commanded by Captain Stephanie Vega and owned by Jacob Valent. Our role in this fight is to provide assistance so you have a chance to fight and to do as much damage to the Order of Eden as possible, especially an old enemy, Eve, who is not what she seems," Liara replied.

"Why should we trust you more than the Order of Eden?" Trey asked. "I know, we're probably short on time, and we might not have a choice, but you could be worse."

"That's true. I wish we had time for a proper introduction, and to make our case, but there isn't time. Your attack on the Messenger caused significant damage to their defences, but Eve will realize that the centre of your compound wasn't destroyed soon, and they could launch another volley. This probe's systems are burned out for the most part, and there are no energy reserves left. It won't be able to protect you again."

"It's all gone! We're in a pit! It's all gone!" Daro panicked, red-faced, tears streaming down his cheeks as he ran for the door again. It opened, and he came nose to nose with two guards. He stopped, pointed at the probe and shouted; "Shoot it!"

To Trey's relief, the guards looked to the Minister, who waved the order off as he stared out the window solemnly.

"Someone find a sedative for Daro, please. In the meantime, can you check on my family?"

"Yes, Minister," one of the guards said as the other led Daro out of the room.

"It's the end! This is punishment for the corruption of technology! What He has made, He will unmake!" Daro shouted as he ineffectively resisted the guard.

As Trey saw through the windows, nervous sweat emerged on his forehead and back. Daro was right about one thing. It looked like the end of all things. Past several paces of pristine lawn was a new cliff. A yawning circle of absent earth that was at least twenty stories deep and still red hot extended outward from there. "It's four times wider than the entire complex," he said quietly.

"Minister, we're in the middle of a crater, on top of a pillar that's holding up the central building. Everyone inside the Minister's Mansion is alive," a guard said as he rushed in.

"My family?" The Minister asked.

There was a moment's hesitation before the guard replied; "They were in the museum. I'm sorry."

"You have my condolences, Minister," Liara said through the probe, her voice soothing even though she pressed; "There is another site like this one some distance to the north. I couldn't do anything to protect whoever was there."

"The command bunker, most likely. It's safe to assume that the two largest countries on this planet are now headless," Minister Haas said. He seemed numb, as though it was all too much. "What do we do here, Logi?"

"We need time and allies who can counter the Order," Logi replied. "Our guns have stopped. They've either run out of ammunition or are waiting for orders. The former is more likely than the latter."

"So we have no edge in this fight," Minister Haas said, nodding to himself. "No one living who can stand for two billion, and no way to defend them."

"We are ready to launch a rescue for you and an attack on the Messenger, Minister," Liara said quietly.

As though struck by all the emotion of the moment at once, Minister Haas turned towards the probe and pointed towards the sky. "You have the power to fight that and you're waiting on my word?" A tear rolled down his cheek as he stared at the device. "You won't even attack without my order?"

The Minister's reaction was surprising to Trey at first. It looked like outrage, and surprise, but then he realized. Minister Haas was a go-between for the most part until that moment. Other than bringing Trey in as an advisor, he was probably only relaying decisions for the Prime Minister. Beyond that, the Order of Eden came and did whatever they liked. They didn't ask anyone for permission. Seeing that this new ally may be different almost made Trey smile, but he felt nearly as surprised as his Minister when he heard the answer from the drone.

"That's... that's right. It would benefit us to attack the Messenger, but the leaders I'm representing know that it would seem like you have new allies, and that could change things for the better or worse. We aren't sure. So the decision is yours," Liara replied. "We can't make it for you."

"What would you do?" Minister Haas asked Logi. Then he turned towards Trey, who was looking past him to the ruin outside. "And you?"

"I would buy time, tell them to send their ships," Trey said.

Logi nodded. "We need a leader. That's you right now,

especially since you would have voted not to attack. You were right."

"And should our new friends attack?" Haas asked, calming down already.

Logi turned towards the probe. "Will your attack prevent another bombardment from the Base Ship?"

"There is a chance, yes," Liara replied.

"Then I suggest you order an attack on the Order of Eden Base Ship, Minister," Logi said.

"It would be the start of a real war. The civil war that split our country was only seventeen years ago, we're still recovering," Minister Haas said mostly to himself.

"The other option is surrender," Trey said. He was unable to see how his country could even participate in a conflict at that level. That was unless the people Liara represented were looking for recruits too.

"No," Minister Haas said, his expression souring. "We fight by any means, even if we have to ally with people we don't know at all against this enemy. Send your attack, Liara. You're right, we need time, and we need rescue. There should be about three dozen people in this building. I want everyone taken to safety."

"I'm told the rescue ships will be there in seven minutes, Minister. There will be more than enough room for everyone," Liara replied through the probe.

"Do you have people who can look for my family?" Minister Haas asked.

"We'll perform a scan when the rescue ships are close. It'll be better than any search party." There was sympathy in her voice as she replied, but Trey's heart ached for the Minister as he didn't hear a hint of hope.

Chapter 27

The First Launch

IT HAPPENED SO QUICKLY that Cooper barely had time to double check the route he had to take to the fighter launch tubes. He had to depend on the instincts he honed as an alert pilot in his earlier days and in the simulated environment that he spent weeks in not long before he joined Samurai Squadron when he remotely checked the fighter's computer systems.

The weeks Cooper spent in the training pod, or Egg as it was called because of its outward appearance, passed like months. Haven Fleet had a special technology that could do that - make someone connected to the simulated environment experience between five and seven times the number of hours that were actually passing. It allowed him to finish his uptraining as a fighter pilot in a month.

The last phase of that virtual time was spent on a starship that existed only in the simulation. He was a Lieutenant in

Ghost Squadron, a part of the fighter wing that existed only in training. The simulation felt so real that he forgot his body was actually in a suspension pod for a few weeks. They flew countless combat missions and had to defend their carrier often. When it was all over, he graduated with the rank he earned in training and was waiting to hear from Haven Fleet about his posting when Minh-Chu approached him for the second time.

Responding to an alert, running for his fighter was exciting in the simulation, but he realized that doing the same thing aboard the Triton was exhilarating in a more familiar way, and Cooper found himself focusing on every task more sharply. Perhaps his subconscious knew he was in a simulation when he was flying with Ghost Squadron. There was no doubt that what he was doing was very real aboard the Triton.

It would have been easy to get carried away by the excitement as he ran down the hallway to the loaders. His fighter, its cockpit painted like the head of a Blue Jay, was lowering into place at the end of the short loading corridor. The punters loaded like a magazine, so the nose of his ship was angled downwards and he could climb into the fighter without a ladder, just step in so his feet rested on the pedals and his butt dropped into the seat. He did precisely that. The harness connected to his fitted vacsuit armour, the canopy closed and the fighter finished rotating so it pointed straight down towards the launch doors. Each punter line could only take three fighters at a time. It was a safety measure, just in case one jammed. There were twenty-nine other tubes. Most were empty this time since Samurai Squadron was low on pilots. There would only be fifteen on this mission.

The mental link to his fighter's computer gave him a shiver as it made the connection, and he could feel the ship like it was a part of his body. The computer reported the results of the automatic checklist. Everything checked out, and for the first time, he realised that he was about to fly a real Archangel Fighter into combat. As far as anyone knew, it was the most formidable fighter in the galaxy, and the enemy hadn't had a chance to see it.

It looked like most of the other Uriel models over the last thirty years or more, so the Order of Eden was in for a surprise. "Breaker, you settling in for the punt?" asked Ronin, the Wing Commander.

Cooper smiled at hearing his call sign from his favourite Commander so far. "Ready here, Ronin. I saw the mission brief, all three minutes of it."

"You have the honour of escorting the Raven while it rescues the pod that launched from the Base Ship. Our comms people are in contact with the occupant, and we're sure he'll cooperate. Pixie is flying the Corvette, and you're flying with your favourite Mergillians," Ronin said. "You will not be returning to the Triton when you're finished, at least not right away."

"My first mission for Samurai Squadron and the Triton. That's big," Cooper said without thinking.

"You ready, Breaker?" Ronin asked.

"Damn right, I'm ready," Cooper replied.

"Good. Get to that pod first and take whatever comes your way out," Ronin said.

"Will do. Good hunting, Ronin," Breaker replied, then he regarded his wingmates. "You two ready to go?"

"Ready for my first non-simulated escort mission in this fighter," Garma said.

Her enthusiasm was shared by her brother, Gren, who added; "The Order doesn't have a chance. I was wondering something, though."

"What's that?" Breaker asked.

"Where does the term; 'punting' come from?"

"It's an old word for kicking a ball as hard as you can, I'm pretty sure," Breaker replied as he watched the heavy launch doors part quickly in front of him. The fighter jerked into its final position. "Counting down from seven now."

A status alert scrolled across his screen. UPDATE: *Raven launched, in position, updating as Ra1 on your Tactical Display.* A moment later the punter system sent his fighter into space so quickly that it seemed like the magazine around him simply disappeared, and he engaged his thrusters. "Wedge One formation," he announced as his wingmates took positions behind him to his left and right.

There was other chatter. Ronin was leading a larger group of fighters to another target, but it was in the background, quieter than Gren and Garma, who acknowledged his order. They followed him as he guided his fighter towards the Raven, which was already accelerating towards the escape pod in the distance. "How are we today, Pixie?"

"Having a great time, Breaker," she replied. "I've been listening to the story the pod's occupant has been telling Triton Communications. Sounds like a great guy who's been burned by the Order pretty hard. Oh, and he snapped Eve's neck. I need to shake his hand."

"What? So, Eve is dead?" Breaker asked, making an effort on keeping his attention focused on the task at hand.

"We didn't even get to fire a shot at her Base Ship," Gren groaned, disappointed.

"Oh, apparently she got right back up. Probably framework tech. Anyway, good to have you guys around. I've gotten used to flying without support," Pixie said.

"Glad to be here. We will be in position, three hundred

kilometres from your nose in about eleven seconds. These fighters have some real power," he said, the increasing thrust of the engines was barely detectable inside the cockpit.

"Are you riding afterburners?" she asked.

"No, standard military acceleration so far," Breaker replied.

"Damn. Well, maybe you can keep up with the Raven," she replied as the trio of fighters slipped into position ahead of her.

"This is Triton Flight. We just confirmed launches from the Order Battlegroup and the Base Ship. Hurry this up or you'll be caught in the middle. Stay on your planned course as you enter your next thrust phase or you will be caught in our long range counter attack."

"We will stay on course," Pixie replied.

"Did I hear you right, Flight? The Triton is engaging?" Breaker asked.

"That's right, Breaker. We're coming about and launching," Slick replied from the Flight Deck. "Captain Vega is ordering us right into the fight. You won't believe your eyes in a few minutes. Just follow the plan."

He'd heard stories about the Triton, and was aware that it had the latest dependable technology aboard, and wished he could be closer during the action. The Order Battle Group was hundreds of millions of kilometres away, only visible on his tactical display as a dash shaped marker. Minh-Chu and the rest of Samurai Squadron rushed past the Raven towards the Base Ship. Once they were closing faster than the Clever Class Corvette, they deactivated their afterburners so they were still gaining distance, moving ahead, but not as fast as they could. He hoped that they and the Triton weren't taking on more than they could handle, regardless of the stories he'd been hearing.

His tactical computer alerted him that the Triton launched fifty-six fully cloaked torpedoes that would pass them in several seconds. He didn't have the time to count the launchers on that ship, but if that's what they could put in space at one time, it was more heavy torpedoes than anything he'd ever seen push out in one volley. Then the Clever Dream blasted clear of the Triton with a smaller ship on its heels that was marked simply as V1 before it disappeared.

It was cloaked before, but most allied cloaked assets would be marked on tactical displays so they didn't run into each other. That would be a highly unlikely accident, but it was worth preventing. This ship, the V1, was something that hid itself from everything, and Breaker had to tear his curiosity away from the question of why.

The first volley of torpedoes burst open and he saw the first phase of his mission complete as fifteen drones decloaked around the Raven and their three fighters. They didn't have much in the way of armament, but each unfolded to have the same shape as a Uriel Fighter, so it looked like there were actually nineteen ships in their group including the Raven. They also had systems that could fake mass, power output and a pair of anti-fighter guns. The technology was fairly simple compared to what was inside his Archangel, and they were easy to produce. The fifteen decoys all came from five torpedoes. The rest of the heavy munitions continued on, still cloaked.

"Looks like we have a great big force over here now," Pixie snickered. "Launching medium range countermeasures."

All three of the gun emplacements on the Raven that could face forward started firing small, high-density rounds that were aimed at the missiles the Messenger were sending after them. "Fighters coming in from the larger battlegroup. They're nine minutes away at top acceleration," Gren announced.

"Plenty of time," Pixie said.

"Wait, I just got a glimmer from something closer," Garma said, highlighting it on her tactical display.

"Point a focused scan..." Breaker started, but was interrupted as the Sciences Officer aboard the Raven finished the task before he could request it and the shapes of a pair of Uriel fighters appeared. Two pairs of smaller, single-seat Ramiel fighters appeared behind them, their cloaking systems defeated.

They were charging in from their left, so he rotated his ship to face them. "Markings designate them as Citadel fighters. They're coming in fast!" he saw that Garma and Gren had turned their ships in the same direction, and they opened fire.

The Citadel pilots must have detected the high-energy scan that found them out, and as the Ramiel fighters split off, the heavier Uriels tore into their decoys with their rapid-fire guns.

Anti-missile decoys launched from the lower and upper aft sections of the Raven, and drew the missiles the Uriels launched as soon as they left the pods. A drone intercepted the only one that looked like it was about to get through sacrificing itself to protect the Raven.

The original intention of the drones was to intimidate the Order Battlegroup and the crew aboard Eve's Base Ship into leaving the Raven alone, or at least thinking twice about launching fighters against them. It was sheer luck that the Citadel fighters were fooled as well, at least for long enough to lose the advantage.

The turrets aboard the Raven's port and dorsal sides roared to life, switching to explosive railgun rounds that could pierce armour if they struck, but would burst if it was a near miss or they were about to fly past. "Break formation, I'm on the heavies," Breaker announced as the pair of Uriel fighters passed by. All the enemy pilots were making sure to stay above the Raven, so the lower and forward turrets didn't have a shot. They also split up, and he could see a pattern already. "They're staying relatively close and waiting for us to go after one of them so the others can get behind us. It's old school."

"I see it," Garma replied as her fighter went after one Ramiel fighter, seemingly taking the bait. "Some of their training must have been focused on atmospheric flight. That is a mistake."

Gren made an even greater show of falling for the trap, pulsing his Xetima afterburners for a split second as he started firing at another agile Ramiel fighter. "If this is their strategy, then they shouldn't be here."

A barrage of gunfire struck the nose of Breaker's fighter as he went after the pair of Uriels. He suffered damage to his shields, but they were using a smaller type of round made to take out conventional fighters. They would have taken him out if it wasn't running next-generation shields. Even still, it cost him half of his forward shielding.

His ship reacted at the speed of thought as he mentally commanded it to distribute more available power there, increase the reactor output, and set his reserve shielding to recharge. The Uriels split up, and he chose to follow neither one, flying right between them instead while he marked both with his targeting system. Being able to see the tactical map in his head made it easy to order his auto-turret to track and fire at one while he tried to lock on to the other fighter with missiles.

Both of the fighters spun towards him and opened fire with their main guns. Breaker fired his starboard thrusters then strafed in a jagged pattern, sending his fighter away from the anti-fighter rounds as he watched his shields take significant damage from a trio of small, fast missiles as they struck the nose of his ship. "They've got upgrades too, watch it!" he said as he rotated his Archangel away from them and accelerated in an evasive pattern away from the Raven. "Come on, get frustrated, get closer," he said as a loud five hundred hertz tone informed him that they both had missile locks on him.

The vibrations of the heavy rotary gun on his turret rumbled under his feet slightly as it found one of the Uriels and spat thirty-five rounds per second at it. He flipped a switch, adding a jammer round to its firing rotation so one in five of the bullets flying towards the Uriels would be highly charged, sending sensor jamming signals along with the more deadly explosive armour piercing rounds.

With a mental command, he activated a directional sensor-jamming device mounted on the top of his fighter. There was a noticeable tax on his power generation, but the tone indicating that his enemies had missile locks on him diminished, meaning that only one of them still had a lock. The other, the one his turret was ignoring, was coming after him, accelerating as quickly as he could. "There we go!" Breaker said to himself as he deactivated his afterburners and waited. Three fast Spear Nine missiles were launched at him. His turret took care of two, and his aft shields absorbed most of the impact of the third. Some shrapnel made it through, piercing his emergency supplies compartment. *That's why they put that stuff at the back. Just a little more dense stuff to absorb damage.* He thought to himself as he flipped his fighter end over end to face his pursuer. If he waited until his eyes caught up to pull the trigger, he would have lost whole seconds while he took his aim, but Breaker knew that his reticule would be spot on his enemy's nose. It was a maneuver he'd practiced a thousand times or more in training, so he squeezed the trigger the instant a six hundred thirty hertz tone that told him that his guns were lined up sounded in his helmet. It only lasted a second, but it was enough to loosen the chase up and turn things around. Both Uriels were second guessing their positions and he was able to guide them back towards the Raven's course so they wouldn't get in the way of whatever the Triton was doing.

He glanced at Garma and Gren, who were in hot pursuit of one Ramiel each. As predicted, they were both pursued by another Ramiel in turn and without signalling to each other, the Mergillian pilots rotated their fighters so they faced their pursuers and opened fire. The aggressive Ramiels resisted the heavy anti-armour rounds at first, their shields holding firmly as the enemy pilots panicked. It didn't last, and both Garma and Gren's rounds struck bare metal, then broke through, tearing the Ramiel fighters to pieces.

"Ramiel Four eliminated," Garma announced.

Ramiel Two eliminated," Gren cheered. "Going after Three."

"Going after Ramiel One," Garma said. That was their strategy. Chase two, eliminate the fighters that went after them, then they'd finish their chases.

The Triton, still cloaked but marked on his tactical display, passed within thirty kilometres of Breaker, and he had to make an adjustment to his course that shed his advantage. "Wherever they're going, they're in a great big hurry. Good luck,

Triton," he said to himself as he tried to keep his fighter from passing right through either Uriel's gunsights.

The lead Citadel pilot who was closest to Breaker closed with him even more, its guns firing as it started landing hits on his aft shields. Breaker sent the last of his energy reserves there to recharge the barrier. It would be just enough, unless the Citadel Uriel dumbfired a missile and got lucky.

Breaker's enemy was in position, too close to easily dodge a counterattack, and he flipped his fighter over and opened fire at the pursuer. He blasted his starboard thrusters, sending him into a strafing manoeuvre so he could have a long moment to fire on him as the Uriel flew past him. His rounds burst through his target's shields. The pressurized compartment of the enemy ship sent bursts of gas into space as the armour-piercing anti-capitol ship shells from his main guns passed all the way through the Uriel fighter. The pilot in the fighter that was hanging back as it tried to launch missiles after him, ejected as rounds from Breaker's auto turret burst through her energy shields.

A second later, a Ramiel fighter was torn to shreds as two of the Raven's turrets scored hits.

"Hey! Not cool, Raven! That was mine!" Gren shouted.

"We couldn't let you guys have all the fun," Pixie replied.

Breaker checked the tactical screen and saw that two gunners aboard the Raven destroyed the Ramiel Fighter Gren was chasing. "You ran them right into their firing arc, Gren, good work."

"You don't get an ace star for assists," Gren grumbled.

"My target's gone too, our immediate engagement area is clear," Garma said.

"Raven, this is Triton Flight. We're buying you some time. Get the pod, and then pick up that pilot."

There were two drones left, and they flew alongside the Raven as it opened a lower rescue hatch, tilted, then took the whole escape pod in. "I hear you, Flight. We have the pod, I'll pick the pilot up on the way back. Get ready for a hostile combattant, everyone," Pixie replied. "I'll blast her with a Directed Electromagnetic Pulse beam before she comes in, so she may be gasping, but shouldn't have any working weapons on her. You know what to do from there."

"I know what to do," replied Remmy. "I bet my cushy new quarters that it's a framework."

"Form up, recharge reserves," Breaker told Garma and Gren. They took positions around the Raven as it rushed towards the ejected pilot. To his surprise, Pixie flipped the ship at the last moment and caught her in the large rear cargo doors, closing them behind her.

The torpedoes the Triton launched struck the Base Ship in the distance, devastating its shields as a series of nuclear flashes lit his sensors up one after another. Samurai Squadron swept in as soon as the blasts came to an end.

To his surprise, the Triton de-cloaked within five hundred kilometres of the Ascendant, the flagship of the other Order of Eden battlegroup and let loose with a full volley of fresh, deadly torpedoes that eschewed cloaking for faster acceleration and armour piercing power.

The Triton was upside down relative to the battlegroup, and dozens of rapid-fire turrets mounted across the dorsal side of the ship opened fire. "God, I wish we could stick around," Breaker said with a smile, imagining the panic on the bridge of the Ascendant.

"Time to hitch on," Pixie announced, her tone all business.

"Yes, Ma'am," Breaker said as he rotated his fighter, retracted his auto turret, lowered his landing gear, then activated the latching system. With a little touch of the stick, he made contact with the top of the Raven and saw that his fighter was firmly affixed. "Breaker ready."

Gren affixed to the other side of the Raven's dorsal hull. "Gren ready."

Garma touched down near the Raven's nose, and before she could announce that she was affixed and ready as well, Pixie burst; "Hey! Watch it! Even regenerating hulls can get scratched!"

"Sorry," Garma replied. "Ready."

The defence drones sped away, leaving to attack their secondary target, the Base Ship. A split in space revealed a slightly more luminous place in front of the Raven and it accelerated into it. "Entering Transit Space," Pixie said as a trans-dimensional wormhole surrounded them.

Chapter 28

The Zhan Class Close Combat Carrier Triton

IT WAS NERVE-WRACKING. Ayan had been in many tense situations. Memories from her predecessor, Ayan Rice, had experienced enough of them to fill two lifetimes as well. It still didn't change the fact that Captain Stephanie Vega could swear that the Admiral started looking worried the moment Alice and Jacob left the ship. It was only when Ayan thought no one was watching, or when she looked at the tactical map, but Captain Vega could see it. She wasn't sure if anyone else noticed.

Every officer aboard the Triton was worried about her being aboard. Some saw her as a symbol of Haven Fleet's overreach, someone who was put there to watch over the crew as they separated from the military. The rest of the officers realized that what she told them was true. She wasn't there to police them, but to help put the Privateering effort together and supplement the Sciences Team aboard the Triton. They were also terrified to see any harm come to her.

On one hand, she was an active Admiral in Haven Fleet and one of the new founders of the solar system, largely responsible for designing its continuing modernization. The fact that millions of people saw her as their beloved Queen made the situation even more delicate.

On the other hand, she was Jacob Valent's Fiancee and Alice Valent's mother by adoption and then genetically thanks to a moment of severe modification that was brought on by Alice herself. Alice and Jake had both shown that they had a tendency for taking drastic retaliatory action when someone they loved was in harm's way, or worse, actually injured or killed. If anything happened to Ayan, all hell would break loose, and no one crew member had a clear picture of what that would look like.

No one was more aware of all that than Captain Stephanie Vega, who sat in the central command seat of the Triton with Admiral Ayan Anderson to her left. At her side was a resourceful trained officer who was also an incredible engineer. She'd also gotten to see the woman's softer side, as she visited whenever she could, rarely seeing Ayan without her other adopted daughter, Baby Laura. Named after a friend who was murdered by a Citadel Agent as a target of opportunity, it seemed like Laura was the centre of Ayan's world. It was a very big deal that Ayan took time away from motherhood to help the Triton, but Stephanie still hesitated to ask the Admiral to do anything for her.

"Our shields are down to eighty-four percent," Chief Finn reported from her right. Holographic status screens surrounded all three of them with the tactical map in the middle. "We can't recharge, there's too much firepower coming at us from the Battle Group."

The Order of Eden Battlegroup was above them, relatively. They had closed to within two hundred twenty-four kilometres, too close for most of their heavy torpedoes and other long-range munitions. The Ascendant, Admiral Scanlon's flagship, was centred directly above. It was a brute force tactic that she proposed, knowing the capabilities of the latest revision of the Triton well.

The rest of the battlegroup was moving to surround them. It was a surprising gathering of ships including six destroyers, two heavy cruisers and thirteen corvettes. They were missing two carriers and at least five battleships. All of which were probably deployed somewhere else in the Cluster. That would be a problem worth addressing later. Stephanie highlighted a trio of corvettes and looked over her shoulder at Shamus Frost, her fiance and the Tactical Chief. "Take them out. Use our port flank guns to launch a nuclear series."

"Aye," Frost replied, ordering those guns to switch munitions and fire three nuclear shells each, one at a time. There would be nine nuclear explosions just out of harmful range for the Triton if they hit, and those Order of Eden Corvettes would be gone or not worth saving. "Crews are switching over, launching in about fifteen seconds. I'm getting ready to fire a rack of Fast Javelin Missiles at 'em right ahead of the torpedoes so the chance of interception is lower."

His demeanour around Ayan was always more professional. Stephanie enjoyed seeing him on his best behaviour, but she wasn't about to tell him because it might stop or worse, he could start policing his speech when they were alone together. "How's the gunnery deck?"

"Down three turrets, one casualty," Frost replied. "Fifty-three main turrets firing on the Ascendant."

"Shields down to eighty-two percent and we can't recharge fast enough to recover, Captain," Finn said. "We need to get out of here or find a way to take fewer direct hits."

They were following the mission plan and making progress towards the moment when they'd be able to break away, but they weren't there yet. Captain Vega and her staff had done everything they could to reinforce their shielding, protect the ship as it held its position above the Ascendant, and provide a massive distraction for the rest of the small force with them. "Advice, Admiral?" Stephanie asked the woman to her left.

"Conservatively, you could reduce power to the gravitational shielding. It's not stopping much at this range, and the other shields could use the input. I'd switch the perimeter guns to burst fire as well. They only have light fighter drones guarding the battlegroup right now. I wish I could give you something more, but you've cut power to everything that doesn't need it and made every other preparation, so there isn't anything to do, conventionally." Ayan added that last word with clear intention.

"Make the adjustments," Captain Vega said, nodding at Finn. Then she turned back to Ayan. "What about unconventional suggestions?"

"Well, our gravitational shield emitters are still untouched. Instead of using the power generation for those to help with the other types of shielding, you could turn one side of the gravitational shielding into a weapon. Angle them towards that Heavy Cruiser," Ayan replied, highlighting Heavy Cruiser 01 on the tactical map. "If we tighten the geometry into a beam, we can strike it with a hit equivalent to a little over three hundred gravitational units for about four milliseconds. I say we point the strike here," she highlighted a section close to the middle of the ship.

"That might burn the port side array out completely," Finn countered. He was doing his best not to sound dramatic, but there was an edge to his tone that everyone caught.

"It is an option while you have power reserves for Grav-Shielding. If you want another aggressive suggestion, you could shunt power from the Grav-Shielding to the main energy barriers and get so close to the Ascendant that you risk a shield clash. I've looked at the Ascendant's power profile, and I'm sure our shield emitters can handle it."

"That's…" Finn considered it for a moment then shook his head. "You're right, we'd come out with more working shield emitters, but we'd definitely burn something out."

"We'll be here, getting hammered for another three minutes or more if we don't do something drastic," Frost said from behind and above them at the Tactical station. "We've got a lot of firepower, but more than half is focused on countermeasures and we can't use our forward torpedoes."

"I know," Captain Vega said, considering Ayan's suggestions. Using the gravitational shielding as a weapon seemed too offensive. There was enough energy there to shore up their other shielding significantly, even if they clashed with the enemy's larger energy barrier. The Ascendant had twice the length, but only two thirds of the width and half the energy dedicated to their protective barriers. The Triton also had a centralized energy projection system for their energy shields. If worst came to worst, they would still have protection if every emitter they had burned out, it just wouldn't be able to take nearly as much punishment.

"The battlegroup is trying to get between us and the Ascendant," Frost reported, projecting the new flight paths for the ships surrounding them. "Except for one of the Heavy Cruisers. That bugger's backing off and pointing her guns at our lower hull."

Captain Vega could see that the Ascendant was trying to get away, rotating so their port side shields could take damage instead of their slowly failing dorsal bank. The main thrusters at the rear of the ship were increasing to full thrust, as the two-kilometre-long vessel turned. "Rear torpedo launchers, concentrate fire on Cruiser One's launch bay," Captain Vega ordered. At best a strike on that section of the enemy ship would destroy their launch bays. At worst, they'd rotate the lumbering vessel to protect that side and they'd launch fighters.

"Aye, full volley away, reloading," Frost said. At the range they were fighting at, the torpedoes seemed to go off right away, showing a significant strike against the ship's shields.

As Cruiser One's hangar bays momentarily disappeared in a hail of conventional explosions, Stephanie addressed the helm; "Ash, keep us in position above the Ascendant. Get us to within a hundred meters, with our nose pointed towards clear sky and our gunnery deck facing the middle of that ship."

"Aye, closing to shield clash range," Ashley said as she guided the Triton along a parallel course that took them even closer to the enemy ship.

"Get us any closer and we'll be launching lines so we can swing aboard," Frost said from the Tactical Station.

"Status?" Captain Vega asked him.

"We'll be through their shields in about one minute, fifty seconds," Frost said.

He continued; "Cruiser One is maintaining position. That trio of well organized corvettes that scratched us earlier is trying to evade."

"Cruiser One's fighter bay is almost ready to launch

again," Kadri said from the Scanning and Sciences section. "Inner doors are opening."

"Hit them with another volley from the rear launchers," Stephanie said. "Where's V1 right now?"

"No idea," Ayan said. "Still off all scanners."

"Congratulations, the new hull your division designed is working," Captain Vega said. "The Clever Dream?"

A holographic image of Slick replied from the translucent status screen surrounding them. "Entering Tiy's atmosphere. There is a very nervous communications team aboard, but I think they'll do fine."

"I'm sure Liara will do just fine without Alice," Ayan replied. She seemed on edge as soon as Alice decided to go with Jake moments before V1 launched.

Stephanie didn't blame her, only she wished that she was on V1 as well. A cluster of explosions raged against the Triton's lower hull. "That's it, they're using nukes and small antimatter torpedoes," Finn reported.

"The lad's right. Cruiser One's launch bay has been shut down for now, and she's getting more distance. So are the corvettes and the other destroyers. They're abandoning the notion that they can get between us and the Ascendant."

"Some of that hit the Ascendant," reported Kadri from the Scanning Station. "Energy curve for their shields indicates that they're close to a main burnout. We have a clear firing solution on bare metal."

"It's about time," Frost said. "They could still get things running well again if we let up at all. I have five more gun emplacements down. They've got some kinda shield piercing rockets that are good at close range."

"That's it," Captain Vega said. "Set dampeners to emergency mode."

"Done," Chief Finn replied.

"Clash with their shields, Ash," Captain Vega ordered.

"Aye. They're trying to get away, but it's too late," Ashley replied as she carefully guided the Triton into the other ship's dorsal side on a merging parallel course. The sound of something snapping several decks above made several of the bridge crew jump.

"Their shields have failed," Frost announced. "Not just the dorsal ones, either. They are bare metal in every direction."

"We lost nine dorsal emitters. The rest are next to overheating. That pop was a power distribution node buying it. Instructing damage control to re-route," Finn reported.

"We have shields all around?" Captain Vega asked, looking at the ship status section of the holographic display.

"Yes, calculating integrity," Finn said.

"Twenty-eight percent and rising," Ayan replied. "Concentrate on damage control, Chief. I'll translate the rest of this mess."

"Thanks, Admiral," Finn said as he worked feverishly to direct damage control personnel to different sections of the ship while he got the instructions for what they should do when they arrived together.

"Cease fire on the Ascendant," Captain Vega said, her lips curling into a smile. "Ash, get us lined up for the strike."

"All our emplacements have ceased fire on the Ascendant. Assigning other targets. Corvette trio One is down to a single ship. The others have been destroyed by our nuclear volley," Frost reported, highlighting the devastating strike on the three ships. "Tracking two escape pods."

"Are there any from the Ascendant? Any escaping ships or other launches?" Captain Vega asked.

"None, but a rear bay is opening," Kadri reported.

"Sighted: There's an Advanced Scout Class ship in there. The Peerless," Slick reported from the Flight and Strategic Deck.

"Regent Galactic made, it has a combined hyperdrive wormhole system. It's one of their fastest armed ships," Ayan said.

"Fire our special torpedo volley at the dorsal side of the Ascendant," Captain Vega said. It was their primary mission, to fire all fifty-six of their forward-facing torpedoes at the bare metal hull of the Ascendant. These munitions weren't meant to destroy the ship, however. Each included a trio of heavy attack androids they'd printed using the Triton's fabrication centre.

"We're almost in position," Ashley said. The Triton rotated so the front of the ship faced the dorsal side of the Ascendant, staying in position as the Flagship tried to turn so a shielded area of their hull would face their enemy.

"Nice work, Ash," Frost said. "Firing!"

Every torpedo tube along the front of the Triton opened and let loose twice in quick succession, pushing one hundred twelve torpedoes towards the top of the Ascendant. Less than three seconds later, ninety-one of them struck home and started drilling into the enemy vessel's thick hull.

"Shields are down to nineteen percent," Finn said after a pair of large antimatter torpedoes detonated against the Triton's aft section.

"Where are my countermeasures?" Captain Vega snapped.

"There's heavy fire coming from all sides now that we're backing away from the Ascendant. Every countermeasure we have is running at max levels or running out and being reloaded," Frost replied. "Someone transferred all the power away from my beam weapons too."

"Sorry, needed it for shields," Finn replied. "Aft Prometheus Beam Three and five were down anyway. Main Thruster Two isn't responding either."

"This is about to come to an abrupt end," Frost added.

"Signal V One and get us to Retreat Point Alpha," Captain Vega ordered. "The Ascendant is vulnerable. Oh, and fire on their aft bay. We need to shut that down."

"Already locking on with guided Trident Missiles," Frost said. "Firing three."

"Fire the rack," Captain Vega said.

"Firing fifteen," Frost said with a pleased smile.

The Triton reoriented itself on its axis so it would fly past the Ascendant and accelerated, all four of its main engines flared brightly. "Shields down to eleven percent, Ash!" Finn called to the front of the bridge. "I'm going to have to start borrowing from one angle to reinforce others here."

"Impact on aft quarter, section one-zero-five, frame one-forty-seven," added one of his subordinates. "Viewing cabin, venting, sealing it off now. No one was in there."

"No need to call that one out," Finn told him.

The Triton was rapidly splitting off from the battlegroup, rolling to spread the damage it was taking from rounds and missiles that made it through the pulse weapons and auto cannons that were destroying most of the incoming projectiles. "We're almost clear," Ashley reported.

"Main D-Transit Drives are starting up, but we need more power," one of the staff at the helm reported.

"You've got it," Frost said. "There's everything I've got left from forward countermeasure reserves."

"That'll do," Ashley said.

"Okay, Jake, it's up to you guys. Good luck," Captain Vega said as she watched the blackness in front of the Triton split open the instant before they escaped into transit space. They were away. Their mission was complete.

"We've either terrified or enraged Scanlon and the crew of the Ascendant," Ayan said. There was an uncommon seriousness about her that was completely absent when the Admiral was at home.

"I'm going to go help with damage control. There's a gunner stuck in his turret. The support frame is making contact with a live line from below. No one can give me enough information to shut it down from here," Finn said as he looked at Ayan. "Can you man the Engineering Station and help me trace it, Admiral."

"It would be my pleasure, Chief. Oh, and I'm not your Admiral," Ayan replied, glancing at Captain Vega, who was his actual commanding officer.

"Aye," Finn said. "Permission to go, Captain?"

"Go ahead, just don't get fried," Captain Vega replied.

"Ready at the Engineering Station," Ayan said after she looked the status screen over. "Give me a moment to take a closer look at our status, please."

The Triton emerged from transit space on the other side of the solar system. "How is Samurai Squadron doing?" Captain Vega asked Slick's hologram.

"Two fighters have taken serious damage and are flying to retreat point Beta. Easy just made his fifth kill, making him the Ace of the engagement," Slick's hologram replied from below. "Dame's right behind him. They just signalled V1. There is enough of an opening for them to run their mission on the Base Ship, and they've located Eve with scanners."

"How are our cloaking systems?" the Captain asked.

"Ready," Ayan replied.

"Time to disappear," Captain Vega ordered as she sat

back. The Raven and her escort of three fighters were nearby, right where they were supposed to be.

"Activate all cloaking systems," Ayan said to the Field Specialist Team who were at their stations against the left side of the bridge.

"Activating refraction, dissipation and bypass fields," announced one.

"Shifting hull plating to stealth mode. Marking three failures in sections smaller than four square metres each," reported another.

"Activating signal repeating array," announced the third.

"Closing all venting and emission shielding hatches, no faults reported," said the fourth crewmember.

"Forwarding the locations of damaged hull plating to emergency repair teams," Ayan said as she looked at the ship's cloaking status. "We are cloaked."

Slick's hologram whistled and shook his head. "Man, that was quick. The Clever Dream jumped from the upper atmosphere and they're already with us. Tiy's leadership is on board."

"Captain, we're receiving a direct signal using Haven Fleet Security Encryption," the temporary senior communications officer reported. He was a mergillian named Lagarik. "It's Captain Paron of the Lorander Battlecruiser Varcan. He is addressing the Captain of the Triton and Admiral Anderson."

"Put it through, please," Ayan replied.

Lagarik looked to Captain Vega with big dark blue eyes that were round with surprise. She nodded. The holographic image of a man in a uniform she'd never seen before - a high-collared jacket over a shimmery dark skin suit - appeared. "Captain Vega, Admiral Anderson. I see you've already done most of the work for us. We - the Varcan along with one of the newly arrived British Alliance Battlegroups - are taking responsibility for the security of Tiy. We will arrive in twenty-eight minutes."

"How did you find out about our operations here?" Captain Vega asked. She was grateful that there was a relief force on the way to clean up the mess the Order made, but it was too soon. It was just as likely that they'd sweep in with a superior force and claim credit for the battle as well.

"Admiral Anderson has kept Haven Fleet Command aware of the status here. Her short briefings started coming in minutes after the Citadel Shuttle was discovered."

"Did she tell you anything about V1?" Captain Vega asked, seeing Ayan shake her head right away.

"No, I'm afraid I don't know what you're referring to. Are you currently in combat with the Order?"

"Our part is finished for the moment, we're making repairs," Captain Vega replied. "Why?"

"We were hoping to arrive in time to fully engage and assist you in defeating the enemy. I know you've become a sort of bounty ship, but this stands to be a larger victory," Captain Paron said. "Will V1 become significant in our strategy?"

"Yes. We'll keep you updated as the situation develops," Captain Vega replied, using a phrase that she'd heard just as much in the news as from senior officers in the past. "You'll be contacted five minutes before you arrive with more details. Be ready to fight." She ended the call and then turned to Ayan. "Did Jake know you were telling the Fleet what was going on?"

"Only after Oz informed me that the Alliance wanted to be involved. I convinced Jake that shutting the Fleet out would be a mistake here. I'm glad I did, because Tiy could become a very large problem. I still didn't think assistance would get here so fast. I was sure it would be another two days at least."

"Why did you keep me out of the loop?" Captain Vega pressed.

"So you could concentrate on making sure the Triton was ready. You did better than anyone expected," Ayan said. "Finn traced the powerline, by the way, it's deactivated and the turret gunner has been extracted. He's moving on to the power node that we may have lost."

"Good," Captain Vega replied. She contacted Finn directly then. "How long do you think it'll be before we get dorsal shields back to full capacity, Chief?"

"That depends on how bad the burnout is. My people are already transporting replacement emitters though," he replied.

"Thank you," Captain Vega replied, ending the call then looking at Ayan. "Maybe you should go back down to the Flight Deck. They probably want you in the Sciences Section."

"Yes, Captain," Ayan said as she handed responsibilities for monitoring the Engineering Station to Finn's subordinate.

Chapter 29

Impact

THE DECISION WAS MADE. Given the choice to go after Eve aboard her massive Base Ship or Admiral Scanlon on the Ascendant, Jacob Valent was certain that taking out the Admiral was the right thing. He waited until the Breaching Attack Ship, or BAS, was at the point of no return. It slipped through space, a featureless needle in the dark, finally coming to a point along their course where turning to port or starboard was unavoidable.

"The Ascendant," Jake Valent said flatly over their low powered laser link. Noah guided the new Breaching Attack Ship towards it and started preparing for final acceleration.

The interior of the ship was so dark that if it weren't for the tactical map on his in-helmet display marking the other people in the cabin, he would have sworn he was alone. He was connected to a pilot seat that looked like it had grown out of the ship's deck. It was as sturdy and immovable as the hard internal armour that surrounded them all. The manual controls were old fashioned, plugged into a mechanical box that sent impulses down wires leading to the few thrusters and other systems built into the vessel. The stick, throttle, and pedals were stiff compared to what he was used to, but there was something incredible about the feel of them. There was no instrument panel or other emissive displays. Everything he needed to know was all in his helmet display.

The needle-shaped ship was almost all armour with a layer of stealth material that eliminated the need for several systems that used a great deal of power to do the same job. Once the forward hatch was sealed, the thick coating was seamless. It worked. They managed to slip past starfighters and sensor sweeps without detection as far as any of them could tell. So many systems had to be sacrificed so the ship wouldn't emit detectable energy that it was no longer a modern vessel by any stretch. There weren't even emergency systems, life support or lighting. The utter darkness was more isolating than Noah expected. Somewhere in front of him Alice, Jake, Iruuk and Alaka were in their heavy armour, fastened to the sides of the inner hull. He used the visual and aural quiet to focus on the task at hand.

"Final approach, activating solid Xetima booster," Noah said as he finished laying in their course. The Triton was out of the way. The Ascendant's dorsal side shield emitter array had completely burned out. It was time to do something he'd been avoiding his entire career - crash into a ship at the highest speed he could achieve. He flipped the safety cover off the end of his throttle, then toggled the switch that started the all-or-nothing rocket engine at the rear of the BAS.

For a moment nothing happened. "You know, to be honest,

that's kind of a relief," Iruuk said over their close proximity radio. "I really wasn't looking forward to…"

Then the entire ship started vibrating so abruptly and violently that it felt like they'd been hit by a bomb. Noah watched as their speed relative to the Ascendant climbed into the triple digits, then quadruple digits. When it was about to pass fifteen thousand kilometres per hour he activated the secondary inertial dampener array. The high-powered system would save everyone inside once they struck the Ascendant. They were the second largest system aboard, right behind the main rocket engine that was propelling them towards the softest part of the Ascendant's dorsal side. Between the two systems, they'd look like a flaming comet that came out of nowhere. It was a simple trade of stealth on approach with speed during the last seconds of their journey.

"Impact in three, two," Noah said, the last digit drowned out as the sounds of a horrific crash filled his ears and shook his body despite the anchoring of his heavy suit and the massive impact-dampening system. The BAS' forward armour was gone, its pieces broken away after the hard needle tip pierced the outer hull, exploding to the sides of the ship as it came under pressure. Another layer of material behind that broke away as it pushed protective metal inside the Ascendant aside and finished slowing the BAS.

The rocket booster was cooling off. It ran out of fuel during impact as planned. The exposed mid-hull of the BAS was activating, quickly bursting into expanding liquid that hardened, filling all the cracks around the BAS so it became a plug. The front of the ship opened and the last of the BAS's systems went into standby mode. "That wasn't as bad as I thought," Noah said as light from the hallway below spilt into the simple hull of the breaching ship.

The silence following the violent breach through the enemy ship's hull and several decks was eerie as his suit separated from his seat. Two large shadows moved into the opening at the front of the ship and dropped into the hallway beneath.

As the light struck them, Noah shuddered at the sight of Alaka and Iruuk, both standing over two metres in thick armour that looked like blackened liquid metal. They carried beam weapons that required a backpack with a cold micro fusion reactor and power storage system. Light filled the hallway as Alaka fired down the corridor for a second then shouted. "Clear!"

Jake and Alice dropped down to the deck beneath the nose of the BAS. Their footing never looked uncertain, and they were ready the instant they dropped, their Knight Killer rifles in hand. Their armour was midnight black, made of flexible horizontal slats over military vacsuits. The bands of metal hid rows of tiny multi-purpose emitters that could be used for energy shielding, to generate thrust, dampen impacts or gravitational force. Providing impact resistance was the least of its capabilities.

Noah let his armour disconnect from the seat and hundreds of firm points of contacts let loose at once. He managed to brace himself against the dead control stick instead of falling directly onto the controls, then slipped around them so he could slide down the deck past the cooling inertial dampeners into the hallway. He landed between Jake and Alice on his feet. His armour's systems made it feel like a light impact instead of a two-storey fall. He unslung his rifle, made sure it was set to marksman mode and said; "Set."

"We have ninety-two heavy combat androids moving through the ship, prioritising Order Knights and other heavily armed units," Alaka reported. "They're marking themselves on our tactical maps now."

"Is that what you've been up to all this time?" Noah asked, watching as his tactical map updated with the schematic of the Ascendent's interior, then green dots in groups of three and five that showed where their combat androids were moving. Half of them were meeting resistance, shown by flashing red dots. Most of the others were scanning, moving through the ship, connecting to computer systems, and capturing data as they attempted to hack into the ship's main control and secure storage systems. They marked retreating crew members and soldiers who weren't providing resistance that was as effective as the Knights as yellow dots that occasionally flashed red.

"A hunter should never stop developing and mastering his tools," Alaka replied.

"Where is she?" Jake asked over their secure laser link.

"I'm checking. There's a lot of panic, it's hard to pick her out," Alice replied, her head down.

THE ACTION around Admiral Scanlon on the bridge of the Ascendant was noisy and near chaos as every station tried to repair and maintain control of systems. The combat androids were well equipped. Groups of three could stand against a pair of Order Knights long enough for others to infiltrate key areas of the ship and make trouble. As she understood it, the combat androids that were sent aboard using torpedoes that were launched as soon as her Flagship's shields failed. She didn't understand how a captured ship like the Triton could break through the defences of a battle group - even an underpowered one - and win an engagement with the Ascendant. It should not have been possible.

Nothing smaller than a juggernaut should have been able to accomplish that alone.

"Where is the heavy fighter support from the Base Ship?" Rear Admiral Rinder asked his lead tactical officer.

"They've been intercepted by Samurai Squadron. The Uriel fighters they're flying are some kind of sleeper craft; the same old shell with new capabilities and intelligent armour," he replied. "The Base Ship won't be recovering the fighter wings, though. They'll come to our aid once the Base Ship completes its emergency wormhole jump. That is, if Samurai Squadron doesn't finish them off. They're taking them out at a ratio of one to six."

"I'm guessing we're on the losing side of that ratio," the Rear Admiral said, satisfied with his subordinate's cringing nod as a response. "Send our destroyers their way. Maybe we can turn it around with a little cover, or at least recover a few of our pilots.

"Yes, Sir," replied the Lieutenant.

"No help there," the Rear Admiral said as he looked at Scanlon. "Any contact from our other allies since their fighter patrol was taken out?"

Admiral Scanlon turned towards the communications section of the bridge. They seemed too busy accomplishing nothing. "Try to contact the Saratoga, immediately!" she barked, not for the first time.

"There's still no response, Ma'am," replied a frazzled communications officer, shaking his head. "They've either left the area or are running silent."

"Reach out to the Rixe," Admiral Scanlon ordered. It was unlikely that the ship was anywhere nearby after completing its mission to assassinate the royal family in the Cefa System, but she had to try.

"Aye, I'll try to raise them," the communications officer replied, a glimmer of hope showing in his eyes.

"Admiral, it's time for you to go," Rear Admiral Rinder said, gesturing towards Gisa, who was already wearing a stealth suit that seemed to negate light.

Scanlon looked to Rinder in surprise. "Are you saying that we're about to lose the Ascendant?"

He nodded. "I'm about to order the crew to re-crystalize our main data storage units and abandon ship. I'll stay here so I can slow the enemy's progress, but the androids just got control of propulsion and power distribution. Your secondary egress route is about to be blocked."

"There's nothing you can…" the question died on her lips as she felt something in her mind. She, like most modern admirals and high ranking officers in the fleet, had some telepathy training. Only one had actually exhibited active talent, but most could sense when they were being read. Scanlon had no telepathic abilities save for the most minimal mental awareness. For the first time in her life she felt someone who meant her harm touch her mind. It was like feeling an emotion - aggression - that was not her own rise up then fade away. What Mikan told her about Alice must have been true. Her encounter with a powerful Geist had forced a door in her mind to open and she was probably a telepath. That, or they had another telepath aboard the Ascendant that didn't follow a strict moral code. But then, why would a random telepath feel such animosity towards her? The touch of another mind could only lead her to one conclusion. "Alice is here. She's coming for me."

"They won't get you. Our remaining corvettes are getting ready to take our escape ships," Rear Admiral Rinder said.

Gisa was already leading the way to one of the heavy

bridge security doors and Admiral Scanlon was right behind her, doing her best to keep up with her at a dead run. She stopped as the door started to close behind her so the bridge would be perfectly isolated. "Don't go down with the ship."

"It's been a pleasure serving you, Admiral," Rear Admiral Rinder said as the thick armoured door closed between them.

"We have to go," Gisa said as an entire squad of fifteen Order Knights in new heavy combat armour formed up around them. They started running towards the lift that would take them to the nearest uncompromised escape shuttle.

Chapter 30

Chasing Scanlon

MENTALLY TRACKING Scanlon wasn't like any of the other things Alice had used her gift for. The practice she'd had with Quan at determining who someone was depending on what their mind or presence felt like had honed that ability, but actually searching for someone who was on the run wasn't something she expected to do. Now that she was doing just that, it felt like an obvious use. Perhaps it would have been the first thing her father would try if he was given the empathic gift. It didn't feel wrong to Alice, but it wasn't something that she'd talk to other people about unless she had to and she felt it could be a way to misuse the talent. Above all else, the notion that she could track someone by reaching out with her mind would probably inflate the anti-telepathy paranoia to absolute hostility.

It was difficult at first, and Alice was sure that she tried too hard at the beginning, mentally alerting Scanlon when she found her, but it was unlikely that the Admiral had anything but an eerie 'I'm being watched' kind of sensation for a moment. Alice backed off the instant she was sure Scanlon was the one she was sensing. Alice was also certain that the Admiral was alarmed and ready to run. That was expected, but she was surprised that tracking Scanlon once she relaxed her efforts to seek her out became easy.

As they rushed down a corridor and met half a dozen Order Soldiers in armoured vacsuits that looked like their own except for their dark green colour and markings, Alice was surprised that she was still aware of Scanlon even after dropping back and taking cover for a moment. "Save your energy," Jake said as he pulled a pair of grenades from inside his jacket and tossed them around the corner. They were small, no longer or wider than her middle finger.

A concussive thump made the air pulse and they rushed down the hallway. Alaka dropped a tiny capsule filled with nanobots into the middle of the scattered soldiers. Their vacsuits saved them from broken bones and worse, but the grenades Jake used put tiny holes in each of them that their knockoff uniforms hadn't repaired yet. If any of them were framework soldiers, the nanobots Alaka released would knock them out and stop them from regenerating. "Next time we run into grunts like these, we cut them down."

"I agree," Alaka replied. "Taking cover once we saw them lying in wait was wise, but our energy shields and weaponry would have given us a clear advantage."

"Still have a lock on Scanlon?" Jake asked.

Alice didn't have to think about it, she just knew where the Admiral was, so she marked her on their shared tactical map.

"There. She's going towards one of the main transit tubes from the bridge."

"That one's shut down, our androids got the inner transit system," Iruuk said.

"Then she'll be going for the outer one or the stairs nearby," Alaka added. "There are no airlocks on that level though."

"The escape shuttles are two levels above," Iruuk said as he pinged the map to show where they were.

"Then we cut her off from below," Jake said as he, Alice, Noah, Iruuk and Alaka started running through the hallways. They moved two-by-two with the Nafalli at the front, Jake in the middle with Alice and Noah taking up the rear. "I'll tell you if she changes her mind," Alice said.

That section of the ship seemed largely empty. The androids that were hacking into the systems aboard opened the blast doors for anyone but Order Knights, letting them take the escape shuttles and smaller emergency pods. It was intentional. They only used the doors to hamper and coral the few Order Knights they found.

Being able to race through the hallways of a ship unimpeded even for a minute seemed strange. Alice expected a whole squad of Knights to jump out at them at any moment, and the expectation only grew as time went on and they only encountered panicked crew members who wanted nothing more than to get away from the terrifying group of five.

Maybe that's why Iruuk tried to start a conversation. "So, I was talking to a few of the people in the Command Centre yesterday, and they were all impressed with how you're taking being retired from the military."

"This may not be the time," Alaka, his father, said.

"I was just going to ask him how he likes being free to pursue his own goals," Iruuk explained.

A group of four Order of Eden soldiers rushed into the next hallway intersection. Alice's tactical scanner only saw them half a second before they ran into position. They were in armour that looked similar to the type that Jake and his team wore, but they all knew it was several generations behind. Each one of them had one of the heavy rifles the Order Knights were famous for, but they didn't seem as organized or as quick as the elite soldiers. Alaka and Iruuk activated their beam weapons, sending lines of blinding light and destructive heat against their assailant's energy shields.

Stoic, seemingly fearless, the Order Knights fired back and their explosive rifle rounds took the Nafalli father and son's energy barriers down to sixty-three percent before Jake charged between them, holding a secondary shield in front of him like a shield strapped to his forearm. He had slung his rifle so he could switch to a newer handgun that he blasted through the one-way barrier at one of the Order Knights.

The Nafalli charged into the intersection, moving in long steps that allowed them to outflank the Order Knights. Alice and Noah moved closer to either side of the hallway as they opened fire with their rifles, shooting past Jake as he roared, running towards the innermost pair of Order knights. With a loud crack, the energy shield projected from his left command and control bracer burned out, but he'd already closed to point-blank range.

Using what must have been every newton of force that his vacsuit and heavy armour could give him, Jake pushed the Order Knight on the left so hard that he was sent through the left wall of the corridor behind him. Jake's sidearm was out again. He gripped the top of one soldier's head with one hand while he put the muzzle of it against the Order Knight's faceplate.

"Surrender!" Jake bellowed loud enough to make the microphone in his helmet crackle.

The Order Knight's response came as an attempt to cut through his assailant's suit shields with a nanoblade that spat orange sparks as it failed to penetrate. Jake pulled the trigger once to little effect. A second shot in the same place cracked the Knight's faceplate. A third had it almost shattered, and a fourth destroyed his enemy's head.

The Order Knight who Jake had sent through a bulkhead came charging back into the hallway, and a powerful armour-piercing explosive round stopped him before he took his third step. Alice smiled a little as she realized that the precise shot came from Noah, who had always been a good shot, but she'd never seen him in sniper mode. With very little space to shoot past her father, the knight wasn't an easy target to hit. "I've been practising," Noah said calmly before sending another high powered round at the Order Knight as he stumbled. It sent him tumbling back to the deck, his shields depleted.

Jake picked the Order Knight up and tossed him through the wall opposite the one he'd been put through. Without taking a moment to enjoy the spectacle, he threw a trio of low-radius fragmentation grenades after the soldier. They detonated with a loud pop, which isn't what made Alice flinch. It was the unexpected shot that Jake finished the Order Knight off with using his sidearm. "Make sure none of these assholes regenerate. Shoot 'em with M-Twenty-Eight."

Munition twenty-eight was an intelligent round that had a counter-pulse mechanism that depleted shields, a point that could pierce armour, and an explosive finish that went off before passing through a target, releasing a package of nanobots that forced framework soldiers - especially Order Knights - to regenerate one more time, leaving their framework system behind in a way that prevented them from doing it ever again. Alice knew it well and had already shot several Order Knights with the ammunition type on previous missions.

The Order Knight Iruuk was firing on fell half a metre in front of him as the Nafalli's beam weapon burned through his chest. Alaka's target lunged at the last instant, knocking the beam weapon aside. The Nafalli grasped the soldier by the neck and threw him over his shoulder. He bounced against the ceiling, tumbled through the air, then landed in a heap on the deck. Before the soldier settled there, Alaka turned and ran after him. Alice lost sight of the enemy and the large Nafalli, but felt the deck shudder three times before there were three gunshots. "That one won't be regenerating," Alaka said as he emerged from the mouth of the hallway. "Perhaps that answers your question, Son."

"What? What was the question again?" Iruuk asked as the pair of Nafalli, Alice and Noah checked each direction of the four-way corridor intersection to make sure no one else was coming.

"How Jake is taking his sudden freedom," Alaka said.

"Oh, right," Iruuk said. Then, after a moment he added; "I didn't hear Mister Valent answer though."

"He just threw a guy through a wall," Noah replied. "Twice."

"I thought that was normal combat for someone of his stature," Iruuk said in a whisper that they could all hear clearly.

"That is not a normal fighting style," Alaka sighed. "Jake is an exceptional fighter, but also a passionate one at times."

"Those weren't fully trained or armoured Order Knights," Jake said as though he didn't hear the conversation. "Stay focused. We'll probably run into a few. Which way?" Jake asked.

Alice could still feel Scanlon and pinged the map to indicate that they'd moved, but were forced to go around a few bulkheads that the androids had dropped in their way. Alice sensed frustration and fear. There were six other people with her. "The quickest way would be down this corridor, left, then right to the stairwell."

"Good," Jake said, starting into a run. The rest of the group caught up and re-formed. He pulled a thin puck-like shield emitter from his left arm unit, tossed it away and replaced it with another. "To answer your question, Iruuk, it's a relief, being out of Haven Fleet, but only because I wasn't a fully qualified Admiral. I didn't have the experience, and didn't serve as much time as I should have before I was promoted to the rank. I did my best, but never thought it was my place, so it's good to step aside."

"That's not what you told me last month," Alaka countered.

"Okay, so sending people on missions that I wanted to go on myself was pissing me off then, but I guess that's not the biggest problem with me being an Admiral. Now I'm happy to do things my way, but I have other problems."

"Oh? Like what?" Iruuk asked.

Alice cringed. The younger Nafalli didn't seem aware that it wasn't the time for this kind of conversation. He also didn't seem to realize that what he was asking was intrusive, personal, and even inappropriate to ask someone like his father. Sure, it would be fine for her to ask for more personal or career details from her father, but she would have picked the right time. That was why she was surprised when her father actually answered.

They were still running. Crew members scattered as they passed down one long hallway, a few were about to emerge from bunk rooms, but retreated hastily, closing doors behind them. Ideally, Alice and the group would have a much larger force, so they could clear those rooms, and make sure that the crews were isolated and secured so nothing could surprise them from behind. But they were depending on speed this time out, which was reckless, but they'd all done it before. That was except for Noah. Jake's reply sounded like it was something he'd considered more than once, it even seemed a little practised. "Now I can build whatever I want. I have the money, the ship, even the tech, but it's no good unless I take it all far away from home. Ayan's going back to the Haven System in a couple of days. Part of me wants to follow her so I can be with her and Laura, but I know I'd get restless before long. Ayan knows it too. Besides, I want to be with Alice, to see what she's built. I know, I can contact Ayan whenever I want, but she's shown me that it's just not the same. I can't imagine how much she misses Laura, or how much I'll miss Ayan when…"

Alice was shutting him and the rest of the team out. It was part of how she was able to mentally reach far enough to be aware of Scanlon. Even still, as Jake was about to change the topic, she sensed something unusual from him - a mix of joy and anxiety. "What's going on with Mom?" she asked.

"Are you going full telepathic now?" Jake asked. "I couldn't hide this from Oz, either."

"No, you just poked through the block I have on you with some kinda… Janxiety. A combo of happiness and nervousness."

"Janxiety, I like it," Noah snickered.

"Ayan's about a month along," Jake replied.

"Congratulations, Jake," Alaka said.

"What?" Alice asked, stunned. She had to concentrate on holding her focus enough to be aware of Scanlon. "That's amazing, Dad."

"We'll talk about it later," Jake said as they turned towards the stairwell. The doors opened and their tactical maps populated with nine markings, indicating that there was almost a full squad of Order Knights.

They'd set up in two lines that filled the double door passage into the stairwell. The first line was kneeling with a second standing. All eight of them had their rifles trained on them the moment Jake and his team stepped around the corner.

The Nefalli and Jake were caught by the brunt of the hail of anti-shield armour-piercing rounds. These Knights were in the latest armour, the ammunition they were using tore through walls like they were made of paper and actually dented the advanced suits Jake's team wore.

One pierced Alaka's thigh, painting the wall behind him with a spatter of red as they retreated around the corner. He stood on the other as nanobots and a regeneration serum rebuilt the limb quickly. His armour regenerated, using energy and a mass reserve to re-seal. "They were ready for us," he said.

Iruuk stared at the wound, frozen for a moment. The memory of losing his own leg brought a wave of anguish back, and Alice was almost just as stunned when she sensed it. She was there when it happened, it was the darkest point in their relationship. Alice reached up and turned his chin towards her. "He's all right. We're okay."

"Almost healed right back up, Son. Focus on the hunt," Alaka said.

Iruuk stiffened and nodded before slipping into a hunting stance with his beam weapon at the ready. "I'm ready."

"No more distractions," Jake said, leaning around the corner to fire several shots. At first, Alice thought he missed, then she realized that he'd taken out the door controls so they would stay wide open. "We got complacent because the androids hacked the turret and defence systems."

"There are ways around the stairwell," Noah proposed. "And holy crap, does that hurt like nothing else."

Alice looked at him in time to see his armour repair itself over his left shoulder. It had been dented inwards. There was a burst of black where more than one of a Knight's rounds exploded against it. "You're all right?"

"Yeah, suit's regenerating and my ribs are back in one piece," Noah said. "That was close."

"I'm sorry," Alice said, remorseful that she didn't notice that he'd nearly been killed.

"I'm good, no worries," he replied, straightening, holding his rifle across his chest. "What's next? We go around?"

"I think I've got an idea." With a few icon selections made with eye movements over images in her visor display, Alice loaded her rifle's grenade launcher with another ammunition type and then nodded to herself. "We don't have time to fight them. We should use supression."

"You're right," Jake said. "Specifics?"

"We hold them up with metal suppression foam and go up the transit line," Alice said as Noah nodded.

Iruuk's long snout bobbed up and down as he nodded. "I like it."

"Good plan," Jake said as his shields finished recharging. "You all right, Alaka?"

"Ready," he replied.

"Alaka, Iruuk and me will lay down cover fire while you and Noah launch suppression rounds," Jake said. "On three."

"Okay, getting it loaded now," Noah said, then nodded and said; "Good, ready, I'm good."

"One, two, three," Jake counted. As he said the last, Iruuk and Alaka stepped out into the open firing their beam weapons. They were set to their maximum charge. Channels of molten metal were burned along the walls as their beams of white light found their marks. Jake's shields were running as hot as theirs as it added energy to their defensive barriers. He fired his Knight Killer rifle between them.

For the first moment, there was a wave of return fire, but when a few of the Knights saw how quickly their suits' energy shields were being depleted, they started to move to cover at the left and right of the stairwell's double doors.

"Now, fire all five rounds," Alice said as she moved into position so she could use the grenade launcher to pump out the largest ammunition type it could take. Alaka and Iruuk stopped firing. Ten heavy three-millimetre wide cylinders were sent down the hall, through the yawning double wide doorway. The launcher was set to its lowest mode, so she could see the next four rounds leave the end of her rifle with a loud thrumming.

The Order Knights were standing out of the way, so the grenades bounced off the back wall to the left of the stairs. Before they could tumble back out into the hall, they burst. A foam made of liquid metal and monofilament wire burst from all the grenades, filling that section of the hallway and trapping the Order Knights as a charge meant to deplete their energy shields and other systems went off.

"That'll buy us at least a couple minutes," Jake said with a chuckle. They rushed back the way they came then towards the outer transit corridor. Someone had sealed the containment doors that would take them inside. "These are armoured bulkheads," Iruuk said as they stopped.

"Then we cut," Alaka said, starting to burn a line through the sealed doors. Between his and and his son's efforts, they cut a neat square door in a little over twenty seconds.

It was then that Alice realized why she was feeling occasional spikes of frustration from the enemy Admiral. "Scanlon's people have had to cut through the blast doors our androids have been dropping in her way," Alice said with a little smile. "We're going to beat her there."

The thrusters built into their suits had survived the brief encounters for the most part. Only the barrier emitters on the right side of Alaka's armour weren't working, so his son had to fly him up the three levels as Alice and Jake planted traps below that were set to detect Order Knights. If they tried to follow them, they wouldn't get halfway down the corridor thanks to several cloaked anti-tank mines.

"Scanlon is afraid. I think she's trapped," Alice said as they rushed down a hallway near the edge of the ship. They were between the Admiral and the escape ships.

"How many with her?" Jake asked.

"Two. Only two now," Alice said as they turned down the second-to-last corridor before they'd be able to lay eyes on her. "Urgency and dread."

"Stop," Alaka said, and the five of them halted on the spot.

"You're right," Jake said, turning the gain of their scanners all the way up.

The tactical display was muddied with extra energy readings and clumped motes of dust, but Alice made out the wavering shapes of four figures. She raised her rifle to aim at the one behind her and was surprised to see that Noah was doing the same. There was one right above him, and he either hadn't seen it or didn't see it as a priority.

Alaka and Iruuk blasted the other two Order Knights at close range with their beam weapons for a moment. Alaka swiped at the one in front of him. Long claws made from nanobots swirling around spades that jutted from the end of his suit's fingers slashed across the Knight's helmet and then his neck guard. It was enough to weaken the armour at least, and his son finished the task of defeating the Knight as his father stepped back. Iruuk's beam weapon burned through the gaps in the armour, burning the flesh beneath away. Alaka and Iruuk finished the last one off with their beam weapons as the Order Knight tried to fire back.

Alice and Noah were able to fire through their target's armour, which was set to emit a cloaking field, not his energy shield. Jake made the one who was about to drop onto Noah from above his priority, pushing the younger man out of the way so Jake could grab the Knight on his way down. Point-blank shots from Jake's sidearm finished him quickly. "Always take care of yourself first!" Jake shouted at him as soon as the action was over. "You aren't worth a damn to anyone else dead."

Jake didn't wait for a response but activated the energy shield mounted to his arm. Then he turned and started striding down the hallway that would take them to Admiral Scanlon.

Chapter 31

The Turn

ADMIRAL OLIVIA SCANLON'S mind raced as she realized that she was about to be caught. Her thought process threatened to devolve into chaos, like a kicked hornet's nest of useless ideas and regrets.

The most recent regrets led her directly to the situation she was in. Like escaping early while her most faithful subordinate covered for her. Then there was the idea of sending her protection detail of Order Knights after her pursuers instead of keeping them close at hand.

Even the thought of coming to Tiy in person instead of staying on Iora where she could monitor the situation seemed foolish. She watched the Order Knight turn his laser tool off and give up on cutting through the door. "I'll have more luck hacking the controls so the blast door will open," he explained as he opened the large access panel.

Admiral Scanlon watched as Gisa looked into the small compartment. "Is there anything I can do to help?"

"I'm trained for this, you'd only slow me down," the Order Knight replied.

"You have a more important job," Scanlon said to Gisa. "When they come, be passive. Stand still, put your hands up and stay behind me unless they order you to step away. I'm going to try to earn the mercy of the Haven soldiers, but they'll probably execute or imprison me in a place that I won't be able to get out of. You aren't as important. You will cooperate with them while you use the opportunity to observe, learn everything you can, and then, when you're sure you can escape, run back to the Order. Tell them everything."

"What do you mean? Earn their mercy?" Gisa asked.

What came next was thanks to the clear, disciplined kind of thinking that Scanlon was proud of. An idea was coming together as she spoke. "Above all else, survival is our goal. When superiority, control and charm fail, we must do anything to persevere. Buy time until you can find your way back on top. That's what's gotten me to my position above all else. If you base everything you do on that, you'll be fine."

"I understand, but what are you planning, Admiral?" Gisa asked.

"Don't worry," Scanlon said as she realized that the only way to follow her own advice was to surrender completely. "They'll be focused on me. You'll probably have a chance to escape, and if you don't, I want you to follow my lead."

"What are you going to do?" Gisa pressed.

The sound of heavy boot steps coming around the corner drew Admiral Scanlon's attention. The Order Knight was utterly failing at hotwiring the door to open, as he should. Those were security doors, not just meant to isolate sections of the ship to prevent damage from spreading. The designers of the Ascendant were excellent, of course, it would be difficult or even impossible to circumvent her security measures.

Then there was a voice in her ear, Rear Admiral Rinder. "There's a larger enemy force coming in, and only three of our corvettes remain. The heavy cruisers are holding, but the enemy corvettes have rejoined the fight. They've taken most of our fighter screen and point defence systems out completely with the help of their fighter squadron. There's no cover, and every shield we have is failing, Admiral. What are your orders?"

"Retreat. Abandon the Ascendant. Melt her data storage drives down and deactivate all reactors," Admiral Scanlon said. "I hope you're not still on the bridge."

"We relocated to a conference room close to an airlock. The bridge staff is mostly intact. What about you? Are you close to an escape shuttle? I can't see you, the internal scanners aren't under our control," The Rear Admiral asked.

"Worry about yourself. Get the crew out," Scanlon replied. "That's an order."

"Yes, Admiral," Rear Admiral Rinder replied. She could hear the sounds of a ship roughly docking in the background. At least one of the corvettes was probably already there to pick them up.

It was time. The decision to save herself, to leave early and not stay with her faithful Rear Admiral had put her in a corner. The option of surrender and what it would mean ran through her head in a rush. She would be isolated in the brig of the Triton if they were smart, not allowed to speak to anyone. There would be a hand off with Haven Fleet. Then she'd be in the hands of their Intelligence department and allowed to speak with expert interrogators. One would probably pose as a kind of therapist who would monitor her well being and try to earn her friendship. It would be a mistake to let her speak to any of their leaders, but it might happen. Some of them were prideful. They'd want to see her in captivity. Whatever happened, Olivia Scanlon knew that she'd have to befriend the right captors, and it would take a lot of betrayal to earn their trust.

They'd perform a deep scan on her mind if they had the technology to do it safely. Everything she said would have to line up with what they found perfectly. Scanlon's planning was interrupted by an explosive thought. What if switching sides would benefit her more than staying with the Order of Eden anyway?

Perhaps it was time for a change. The Order of Eden was starting to feel more like a cult than a corporately owned military force. Eve was fanning the flames of zealotry and they were catching. The woman seemed to believe that Hampon was still alive, somewhere in the future, sending whispers to his brother, Overlord Dron. The mad fire of zealotry seemed pure in her eyes, and that would either make the Order more dangerous than ever or it was the beginning of the end. Scanlon couldn't be absolutely certain, but her method of infecting worlds with her kind of culture wouldn't survive. Her command would become about destroying anyone who stood against the Order of Eden and nothing else. That was always her last resort, not the second step in a strategy of domination.

Citadel wasn't interested in helping. Whatever they believed, and she still hadn't determined exactly what that was, it didn't line up with the kind of culture war she had become used to winning. Olivia Scanlon started to feel calm as the sound of those boots against the deck grew louder. "Follow my lead. It'll be all right," she said to Gisa.

. . .

WHEN ALICE, Alaka, Iruuk and Noah followed Jake around the corner, the first thing they saw was Admiral Scanlon, who stood in a vacsuit. It was similar to the one Alice wore under the heavy armour, and she was staring right at them through her faceplate.

The Order Knight behind Scanlon froze mid-task, his hands buried in the electrical panel beside the door. His simple mind wasn't filled with panic, but he was eager to get that door open, irritated at being interrupted.

The Knight's mind felt simple to Alice because the woman who was trying to help, one who was even a little shorter than she was, had tamed her fear with discipline. Then there was Scanlon, whose emotional state became clearer as she came into sight.

Admiral Scanlon's fear was only background noise compared to the determination and what Alice would describe later as a clear expectation that she would persevere. There was no indication that the woman was panicked by the sight of five heavily armoured enemies closing on her, or that her fear was about to overtake everything else.

In her place, Alice could only hope that she could be as calm and collected. Admiral Scanlon's short companion was standing behind her. The Order Knight moved to pick his rifle up from where it was leaning beside the open panel and Scanlon stopped him with a hand on his shoulder. "You'll only get us all killed. You and your entire squad have failed."

"No, I will not surrender!" he shouted. It was the last thing he'd ever say.

Admiral Scanlon tapped a display that was tattooed on the back of her hand then put her hands up.

Jake raised his sidearm and was about to ask what she'd done then the Order Knight began to scream. He scrambled to get his helmet off. It came unlatched and then rolled across the corridor as his flesh slipped off the silver framework skeleton beneath. The Admiral took one step away from the slowly spreading pool of red and black remains. "I'll come quietly."

"She's way too calm for someone who's about to get captured," Alice whispered to Jake.

He stopped five metres away from the Admiral. "You're surrendering?"

Admiral Scanlon nodded and retracted her headpiece. The faceplate retracted to the side, turning it into a hood first, then it rolled down into her collar. She smiled a little, and there was a hint of relief in her mind as she took a careful step forward. "I'm ready to join Haven. I realize it'll take years for me to build trust, but you'll eventually see that I've grown to detest the cash cult zealotry that..."

Alice couldn't believe what she was sensing from the Admiral. It was true. Scanlon was willing to flip, then, where there was a neatly organized chorus of emotions, she could only sense an absence.

"Put it down!" Jake said, raising his sidearm and taking aim at Scanlon's shorter companion.

The Admiral sank to her knees. Her limp, lifeless body fell face first, revealing the back of her head where a small group of wounds bled through her hair. Her companion was holding a blade gun. Those were usually used for stealth since their thin rounds didn't travel fast enough to break the sound barrier. They were known for shattering once they entered the target and Alice was certain that whatever was in the Admiral's head had been reduced to a shredded mess.

The woman dropped her pistol and Jake fired a containment round at her. In an instant, she was enclosed in a black bag that held her still. Jake let his sidearm fall back into his holster instead and then rushed to the Admiral's side. He scanned her with his enhanced command and control bracer. "Tell me she's still in there."

"No, I don't feel anything from her," Alice said.

"She's not regenerating, either, so there's no framework technology," Iruuk reported.

"I know," Jake replied quietly. "This is the only Scanlon you could find aboard? This isn't a decoy?"

"I'm sure. If there's another copy, then she's not on the ship. Probably not even in the Battlegroup," Alice replied, adding. "I'm sure."

"Dammit," Jake said, rising to his feet. "Was she really about to turn?"

"Yeah," Alice replied, still surprised.

For a moment, her father was furious, then he lashed out, denting the corridor bulkhead with a savage punch. Seconds later, he was focused and calm again. Alice blocked him out then, as she often did. "Ronin, what's happening out there?" Jake asked.

"We just stopped one of the corvettes that picked up the Ascendant's officers. The other got away," Ronin said. "The Triton's coming back now that the heavy cruisers are holding position. Get the Admiral yet?"

"Sort of," Jake said as he fired a containment bag round at the Admiral's body. Its stasis system engaged the moment she was fully encapsulated, though Alice was sure it wouldn't do any good. She dropped a capsule of nanobots onto the framework skeleton that would prevent it from ever activating again as Iruuk took high-powered scans of its equipment and the remains.

"Well, I guess the details can wait. Ready for pickup?" Ronin asked from the seat of his Archangel fighter.

"We'll be coming out on the dorsal side, near frame one-thirty-one, section fifty-nine," Jake replied as he put the Admiral's body over his shoulder. The bag was affixed there and held her in place so his hands were mostly free.

"A Clever Corvette will be there in three minutes," Ronin replied. "This party is winding down fast."

Chapter 32

Chasers

ADMIRAL SCANLON'S battlegroup had re-formed with the largest ships to either side of the Ascendant. The Admiral's flagship was remotely controlled by a small crew aboard the Triton using the ad-hoc connection installed by the assault androids that raided the vessel. It led the way to Tiy, where it was trying to establish a high orbit. The damaged ship was at the mercy of the pair of heavy cruisers that once escorted it. Every anti-capitol ship weapon they could point at the flagship was being turned in its direction. It was clear that the Order of Eden would rather see the Ascendant destroyed rather than have it fall into enemy hands.

Without help from the Triton, which had retreated to the other side of the solar system, the Heavy Cruisers dominated the field, making it impossible for the Clever Dream to dock with the Ascendant so Alice, Jake, Iruuk, Alaka and Noah could escape.

Breaker was tracking the progress of the last three fighters from Samurai Squadron using his tactical system. Four pilots had to eject, while the rest were ordered to return to the Triton because they were too badly damaged to continue. They'd lost no one so far.

The members of Samurai Squadron who remained in the fight were Ronin, Easy and Maid. Breaker Garma and Gren re-armed at the Triton and were punted back into battle. The trio made a short wormhole jump that made Breaker feel like his stomach flipped for a moment and they emerged near Tiy with the last of the enemy Battlegroup in sight.

He was in time to see Ronin guide his Archangel fighter under the main thrusters at the rear of Heavy Cruiser One. "Launching one EMP FS-Three Missile. I hope this is the needle that makes the giant flinch," he said as he launched his last electromagnetic pulse missile at the most vulnerable spot he could find.

Samurai Squadron had already taken out most of the lumbering ship's close-range countermeasures, and Minh-Chu's missile reached its target unobstructed. It flashed three times, blasting the lower aft shields of the Cruiser before colliding with a small explosion. "I'm out of missiles and the shields are still up! How about you blow this candle out for me, Breaker?"

The Clever Dream was drawing fire from the few smaller guns that were still operable on Heavy Cruiser One as its turrets fired bolts of blue energy back, taxing the large ship's shields enough to make them pay attention. That gave Breaker's small team of three a clear path to the aft of the large capital ship. "Man, we came in close to this thing. I've got this, launching a pair of EMP FS-Three missiles in ten seconds."

"The Cruiser would have made us splat if we jumped in further out, no?" asked Gren.

"I know, I'm just saying, I've never come out of a wormhole within ten kilometres of anything before," Breaker said. "We're launching two missiles at a time on this run."

"Two EMP missiles," Gren and Garma replied at the same time.

"I'll fire second after you," Garma announced.

"Firing third after Gren if there's anything left of their shields," Gren added.

"Switch to Javelin AP Sevens if the shields go down," Breaker said.

The aft side of Heavy Cruiser One loomed large before Breaker launched a pair of electromagnetic pulse missiles. His aim was true. He didn't wait to watch them reach the target. Instead, he veered away and accelerated into a curve that would take him across the side of the Cruiser facing away from the Ascendant. "That was a good shot," Dame said from the bridge of the Clever Dream. She was flying the fast corvette in and out of the Heavy Cruiser's starboard firing arc, giving her gunners opportunities to fire back at the massive ship's cannons while avoiding most of its firepower.

She was already a famous pilot. An ace and an adventurer who followed Alice Valent on a secret mission that, according to rumour, ended in victory, but not without a great sacrifice. Just as Breaker was about to thank her, Heavy Cruiser One's hangar doors exploded outward. The ejection of thick metal almost caught him. He was certain that whoever was in charge of triggering it waited until he was in the path of the tumbling chunks. A group of five fighters launched at full thrust, following the burst of steel closely. "Five ships just came out of the starboard hangar. Four Uriels and one heavy fighter I've never seen."

"This is a day you will all regret," said a voice over the emergency channel. It was unencrypted, coming from the new fighter type flying at the lead of the new group. Its large engines flared, sending it on a broad arc. Its four accompanying fighters followed as they provided cover fire, scoring several hits on Breaker's energy shields.

"Now that guy sounds serious," Ronin quipped on the Samurai Squadron encrypted channel. "Easy, Maid, let's break his group up."

The Raven arrived, emerging from a wormhole only five kilometres from Heavy Cruiser Two. The large, lumbering Cruiser was firing on the Ascendant using its port cannons, opposite. The ailing Flagship's armour was starting to come across the top.

"The lower aft quarter section of Cruiser One's shields are down," Breaker said as he evaded gunfire from the new fighters. His shields dropped over thirty percent before he managed to get out of their sights. "These are not newbies. Their guns are normal for a modern Uriel, but they're hitting like marksmen."

"I see this," Gren said. "The other Uriel pilots used a lot of missiles and rarely hit us with guns. These have hit all three of us now with no missiles."

"Follow me, I'm taking a run at Cruiser One," Breaker said, sticking to their mission. "Same firing order. Anti-Capitol ship torpedoes. Close range."

Two of the Uriel fighters broke off from the new group and moved to intercept him the instant he started towards Heavy Cruiser One. "You may have eliminated the Ascendant, but you will not extend your victory to the Farlight," said the voice over the emergency channel.

"Oh, is that what this ship is called?" Ronin asked. "Good name. Too bad someone forgot to paint it on the side. At least we know what to call it when we recycle its expensive bits later."

"It's good to hear that you're in good spirits at the end," the enemy pilot said.

"I'm sorry, this channel is reserved for emergencies only. Please stop reciting old one-liners from fighter jock dramas," Ronin quipped.

"Ronin. I'm looking forward to our first and last dogfight." Breaker could hear the smile in the speaker's words. He could also confirm that the transmission was coming from the larger fighter, which had a higher shield rating than their Archangels, but was less maneauverable thanks to extra mass. There was a cockpit pod at the front with two other pods built into a fixed-wing hull shaped like a wide, blunted A shape.

There was no need to pass the information on. Everyone who was in scanning range could see the details for themselves, so Breaker concentrated on his mission and fired a pair of Javelin Torpedoes at the unshielded section of the Farlight's aft section. They dug into the bare metal as he veered away, and his tactical display showed Gren and Garma's torpedoes doing the same, less than a second behind.

The impacts happened quickly. His torpedoes failed to penetrate all the way through the thick armour but exploded as they were designed to, thinning a part of the hull with a shallow crater that was several metres wide. The second pair of missiles made it through, and a small burst of material from the inside of the ship and a shudder indicated that they exploded inside the aft section of the ship. Garma's torpedoes were the most devastating. They passed right into the hole her twin's torpedoes made, then dozens of metres into the ship's interior before exploding. One of the vessel's massive main thrusters flickered and then went dark.

"Cruiser One's lower shields are failing, you guys hit something important, nice work!" Dame said as she guided the Clever Dream down so her gunners could strafe along the bare metal there. As if to further taunt the enemy, they peppered the hull with armour-piercing rounds right where the name of the ship - Fairlight - should have been painted. A few of their rounds even made it through, causing little eruptions of white gas as whatever was being stored there escaped.

"Its guns have stopped firing," Maid said. "Damn, I'll be impressed if we killed this capital ship without using antimatter."

The Heavy Cruiser Farlight opened a wormhole and its remaining pair of thrusters flared brightly, pushing it inside. The Clever Dream was on its way to the starboard side of the Ascendant before the massive ship that was keeping it from docking was halfway into the wormhole. "Time to pick our team up," Dame announced. "Cover me."

"Sorry, we can't get into position. Heavy Cruiser Two is still here, in case you didn't notice. They're trying to launch fighters, so we're holding that back by strafing their hangar doors," Pixie replied from the bridge of the Raven "Ronin's right: We could use another thirty pilots in Samurai Squadron. It would be great if they could get here right about now."

"Working on it, but I don't think I can get them trained in time for this fight," Ronin replied. "The Uriels from the Farlight are getting right in my way here."

The fighters that tried to chase after Breaker switched to Gren, and Garma was backing him up, launching signal-seeking missiles at both of them as she tried to get the rear-most one in her gunsights. "I can't keep running, Garma. I'm firing back. Do not get into my sights," Gren said as he flipped his fighter end over end to return fire on the fighter that was closest to him.

Garma was forced to move aside so she wouldn't get caught in his stream of bullets. "Coming in, watch for me on tactical," Breaker said, watching Gren's shield integrity drop to twenty-one percent on the front side. His rear shields were almost gone.

From Breaker's position, he was able to get a missile lock right away. The tone sounded like a sweet song in his ears as he launched a pair of fast seekers at each of the enemy fight-ers. They spat bright countermeasure capsules behind them, and all but one of his missiles followed the enemy ship.

Without hesitation, Breaker locked onto the enemy closest to Gren with his auto turret, fired another pair of fast seeker missiles at him, then opened up with his rail guns. Garma, repositioned so she wouldn't catch rounds from her comrades by mistake, opened fire as well. The lead Uriel's cannons burned through Gren's shields, momentarily ignoring the hail of gunfire it was under. It was just long enough to damage the Mergillian's main thrusters and pierce the hull across the aft side. His ship was sent spinning.

Breaker and Garma's attack on the fighter pursuing Gren sent it to pieces in the next instant. Maid strafed past from the opposite direction, sending a pair of fast seeker missiles after the surviving Uriel as it started breaking away. There was another one on her. "Gren! Gren!" Garma cried.

"My fighter has been destroyed. I am not well," Gren replied. "Stasis. Emergency Sta…"

"Gren!" Garma called one more time in a screech. She

piloted her fighter up to the remains of his, used her grappler to take hold of it and started charging her wormhole generator. "I'm taking him to the Triton."

"Wait. It'll be safer if we pick him up with the Clever Dream. Provide cover until we get there," Alice said over the secure communications channel.

"The boarding team is aboard the Clever Dream. Airlock sealed. We are on our way," Dame added.

Breaker gave chase to Gren's surviving attacker, who was about to come around for another pass. That was a mistake. Before Breaker could get a shot off, Garma launched half a dozen seeker missiles at the enemy Uriel. She was in turret mode, extending her ship's shields around her brother's broken hull, turning her ship so she could fire at any enemy that came near them, her auto turret adding to the hail of firepower she assailed them with. As the enemy Uriel struggled to dodge and launched countermeasure capsules, Garma took her turn to speak on the emergency channel. "Don't you come near him! I'll kill everyone who comes near him, then I'll hunt the rest of you down."

The Uriel fighter exploded in a burst of escaping air and debris. "I've gotta take care of this bugger on my back, breaking my pursuit of Mouthy One for a second," Ronin announced.

Breaker saw what was going on in an instant. Ronin had marked the new enemy heavy fighter as Mouthy One, and it was rushing towards the Ascendant from the aft side. A pair of rear-firing guns were taxing Ronin's shields from the front, while the remaining pair of Uriels were taking every opportunity to fire on him from a distance as they harassed Maid. The Clever Dream was seconds away from picking Gren and his wreck up. "I'll pick up the pursuit, Ronin," Breaker said, lining his nose up with the new enemy fighter. He pushed his main thrusters to full throttle then engaged his afterburners.

"You won't catch me in time," said the enemy over the emergency channel. "I am Stas. You'll never forget my name." A compartment opened on the lower side of his ship and released five torpedoes. As his heavy fighter veered off, the thick munitions accelerated towards the lower side of the Ascendant. Breaker's experience as a Bullet Chaser paid off then, as he used his computer's automatic aiming assistance program to lash out at the enemy torpedoes.

All but one were reduced to ruined shreds of metal that harmlessly bounced off the Ascendant's battered hull. A heat alarm chirped in Breaker's helmet as a half-globe of white light filled his view for a millisecond. When it cleared he realized that the munitions Stas fired were meant to change the Ascendant's course. "Holy shit, he's here to make sure that thing burns up in the atmosphere," Easy said. "I barely managed to stop him, and there's no way he has more of those torpedoes. He's moving on to assist the fighter that's after Maid."

"This guy's good too. I damaged him, but he's sticking to me like glue, forcing me to run. I can't get a good shot off," Maid replied. "Looks like not all their pilots are green."

"I already have sights on him, hang in there," Ronin said.

"I'm after the leader," Breaker said as a tone informed him that he had a full device lock on him. As he activated his turret and got ready to fire a pair of missiles at Stas, his computer failed to maintain the lock. "He's got jammers, they're working," Breaker announced. It made sense. Stas couldn't use sensor jammers until he'd launched his torpedoes. Now that they had struck their target, he could mess up everyone's readings. It was the size of his ship that gave Stas the ability to load up on extra equipment. This was some kind of bomber class, and Breaker hoped that it was out of surprises. "Switching to guns." he said as he reduced throttle and looked through his canopy, realizing that for the first time in his career, he'd gotten close enough to clearly see an enemy fighter while it was manoeuvring to fire at him.

He was able to get a quick shot off before his gunsights slid past Stas's heavy fighter. Breaker spun to line his shot up again only to see that his enemy was lining up a shot at the same time. His triple railguns activated. His enemy's shields shuddered, a shifting haze of blue as rounds raked across them. Stas returned fire at the same time, sending a steady white ray from an emitter on his ship's nose along with a hail of bullets. "Breaker! Do not get into a knife fight with this guy!" Ronin said. He'd never heard the Wing Commander say anything so urgently.

Knife fight. It was a term that he'd heard several times in training that applied to zero gravity ship-to-ship combat where two attacking vessels were too close, facing each other while they tried to outmanoeuvre each other. It usually happened when two skilled pilots refused to run. It was a rare thing. Engaging the enemy from many kilometres away was always best, even if you were being led on a chase. Most pilots refused to engage in a knife fight, using countermeasures instead to get away from their opponent so they could fight another day. "I'm going to kill you now," Stas said.

Breaker didn't realize that he was in a knife fight until the enemy pilot's first round tapped his nose shields. White knuckled at the controls, he set all his power reserves to recharge his forward energy barrier, locked his auto turret forward, and worked to shift his ship to one side, the other, up and down in an attempt to get out of his enemy's sights while trying to get a shot. Stas did the same, and for what felt like minutes, it seemed like Breaker's sights kept on sliding past, moving around, and jerking across his ship. When Breaker tried to back off, Stas would accelerate just enough to keep him within fifty metres. "How is he doing this?" Breaker asked in frustration. The enemy pilot wasn't good, he was great. On par with Ronin or Dame or any of the aces that had been a part of Samurai Squadron.

The beam weapon from Stas' ship flashed as Breaker got the enemy in his sights and fired his three railguns along with his auto turret. They taxed each other's shields, and Breaker activated his right thruster the instant he felt the vibrations of rounds striking beside the cockpit. The sudden, jerking thrust wasn't enough to shake Stas, who was lining up a final barrage.

Breaker sent all available power to his rear shields, finished turning away from the enemy ship, and activated every thruster he could point aft. Stas was already manoeuvring to get in front of him, and he was coming around to get behind his ship, guns already firing. Then a hail of rounds struck Stas' ship from above. "Break this up now," Dame said as the Clever Dream came into view.

To Breaker's relief and frustration, Stas accelerated past him and began charging a wormhole generator. He was gone before anyone could give chase. "God dammit!"

"Heavy Cruiser Two is jumping out. All we've got are the two corvettes we managed to capture," Maid said.

"And one hell of a show while we wait for the British Alliance to arrive. There won't be anything left of the Ascendant, but it'll be a once-in-a-lifetime thing to watch it burn up," Ronin said.

"How's Gren?" Breaker asked.

"Alive. He's going to get to know what the inside of a

regeneration pod looks like, but he'll be all right," Alice replied. "We're not sticking around for the view. Headed back to the Triton."

"Permission to escort the Clever Dream?" Breaker asked.

"Granted. You and Garma can make sure he gets to medical," Ronin said. "We'll make sure the Ascendant doesn't make a descent towards the planet."

"Oh, that's a bad one," Easy groaned.

"What?" Ronin asked.

"Ascendant, descent?" Easy replied.

"Wow, that wasn't even on purpose. I should ask Ash if I pun in my sleep."

Chapter 33

Answers For Tiy

THE SPACE THAT TREY, Minister Haas, and Logi were locked into was more like a very upscale apartment in one of the growing cities on Tiy. It was built with metal and a kind of plastic that felt more like wood, and the colours were light brown, black and white with furniture that was almost too comfortable, but it had a feeling of luxury that he'd only seen pictures of.

Logi spent all of his time looking through one of the floor-to-ceiling windows. There was a view of stars, and they could see across a part of the Triton's hull where repair drones were assisting the regeneration of its outer armour. Past that strange metal landscape was a conspicuous dot that was, if you stared long enough, brown, blue and green. That was Tiy.

Trey boggled at the sight of it the first time Logi pointed it out. His home planet was so small at a distance. Everyone he'd ever known was there. It didn't fascinate him as much as Logi at the moment, but Trey knew that he'd think about that sight in the future. It was a humbling thing to experience, being separated from your home and shown how small you were in the galaxy. "How many people did the man who escorted us here say there were in the galaxy?" asked Minister Haas.

"A little over two trillion humans now," Logi said without looking away from the window. "That's after the disaster we watched a movie about. One trillion dead."

"By the Order of Eden. Everything I've seen backs that up, too," Trey said, finishing the line that stood out for him in the two-hour educational film. It was more convincing than the propaganda that the Order showed them. He'd also been given access to something called the Stellarnet, which he'd become lost in. The stiff, paper-thin tablet behaved a little like a paper book, only it was in perfectly realistic colour, he could summon up holographic versions of anything he saw, and he was able to navigate around by tapping on anything that caught his interest.

The first thing he looked for was the negative facts about Haven and the people who had come to their rescue. The man who owned the ship they were on was Jacob Valent, and he had been dismissed from the military only days before. He dug for details, finding so much information that he had to skim through to find the information that would tell him the story of Valent. That led him to the re-founding of the Haven System and the formation of its government. The only thing he found unbelievable is that it all took years, not decades. Nothing moved that fast on his world, but all the information about how it happened was there, and he believed what he was seeing before long.

"I keep seeing you shaking your head," Minister Haas said,

dropping his interactive page onto the coffee table and sitting down.

"It's…" Trey said, finishing skimming through a report about the Order of Eden's occupation of the Haven System. "It's all here. Not just a string of reports and propaganda stories about these people and where they come from, but the ugliness, the strangeness. I just finished reading a number of public reports and recountings from the occupation the Haven Solar System suffered a little while ago." He brought a holo-gram of a large statue being pulled down and then cut apart. "Their enemies had them right in their hand, and these Havenites, or whatever they call themselves, rallied and took their whole Solar System back. That's remarkable from a historical standpoint, but what I find interesting is that if you peel back the available information you find more. A story about how Haven Fleet screwed up during the battle, costing them hundreds of soldiers. Then something more current: an activist group who believe that the Haven System should have remained in the Order of Eden's hands. They're allowed to speak on this forum and to attend official meetings even though most of the people who live in the Haven System think they're crazy, even offensive."

"True free speech," Minister Haas mused. "But what about the people who have us in their hands?"

"Oh. This ship is owned by Jacob Valent. A former Admiral who was thrown out of Haven Fleet only days ago for committing a war crime against the Order of Eden. It was a galactic scale war crime because he used some outlawed weapon, a smart computer as far as I could tell, to make an attack on the Order that was too general. Civilians were caught in the crossfire, and no one was given a chance to defend themselves against it. He's out here as a corsair, a kind of Captain for hire. He was a bounty hunter years ago, so that makes sense. I think he has a lot to prove. Maybe he's trying to show everyone in Haven Fleet that they shouldn't have kicked him out. That's not the point though. Everything I see tells me…"

"…that he's here to continue the fight against the Order of Eden," Minister Haas said with a sigh. "I was looking for any information that counters that. That makes that seem like more propaganda."

"You'll find it," Logi said, not turning around. "If you look for something negative about a person or organization long enough, it will appear. The difficult part of putting someone else's story together if you look for too long is determining what is true, and what you've assembled using parts that only add up to something damning when they're taken out of context. That is how a lie can seem true, especially if you're trying too hard to prove a negative."

"So, you're saying that I'm trying too hard to make an enemy out of a potential friend?" Minister Haas asked.

"Yes. From what our resident journalist has found, Valent definitely has a past that includes some wrongdoing, but he was willing to be accountable for it. He was punished, and now he's making the best of things. That is, if I understand your summary correctly?" Logi asked.

"You do. He still owns a part of the Haven Solar System, that's how he's funding this venture," Trey replied.

"He owns a part of a Solar System?" Minister Haas asked in disbelief. "That's insane."

"It's true. Even the Order of Eden's news threads mention it. He could be living in luxury, but he's out here instead," Trey said.

"This isn't luxury?" Minister Haas asked, gesturing at the main room.

"That is sacrifice," Logi said, pointing through the window at the damaged section of the hull. "A willingness to take a great risk, to make a great sacrifice for something. If it's a fight with the Order of Eden, then we should listen to whatever they say. The Order has laid a heavy hand on our world, and I suspect that they disguise their intentions with generosity."

"On that, we definitely agree," Minister Haas said. "I still wonder…"

He was interrupted as the main doors opened and Orner entered. Trey didn't hesitate in crossing the room and embracing him.

"I'm sorry," Orner said as they parted. "I thought going with Moxa to see the Order was the right thing to do. I was wrong. They only brought the worst of me out in the end. When I thought you were dead, I did something I'll never forget, but it didn't break our enemy in the least."

"What do you mean?" Trey asked, worried. His little brother seemed tired and looked as though he was being weighed down by guilt.

"I met Eve," he whispered. "She ordered the attack on you. Trey, I broke her neck when I saw it. I was so angry, so frightened for you. Then I escaped and I saw her stand up. Their technology is so advanced, it's like they're immortal."

"Then how is there any hope to defeat the Order?" Minister Haas asked.

"They aren't so different from us," Orner said, giving no greater respect or reverence to the Minister. "They have lazy rich just like our culture does. I saw them. They were there to greet me like I was some exotic arrival at a zoo. A new convert. I had time to think in the escape ship I stole. Eve was dressed like our lounging rich, the ones who look down on the rest while we provide everything for them."

"I know the phenomenon," Minister Haas said, guarded. "Not all wealthy people are inconsiderate of the less fortunate, not where we come from, at least."

"Maybe, but the room I was taken to on that ship was filled with people who looked pampered. If that's who leads them, then we have a chance," Orner said.

"I see what you're getting at," Trey said, proud of his brother. "They may be easily distracted, selfish, and they take every attack - verbal or literal - personally. Most of all, they want to protect their privilege."

"Good strategy takes people like that down eventually, but their technology is so advanced, I can't imagine we'd have a chance without help," Logi said, finally turning around to face the door. "I'm assuming this is your brother."

Trey nodded. "Yes, this is Orner."

"Who have you been talking to, Orner?" Logi asked.

"Come in please," Orner called to the door. "They are not the founders. They are Lorander Corporation representatives and our cousins from the British Alliance."

A pair of officers in grey and white uniforms entered. The man and woman looked like they were in perfect health. "We are the Commanders placed in charge of the Tiy Effort," they said in unison. Then the woman spoke. "I'm Ouadi, and this is my partner, Edarm. We represent a Unit and a selection of resources from the Lorander Corporation that have been allotted to help you and the people of Tiy rebuild and catch up to the galaxy's general level of technology."

They were strange. Not in their general appearance with dark hair and healthy features, but Edarm's expressions matched Quadi's perfectly as she spoke. The only difference was that his mouth didn't move. "Are you human?" he asked, not knowing how to phrase his question more politely.

Edarm laughed a little. It looked like he was trying not to be condescending as he replied; "I'm sorry. There is something strange about us to new people. Quadi and I have been tele-pathically bonded for nearly thirty years. Our minds are one most of the time, so we tend to synchronize our modes of appearance, expression and speech at times. I'm sorry if it's disconcerting."

"Not at all," Minister Haas said, nodding and approaching the pair.

He was intercepted by a thick-bodied man in a navy blue uniform as he entered the room. "I'm Commodore Thomas. You'll be speaking to me for a while. I suppose I'm the cousin that Orner was talking about, and you're his brother, Trey."

The accent was familiar. Everyone Trey ever knew had a little of it in their speech. "I am, it's good to meet you, Commodore." That rank was another commonality. It was in their military and police force.

"Fine," the Commodore said with the weight of finality as he moved on to Minister Haas. "And you're one of the highest remaining authorities on your world?"

"Minister Haas, and this is Logi from Strategic Intelligence," Haas replied.

"Funny, the Loranders have the same rank in their organization," Commodore Thomas said.

As Trey had more time to observe the Commodore, he saw that the man wasn't fat, but muscled and short. It really was like he was looking at a cousin since he had a similar build but a different skin colour. The Commodore was much paler. "So, it was your people that settled here?" Trey asked.

"Right to the point. Good," Commodore Thomas said,

turning towards Trey. "I hope the Minister here puts you on his staff."

"We do as well," Quadi said.

"Well, I'll answer that question first," Commodore Thomas said. "Yes, Risago and the rest of his misguided bunch were from British Alliance worlds. They paid a Lorander Corporation Colony ship to gather his people up and bring them to a surveyed world that didn't have any intelligent occupants on it. Risago's followers hated technology so much that they made sure that the colony ship was destroyed. He did such a good job that Lorander never did find it."

"The ironic thing is that it would have taken a great deal of technical understanding to accomplish that, so Risago and some of his people must have been highly proficient," Quadi added.

"The British Alliance's archives have plenty of information on Risago and his strange bunch. They were terrorists who tried to halt progress on several worlds before they gave up and left. We're gobsmacked that any of you survived, but I'm not surprised at all at the wreck you're making of Tiy. What a toxic shithole," Commodore Thomas said directly to Minister Haas.

"We've advanced great strides considering our handicaps and what we had to work with," Haas replied, raising his voice.

"The Commodore is right," Trey tried to interject calmly.

"No, no, you have to consider the ingenuity of our people now," the Minister pressed. "We are finding new ways to improve the quality of life all the time."

"Please be calm, Minister. We don't have much time," Quadi plead. "There are plenty of causes in this part of the galaxy that our Unit can respond to. Yours is only one."

"We do acknowledge that the People of Tiy have made impressive advancements considering the circumstances," Edarm continued. "But we need to alert you to the increasing toxicity levels as you pollute your planet with substances from spent industrial batteries and push millions of homeless people into the forests. They use dung and wood for fuel there, exhaust the resources and move on. That's all we can determine from initial observations of your world with scanners, but you will quickly deplete some resources while ruining others if you continue as you are."

"The Commodore's disdain, while a little crass, is understandable if you consider his point of view. The records he provided concerning Risago show the behaviour of an egotistic tyrant who executed people who crossed him. He left because he faced prosecution, not because he wanted to create a better civilization. He did hate technology, but the evidence points to a specific reason for that. Risago wanted to restrict access to it so he could control his people. So he could create what the British Alliance calls a 'peasant class.' I'm afraid your society is still recovering from that," Quadi said.

"Well, that may be true, but that's not why I have no respect for the people of Tiy," Commodore Thomas said. "I'm pissed because I come from Elport. You want to see a toxic swamp? That's the spot. The scans show that huge tracts of Tiy will be just like that if you don't smarten up and start cleaning up. I'm not sticking around to help, but the British Alliance are willing to defend your planet while this Lorander Unit, which is made up of thousands of important, smart people, by the way, stick around. In trade, we want point three percent of the resources from the solar system - except Tiy, you get all that - and we get to build five bases."

"On Tiy?" Minister Haas asked.

"No, we don't want a foothold on the future site of your wasteland. Elsewhere in the solar system. It's a good deal. Oh, and Haven Fleet has a proposal for you too, which is even better, but it's contingent on you accepting what Lorander's offering." Commodore Thomas pulled a short rod from a pocket and put it onto the table. "There it is, all the details, and you can contact the officer I'll leave in charge of the defence here anytime. I don't like the shape of Tiy, and I think your people need education, so I hope you take the deal. It would be amazing to see things on your planet turn around in my lifetime. I may not like you, but I'm rooting for you. Having said that, you have a week to decide. That's seven twenty-four-hour days, then we have to move on to another crisis. There are billions of people in trouble in every direction. I hope we get to you first. Oh, there's one more thing that no one has thought to tell you."

"What's that?" Haas asked, scowling.

"Ships filled with outsiders will come to your solar system one way or another. If you take a deal, you'll have some hope of a defence and recovery. If you don't, then whoever comes will be random, they won't give a shit about your people. They may as well be primates to them. At best there will be traders and people who plunder your solar system for resources. At worst - and this is bloody likely - you'll be attacked by slavers and invaders who want your land and who knows what else. That's if the Order doesn't return. They already have an army down there, they just haven't activated it for some reason. Take a deal. Good luck." He nodded at the Minister and then left the room.

"He's a busy person," Edarm said.

"A very busy man," Quadi added. "It is important to remember what he said, however, because he's right."

The Minister turned away and stared through the window for a long moment. Trey was about to say something when he finally returned his attention to Quadi and Edarm. "So, before I look closely at any deal, I suppose you want some kind of restitution for your lost ship," Minister Haas asked.

"No," Quadi answered firmly.

"That act of sabotage that destroyed our colony ship was committed by someone who died a long time ago," Edarm said.

"We are offering to remove the Order of Eden soldiers from your world, with the assistance of the British Alliance. While that's underway, we hope to help you devise a way to solve homelessness and starvation. We see undernourishment in a near majority of citizens. The final phase of our proposal involves mass education and a considered pace of technological advancement."

"What do you mean by 'a considered pace?'" Trey asked.

Quadi turned towards him as her partner watched the Minister consider the proposal. "We will work with your government to assess the cultural maturity of your people as we teach them how to responsibly build and use advanced technologies. This is something our people used to do for small pockets of humanity that showed great promise. Most of them were already on their way to interplanetary travel, like your people."

"Yes, we were well on our way," Logi said. He was quietly listening to every word.

"What do you want in return?" Minister Haas asked.

"This is not a trade," Quadi said.

Edarm spoke then; "We will learn from you. Every time Lorander or another group of our people assists a civilization of any size, we gain knowledge, compile stories, and connect with other cultures. We are here to build a future for you that is adjacent to us and the rest of the galaxy. The Lorander Corporation has learned a great deal from the Haven System and the people we came to know there. At one time we were afraid to assist with more primitive cultures, but they've shown us that the right people can learn about our technology and use it to create safe places in this galaxy. Places where your people can thrive. We are offering that to you."

"I have to admit, I don't like being insulted. You and that Commodore treat us like we're helpless children. He's direct about it, and you're condescendingly kind. I don't much care about your history right now. I'm trying to figure out whether or not you're lying to us," Minister Haas said.

"I understand that you're wary," Edarm said, raising his hands. His companion did the same, it looked like a pleading gesture. "We propose that we include a trial period in our arrangement. We will limit our assistance for that amount of time so there are no permanent structures or changes on your world so you can send us away if you're still suspicious or if your people reject us."

"That is a good compromise, Minister," Logi said. His voice was firm for the first time since Trey met him.

It gave the Minister pause, and he calmed down. "And if we don't accept whatever terms we discover during the negotiations? What if we turn you down completely?" Minister Haas asked.

"Then there will be only one piece of evidence that we were ever here after we go," Quadi stated.

Edarm spoke with less finality. "The Lorander Corporation will leave a beacon behind if you like. You can attempt to contact us if you need help in the future. Other than that, we will leave you completely alone."

"There is no guarantee that we will respond if you activate the beacon. We may not have the resources to aid you," Quadi added. "We expect that you will not contact us until your world is nearly completely destroyed, so I can't say what will change between now and your inevitable request for evacuation."

"Evacuation?" Minister Haas asked, openly surprised.

Orner shook his head. Trey understood why. The other worlders were loading Haas down with a lot of information all at once, and it was starting to feel like a scolding session. "They're predicting that there won't be many of us left by the time we ask for help."

"That's how these things turn out, in our experience," Edarm said.

"To be clear, your world looks healthy at the moment, but you stand at a precipice. In only one generation there will be more people building in the wild - the homeless you send there now - than there will be in your organized society. Civil war will erupt. Meanwhile, the damage you're doing to the ecosystem will only worsen as political and economical concerns distract you," Quadi explained with such certainty that Trey found it chilling.

"We have historical records that prove that this has happened to humanity and many other species many, many times. We'd like to prevent it. Lorander has done it before," Edarm said.

"All the information you need to consider our offer is on the data rod that the Commodore gave you. We can send two of our representatives to help you browse and understand the information if you like. We'll understand if you turn us away. Pride is commonly the reason why a human outpost does so. We'll hold a lamentation ceremony, which you'll be invited to, and then we'll depart," Quadi said quietly. "I'll leave you to decide."

As soon as the doors closed behind them, Minister Haas shook his head and spat; "Pride! They think my caution is just pride!"

"They're right," Logi said. "It's why Tiy is divided into two major nations and five minor ones."

"They could have presented their offers better," Trey mused.

"I don't see how," Orner said. "We've done the damage. People are suffering. How many homeless folk came to our back door last winter, asking for food?"

"I lost count at twenty," Trey said. "I thought we were running a shelter for a while there, with people sleeping between the presses. I guess the real thing to consider is that there were more than the year before."

"And that we almost went hungry too," Orner said.

"I've been to your farm. It's nowhere near the Lower Woodlands," Minister Haas said.

"Then imagine what it must be like there?" Trey asked.

"We don't send homeless people into the forest. We transport them to the outskirts of town with tools, where they can build their own homes," Haas countered.

"Thus, sending them out of our towns, to the outskirts of our woodlands," Logi said. "I'll stay if you like to discuss the offers, but I'll be leaving if we don't take them. I'm not going to stay on Tiy if it means living in the dark."

"The void!" Minister Haas burst, pointing at the blackness of space through the window. "That's darkness."

"That's potential, and a place to find people who are willing to consider things that our culture can't even grasp. That's my future, and I hope I can achieve it by helping

Tiy's citizens elevate themselves through education. I think that's what they're offering, really. Security, for now, education so we can better ourselves in the long term," Logi said calmly.

Minister Haas considered that for a moment as he looked down at the data rod on the table. "Maybe. I need to know more. There's a lot to consider, maybe too much for one week, and there has to be some kind of vote."

"Convene a council," a woman said as she walked in. She was in a simple one-piece black uniform. A savage-looking sidearm hung on one thigh. It was balanced by a pouch on the other. The wrist units that Trey had seen several times were there too. Trey was immediately enchanted by her dark eyes when she smiled at him for a moment. Orner nudged him, a knowing look on his face that made it perfectly clear that he noticed Trey's jaw drop.

Trey cleared his throat and replied to her. "I'm pretty sure we could do it if we had help getting people together down there. Good idea."

"The British Alliance has plenty of shuttles," she replied, nodding.

"You'll probably see the inside of one soon. I think the BA are taking their turn playing chauffeur," said the young man beside her. He was wearing a similar uniform, only he didn't have a sidearm. "You'll be welcome to bring people to you or go back to your world as soon as you're transferred to the Denwas. I'm Alfas, from the communications department here. This is Tammy, from the security staff. We're here to make sure you have everything you need. Then we'll escort you to a shuttle that will take you to a Lorander Ship or down to Tiy."

"You're not going to keep us here?" Minister Haas asked.

"No, the Triton is moving on. You know what they say…" Alfas started.

Tammy interrupted him. "They don't know the three D's. Anyway, we're getting underway in a little over twenty hours. Anyone who's still aboard when we do will become a part of the crew. We're not ferrying passengers out of the system, at least not to where we're going, anyway. Until then, we'll help you out with supplies, get you some really basic gear, and show anyone who wants to join the crew of the Triton where to go next."

"Oh, and tell you what you'll probably be doing, what you'll get paid and what life aboard is like," Alfas added.

"In short: working your butt off, earning lots of platinum, and having fun when you're not doing the first thing," Tammy said, pulling her black hair into a ponytail. "We'll be out there if you want anything, and you can leave, you just can't go anywhere alone. It's a warship. We don't want you to get into trouble."

"Thank you," Minister Haas said as they stepped outside.

"So, what? I stand on this side and you stand on the other?" they heard Alfas ask as the doors were starting to close.

"Yup. We stand here so we can pay attention to the hallway and that door. Exciting, huh?" Tammy asked.

After the doors slid closed, Trey regarded his brother, who was contemplating something. "You don't want to go back to Tiy."

"No," he said in a whisper. The Minister and Logi were having their own discussion as they activated the data rod. A holographic circle of screens surrounded them. "I don't think any option they choose will be easy. It'll take most of our people a decade at least to adjust to the idea that humans have come from beyond our world to help. They won't trust them, even if they're really just here to help. Not at first."

"Meanwhile, there will be bigger things happening out here," Trey said, nodding. "I can't say I understand everything I've seen, or that I know where I'd fit in if I joined up, but I've seen Valent, heard playbacks of his speeches. I understand the war they're fighting. Well, as much as anyone like me can in a few days."

"But you want to stay on Tiy so you can help our people," Orner said. "I understand. I'll go where you do."

"I love you, little brother, but I don't want you to stay if you feel like you're missing the biggest opportunity of your life. I can't say I wouldn't want to get to know you as you are, as a peer, and I'd miss you, but don't stay for me."

Orner stared at him, thinking. After a long moment, he turned towards the door and walked into the hall. Trey followed him and watched as he asked Alfas; "If I join the crew can I come back to Tiy? Will there be a way to visit?"

"Probably. I mean, especially if your government accepts help. There will be regular transports from a few places before long," Alfas replied.

"The Triton has started a shuttle rental program, too," Tammy added. "You'll be able to borrow one if you can fly one. Well, after you've served for a while and earned a little platinum, I assume. The details aren't all out yet."

"Really? A rental program?" Aflas asked. "Why didn't I hear about it?"

"It's not official yet. Agameg and a few other officers are putting it together. I heard Slick talking about it," Tammy explained.

"Oh," Alfas said as he returned his attention to Orner, looking up at him. "So, there's your answer, big guy. If your folks sign up with the Alliance as a Beneficiary Junior Member, then it'll be pretty easy to get back home if the Triton's not in the thick of it."

"Thank you," Orner said, returning to the room.

"So, what are you thinking?" Trey asked in a whisper.

"If Tiy accepts help, then I would like to stay aboard," Orner said. "That is if you are all right with it."

"You can go wherever you want, but I'll miss you." The pair embraced, and Trey knew that his brother would be going further away than he could have ever imagined.

Chapter 34

Stage Two

THERE WAS something about shifting the colour of her vacsuit back to blue that made Alice feel like everything was calming down. That wasn't something she had to convince herself of, it actually was. Scanlon was dead. Half of the Ascendant's bridge staff was in custody. The flagship was in a stable orbit and crews were salvaging every scrap of data that was left behind. Samurai Squadron had lost several fighters, but every pilot survived. There were so many things to celebrate, and she was sure there would be a hell of a party in the Pilot's Den.

The British Alliance were forming around Tiy and working on a plan to secure as much of the space around it as they could. The Lorander Corporation had stepped in to support the population there. Alice hoped the people of Tiy would take every offer they could.

She waited outside the main armoury of the Triton, nodding at crew members who noticed her, and most of them did. Their emotional states ranged from excited to purposeful, but morale was higher than it ever was on the Merciless, where most of them had served previously.

Noah finally emerged from the armoured doors. When he noticed that she'd changed her suit's colour, she felt that he liked seeing her in it, and that explained part of why she liked it too. Feeling affection and attraction from people with her empathic abilities could lift her spirits too high. It could become intoxicating, and she loved it, most empaths and telepaths did. It was also addictive, and a person could depend on that to feel anything good about themselves after a while. That's why most sensitives, including her, learned to tune it out after recognizing the rising feeling. She held onto it a little longer as she gave Noah a hug and felt his affection spike.

Instead of only shutting him out, she gave him a kiss to show him how she felt about him. "What was that for?" he asked as they started down the hallway.

"Just noticing that you still like me in blue and saying thank you," Alice said under her voice so the crew members they passed couldn't hear. "How were things in the armoury?"

"Stern. They let you drop your extra gear off then leave without a second thought, but I had to answer a few extra questions when I put the rifle back but told them I was keeping the sidearm. I guess it makes sense. They've got a few weapons missing, they wouldn't tell me more than that," Noah replied. "They were trying to get it straightened up before Agameg arrived. That is one busy guy. He's on the Ascendant right now."

"I think he likes it that way, being busy. Maybe I should

help the security staff track those missing weapons down?" Alice mused.

"Oh, no. We just got out of heavy armour. We're getting something to eat after this next meeting. I think those small arms walked away because a few crew members forgot that there are still rules aboard. They'll get it figured out," Noah said, putting his arm around her shoulders. "I didn't forget about the regulations, and I've been away from the fleet for months. Those guys won't get away with lifting a few guns."

"Someone stole guns?" Remmy said as he rushed to fall into step beside them.

"Yeah, just a few small ones as far as I could tell," Noah replied.

"That's a bad idea on this ship," Remmy snickered. "There are a lot of people here with a very clear sense of right and wrong."

"Hey, how are you?" Alice asked.

"Better than ever. Just had a little complication that took me out for a bit, but I'm fine. So, any idea what this meeting is about?"

"Probably some after-action kind of thing," Alice replied.

"Then why am I going? I was in medical the whole time," Remmy countered.

"Maybe they want to keep you in the loop?" Noah suggested. He colour-shifted his vacsuit and long coat so it was a dark purple and a little looser.

"Makes sense. If I'm around for all the meetings, then no one has to catch me up on anything later," Remmy replied. "You sure you want to go in all colourful, though?"

"This is my crew colour," Noah replied. "Besides, I thrive on attention."

They arrived at the double doors. They were the old-fashioned Earth Defence-style armoured sliders with a full metre of armour and arms to draw them in and out. Their command and control bracers vibrated for a second, informing them that they were being scanned, then flashed green before the doors parted.

As they crossed the threshold they saw a circular room with a ring of swivel seats that were retracting into the floor. Every surface was black at the moment and there was a timeline that was fifteen hundred years long across one wall. The first two-thirds were heavily marked with events. The last, representing the next five hundred and one years, barely had any marks on it.

Ayan stood in a green vacsuit that had a loose wrap layer on top at one end of the inner circle. Jake and Minh-Chu were on her left. Stephanie and Frost were on the right. Across from them was a thick bodied man in a British Alliance uniform and two younger Lieutenants who were listening closely to everything. Alice focused her empathic sense on her father, Ayan, and the top British Officer.

"...we could come to an agreement, Commodore," Jake was saying to him. He was calm, confident.

The British Alliance Commodore was feeling pleased, but not to the point of outright joy. "We'll make good use of what's left of the Ascendant. Thank you for keeping it from being completely demolished. We'll transfer the funds to your base in the Haven System within five days. I could credit you right now if you'd accept anything other than platinum."

"I need to build a reserve up that doesn't tap into Haven's resources," Jake replied.

"Still a patriot, after all that," the Commodore said, shaking his head. "I wonder if I would be if my government sacrificed me. I can't be sure, if I'm being honest."

"Some of us don't know until we're tested," Ayan said. She was feeling a little impatient with the Commodore.

"Well, good luck out there. The whole British Alliance is looking forward to seeing your Priveteering Program at work. I'm wondering something, though. Is the Triton going to gather a fleet of privateers around itself? A more official group to coordinate with?"

"No. It's important that the Triton remains mobile and independent for the time being," Jake replied. He was lying. Alice was sure she was the only one who could tell, but she could feel it.

"Well, it worked for you this time. Good luck," The Commodore turned and left, walking past Alice, Noah and Remmy.

When the thick doors closed behind him, Remmy walked further into the room and dropped into a seat. "So, did we just witness the sale of Scanlon's Flagship?"

"That you did," Frost said, cracking a grin.

"What does that kind of tonnage go for?" Remmy asked.

"Enough to pay for this mission for another seven months, a year if we're careful and source our rare materials from unclaimed scrap," Jake said, looking more than a little pleased.

"We're pulling an extra bonus since it's still functional and we're leaving our androids behind to help with repairs," Stephanie added.

"Over the next ten hours we'll be moving supplies and any equipment that isn't nailed down from that ship to the Triton," Jake said.

"I guess I know what I'll be doing for a while. When do I take off?" Remmy asked.

"You don't have to be aboard the Raven. I'm sure there's another crewmember who can take that watch," Jake said.

"I'm her Captain, I should be on board," Remmy sighed.

"Good." Jake was pleased to see that Remmy was taking responsibility for the ship, even during fairly boring tasks. "I have a request for you."

"Another one?" Remmy asked. "Okay, but can you start paying me by the hour? I think I'd like the overtime."

"No," Jake replied. "But you do get a share of the Ascendant's sale. Not a really big one, but enough to make most people in the Cluster jealous."

"All right then. What do you need, Sir?" Remmy asked.

"I'm going to need a crew for missions. I was about to start printing a small corvette of my own, then Ayan made a suggestion. Why don't I team up with you and the Raven crew, since it's a tested ship and a green group." Jake was actually a little nervous. Alice doubted that anyone could see it, but it was as if he was afraid that Remmy would turn him down.

Alice was surprised that her father didn't make the same proposal to her, especially since she was a few members short on her crew and, well, it was her Dad, after all.

Ayan added to the proposal. "I know this may seem a little condescending, but I think your crew could benefit from working with Jake. We know they're good, and they've been well trained, but you two have different kinds of out-of-the-box thinking that I think could complement each other. A young crew who gets to see that can only benefit." Then she turned towards Alice and Noah. "I was going to suggest you and the Clever Dream, but I realize that you already have a lot on your plate. I'm not proud of this, but we keep forgetting that you own at least two ships - the Clever Dream and the Advanced Destroyer that you've left with Yawen."

"No worries. With a Captain like Yawen in charge over there, it's easy to forget that it's my ship," Alice said. That reassurance landed well with everyone in the room. "But keep us and the Clever Dream in mind any time you want an extra ship on a mission."

A slender door to the side opened and Ashley entered with Alaka and another tall, dark-furred Nafalli. "I'm sorry we're late," she said, tapping a spot on the floor. A stool with a short back rose up and she sat down.

"How's Zoe?" Stephanie asked.

"Good, she sang me three different alphabets. She wouldn't let me go until she finished," Ashley replied.

Alice remembered the little Nafalli as a toddler and felt the same way the rest of the room did - happy that the little one was doing well. She wondered why Ashley was there, however. She was the Master of the Helm, and a full Commander, but she rarely attended upper command meetings. The answer was coming, she was pretty sure, so she and Noah moved to the inner circle, where she stood across from her father and Ayan. Ashley went on. "Panloo says the talks with the Nafalli Council are going well. They don't know how many ships will be joining us, but they want to pledge more than one. We'll know in the next two weeks."

Alice was surprised by the black-furred Nefalli when she spoke with a soft voice. She was muscled like one of Haven Nafalli's top warriors. "There are many leaders who want to represent our people in this new phase of the war. The only reason why they aren't with you already is because we have to join you quietly. The Council is afraid to send too many of our ships out as privateers. They expect that too large of a move will suggest that they're supporting a war criminal."

"They will be," Jake replied. "But I understand why that's a bad look. Make sure they know I don't blame them."

"They already do," Ashley said. "Or they will when Panloo passes our messages on."

"Why is Panloo representing us with the Nafalli? I was never clear on that," Frost asked.

"It's so we can keep this part of the chatter secret from the Admiralty and any Order spies. I call her up all the time and babysit Zoe when we can, so no one will suspect a thing," Ashley replied with a shrug.

"Panloo also understands us better than most humans and knows the language," Alaka added.

"You speak Nafalli?" Frost asked, surprised. "I mean, I know a few words, mostly curses, but it's not an easy language."

Alice was surprised too, especially since Ashley had a persistent lisp. Most people thought it was cute, but she imagined it could get in the way. "I know Lowroo well, and bits of a couple other languages," Ashley replied. "Lowroo's the key one."

"That's impressive," Alice said, agreeing with the common sentiment in the room.

"Thanks," Ashley replied.

A bigger picture was forming in Alice's head. "So, why are we here?" she asked, looking for more pieces to the puzzle.

"Wait ten seconds," Minh-Chu said, looking at his left command and control unit, holding a finger up.

Everyone in the room fell silent for an increasingly awkward ten seconds. "Are you..." Jake started to say as he looked towards Minh-Chu.

"Shush. Ten more seconds," he said. "Damn, I thought I had this timed down to the..."

A hologram of Defence Minister Terry Ozark McPatrick

appeared on one side of the inner circle. "Sorry, it took me a little extra time to secure my office."

"Oz, you screwed up my timing," Minh-Chu said with exaggerated irritation.

"Sorry, Ronin, there was a Haven Shore Council Member who thought that running an industrial transit line through the heart of the southern jungle was a good idea. I had to tell him that he wouldn't get that passed," Oz replied.

"You're right on time," Jake said.

"How are things going with Nafalli support?" Oz asked.

"Good," Ashley replied. A moment later she realized that he expected more. "Oh, I can't give you any more details right now. Sorry."

"I understand," Oz said. He looked at Ayan then. "Your replacement is on his way. He comes with a small staff, not from your Sciences Department, but they're experts in grading ships and assessing commanders. He's eager to build on the foundation you've built for the Privateering program."

"Good. I'll start packing," Ayan replied. "The Lower Bridge will be pretty empty without my Science Staff."

"It had to happen sometime," Jake said. "The Admiralty would get suspicious if half the senior Science staff was serving on the Triton along with the Admiral in charge."

Another piece of the puzzle. "Suspicious of what?" Alice asked.

"I was just about to ask that," Remmy said, snapping his fingers.

"Same here," Noah added.

"I'd like to say that was on my mind, but I suppose I'm a step behind," Frost said, looking at Stephanie. "What's going on, my dear?"

Jake looked at her and nodded. "You're the one who sacrificed the most, you should start us off."

Stephanie took a step towards the middle of the circle and regarded the side where Remmy, Alice and Noah were. "I'd do it again. When Jake realized that he would have to be convicted of a war crime before the alliance with the British, Mergillians and Lorander could be formed, we started talking about the future of the fleet. The need for defence is high, so the Defence Minister, Oz, stuck to his guns on that. We couldn't send much out into the galaxy to fight, especially since he predicted that the Cefa System would be in trouble again soon. He didn't know how, but Oz was sure Haven Fleet would have to move in to guard the region or it would descend into lawlessness. It turns out that he was right, and now we have to find another way to fight the Order." She looked at Ayan then.

The reminder that the Prince Alice had guarded for months was dead along with his entire family burned. She found out on her own when they were on their way back from the Ascendant, and said nothing about it. The people she had to blame weren't nearby, so the reckoning would be carefully crafted and then delivered to Oz when she managed to get him on a call alone. He was the one who could have made sure that the transition from her team to another was more secure. She realized that her hands had curled into fists, and breathed deeply, letting them loosen.

"You all right?" Noah asked.

"I'll tell you later," Alice said, nodding at her Mother who was about to speak.

Ayan picked up where Stephanie left off. "Stephanie told me what was on her mind - that the end of the military that her and Jake were holding together was about to fall apart and I suggested an old idea. A shadow fleet. Freeground had one, and just because it didn't work out for them didn't mean we couldn't do it properly. We all started talking about it."

Minh-Chu got to his feet then. "She called me when Ashley and me were babysitting Zoe. We'd just played this trick on her that was hilarious. See, when she sneezes, she points her nose straight up into the air and makes these 'uh-uh-uh' squeaks, so Ashley and I dove for the deck like a bomb was bout to go off. I yelled; 'She's gonna blow!' and we distracted her so much that the itch went away. She looked at both of us and said; 'you stole my sneeze.'"

Remmy and Alaka burst out laughing. Jake looked at him and said; "Maybe start after that?"

"Right. As Ashley was apologizing, I got the call," Minh-Chu said. "I liked the idea of a shadow fleet, but I agreed with Ayan. Just starting one up right after Jake got kicked out would be conspicuous. We might be able to divert resources without drawing too much attention, but people would figure it out the moment we had a public victory. I mean, we like to say 'Deploy, Dominate, Disappear,' but how many times can you do that before there are witnesses?"

"That's when you came up with the idea of a corsair fleet," Stephanie said.

"I was getting to that," Minh-Chu said.

Stephanie continued the story. "So, Jake gave the Tribunal all the evidence they needed to back up his conviction and began working on a deal for his sentence. That's where I came in. Liara and I did most of the bargaining, using a secret staff aboard the Merciless to justify the transfer of the crew to the Triton, since Jake still technically owned the ship. We also put a proposal for the Privateering Initiative together with Ayan's help. She saved us a lot of time as an Admiral because she was able to find out who would support it without drawing too much attention."

"So, the whole Privateering Initiative is really a direct arm of Haven Fleet?" Alice asked.

"Good guess, but there's a little more information to take in here," Minh-Chu said, sitting back down and spinning in his chair.

That is when Jake stepped forward. "My removal from the fleet is real. Anything less would have put the new alliance in jeopardy. Instead of a new branch, we're starting an entirely new force using the Triton as an anchor. The crew will be given a new set of regulations that match what they're used to from Haven Fleet, for the most part. The difference is that we are an offensive force that will establish bases in key areas. Eventually, we'll be headquartered somewhere else. The Privateering program will give us the opportunity to bring new captains and ships in. I knew that we'd need you at this point, right before we really get started. You have already done it. When you joined the Captains of the Oasis and Last Crisis, bringing them together, you reminded us that rebel elements could come together by showing us how. I wish I had more control of the Special Combat Unit, but I had to leave you out of all this, and someone else had to serve as your superior officer," he was looking directly at Alice. "I fought the decision to have you placed in the Cefa System, but they thought building a reliable government there was more important than having you out there building a fleet of rebel ships."

"They're still out there. Yawen and I have a lot of credibility with the Rebel Captains," Alice said, feeling her Father's regret start to ease.

"Then there's Noah," Stephanie said. "I've enjoyed Knud's reports about your gun-running operation. He's been reporting to me since he switched to your crew. I can't believe the intelligence you've gathered on the Rose and Doxan Systems. You even have good intelligence from Iora. All by selling and trading weapons and gear to people who like to shoot at anything that's associated with the Order. We need you more than anyone."

Noah gasped and shook his head. "Ohmygosh, you spied on me! I did not see that coming." He was kidding, of course, but it took Stephanie a moment to recognize it. "No worries," he continued more seriously. "I'm going to prank the hell out of Knud when I get back though, so don't tell him I know."

"Just record it for me," Stephanie said, nodding.

"She told me what you were doing out there," Frost said, nodding as he rubbed his grey stubble. "I admit, I wished I was with you on that venture more than once. It's going to be interesting when the Triton goes right into the Shattered End for all those gangsters, mercenaries and rebels to see. There might be a bit of a ruckus."

"Exactly, so we need an in," Minh-Chu said.

"We need the crew who stole three brand new Order of Eden Advanced Destroyers right out of the docks," Jake said with a proud smile. "Along with their favourite gun dealer. I want the Triton to join the Rebel Captains. Not lead them, but sign up. All we want are three votes at the table. One for the owner."

"One for the Fighter Squadron," Minh-Chu said.

"And one for the Captain," Stephanie finished.

"Then this Shadow Fleet will start to grow, and we'll drive the Order of Eden out of the Cluster," Ayan said.

"Meanwhile, Haven Fleet will turn all its attention to defence and exploration. The Shadow Fleet will be legitimized as a separate force, and will remain on the offensive until our enemies surrender or are neutralized," Oz said. "I wish I could be with you. Maybe when I get voted out."

"You'll have to bring a ship so you can join as a Captain," Alice said, barely able to contain her excitement. The whole room was buzzing, she had to turn her empathic ability off entirely.

"Will do, Captain Valent," Oz said with a salute.

"Does anyone else have goosebumps? This is exciting," Remmy asked, rubbing his arms.

"Well, I hope it lasts, because we're going to be here for a few hours," Ayan said.

"It's time to figure out how we do this from this point," Jake said. "News is about to get out that we captured the Ascendant, that Scanlon is dead, and have collected bounties on her as well as several high-ranking Order officers. I knew we needed a win before we moved ahead, but I didn't expect one so soon, so we've got planning to do. Are you two ready?"

"Absolutely," Noah said with relish.

"I've never been more ready," Alice said, tapping her comm con. "But I need Iruuk in here. He's got a good brain for this stuff. Besides, I want to see the look on his face when you guys do that whole thing over again for him."

"I told you," Minh-Chu said, pointing at Jake. "We should have recorded it."

Epilogue

The Rixe Zhan II Class Combat Carrier

VOLLIS MIKAN, Captain of the Zhan II Carrier Rixe, missed all the action near Tiy. The fighters from the Saratoga, the sister ship to the Rixe, left behind to monitor the situation were destroyed early. The Ascendant had been taken. His First Officer delivered the news to Captain Mikan as he sat in the command chair.

The information was old already. Nearly half an hour had passed since the data burst was sent. The next one would come soon, and it would only be seven minutes old. They were closing on Tiy quickly.

Captain Mikan thought about what was reported there, especially the Triton. It had been upgraded multiple times, and was only a Sol Defence ship in form. He would give anything to get real information on her systems. The combat data collected from its attack on the Ascendant was fascinating.

The Triton had superior shields, a stronger hull and more redundant systems. There were indications that her fighter wing was small, but there were some brilliant pilots in Samurai Squadron and their fighters were more resilient. He turned his attention back to the Triton itself and shook his head at the usage of a Gunnery Deck. It was something Sol Defence had left behind in their designs, a vestige of another era. He was happy his ship didn't have one.

Built in the shape of a stingray, the Rixe had the same large triple recovery and launch bays beneath it as the Triton. Many other of his ship's main systems were different from the older ship, but to the average onlooker, the Rixe was a close match except for the colour. Instead of a glassy black hull, Vollis' vessel was dark green and white. His ship was only three years old, however, and there were hundreds of other differences. He considered them for a moment longer as he listened to the dire news.

"I predict that Tiy will be a complete loss to us. Fighting for the planet would be a mistake, in my opinion," his First Officer finished.

"Where was Admiral Scanlon at the time of the data burst?" Captain Mikan asked.

"Aboard the Ascendant. Rear Admiral Rinder reports that she should be safely away by the time you received the transmission," his First Officer reported. "The Rear Admiral has ordered all ships away from Tiy."

"Helm," Captain Mikan addressed. "Change course for the Rose System. Take us in a long circle around it. Decelerate slowly."

"Yes, Captain. Slow deceleration course around the Rose system," his navigator reported back.

Mikan looked to his First Officer, one of the better-fabricated beings that had come out of his facility. He was slender, disciplined, and attentive. Danton was his name. He was one of the few who were made aboard the Rixe who chose it himself. "You will connect to every available hyper transmitter and Haven Node relay so we can collect as much news concerning Tiy, The Ascendant, and Admiral Scanlon as we can. Send coded messages to all our assets in the field with the Rear Admiral's orders. Include a query. I want to know who told Eve about the planet and the state of the people there. That leak came from Citadel. I will repair it."

"Should we send an update to the Overlord?" First Officer Danton asked.

"No. That is beyond the scope of our mission here. Admiral Scanlon will report these events herself," Captain Mikan replied.

"Yes, Sir. I apologize." The youthful visage of the First Officer made the apology seem more dramatic than it ought to be.

"You assume the worst, that the Admiral has been captured. I understand. Given time, you'll become better at acting only on fact rather than assumption," Captain Mikan said, hiding his worry in a show of sympathy.

"I can only hope," the First Officer said as he bowed and returned to the Communications Station.

Captain Mikan leaned back in the command seat. There were updates from several spies located across the Cluster and from the Rixe's Fighter Wing, but he saved them for later. It was difficult for him to focus on anything but the news coming from Tiy.

The taste of something rotten, subtle but unmistakable, started at the back of his throat. It was a misfiring of nerves, a sensation that always came with an ominous feeling. A notion that something had gone terribly wrong. That was a misfire too. Anxiety. The few times he'd had it after he left Earth, Mikan resolved it by figuring out what or who he was nervous about. No effort was required this time. He knew exactly what his stressor was.

Admiral Olivia Scanlon was a great strategic thinker who he'd come to appreciate quickly. Her record was so good that he expected to be disappointed when he met her. Mikan found that he was impressed instead. In her, he found a fellow thinker, and they agreed on most things. The topics that they were out of alignment on, such as when to apply military force, were fertile ground to explore in conversation. Regardless of how far apart their philosophies were, she was always willing to discuss their differences so they could learn from each other. Her more logical view of the Order of Eden and its purpose was another thing he found refreshing. Those long conversations were the building blocks of their friendship. It was the most valuable relationship he had. Not only in that region of space, but anywhere.

Most Order of Eden members judged him because of his service with Citadel, or saw his facial markings and assumed a professional killer had nothing useful to say. The Admiral was the opposite. The first time she met, Scanlon said; "In a few weeks we'll know each other well enough for you to tell me the stories behind those tattoos."

It was a brief meeting, but an encouraging one, and Captain Mikan couldn't resist looking forward to sitting down with her again. His First Officer looked over his shoulder at him. "I have a coded emergency message from Admiral Scanlon with a holographic component and a high-priority notice from the Ascendant, Sir."

"They came in separately?" Captain Mikan asked.

"Yes, Sir. One from the Ascendant, the other from the Heavy Cruiser Farlight," he replied hurriedly.

"Send it to me," Captain Mikan said, tapping the back of his hand as he stood. "You have the watch."

"Yes, Sir," his First Officer said as he stood and crossed the bridge to the command seat.

The doors to his ready quarters opened silently. When they were closed behind him, he called up the message from the Farlight and shook his head. The report detailed and updated what he already knew. The confrontation near Tiy was a disaster.

The Triton had defeated most of their armaments, which were made for medium to long range, by moving in very close to the Ascendant. Admiral Scanlon's flagship didn't launch enough fighters to slow the Triton down, and damage to the Farlight as well as her sister ship kept them from launching most of theirs. The enemy launched only a few fighters, and they were equipped to attack large and small targets, which they did well, harassing Eve's Base Ship until it left, then turning on Admiral Scanlon's battlegroup. "Starfighters could tip the balance in their favour," he said to himself, finally getting to the final statement from Rear Admiral Rinder.

Boarders on the Ascendant intercepted and killed Admiral Scanlon. There was no footage or audio file associated with the event. Instead, there was a list of the lost and assumed captured tagged onto the end of the early report. Mikan wondered if Scanlon would still be alive if she still had her Justicars. They were her well-trained Order Knights. If they hadn't been defeated, then she would have been safe, he was sure of it. The knights that remained from that unit had been disbanded. Mikan considered gathering them.

Alice Valent was the one who exposed them and defeated

them. He added her to the top of the list of people who were responsible for murdering Olivia Scanlon. There were others, including the ones who pulled the trigger.

"Who is it? You have to tell me who killed her! I need to know!" he stabbed at his chest with his finger, shouting at the screen on the wall. He stalked the room for a moment, knowing that he'd seen the whole preliminary report from Rear Admiral Rinder. There would be no more information there. A full report would be submitted eventually, but his lower rank may prevent him from seeing it. Vollis silently decided that he would use unofficial channels if he wasn't given the identity of her killer.

He hoped there would be something in the other message, the one that came directly from Admiral Scanlon, but let himself seethe for a few more moments. When his fists finally unclenched and he didn't feel like tearing his own quarters apart, Vollis Mikan activated the second message.

Admiral Olivia Scanlon appeared in his quarters as a full-sized, high-resolution hologram. Instead of a uniform, she was wearing a white business suit. "Hello, Vollis. If you're seeing this, then I've been killed."

"Yes," Captain Mikan replied, the single word loaded down with so much anger and grief that it made him shake.

"You know, I always wondered what it would take to break your composure. I'd find this moment interesting if I were still alive. Before you get any ideas about recovering my conscious-ness from this artificial intelligence or from any database that may have a neural scan, stop. There will only ever be one Olivia Scanlon."

Captain Mikan regarded the image of Scanlon, his heart sinking. She was cool, collected, and barely paying attention. "What?"

"That's right. Any attempt to reproduce me will end in tragedy for whoever is involved. I have ensured it," she said with dark certainty.

"I volunteered to come to The Cluster because you, someone with real intelligence, were leading the way here. Why would you eliminate yourself?" Mikan asked, his voice rising.

"Ah, but that's the thing. I didn't eliminate myself. I would never commit suicide. I was killed. Whether by murder or misadventure, my life is over. Anything that could be made with my memories and personality would just be something else. What could be a larger threat to our individuality than a copy? Who could imagine that I would surrender control by letting myself be remade by a framework or something else that could be used by someone else like a puppet? I would never allow that."

"What about your legacy? The plans you had in motion?" Mikan asked.

The Scanlon hologram laughed and stood. "I was the most selfish person I ever met. Not psychopathic, but greedy. I had more money and power than most people could even comprehend, but not a bit of that matters now that I'm dead. I suppose you want some detailed report, or map to show you what was in the works?"

Mikan didn't answer. He only stared, unbelieving.

"You won't find it," Scanlon's image said with a little smile. "You and the entire Order of Eden failed to protect me, so you don't get to benefit from any of my work. You can learn quite a bit from my Officers, that's true, but they only know the next two, maybe three steps of any of my plans. No one was given information about where to go from there. When it all starts falling apart - and it will - most of the Order in the Cluster will become segmented. Their commanders won't know how to group their forces to work towards a common purpose. They won't know what to protect other than their own bases, and my influence will fade, leaving assets to do whatever they like. Imagine Planet Rodus, which is recovering quickly, thanks to me, under the independent rulership of the shaved baboon they call a president? Watch. Even the wealthy will begin to rebel. If Eve and the other Sycophants the Overlord sent here try to interfere, I foresaw that they would make critical missteps. The kind that lead to open aggression. That's just Rodus and the Rose System."

"For revenge?" he asked, anger competing with shock.

"To inflict a cost for the negligence that led to my absence. I didn't believe in legacy, but everyone should know that all the right people had my name on their lips as I grew the Order's influence in the region. I also hoped that I could show everyone that we didn't need the Order of Eden to be some kind of cult. It works as a conglomerate much better. If I had lived, I would have managed that even if it took years, and it probably would have. Now the ruin that my absence brings will teach that lesson."

"The religious aspect of the Order only draws more people and reinforces the whole with faith," Mikan countered, realizing at the end that he was arguing with a simple program. Nothing he said would change a thing.

"I saw enough evidence in my life to know that it took horrible manipulations to create the core of that faith. The Overlord did something to Eve and many others at the top. Maybe it was some kind of telepathic reprogramming or he frightened them into unquestioning service. I was going to demonstrate that zealots are ignorant, and stupid because of their unquestioning nature over time. I'm out of time now, so the Overlord will have to learn that lesson by watching them fumble in the absence of a reasonable mind to guide them. The Order of Eden will probably take the Cluster eventually, but it'll take longer, and the entire organization will suffer because of my death. I hope it brings him here, and that the people who murdered me do the same to him. I hope he sees it coming and is killed in the most helpless state possible."

The rumours that Scanlon was unpatriotic and that she doubted the truth of the Order of Eden were commonly repeated. Mikan didn't believe that the Overlord would put someone like that in charge, but there it was. "You really do doubt the Truth," the Captain said.

"Of course I did! The Order of Eden did succeed in delaying the Edxi's revenge. Those insects acknowledged the penance of a trillion humans. Anyone who sees reason can believe that. What I will never believe is that Hampon whispers to the Chosen from the future and that he'll return to lead us all into living eternal life. What a complete, ruinous lie. It is an insult to anyone of average or greater intelligence. After seeing that the Order of Eden is leaning into superstitious nonsense, I made sure my death plan would be as devastating as possible."

"Your reach couldn't have been that long," Mikan said.

"You'll see how much influence I had here. My retribution of ruin will begin with the five civilized worlds that the Order had regular contact with, but didn't have a base on. I was building a brand, one that would appeal to the wealthy and powerful. I invested in their companies and political careers. It was a significant amount. The Order is controlling thousands of top-ranking people through financial leverage and blackmail. When my signal reaches those worlds, my treasure will be withdrawn. Companies critical to the wealthy will collapse.

The sensitive materials my people gathered and safeguarded will be released."

"Why?"

"Because you failed me," Scanlon replied angrily. Then the hologram twitched and was calm again. "Oh, right. And this is for you, Vollis. There is a politically trained royal family in the Cefa System. An offshoot of the Rishen lineage. They're already wise low-level politicians who believe in democracy, but they lacked the resources to make a play for planetary leadership. An information packet along with a significant contribution to their coffers has been sent to them with all the details they need to make a bid for the throne. Stability will be restored there within the year. They will become significant to the Cluster right alongside the Haven System, and that will cause incredible disruptions and chaos for the whole region. These stars will fall when the Edxi and the Order's other enemies see the weakness democracy and sympathetic ruler-ship brings."

Killing the Royal Family in the Cefa System wasn't easy. Having his work undone made Mikan burn, and he refused to repeat the question of; 'why?' even though it was on his lips. Instead, he asked; "What about the Haven System?"

"Well, there's every chance that someone from that tamed place was in some way responsible for my death. In fact, after Alice ruined my Justicars, I was convinced that they'd be the only ones capable of ending me. I don't have to do anything to get revenge on them myself. The Overlord will send a tide of Order ships here with aggressive leadership. It'll only add to the short-term chaos, and I hope the Haven Government tries to step in to aid the people who will starve or freeze when shipping routes grind to a halt. It'll make them vulnerable."

Mikan used the computer interface on the back of his

hand to check the personnel archives aboard his ship. He was growing impatient with the hologram. There was a chance that there was a copy of Olivia Scanlon's mind in storage. He brought it up and started looking.

"I was wondering how long it would take you to do that," the Scanlon hologram said. "Thank you for accessing my neural scan."

A command he didn't enter replaced the file with someone else's neural data and then initiated a sequence that cascaded across the database. "What are you doing?"

"I'm overwriting every neural image aboard your ship a few thousand times a second and initiating a full backup routine that will make sure those are ruined as well. By the time I've finished telling you about it, my neural data, along with everyone else's, will be replaced with the standard framework soldier's template. You won't be able to retrieve anything and the only thing your ship will be able to produce will be standard infantry units."

"You couldn't get access to my data until I checked it," Mikan realized aloud, aware that it would take weeks to rebuild his archive of duplicatable scientists, soldiers and workers. "I didn't fail you. I was nowhere near the Tiy System."

"You're right. The only thing that made you important was the personnel fabrication facility aboard your ship. I'm not taking revenge on you, but Citadel, for its part in retaking Earth and ruining it for everyone. I hoped to visit one day, and I died a little inside when I discovered that it had been reduced to a ruined husk. You had the most advanced personnel production systems in your fleet. Now you don't."

"Why appear to me?" Mikan asked, his frustration boiling over.

The Scanlon hologram laughed and shook her head. "You

still think you matter. I wish I was alive to see it. Don't get me wrong, I liked you and thought you could do great things for me, but you're not special. This hologram is appearing to dozens of people. It's an adaptive program that Olivia created so she could have the last word. Speaking of which, I think it's time. I hope that you and the Order are destroyed by all the bleeding hearts. Haven, the Cefa leadership, the Nafalli and Lorander. I hope it happens right before the Edxi turn humanity into a slave class. It's what you all deserve, and I know it for a fact. I was just as greedy and self-centred as the worst of you." The hologram twitched, froze on an image of Scanlon smiling smugly, and then disappeared.

Mikan checked his display and saw what he expected. The program was deleted and that section of his computer's drive had recrystallized itself so it couldn't be recovered.

At first, he was furious, stuck still on the spot and seething. That faded quickly and he dropped into the chair where the hologram pretended to sit only minutes earlier and shook his head. For spite's sake, Scanlon had left a message behind that was making its way across Order and Citadel ships. It would eventually reach the Overlord, he was sure, and Mikan wondered what she'd say to him.

Excusing the thought, Mikan wondered at how badly shaken his own faith was. Scanlon was a commander who believed in long plans that added up to great dividends. She was a business and military leader at the same time. He'd never known of one like her. If someone like that wanted post-humous revenge, then it would cut deep. The damage she did to the most important system on his ship alone was devastating. He considered the loss of the Ascendant and the technology they'd find there. It could be devastating. The idea that the Triton and its people, acting alone, were able to take it whole was worse. Once word got out there would be a dip in morale, and they might need someone like Eve to restore faith. They might need someone like him to punish the doubtful.

The feeling that the Order of Eden in the Cluster was about to unravel was inescapable for Mikan. For the first time in his life, he wondered if he was fighting for the wrong side.

A chime in his subdermal communicator snapped him out of it. There was a lot of work to do.

Afterword

Thank you very much for purchasing and reading Spinward Fringe Broadcast 17: Clash. This was one of the more difficult novels to write in the series. It was also incredibly rewarding in the end.

As an experiment, I offered the people who followed the serialized version of the book on Patreon a chance to shape the ending. At a critical moment, when Jake, Alice, Alaka, Iruuk and Noah were about to attack, I asked them if they should go after Eve's Base Ship or the Ascendant. They voted for the Valents and company to go after Scanlon aboard the Ascendant.

Later, when it came time to write Captain Mikan's confrontation with Scanlon's hologram, my first idea was similar to what you just read in the Epilogue. I originally imagined that Scanlon's main trait was greed, which was her motivation all along. Greed for wealth, but especially power.

As time passed and that point of the outline aged, I reconsidered. So, I wrote a different version of the encounter where she gives Mikan all her resources and the hologram becomes like a spirit that follows him into the next book, where it would give him advice and information concerning her plans. It would have been interesting, but I wondered if it didn't make Scanlon's defeat a hollow victory.

It turned out that, according to a couple of comments from the Patrons, my musing was right. It partially negated the effects of Scanlon's death. That's why I looked back at my original outline and re-wrote the confrontation so Scanlon's hologram is there to take revenge against everyone, just to make sure that she holds the people who failed to protect her accountable. Then, knowing that the Order and Citadel will pay a toll while Haven and their allies will face an escalation, Scanlon's ghost disappears.

I enjoy a challenge. That's one of the reasons why I'm still writing this series. It's also the reason why I included the story of Tiy and the brothers. I wanted to write a Lost Colony story that didn't overwhelm the book. Originally I had a group from the Triton landing in a place with 1920's technology, but I was pretty sure that would distract too much from the other points of this novel, so I leaned into the more dramatic option to involve Citadel and the Order of Eden. I also wanted to show a bit of the rivalry between the corporate and religious attitudes in the Order of Eden before Scanlon was gone.

I am happy with the brother's storyline in the end, and it gave me a place to bring Lorander and the British Alliance back into view. I'm happier with the shape of things now that they're back as real allies to Haven. They'll come up again, just like the idea of exploration and of meeting new beings.

The journey to the Shattered End and beyond will be at the beginning of Spinward Fringe Broadcast 18: Samurai

Squadron. You can expect a lot of adventure, starfighters and other exciting stuff from the serialized version on January 1, 2022 on Patreon. I chose that date specifically because it will mark fifteen years to the day since I started writing the Spinward Fringe series. If you'd rather read the whole thing in a finished eBook, then you can expect Samurai Squadron in the first half of 2023.

I should get to work on that.

Thank you again!

Randolph Lalonde

The Spinward Fringe Universe Timeline

As requested by numerous readers on multiple occasions, here's the reading order of every Spinward Fringe related book published so far. Any title with an asterisk (*) at the end of the name is a standalone book that can be enjoyed on its own or in order with the rest of the series. There's a list of Audiobooks that have been produced at the end as well. It's a lot shorter, but we'll work on that if the demand is high enough.

Thank you for reading.

STORIES IN THE SPINWARD FRINGE UNIVERSE

Spinward Fringe Broadcast 0: Origins*

Spinward Fringe Broadcast 1 and 2: Resurrection and Awakening

Spinward Fringe Broadcast 3: Triton

Spinward Fringe Broadcast 4: Frontline

Spinward Fringe Broadcast 5: Fracture

Spinward Fringe Broadcast 6: Fragments

The Expendable Few: A Spinward Fringe Novel*

Spinward Fringe Broadcast 7: Framework

Spinward Fringe Broadcast 8: Renegades

Spinward Fringe Broadcast 9: Warpath

Trapped: Chaos Core Book 1

Cool Pursuit: Chaos Core Book 2

Spinward Fringe Broadcast 10: Freeground

Spinward Fringe Broadcast 10.5: Carnie's Tale*

Spinward Fringe Broadcast 11: Revenge

Savage Stars: Chaos Core Book 3

Spinward Fringe Broadcast 12: Invasion

Spinward Fringe Broadcast 13: Warriors

Spinward Fringe Broadcast 14: Rebel

Spinward Fringe Broadcast 15: Pursuit

Spinward Fringe Broadcast 16: Hunters

Psycho Electric - A Spinward Fringe Novel*

The Last of the Bullet Chasers - A Spinward Fringe Short*

Spinward Fringe Broadcast 17: Clash (Coming in late 2022)

Spinward Fringe Broadcast 18: Samurai Squadron (Coming in 2023)

AUDIOBOOKS

Spinward Fringe Broadcast 0: Origins
Narrated by Adam Verner, Written by Randolph Lalonde

Spinward Fringe Broadcast 1: Resurrection
Narrated by Adam Verner, Written by Randolph Lalonde

Psycho Electric

Narrated by David Berlekamp, Produced by Heather Berlekamp, Written by Randolph Lalonde with music by Patrick D Emond

For information on where to listen to the audiobooks or read these Ebooks, please visit: www.RandolphLalonde.com

www.ingramcontent.com/pod-product-compliance
Lightning Source LLC
Chambersburg PA
CBHW060808030726
47503CB00002B/401